Short Stories From My Heart

Short Stories From My Heart

Larry Wade Livingston

Copyright © 2012 by Larry Wade Livingston.

Cover Picture by Larry Wade Livingston
Cover Graphics by Connie Hughes

Library of Congress Control Number:		2012904275
ISBN:	Hardcover	978-1-4691-7517-1
	Softcover	978-1-4691-7516-4
	Ebook	978-1-4691-7518-8

All rights reserved. No part of this book may be reproduced or transmitted in any form or by any means, electronic or mechanical, including photocopying, recording, or by any information storage and retrieval system, without permission in writing from the copyright owner.

This is a work of fiction. Names, characters, places and incidents either are the product of the author's imagination or are used fictitiously, and any resemblance to any actual persons, living or dead, events, or locales is entirely coincidental.

This book was printed in the United States of America.

To order additional copies of this book, contact:
Xlibris Corporation
1-888-795-4274
www.Xlibris.com
Orders@Xlibris.com
112856

CONTENTS

01. The Magical Ornament...11
02. Biggie..14
03. Amber...17
04. Zeke's Treasure...21
05. Malkar and Tiberius..25
06. The Shoe Box..28
07. The Pond...32
08. Decisions...36
09. Misdirection..41
10. The Sweet Smell of Jasmine......................................44
11. Loyalty..48
12. Mars on the Horizon..51
13. Thank You; But!..57
14. Gatorman...60
15. The Miracle Hand..66
16. Resurrection..69
17. Wishing...74
18. The Impossible Dream...79
19. A Swan's Love..85
20. Land of Skettels Down Under...................................88
21. Escapism...91
22. The Peruvian...95
23. Making Memories...109
24. Complications...113
25. Moving On..121
26. Let's HAve a Talk...123
27. Childhood Memories..127
28. Star Knight..130
29. When the Time was Right......................................135
30. Introduction..139
31. The Guitar...143
32. The Time has Come..148

33.	The Runaround	152
34.	The Loneliness Anthem	158
35.	Final Lap	161
36.	Mr. Hardin Buckley	165
37.	Not as it Seems	169
38.	Black Sand	173
39.	The Vision Within	185
40.	A Heartbeat Away	189
41.	The Four Horsemen	194
42.	Sanctuary	197
43.	Guilty or Not?	208
44.	Destiny's Twist	220
45.	Rememberance	224
46.	Life as I Know It	228
47.	Secret Love	306
48.	From Haunted to Reality	313
49.	Slow Down and Visualize	319
50.	Disparaging	322

DEDICATION

I dedicate this book of short stories to my Mother and my Aunt Ann. Both were wonderful writers up to the time before their deaths. It is sad that they never had the opportunity to have their work published or even read by more than a few friends. I always say that if I can bring out one second of emotion from the reader I have accomplished my goal. To affect a person and get them to react is a wonderful sense of satisfaction to me; I call it the power of words. They can cry, laugh, get angry or even hate what they read; but if it arouses them, I have succeeded in every aspect of writing. I owe my writing ability to so many that I can not name them all. I would like to thank Connie, Donna, Stan, Martin, Debbie and Karen for all their great help and patience's. I must say that I thank the good Lord for giving me the gift to tell short stories.

STORIES

THE MAGICAL ORNAMENT

AS FAR BACK as I can remember my mother would hang a beautiful Christmas ornament on our tree. It was bright red with a gold embossed design. It had silver stars scattered randomly around its surface. She always said it was magical and every Christmas Day it would do something special. It had been hand made by her great, great grandfather. It was a family heirloom and every generation had the responsibility to protect it from being damaged. I was told that when I was old enough it would be passed down to me for safe keeping and to carry on the tradition.

Every Christmas Day my little brother and sister would run downstairs with me to open presents. I was the oldest, then my sister and finally my brother. Our eyes would light up opening our gifts while mom and dad laughed and helped us with the ribbons and bows.

Then someone would always ask when the magical ornament was going to do some magic feat. We were told that the bulb must be saving up its magic for something really spectacular for next year. That scenario repeated itself year after year right up to my wedding day. In fact my brother and sister were married as well. We are all in our forties with our own children now.

The grandparents loved having all their children and their grandchildren over for the holidays. This last Christmas Day was the last one we had with mother. She had been sick for months; but she fought hard to make it to Christmas Day. With fathers help she hung the big red Christmas ornament on the tree for her last time.

The grandchildren have been brought up on the legend of the magical ornament like the rest of us. They were the ones that started asking mother if this was the year the magical ornament would perform its magical feat. I must admit I too was curious as well as my siblings. Mother sat down and looked out over all her children and grandchildren. While holding fathers hand and tears of joy in her eyes she started telling the story of the magical ornament.

"For close to 100 years there has never been a Christmas Day that the entire family has not been together. Not even during both World Wars and all the ones that have followed. The magical ornament has for years brought the family together to see what magic it would display. Look around this room and you will see the magic that it has had for near a century. The magic has always been to bring families together on Christmas Day to see what it would do. The real magic was never the ornament, the real magic is in you and it has been in everyone in this family's legacy for the last 100 years."

BIGGIE & SKINNY

BIGGIE & SKINNY are two rats that live a fine life; that is for them being members of the rodent family. They scamper around mostly at night enjoying the plentiful droppings of food disregarded by their sworn enemies, that being you and I (humans). Now if that was all it was to this story it would be over and not a very good account of Biggie & Skinny's true life or relationship. It seems that the rodents of the world are similar to us homosapiens in far too many ways that we want to acknowledge.

I have to start from the beginning so you understand how this all came about. Biggie was born at 242 Wilson Drive and Skinny was born at 245 Wilson Drive, right across the street. Biggie was three days older than Skinny and that fact was to prove to be a major point in what was to be their relationship. Both of them were 4 months old when they first met as they were fighting over a piece of corndog after a backyard Bar-B-Q. As the fight continued Biggie became victorious due to him being twice the weight as Skinny (thus the names).

Skinny sat and watched as Biggie got his fill. Once his stomach was bloated to its maximum size he nudged what was left of the dog over to Skinny. After that day they hung out together constantly with Skinny always following behind the older Biggie. As the months passed Biggie would take advantage of Skinny. He would make him run out into the street to retrieve food or steal food from the cats bowl. Biggie would never take a chance of getting hurt or killed; he would just make Skinny do it.

Skinny was intimidated by Biggie, yet at the same time he admired him greatly. He resented Biggie for his relentless verbal abuse and belittlement of him. It was a thin line that Skinny lived and walked. Biggie was his protection from other rats as well as giving him a sense of importance. He was Biggies right hand rat and that alone warranted respect from the other rats. However, truth be known, Skinny in his heart wanted to be his own rat and stand on his own four feet.

There finally came a time when Skinny was attracted to a sweet little rat by the name of Saffron. She made his whiskers tingle with excitement. Biggie saw that Skinny was interested in Saffron, but he too wanted her for himself. With a few calculated maneuvers Biggie managed to win the heart of Saffron by downgrading Skinny and making him look like a fool whenever possible. Biggie and Saffron mated and she then disappeared and was never seen again. She didn't even say goodbye to either of them. Maybe she felt ashamed or realized that she had made a huge mistake and should have been with Skinny. We will never know for sure; but I would like to think it was the latter.

As time continued on Biggie got bigger and he slowly went blind. It was now Skinny that led Biggie around. He was more or less like a Seeing Eye dog for Biggie. Skinny got food for the both of them and provided any and everything that Biggie required. However, that did not stop Biggie from still degrading and belittling Skinny. The verbal abuse was to the point that it became intolerable. Skinny thought long and hard on what to do about his situation.

He owed Biggie for all the protection that he had given to him over the years. He thought about the respect that he had had over the years even if it was generated by fear of Biggie. On the other hand Biggie took advantage of him and stole the love of his life, Saffron. Biggie made him a fool and his personal slave in many ways. Skinny was looking for a sign when out of no where it suddenly appeared.

They both entered the garage at the home on 242 Wilson Drive; the exact home where Biggie had been born. There on the floor was six pieces of cheese. Five of them were lying freely on the floor. The sixth one was a large piece of Swiss cheese, Biggies favorite. It was attached to a large rat trap. Skinny led Biggie over to a piece of cheese and he began to eat it. Biggie found his way to another piece and he ate it as well. Skinny sat back as Biggie finally caught a whiff of his favorite Swiss cheese. He went over to it ecstatically and as he bit into it, the trap slammed down on his neck. Skinny heard Biggies neck snap and he watched as the bloated body twitched till it lay motionless. He went over to the Swiss cheese and began to eat it with a grin on his face. As he was walking away he looked back at Biggie for the last time and muttered to himself (Payback Is a Bitch)

AMBER

SEVEN YEAR OLD Amber would sit on the edge of her bed and look out her window. She admired the birds and squirrels that played in the large oak tree outside her window. She often wished that she could interact with all the creatures she sees.

Finally one day she watched as a caterpillar crawled out on a small limb and start weaving a cocoon. It took several hours over the next week before it was completed; but every time that Amber would watch she had moon shaped eyes. She was fascinated by how precise and elaborate the whole process was. Amber didn't know anything about metamorphous. She just liked watching the silky threads being wove into the cocoon.

Once it was completed she sat back and waited to see what would happen to the cocoon. Days past and nothing seemed to be happening. She asked her mother and was disappointed to hear that it may take weeks before the cocoon would open. When she inquired as to what would come out her mother only told her to wait and see.

After a few weeks Amber was looking at the cocoon and it moved. She was excited for sure about this new development. She stared as the cocoon split apart. She gasped as a beautiful Monarch butterfly emerged. It slowly spread its wings and absorbed the suns warmth. It was bright yellow and black with the traditional Monarch pattern markings. As Amber studied the creature she noticed something different about this particular Monarch. It had a bright blue dot on its back. That made this butterfly very special.

Amber reached outside her window and extended her index finger in front of the new born creature. The butterfly fluttered and then lit on her finger. She smiled as she brought it closer for her to examine more closely. After a few minutes it flew away as Amber watched as it disappeared into the meadow across from her bedroom window.

The next day Amber was sitting by her window and to her surprise the same Monarch appeared. It flew in her open window and lit on her shoulder. She raised her hand and the butterfly then lit on her finger. She brought the creature close to her face and said "my, you're a friendly butterfly aren't you? You are so beautiful. I am going to name you Misty and you can be my friend." Misty flapped her wings vigorously with joy as if she understood what was being said.

During the day Misty would return to the meadow; but at night she would come and perch herself on Amber's headboard and watched over her. This scenario continued for four weeks before Misty became sluggish and barely able to fly. Amber didn't understand what was happening to Misty and was worried for her friend.

Late one night Amber woke up to discover Misty was lying on the pillow next to her head. It took her a moment to realize that her friend was dead. Amber was devastated and her tears ran freely down her cheeks. Her mother heard the cries and entered her daughter's bedroom," what's wrong honey," she asked.

"Misty died mommy! Look," she said as she held the butterfly up in her cupped hands.

"Amber honey, butterflies only live two to six weeks. You saw how the caterpillar wove its cocoon and then after a few weeks Misty appeared. Once that had happened Misty only had a short time to live and she spent it with you darling. That is the life cycle of a butterfly."

Amber finally fell asleep; but she was still sad that Misty was gone. Amber's mother put Misty in a small box and the next day she and Amber gave her friend a burial.

Time passed by and Amber had began to forget about Misty. However, summer came and the warm sun shined down on the neighborhood. One day as Amber was sitting on her bed brushing her dolls hair a Monarch Butterfly flew in her open window and lit on her headboard.

She stood up and looked at the butterfly closely. Amber smiled and her eyes opened wide as she saw a bright blue dot on its back. "Misty, you've come back to me," she said. Amber held out her hand and the butterfly flew and perched on her finger. It was like old times and it brought back memories for her. This has to be Misty, all the moments and mannerisms were exactly the same.

The summer was wonderful until like before, this Misty passed away after a few short weeks. No one has every been able to explain how every year at the same time; a Monarch Butterfly with a bright blue dot on its back returns to Amber's bedroom and lands on her headboard. It spends a few weeks and then dies. Amber called them all year after year Misty. She quit wondering why or how and just enjoyed them every year.

When Amber reached adulthood she got married. Her parents moved to Florida and Amber and her husband stayed in the house that Amber had lived her entire life. She told Brad her husband about Misty and sure enough the first summer after the wedding Misty returned. He too had no explanation for it; but he saw how happy it made Amber.

Amber finally became pregnant a year after her marriage and she and Brad were ecstatic. When Amber gave birth to a 9 pound baby girl it was a glorious day and their home was heavenly. They named their beautiful girl Jillian after Amber's mother.

When the first summer came after the birth of Jillian, Amber was in the nursery. (Her old bedroom). As she was holding Jillian she looked up to see two Monarch Butterflies float through the open window and land of cribs railing. When Amber moved closer to have a better look one flew up and landed on her shoulder. She saw that it had a bright blue dot on its back. The other one fluttered its wings and landed on Jillian's nose. Amber could see right away that it had a bright green dot on its back. She put her child in the crib to sleep and as she was leaving she saw both butterflies perched on the cribs railing.

Still to this day the return of the two Monarchs happens religiously. Every year after their life have ended Amber puts each in a small box and continues her tradition. In the back yard along the cedar fence there are 28 little blue crosses and 3 green crosses. Amber had a small placard that hung on the fence above the tiny crosses.

BLESSINGS COME AND THEN MAY GO; BUT THEIR MEMORIES SHOULD NEVER BE FORGOTTEN.

ZEKE'S TREASURE

ZEKES HAS BEEN prospecting for gold for over seventy years. Sure he'd found a small vein here and there; but never that proverbial mother load. He and his mule Sadie would disappear in the mountains for months at a time; only to return with more stories than gold for everyone at the saloon.

Zeke was in his eighties, sun darkened leathery skin and a full length beard down to his belt buckle. What little hair he had left was silver and hung down to his shoulders. The sixteen teeth he had left were yellow, chipped and cavity ridden. That was somewhat common in the year 1848 out in the Wild West, so old Zeke fitted right in.

Carson City, Nevada had many silver mines and even a smelter for the mines ore. Zeke however was a victim of gold fever and not silver. He was mesmerized by the shinny metals color and weight as he held it in his hand.

Zeke told stories about gold nuggets as big as his fist; but they always somehow disappeared, got stolen or he plumb forgot where the dig was. He got free drinks at the saloon and everyone just laughed at his tales while giving him words of encouragement.

The last time Zeke and Sadie left town to prospect was indeed his last. After a year went by everyone thought that he died up in the mountains. They never saw or heard any stories about him again. So I am going to tell you about Zeke's last journey to find his elusive gold treasure. Now this is just between you and I. I am sure you will understand why after I tell you what transpired.

Once Zeke had left Carson City it took him several days for him to reach a spot high up in the Rockies. He had kept a map where he had placed an X at ever location he had found gold at his favorite site. He was following a small creek that originated from the snow line.

Every year he moved higher and higher up the side of the mountain. He would find larger nuggets every time he relocated uphill. Zeke figured that the mother load was higher up and he was only finding the small stuff that was washing downstream. He had decided that he would stop moving in 100 yard increments and now move a quarter of a mile each time.

Zeke was aging fast and time was no longer on his side. If the mother load was there he had to find it on this trip. He worked diligently day after day. He kept to his plan and moved with each find further up the mountains' face.

After a month Zeke was five miles from where he had started. He had worked his way up a ravine and was at a much higher elevation. Breathing was difficult and he labored to take in deep breaths; but he still pushed forward.

One morning he found himself along the creeks shoreline and spotted what looked to be a large gold nugget. He couldn't believe what he was looking at. He picked it up and its' weight made his eyes widen and a smile come to his face. He knew it was gold. He began to dig and the deeper he dug the more nuggets he found. For three days he dug feverishly and the hole grew to four feet across and six feet deep.

Sadie had to pull Zeke up from the hole with the rope that was tied around her neck. Then one afternoon as Sadie was tugging to pull Zeke out of the hole, the ground gave way. She fell into the hole with Zeke. Once her weight hit the bottom of the hole the earth again gave way; both she and Zeke fell a hundred feet.

Zeke found himself in a large underground cavern. Gold nuggets lay everywhere and the walls glitter with gold. Zeke was drunk with delight and visions of being a millionaire. He started picking up nuggets then realized that he was standing in knee deep water. He managed to control his emotions long enough to see that the creek above was flowing in to the cavern.

The water began to rise slowly and Zeke was in trouble. He couldn't swim. He tried to hang on to Sadie; but her saddle bags were full of gold. Zeke cut them loose and that helped for awhile. The cold water started taking its toll. Hypothermia slowly took over both Zeke and Sadie's bodies.

By the time there was eighty feet of water in the cavern Sadie lost control of her muscles and slipped under the water. Zeke tried to cling on to rocks that were protruding from the walls to no avail.

Zeke died that day and his body has never been found. The creek filled the cavern and from the shore it looks like any other pothole good for fishing.

I guess there's different ways to look at Zekes' life. He lived his dream and found his mother load before he died. One could say that greed for gold was what killed him. You might even think it was a freak accident that took his life. It could have been fate or just bad luck.

Whatever the real reason is, one thing is for certain. They all apply at the same time and equally logical. Maybe someday someone will fall into the creek and discover there's a cavern beneath the surface. Personally I hope they don't. This is Zekes' mother load and it should remain his for ever, he earned, it lock, stock and barrel.

MALKAR AND TIBERIUS

IN THE MOUNTAINS of the far away land of Argon,
lived lonely Malkar, the last dragon (because all of his kind were gone).

Hiding amongst the tallest cliffs and caverns up high,
he grew stronger as he practiced daily to fly.

When young Malkar finally mastered the art of flight,
he left the mountains for Argon's attack at first light.

It was the king's destruction he wanted to pursue,
with revenge for the death of all dragons that once flew.

He was justified and fought for dragons' lost honor;
only the King's death would satisfy his deep hunger.

While the Army slept, serpent fire reigned down from the sky.
His war against the King and his army had finally materialized.

Screams filled the air as the peasants ran in total fear;
but Malkar was focused and would never shed a tear.

Man had killed the dragons, so now it would be death to all of them!
Malkar believed that the King's black soul was now his to condemn.

Suddenly there standing alone, atop the highest tower,
the King's best warrior, Tiberius, a man of power.

With a large shield, quiver of arrows and his long bow,
he would face Malkar, hoping to give the killing blow.

Malkar aimed and fired his biggest and hottest fireball;
but the shield of Tiberius held and the man stood tall.

Then he released his arrow and it pierced Malkar's heart,
it was then that Malkar realized that from the start.

His own true destiny was to parish in this way . . .
He was the last dragon, with no mate, how could he stay?

His fate was foretold to you in this story's first line,
as the last dragon, it was just a matter of time . . . .

For you see, no living being can exist happily alone.
They must have a mate who loves them and see it shown.

As Malkar's body slowly spiraled downward towards Earth,
It was only his fate being fulfilled from the day of his birth.

THE SHOE BOX

LILLY UPSHAW LIVES in the Three Rivers nursing home. She just turned 97 years old and the home through her a wonderful party with cake and ice cream. Lilly has lived at the home for the last 25 years. No one on staff can ever remember anyone coming to visit her in that time. In fact according to her chart there are no living relatives.

Lilly is soft spoken when she does speak; but that is only on a rare occasion. She has been like that ever since arriving at Three Rivers a few days after her husband Henry's death. She has been quiet and reserved from that first day she became a resident. She arrived with a shoe box that she held tightly close to her bosom. It never left her grasp and it was by her pillow as she slept.

That's the life that Lilly has lived for the last 25 years. However to be fair, she did help the ladies make blankets and played some cards now and then. It's not that she's unfriendly; she was withdrawn and rarely opened up to anyone.

Staff members will tell you that with each passing year Lilly seemed to become a little more depressed. They would often hear her crying late at night. When they would look in on her she would be hugging her shoe box.

In away it was a sad life for Lilly to have to endure. Some say that it was a blessing when five weeks after her 97th birthday she passed away in her sleep. The morning nurse found her lying in her bed holding the shoe box wet from her tears.

It was determined that she died from natural causes; but everyone at Three Rivers knew it was from a broken heart. She was buried next to her beloved husband Henry at Scenic Hills Cemetery. Their plots had a majestic view of the river and mountains in the distance. Both were things that they loved and were the main reason they purchased these two final resting places.

No one came forward to claim what little possessions Lilly had left behind. She had no will and had never said anything about such matters. Once thirty days had passed, Nurse Erin Ford claimed Lilly's beloved shoe box. Nurse Ford took it home and placed it on her dinning room table. She looked at it for some time while recalling Lilly walking the halls holding it tightly.

Finally she could not resist it any longer; she lifted the lid and folded it back. She reached inside and took out several pieces of paper and began to sifting through them. She found a picture of Lilly when she was 6 years old. Erin smiled as she imagined that little girl being happy and full of innocence. There was also picture of Lilly when she was in her twenties that showed how beautiful she was.

Then there were the pictures of Henry in his Army uniform. It was easy to see how Lilly had fallen in love with him. He was a tall and outdoor type man. Erin continued to view pictures of their wedding and honeymoon.

She finally noticed a newspaper article. The clipping had a title of (A Mother's Heartache). As she read through it her eyes watered up and a tear rolled down her cheek. Lilly had a twin sister at birth; but she died immediately after being born. What emotions Lilly must have had about that terrible night Erin thought. She continued to find sadness in the shoe box as she found a birth and death certificate. They were for a baby girl named Jill and dated two years apart. That explained the pair of pink baby shoes that were in the box. Erin had thought they were Lilly's; but now she knew differently. She saw that baby Jill died from what we now call SID's and that Henry died of lung cancer.

The one major thing that Erin noticed was that there was no life insurance, will or banking information. There were no names of friends, a pastor or some long lost relative. Lilly had been truly all alone all those years at Three Rivers except for staff and residents.

At the bottom of the box was a gold wedding band. By the size, Erin could tell it had been Henry's. She held it up and read the inscription (Love Always) that was inside the band. She carefully placed all the papers, pictures and items in the shoe box. She tied a big yellow bow around it for safe keeping.

The next day she took the shoe box back to Three Rivers Nursing Home. She put it in the glass display cabinet that's located in the front lobby. She took a 3X5 card and in capital letters wrote LILLY. When the staff and residents asked her why she put the shoe box in the display, she told them exactly why.

"We all can learn from Lilly's shoe box. She carried her life on the outside for us all to see. We didn't see or understand it at the time; but it was right there in front of us. Everyone here carries their life on the inside. Many are unfortunate as they develop Alzheimer's and they forget their past. Lilly's life was here for us to see after she left us, it is in her shoe box. We need to start taking the time to learn and discover one another's life by sharing it with everyone.

Before it is too late I am going to start a shoe box of my own. I will put things inside that will tell others who and what my life has been. I want you all to look at Lilly's shoe box and remember to ask the ones around you about their lives. Tell people about your life as well. Better yet, start your own shoe box; because if you ever find yourself all alone with nobody, a stranger might say let's open this shoe box and see what's inside. That may be the only remembrance that your life can leave behind. So protect and cherish the legacy . . . . in YOUR shoe box.

THE POND

WHEN BRADLEY TUCKER was hunting as a teenager deep in the Blue Ridge Mountains of Tennessee; he accidentally discovered a life altering phenomenon. He had cut his hand when he slipped and fell down a steep embankment earlier. After he stopped tumbling to the bottom of the ravine he came to rest at the edge of a pond. It wasn't very big in size, maybe eleven feet across and shaped as an oval.

The water was only two feet in depth and was pristinely clear. He felt a soothing sensation as he looked at the peaceful surroundings. He knelt down and started washing the dirt from the cut on his hand. He suddenly began to feel energized. Then to his amazement the cut on his hand tingled and he watched as it healed right before his eyes. There was no visible scar or pain; in fact there were no signs of it ever being injured.

Bradley walked back to his truck while pondering what had just transpired. He really couldn't comprehend or understand any of it. He even thought that he might have been dreaming after his fall; but he knew better as he looked at his hand. As he drove home he kept looking back and forth at his hand and the road. He decided not to tell anyone about what had happened. They wouldn't believe him anyway. He knew he would have to investigate this more closely and try to prove to himself that this really happened.

The next weekend Bradley returned to the pond to prove that it had the healing properties he had experienced. He took out his pocketknife and made a two inch superficial cut on his forearm. The cut began to bleed. He dipped his arm in the water and as soon as it was submerged he watched the cut slowly close and then heals.

Bradley was ecstatic with a euphoric cerebral explosion. He felt invincible and that he had reached super hero status. He wondered what would happen if he drank the water. He cupped his hands together, gathered water with them and brought it to his lips. It was cool and sweet to the taste. After a few seconds his entire body had a refreshing wave ripple throughout. It was then that he made the decision that the pond would be his secret and no one else's.

Later that year Bradley graduated from high school and got a job at the local sawmill. Whenever he felt ill or had an injury he returned to the pond. He would drink the water and once again feel refreshed and vibrant. He made it a habit to return at least twice a month and drink from the pond. It would be several years before he learned something even more astonishing about the pond's miraculous water.

Ten years after discovering the pond he ran into a former high school buddy. The friend looked at him and asked, "What are you doing Bradley? You look exactly like the day we graduated." Bradley just smiled and went home for the evening.

Bradley had not paid attention to his looks up to that point. He stared into the mirror in his bathroom and noticed that he had indeed not aged a day since school. As great as that might sound; it would obviously become a problem as time went on. He was twenty-seven and he still looked seventeen. He soon found himself telling people that he just came from a good gene pool and that he was blessed in order to explain away his youthful appearance.

When Bradley turned thirty-seven it was no longer easy to explain away his young looks. The company doctor at the sawmill wanted to run some blood test to find out what may be happening metabolically. He was impressed with Bradley's youthful looks and wondered why. Bradley quickly refused the doctors request. He had never been sick in the twenty years since his discovery at the pond. He wasn't going to allow anything to take place that might remotely reveal his personal fountain of youth or good health.

Bradley had to start adding gray to his temples and dressing more maturely than he really was. He wasn't ageing as the years went by. He stayed as a seventeen year old boy. He was afraid to fall in love or get involved in any relationship. He constantly agonized over how he could explain to a wife or serious girlfriend his unique situation. He thought it was easier to be alone with just his dog Bear, a black lab.

As Bradley tried to keep his fake ageing procedures up it became harder and harder to maintain them. He was fifty-seven and having no crows' feet around his eyes and the lack of wrinkles made it almost impossible to keep the facade alive. He sat for days in his living room and came to a decision that would alter his life. He swore that he would no longer return to the pond and let life take its natural course.

After six months Bradley noticed true gray throughout his hair. Wrinkles and crows feet were developing at a rapid rate. Arthritis had attacked his joints and he was slowly growing weaker. After a year he was frail and suffered unmentionable pain. He decided to make one final trip back to the pond. Not to drink of its water; but to easy the pain that was unbearable.

It was all he could do to hobble along a dear trail back into the Blue Ridge Mountains to reach the pond. Bradley was shocked and dismayed when he arrived to find that the pond had dried up. Not a drop of water remained; nothing but dusty soil and weeds. He sat down by it's now dried banks, leaned against a tree and cried while asking aloud, "Why, why, why?"

It's ironic in away. Bradley Tucker died that night there at the edge of the pond that had once given him the opportunity for immortality; but he had rejected what it offered and in the end it was that decision that cost him his life. One thing for sure, Bradley died on his own terms. He decided to experience real life as a mortal man and not one encompassed with magical interference. God bless Bradley Tucker; He may have just discovered a new world with a whole different kind of immortality.

DECISIONS THAT WE MAKE

TYSON BANKS WAS 16 years old as he sat watching Muhammad Ali fighting smoking Joe Frazier on ESPN's classic fights. He was in awe by Ali's shuffle and hand speed. As he heard Howard Cosell scream those famous words, "down goes Frazier, down goes Frazier," Tyson knew in his heart he wanted to be a fighter.

He went to the Gold's Gym, not one of those 24 hour fitness or L A centers. He wanted a gym where he could learn and train to become a boxer. Tyson walked around the ring watching two men sparing with one another. His eyes lit up and a smile appeared across his face as he watched intensely at the skills they exhibited.

An old timer by the name of Cutter saw the expression on the young boy's face. He approached the lad and asked, "What's your name son? You thinking of becoming a fighter?"

"Tyson's my name sir and yes I would like to become a fighter."

"My name is Cutter, glad to meet you," he said as he held out his hand and shook Tyson's hand firmly. "Come over here boy and let's see what you've got."

Cutter took him over to the heavy bag and instructed him to start punching. Tyson punched as hard as he could and even threw in what he thought were combinations.

"Stop, stop!" yelled the old man. "You've got some raw talent kid. With some hard training I might be able to make a fighter out of you. You get along for now and get a note from your mom or dad that it's OK to train you as a fighter. Wait! Better yet, you come back with your mother and let me talk to her. I don't want any misunderstandings."

Tyson felt good about himself, after all a professional trainer said he had talent. Tyson was an only child being raised by his mom, a single mother. His father ran off when he was only two weeks old.

Tyson's mother (Yolanda Banks) was not excited when she heard her son ask for permission to learn boxing. Her first reaction was to have images of her boy getting hurt. It took a few minutes for her to weigh the pros and cons of Tyson's request. She slept on it and considered all the options. She finally decided that she would rather see her son in the gym with Cutter, rather than roaming the streets or in a gang.

She went with Tyson the next day and spoke with Cutter. She signed a few papers authorizing Tyson to participate in a boxing program. Cutter promised that he would care for Tyson as if he were his own son.

Tyson learned fast, he was truly a natural in the ring. Within six months Cutter entered him in a Golden Glove match. He was to fight another 16 year old boy from a competitive gym from across town. Tyson fought as a middleweight so he wasn't surprised to see that his opponent was similar to himself in stature.

As the three round fight started Tyson ran out to the middle of the ring. He was immediately hit with a straight right hand. Tyson hit the canvas in the first ten seconds of the fight. The referee only got to the four count before Tyson bounced to his feet. He held out his gloves to the referee as a sign that he was fine and wanted to continue.

The referee looked at Tyson's eyes and motioned for the fight to continue. This time he laid back and studied his adversary for the rest of round one. He had learned his first lesson when in the ring. He did try a few combinations and made mental notes to how the fighter reacted to them. He especially watched the reflexes when faced with a variety of punches.

Tyson got hit a few times himself during the fight. In fact he had a cut under his left eye. Cutter quickly stopped the bleeding; but the eye swelling shut could be a major problem.

Tyson came out for the third and final round. The two touched gloves in the middle of the ring, that is customary in all fights, even the Golden Gloves. Both fighters stalked one another around the ring. Tyson began to change up his punches based on the reactions he had noted in the two pervious rounds. At two minutes and fifteen seconds of the round Tyson caught the young man with a classic one-two combination. Both punches landed squarely on the chin and with full power. Down the young fighter went. The referee counted to ten and then raised Tyson's hand. He couldn't have been happier, first fight and first knockout all in one night.

Tyson kept getting better and better with time. He also kept winning and winning. He was 21 and ranked number one amateur fighter in the world. Cutter and Tyson thought it was time to turn professional. Tyson would have to let his 67-0-0 amateur record behind and start all over once he turned pro.

Tyson fought more professional fights than anyone ever had in a three year period. He supported a 17-0-0 record. Every fight he had won with a knockout. He was ranked number one contender for the belt; but all the champions in all the boxing organizations wouldn't sign on to a fight. Only the WBC has a clause that the champion has to defend their title within a year against the number one contender. That is if the number one contender has had that ranking for a continuous year. Tyson kept fighting and he held that ranking for the year. It was mandatory now that the WBC champion had to fight for the title or be stripped of it.

The press had enough hype that they couldn't tell it fast enough. With great fanfare at the weigh in Pedro Gondolas signed to fight Tyson for the WBC championship belt. Gondolas record at that time was 84-3-1. Tyson's record was now 25-0-0 as a professional. His total record from the amateur fights plus the pro fights was 92-0-0. The fight was being held at Caesars Palace in Las Vegas on June 9th. It was sold out weeks in advance and everyone that was anyone was going to be there.

Tyson spent over two-hundred rounds with the toughest fighters he could find to spar with. He got tagged good several times himself; but that's the price one pays for being in the pugilistic arena.

Finally the night of the fight came. The crowd's cheers were deafening as Tyson walked down the aisle and into the ring. The reaction to Pedro was exactly the same. It was obvious that the crowd was split 50/50.

After the standard boxing introductions and the ceremonial touching of the gloves had been completed, both men returned to their appointed corners. Clank! Went the bell and the two fighters met in the center of the ring. They exchanged vicious punches back and forth. The referee had to break them apart after the bell ending the round. Everyone could see that this was a grudge match and the rules were going to be tested if not flat out broken by both fighters. The pummeling continued through the next few rounds, each afflicting damage on the other. Both combatants had deep cuts and their eyes were starting to swell shut.

As the fight went on Tyson would manage to knock Pedro to the canvas. Pedro would get up before the count of ten. Pedro would extend the gesture by knocking Tyson down to the bloodstained canvas twice in the eleventh round. Tyson was able to stagger to his feet before he was counted out. It was a blessing that before Pedro could rush in and finish him the bell sounded ending the round.

As Tyson sat in his corner before the 12th and last round Cutter told him he was behind on all three judges' cards. He needed a knockout for the win. Over in Pedro's corner he was being told to finish the fight right out of the box. He was instructed to come out swinging and put Tyson away fast.

The bell sounded and the two gladiators did the customary glove touch for a final championship fight round. Pedro immediately threw a left hook to Tyson's kidney followed by hard right hand that put him down on the canvas. Tyson sucked in all the air he could and managed to get to his feet by the count of eight.

Pedro ran in thinking he would end it all at that moment. He was surprised when Tyson hit him with a thundering uppercut that sent him back and down to the canvas. He struggled to get to his feet; but his knees were wobbly and felt like rubber. Tyson rushed in for the win and he ran into a hard jab and a wicked one-two. Tyson flashed back to his first amateur fight and how he had made that same mistake. They stood in the middle of the ring exchanging blow after blow.

With only thirty seconds left in the fight Tyson unleashed one more vicious uppercut catching Pedro flush on the jaw. Pedro dropped to his knees and then fell forward on his face with his hands by his side. The referee waved his arms signaling the fight was over. Any fighter that goes down in that manner is hurt bad and will never beat the count. The blood thirsty crowd was screaming and yelling because they had gotten their monies worth.

Pedro took six months to recover completely from his injuries. He never fought again. Tyson wasn't much better himself. He was crowned the WBC champion. He doesn't remember the fight. He suffered severe brain damaged and he stutters when he talks, every month he slips further away into the world of dementia. He sits hour after hour in his favorite chair starring out the window from his room in the Glendale Rest Home.

Tyson didn't learn soon enough that sometimes in life we need to ask ourselves if what we seek is worth the price we pay to achieve it. Yes, Tyson is a champion and no one can ever take that away from him. But being a champion took Tyson away and no one can ever bring back the man that he was. I wonder what thoughts Tyson would have today, if only he could tell us.

MISDIRECTION

TOMMY CAIN WORKED at the local brick making factory in Memphis, Tennessee. He started working there two weeks after he graduated from high school. From his first day on the job he had an unusual dream to say the least. He was going to build a replica of Elvis Presley's Graceland; but he was going to build it completely in brick.

Every Friday at quitting time he would load up a wheelbarrow full of bricks. They were ones that had chipped corners or their color was off from being over baked. He would approach the front gate and the security guard would stop him. "What the heck do you think your doing Tommy? I've told you over and over that you can't take those bricks home with you. Dump them out right now" he would say.

Tommy had a dream and one stuck up security guard was not going to be a deterrent. Like clockwork when Friday came around he would proceed with filling up a wheelbarrow with bricks and head to the main gate. Naturally he was met with the same explanation from the guard and forced to dump out the bricks before leaving the property.

Tommy was persistent to a fault; he kept this routine up for several years until the day came when he decided that enough was enough. He marched into the office and proudly gave his two weeks notice that he was quitting. The reason he gave was that he wanted to fulfill a long time dream. Tommy bought an entire flatbed truck of bricks and told the dispatcher to have them delivered to a 5 acre lot out on route 40. He still got his 15 percent employee discount which brought a smile to his face.

When Friday came on the last week of his employment, it was the first time that he didn't try to take bricks home with him. The guard looked in amazement. "I can't believe it Tommy; you finally got it through that thick head of yours. I hear you quit and today's your last time through my gate. I saw the truckload of bricks you bought; that must have really got your goat. You must be ready to build your Brick Land," he said while laughing.

"I'm going to miss you, like the flu," Tommy said. "Yea I'm going to build my Brick Land; but I did have to alter my plans a little." With that said Tommy walked out through the gates for the last time.

It took Tommy a little over three months to build his Brick Land. Then the big day came for the grand opening. It was Saturday, June third at eleven AM. The traffic on the highway was bumper to bumper.

Tommy pulled the rope to reveal his huge sign to the public. As the covering fell to the ground for all to see, they read.

TOMMY'S WHELLBARROWS
HUNDEREDS TO PICK FROM

THE SWEET SMELL OF JASMINE

JACKSON RIVERS MET her beneath the sultry sun of the Georgia Bayou when the inviting looks from her almond eyes captured his interest. Who could resist such beauty standing under the limbs of Magnolia trees with her skin glistening from the southern humidity while her skirt rustled in a gentle breeze? She was tall, slender with waist long black hair that completed her physical attributes that made her a modern day Aphrodite's.

How much can a man endure before he falls victim to lust in his heart or that rare commodity called love? She had a mesmerizing effect on him that day as he slowly approached her. He couldn't help himself from surrendering to her wishes, even though she never spoke aloud. Her eyes said it all and her presence controlled him. It never occurred to him why she would be there deep in the bayou all-alone. She reached out and touched his face as they both fell into a trance.

When he awoke the next morning he was alone and confused, things were blurry and unclear. He did recall the sweet smell of Jasmine mixed with fragrance from the Magnolias. Pictures kept flashing in his mind of much love and intensity. From the bits and pieces that he could see he constructed a vision full of nightly passion. Scratched in the soil next to him was the name Savannah Pearl in capitol letters. It intrigued Jackson how everything had transpired from start to finish.

He hiked back to his truck and then drove back to the room that had been rented for the week. He took a shower and went to the Ma and Pa store next door. An elderly couple, Maude and Emit, in their eighties, ran the motel/gas station/store and post office combination establishment. This little gathering of eight-teen people (including Emit and Maude) lived here at the edge of the bayou in a community called Moss Tree, Georgia.

Jackson had come here to have peace and quite while enjoying the plant and animal life that thrived in the bayou. He walked up to the counter with his selections and asked Maude if she had ever heard the name Savannah Pearl. Her eyebrows quickly lifted and her spine stiffened. Emits eyes squinted as he tilted his head, then asked "what fer, where'd you all heard that name boy?" Jackson knew right away that he had hit a nerve or at least the source to answer all questions. "Tell me about her Emit, please" he responded. Emit looked at Maude and she gave him a nod, so he began telling the story of the woman in the bayou.

"Savannah Pearl was the daughter of General Zackary Pearl back in the Civil War days. The story goes that Miss Savannah loved General Bushnell. A damn good fer nutten Yankee; that about killed her daddy Zackary. The family threw her out and disowned her. She lived in the swamp, cause no true Southerner would even talk to her after that. The General should have skinned her like a bear, that's what I'd have done for sure. Family or not, once you turn your back on the South you don't ever get nuttin no more.

After a couple of years had passed General Pearl went into the swamp to find his daughter to tell her that the war was over and that he wanted to mend their relationship. He found her with that Yankee Bushnell and that was too much fer him to take. He pulled out his pistol and began shouting he was gonna kill himself one more damn Yankee. When he fired, Savannah jumped in front of her lover and the bullet hit her square in the heart. The bullet went clear through her and struck Bushnell as well. Savannah was dead before she hit the ground; but that Yankee was only seriously wounded. Bushnell held Savannah in his arms and that only made General Pearl madder than hell. He pulled Savannah away from that Yankee General, and then made him watch as he buried his daughter right there in the bayou.

Then the story goes on to say that Zackary hogtied that Bushnell fellow to a tree and left him there screaming as gator bait.

Around 1901 after the new century started legend has it that a beautiful lady lived in the swamp. Thousands go looking fer her and some say that they have seen her with their own eyes. Hell some say they even made love to her. Swamp gas hallucinations if you ask me young fellow. Anyway about every 10 years are so someone has come back from the bayou ranting and a ravening about seeing Savannah Pearl and making love to her. You've gotta feel sorry fer them poor bastards. The swamp does funny things to some people. Why you asking about her anyways? Where'd you heard that name?" "I think I saw her last night in the bayou." "God all mighty Maude, another one gone loco from swamp gas."

The old couple laughed as Jackson paid for the food and retreated back to his room. He sat up most of the night going over in his head all that he could remember. He had to know if he'd only dreamed it all or did it really happen to him.

The next day Jackson returned to the exact spot under the limbs of the Magnolia trees and found nothing. No name scratched in the soil or evidence that he had ever been there. His vacation ended the next day so he checked in the rent a truck and flew back home to Portland, Oregon. Every year for the last thirty years he has gone back to Moss Tree and returned to the same Magnolia trees to no avail.

Time had indeed taken its toll and Jackson now approached eighty years old; but he had continued his pilgrimage to the bayou. It's all that he can do now to hike deep into the swamp these days. He got out of his truck and thought to himself that this would be his last trip. Slowly he pressed on through the swamp, even as he felt his health deteriorating with each step. He finally made it to the Magnolias when the sweet smell of Jasmine filled the air. He looked up to see Savannah standing under the trees like she had thirty years before with the same smile on her face. She had not aged one single day since their last encounter. He slowly made his way to her and they fell into each others arms. She whispered to him that she had missed him and that their time had come. Jackson lay down beneath the Magnolias and watched as a young Jackson and Savannah ascended up to the sky. The ghost of Savannah Pearl had chosen him to be by her side for eternity, beneath the sultry sun of the Georgia Bayou.

LOYALTY

ACROSS THE DESERT marched the loyal four-hundred
with blistered lips and lobster red skin.
Never questioning the commands of their Captain
knowing he was of sound mind and judgment.
Each man suffered his parched mouth and cracked lips
while putting one foot before the other in a repetitive motion.

Across the desert marched the loyal three-hundred.
The men that dropped were left by the wayside
where they died and became like dry leather.
Spit was a glorious liquid for those that could still produce it.

Across the desert marched the loyal two-hundred
drawn by the mirage of palm trees and abundant water.
Heat waves shimmering off the sands extreme temperature
baking the minds of the weak ones still in the formation.
Mile after mile, dune after dune they traveled
even the best men experienced wild hallucinations.

Across the desert marched the loyal one-hundred.
Finally the fort that had long eluded them
appeared on the horizon like an Angel of mercy.
The last few miles took their toll as many more fell;
but through the gates walked the loyal fifty.

Was the price too high for the four-hundred and fifty that died?
Or will it serve as honor for the loyal fifty that survived?
Who will go down in history as the most loyal?
the ones that perish or the ones that stayed the fight?
Does it matter if the fort was lost or held in coming days?
or if blind loyalties and obedience is a soldiers duty?

Across the desert marched the loyal one.
The Captain who believed and trusted his orders
and led his men into what he thought was right.
However the ones that gave him his orders
sit in leather chairs in a cool office and never pay
the ultimate price for the loyalties of others.

MARS ON THE HORIZON

LANCE TYLER DREAMED of becoming an astronaut like his father before him. His dad had flown the first manned space mission to Mars. The only physical thing that he had to remind him of that mission was the grainy footage that NASA had recorded. Lance had viewed the video of his father walking on the surface of Mars while verbally sending data back to the engineers at NASA many times.

That was the last time anyone had heard from Captain Jonathan Tyler. Two hours after that infamous contact an explosion on the planet was viewed and recorded by earth's most powerful planetarium telescopes. NASA contracts out some public and also secret issues to the large planetariums around the world. Once the explosion was confirmed Congress immediately voted to stop all monies to fund further manned Mars missions for an indefinite amount of time.

Lance had given his father a little brass spaceship on a chain to wear around his neck while on his mission. It would serve as a reminder of his son throughout his TOUR OF DUTY IN THE HEAVENS.

Lance was twelve years old when his father was standing on the Mars surface that day in history 2022. Lance was obsessed with going to Mars and finding his father's remains. He vowed to find out what really happened that day to cause such a devastating explosion.

He had his life all mapped out before him. He began to take higher math, science and engineering classes as he went through mid-high, high school and M I T. Once he graduated top of his class from M I T he applied for the NASA astronaut training program in Houston, Texas, he was twenty-four. With his father's reputation and his grades he was welcomed with open arms.

The first day that he stepped into the NASA classroom he told everyone that he was going to reinstate the manned Mars program. All the other students at the training facility agreed that they too wanted to go back to the red planet. That turned out to be the first day of NASA's directive to once again gear up for future Mars ventures.

It was hard work with hundreds of hours of classroom time to reach graduation day. Lance was a buff, fit man of twenty-nine as he accepted his pin and diploma that day. He and his fellow graduate alumni had a celebration off base and had thoughts of having Star Trek adventures lying before them. They had a short time before they found out exactly when those dreams would become reality.

It only took a month for Lance to receive the fantastic news that he was to lead a manned Mars mission in eighteen months. He was advised of the rigorous training program and strict diet regiment. He began training in a simulator that was to be the cockpit in his ship. Pride swelled up in the young man when NASA informed him that his ship was to be christened the USS Tyler, after his father.

Those eighteen months were the longest time span of young Lance's life. It finally got to the point that only three weeks remained until the launch date. As the commander of this voyage Lance was promoted to the rank of Captain, skipping Lieutenant all together.

The USS Tyler was completed so Lance and his crew began training in the ships cockpit. They studied the instrumentation and their layout. Even though it was exactly like the simulator the real thing has its own peculiar feeling about it. The crew had to feel comfortable in its presence.

The rest of the USS Tyler's crew was thirty year old co/pilot Jake Hunter and navigator twenty-eight year old Jill Simon. All three had graduated from the same training facility and had been friends for nearly seven years. NASA did not want to send an eight man crew just yet. They wanted to see what was truly happening on Mars and then determine all safety issues. That was the reasoning for only a small crew that could carry out this exploratory mission.

The explosion on the surface of Mars baffled scientist, since as far as they knew, there is no oxygen there. Perhaps the atmosphere has gases that are flammable or even a small amount of CO_2 that allowed enough for an explosion. It made sense in the long run to only send a small crew rather than put a larger number of people at risk.

Lift off of the USS Tyler was on Lance's thirty-first birthday June 23rd. It had taken nineteen years to arrive here on launch day at Cape Canaveral in Florida. In a few months he would be walking in his father's footsteps on the surface of Mars.

As the launch got closer and closer Lance began to have a flood of emotions ranging from apprehension to racing anxiety. Even though he had been trained for any emergencies he still had flashes of fear and doubt about his own ability to command such an undertaking.

On the morning of the launch the technicians helped the crew into their contoured chairs and all those feelings that Lance had dissipated. It was like stage fright. You have butterflies; but once you step out onto the stage and start to perform your training takes over. All the nerves disappear and your abilities take over and do what they were trained to do.

"T minus thirty" and counting squawked out over the intercom system of the cockpit. The crew continued to do its preflight checks. After all the prelims had been completed Lance closed his eyes and said a little prayer as the countdown continued.

At T minus two, Lance dug his fingers into the arms of his command chair. His knuckles turned white when the powerful rocket surged upward. As the G force pushed his body back into his chair, his life began to flash through his mind, from his childhood dreams to this historic moment he was experiencing.

It was NASA control's voice that reported the auxiliary fuel tanks had ejected on time and that the main rocket booster had been ignited that snapped him back to reality. After a few seconds the booster shut off and the USS Tyler found itself in an earth orbit. They would do a couple of earth orbits, gaining speed before their slingshot maneuver towards the planet Mars.

The crew was amazed by the view of earth as well as the moon as they orbited. Then the time came to change the ships heading and lay in the course coordinates for Mars. That was an easy task to apply to the computerized electronic system and in a few seconds they were on the correct vector to Mars. NASA had calculated that the journey was going to take 565 days.

Days turned into weeks and then months by the time the red planet finally was staring the crew in the face. They had arrived safely and without any real negative issues or problems. Spirits were high as lance and Jake began suiting up in preparation for the landing. Jill was to stay behind on the ship as Lance and Jake explored the surface. They landed the ship without incident with exactly the same coordinates that his father's ship had used when it landed almost twenty years earlier.

Anticipation was high as the door's vacuum seal was broken and its loud hissing echoed in Lance's ears. He and Jake gingerly stepped out onto the surface and a tingle of excitement ran through both of their bodies. They immediately saw the mangled hull of the earlier ship that had exploded. It was pristine as far as the metal and components, except for their being damaged beyond working order. Lance was surprised at how much was left and had not blown away into space. Mars has a small gravitational pull; but he thought it was still a lot of debris left on the planets surface.

They both took pictures in the hundreds and Jill relayed them back to NASA for evaluation. Lance and Jake were so involved that Jill had to remind them that their air supply was running low. They checked their gauges and she was correct. They had approximately fifteen minutes of air left. They stopped doing what they were doing and headed back to the safety of the ship.

The crew had seen a large crater to the North as they were landing. The next day's project was to explore the entire crater for any signs that might explain what had happened years before. However, a good night's sleep was in order as well as a squeezable turkey tube dinner. It wasn't Tavern on The Green; but it satisfied the pains of hunger.

The next day Lance and Jake headed out towards the crater with one extra air tank apiece. It didn't take long to reach the craters rim due to the low gravity. They just bounced twenty feet at a time floating two or three feet above the ground. After discussing the best way to descend to the bottom of the crater, they started down.

Once reaching the craters floor they noticed an opening at the eastwardly wall of the crater. It was about a mile away so they set out to investigate it more thoroughly. They were more than surprised to find on their arrival, that it was a cave. It intrigued them and seemed to call out to them, so they prepared to investigate inside.

They hesitated a moment before entering, not knowing what if anything could be inside its dark world. With the help of their powerful flashlights they entered. They had only ventured a few hundred yards when they had to exchange air tanks. They left the near empty ones there knowing they would pick them up on the trip out.

The cave came to an abrupt end approximately a mile after the air tank switch. They were shocked when they found a spacesuit still in tact. Jake lifted the visor on the helmet to discover skeletal remains. Lance pushed Jake aside and bent down to see. He had to know for sure if what he was expecting was true or not. He ripped the suit open and there lying on the rib cage of bones was a small brass spaceship on a chain still hanging from the skeletons neck. Lance scooped up the remains and held them close to his chest. He told Jake that this was his father and that he was going to take him home where he belonged. They quickly returned to the ship with the fallen Captain's remains.

It was disappointing that Lance and his crew could not determine what caused the explosion of his father's ship. They did retrieve some of the ship's instrumentation for the NASA scientist to study. Jake collected forty pounds of rocks and soil samples to take back with them over the eleven days they were on the surface of the planet. They could not see any evidence of water on the planet in their immediate area. They managed to keep all of their samples including Captain Jonathan Tyler's remains under the 100 pound limit. Fuel Consumption was vital and that limit ensured a safe return to earth. It was a solemn voyage back to earth.

The USS Tyler made a safe landing back at NASA several months later. Lance was glad to be home; but he requested to return to Mars as soon as possible. He is scheduled to Captain a return mission in the summer of 2048. This time there will be a crew of eight which will have a scientist, biochemist, microbiologist and a doctor. Their main mission is to set up a livable home base for future missions to live in while exploring the planet.

Lance and his mother buried Captain Jonathan Tyler in Arlington with honors. It was a beautiful ceremony for the family as well as for the five hundred guests that came to pay their respects. Lance and his mother were the last ones to leave. The reason was that they wanted some privacy to perform their own tribute.

Lance took the little brass spaceship still attached to the chain he had once given to his father and put it in a heart shaped porcelain jewelry case that had been a gift to his mother from her beloved Jonathan.

He dug a hole at the base of his father's headstone and buried it about a foot deep. Lance watched as his mother gently smoothed the soil over the jewelry case until it was covered and the ground was level. She and her son would be the only ones to know it was there for all of eternity. Lance thought to himself that just like the first time he gave it to his dad as a boy; the thought was the same. It would serve as a reminder of his son and wife through out his TOUR OF DUTY IN THE HEAVENS.

THANK YOU; BUT!

THIS IS A true story from my younger days. I was traveling southbound on Interstate 5 in southern Oregon one hot summer afternoon. I looked ahead and saw two elderly ladies standing next to their Ford station wagon alongside the freeway. I pulled up behind them, stopped and got out of my car. I noticed that they had a rear flat tire. I asked if there was anything I could do to help them. They pointed to the tire and said they didn't know what happened; it just went flat. I think you should know that I am in my mid twenties, have short hair, dressed well and behaved a complete gentleman. I mention this because it's 1972.

I got a chuckle from their explanation; but I hid it from them. They were in their late seventies or early eighties and each hung on to the other tightly. I offered to change their tire for them and they said that would be fine. It was then I noticed that the back of the wagon was filled to capacity with sacks of groceries. I opened the tailgate and started unloading the sacks one by one. I removed at least 12 or 15 sacks before I exposed the floors trap door to where the spare was.

I lifted the floor panel and lifted the spare out and placed it on the ground. For us old timers; I removed their bumper jack. I placed the base under the back bumper and inserted the long notched pole into it. I pressed the up or down lever and lifted the hooking devise up to make contact with the bumper. Click, click, click it went until it had reached its correct position. I reversed the lever and inserted the jacks handle into the cranking receiver.

I started pumping one click at a time. The car began to move up with each click. I stopped jacking a couple of clicks from the tire leaving the ground. I went to loosen the lug nuts; but they did not have a wrench for the nuts. I went to my car and got my star wrench and then loosened the nuts. Once I had broken them free I continued to jack up the car. When the tire was 4 to 5 inches from the ground I stopped lifting the vehicle.

For everyone who has used a bumper jack you know the problems with them along a busy freeway. The car was already at a slight angle being that it was on the dirt shoulder. Every time a big rig truck would go by at sixty miles an hour the car would rock back and forth. My biggest fear was that the jack would kick out from under the car or that the car would veer to the side and fall off the jack.

I hurried as fast as I could and managed to remove the flat and put the spare on. I hand tightened the lug nuts back on the wheel. I lowered the car until there was enough weight on the tire so it wouldn't spin. I then tightened the nuts the rest of the way using the standard cross tightening technique. I must confess I was sweating profusely by this time. It was a hot day to start with. I put the flat tire in the wagons floor compartment and replaced the jack. I told the ladies to make sure that they got it fixed as soon as possible.

During all this time, not once did either lady say a word to me. The last time one of them said anything was when they said it was fine to change the tire. I then started to replace the sacks of groceries one at a time. I remembered that they were stacked tightly and took up the entire area. As I put the last bag in place and shut the tailgate the car sped away throwing rocks and gravel all over me in a cloud of dust.

I stood there in total amazement and watched the car going down the freeway like a torpedo that was fired from its submarine tube. I dusted off my clothes, cleared my throat as the dust dissipated and had to laugh. I picked up my star wrench and through it in my trunk. To this day I still ponder what those two ladies thought that made them react in such a way. I have never taken it personally; but excuse it as being stereotyped since it was the age of hippies and Aquarius. For those of us that can still recall the sixties; maybe the ladies had no other option in their minds, LOL.

GATORMAN

HE WAS BORN and raised in the deepest part of the swamp
He ruled his world with a mighty boot and a stomp
No sane man would venture into his protected world
Because they didn't know where they would be hurled

Legend has it that he is bigger than an ordinary life
And that he takes what he needs with a Bowie knife
Many have disappeared while they went hunting
We can only assume as a price for their confronting

So the law had to go there, find and question
The man that they hoped would give his confession
Because too many people had lately disappeared
And more deaths were what the locals truly feared

Shots rang out as the lawman approached Gator Man's shack
"Hold your fire," was what the police captain yelled back
But Gator Man didn't live by city rules or any strangers
He trusted no one and was aware of the real dangers

The Captain slowly came forward with his hands in the air
This impressed Gator Man and that was something very rare
But before he could warn the lawman to stop and stay back
A 12 foot gator grabbed him and dragged him under the shack

He learned the hard way what others had before him
That approaching the Gator Man surely would be grim
You see it wasn't the arm of the law that Gator Man had to fear
It was that vicious gator that kept HIM there years after year.

 Gatorman was horrified as he saw the lawman pulled under the water. The thrashing waters turning a dull red, gave proof to the obvious, that the lawman was dead. It didn't take long for Satan's Child, (the name Gatorman had given to the gator years before) to stick his head above the waterline. The gator stared at his human enemy as if to say that his time will soon come as well.

Gatorman looked into the eyes of the big gator as he spied all the scars that he'd inflicted on Satan's Child over the last forty years. He knew that he could recall each one vividly and with extreme accuracy. The long jagged one above his left eye where he had stabbed him the night that he lost his leg. Then there was the two-inch oval chunk of flesh that was missing from the end of his nose. That was the night that he had lost his right arm to the creature.

The swamp man stood on his deck two feet above the water and admired the pot marked hide from repeated buckshot encounters they had experienced. His favorite infliction on the beast was definitely the gator's blind left eye. He had made a spear and stabbed him in it only a year ago. Satan's Child seemed only to become meaner and more deadly after that.

A week before the lawman showed up on his property. The gator came out of no where and with his powerful tail whipped the one remaining leg out from under the Gatorman. He had fallen to the deck and if he had not rolled over immediately, he would have been in the gators jaws for sure. These close calls were becoming more frequent and becoming close to being successful. Age was indeed catching up to Gatorman and his reaction time was slowing him down to the point of possibly being killed by Satan's Child.

He had to come up with a plan to kill his adversary, one that would bring this long time conflict to an end once and for all. He already had tried stabbing, shooting and spearing the big gator to no avail. What could he do now to end this ordeal?

Then it struck him like a driver hitting a three hundred yard golf shot off the tee. He went to the back of his shack where he kept his chicken coop. He grabbed three chickens, took them into the shack and butchered them; smiling all the while, as he was preparing a feast for ole Satan's Child.

Then as the sun began to set that evening Gatorman went out on his deck ready to put his plan into action. He pounded on the railing to draw attention to himself. Sure enough the killer gator raised his head again up above the waterline. Gatorman threw one chicken at Satan's Child and he caught it in mid-air. He swallowed it in one massive gulp. Then the second chicken was tossed and the gator repeated his previous actions.

The gator must have wondered what was happening since this had never happened throughout the years. Could this be a peace offering? The gator was soon to discover the answer to his question. Gatorman threw the third chicken and as soon as Satan's Child caught it in his mouth, it exploded, blowing the huge gators head into oblivion.

Gatorman laughed out loud and hollered in delight at his accomplishment. He was free at last from his lifetime enemy. Why he had not thought of using that one stick of dynamite before escaped him. He hobbled back into his shack and thought about going into town.

The next morning Gatorman woke up with a newly found spirit. He put on his backpack and was ready for the slow and painful journey to town. It would be the first time in forty years that he would see paved roads and sidewalks. He walked his deck over the water with no fear. In the years past Satan's Child would throw himself up onto the deck and block him from leaving.

He breathed a sigh of joy filled with the victory of a warrior when his foot touched the soil for the first time in forty years. It was at that very second that a large growl startled him. He looked up to see four cougars circling him. His only way out was to retreat back across his wooden deck to his shack.

He watched as three of the big cats left while one stayed and guarded the deck crossing. Everyday the cats would return and a different one would stay on guard while the others left. Gatorman had no more shotgun shells or dynamite. A knife or spear was no match for such an agile foe. What now lie ahead for the swamps legendary Gatorman.

Every night Gatorman watched as the big cats exchanged guard duties at the end of his shacks wooden deck. The only thing he could think of as to why the cats wouldn't come across the deck was either their fear of the water, gators or the smell of death that might still linger from the demise of Satan's Child. Time slowly moved onward into days, then weeks, then months; yet the cats persisted in their ritual.

Gatorman had had enough and he was sick of catching fish everyday for food for the last forty-years. He was aging and he swore he wouldn't die a prisoner in the swamp. There was no way that he could kill the four cougars on his own. He had to out think them somehow and quick. He figured he wouldn't have a chance with them on land. That meant he had to stay on the water if he was to have any chance at all.

He began dismantling his shack of forty years piece by piece. Using swamp vines he lashed the boards together. This was a tough job for a one arm, one leg man to do; but determination persevered. The big cats paced back and forth as their anxiety level heightened by all the commotion.

They still however, never adventured onto the deck for whatever reason it was that haltered their approach.

It took Gatorman three weeks to construct a makeshift raft eight by twelve feet and six one inch planks thick. It floated level and true as long as he didn't crowd the edges anywhere. His last job was to take his handrail from the deck and fashioned an eight-foot pole. Swamp water isn't very deep so this pole was plenty long to suffice as his propulsion tool.

Early one morning he pulled the nails from what was left of his deck that was connected to his once shack. He slowly drifted away from the shoreline and into the main current. The four cats began stalking the raft along the shore as he drifted further away. He kept pushing the raft out into the current and eventually left the disappointed cats far behind.

The swamp man knew that he was approximately twenty-five miles from the nearest little town. The good thing was that the slow moving water led right to it. He didn't have to make any turns or complicated maneuvers. He only had to stay in the middle of the current and give a push with his pole every so often. He drifted all day and into the night. He had many obstacles along the way. There had been snakes hanging from low hung limbs. One time he had to poke at two gators with his pole. He almost ran into a large rock that protruded out of the water.

As the sun began to rise, Gatorman emerged from the bayous foliage and into a clearing. There in front of him was the small town of Peachtree, Georgia. This town of forty thousand was completely surrounded by the swamp. There was only one highway that ran in and out of the town, State highway (19). The town was made up of mostly retirees and a few younger people that ran the businesses.

As Gatorman floated up to the pier next to the fish market he caused a stir among the dockworkers. No one had ever seen a one-arm one-leg man, furthermore navigating a raft coming out of the bayou. The men helped him up onto the dock as he thanked them and asked where he could get some hot food and a cold drink. They directed him to the Gator Bar and Grill located right there on the waterfront. He hobbled his way the two blocks required to finally get his food and drink.

Gatorman became a town fixture once he sat down on the bar stool that day at Gators Bar. The owner gave him a small room out back and paid him a salary to clean up; but mostly to tell his swamp stories about Satan's Child and all the victims that he saw killed. Tourists come from all over the country to have their picture taken with him and hear his stories. Who would have ever thought Gatorman was not only a legend in the swamp; but a legend in Peachtree as well? As far as I know Gatorman still lives and spins his tales to this very day to anyone that will listen. If you ever find yourself in Peachtree, Georgia, stop in at the Gator Bar and Grill and have a cold beer and a listen to the now world famous Gatorman tell his tales of the swamp.

THE MIRACLE HAND

I WAS PLAYING in my first poker tournament of Texas Hold-em. I had finally been dealt some semi good cards. A miracle hand that would prove to be heaven sent. It was developing so slowly that I hadn't seen it yet. I thought I had a losing hand in the beginning. My hand was an unsuited pair of deuces. I decided to stay with the hand in order to improve the value of my little pair and not lose my big blind.

After the first round of betting only three players were left in the hand, Big Tiny, Horace the Snake and me the amateur. I could see their delight as they stared me down. They both needed a spittoon for the drool they were salivating.

The dealer laid out the flop while we sat like stone statues. A, K, 2, the trap was set; but for whom? Big Tiny pondered over his pair of Ace's in the hole. Snake played dumb with his pair of King*s in the hole. I showed no emotions with my trip two's.

Ace's led out with a thousand. The kings followed suit. I hesitated as part of my act to slow play and show weakness. Even with trip's, the board was dangerous. Since this was the first good hand I had gotten I put in the thousand then waited to see the turn. It was all I could do to compose myself as the last deuce hit the felt on the turn.

Big Tiny bet $5000 thinking his full house with Ace's over duce's was a winner. Horace saw the bet thinking his full house with Kings was the winning hand. I continued to pause while making small talk about how the pros were running over me at the table (my attempt to act out being on tilt). I raised the pot to $25,000. I immediately saw the wheels turning in their heads. Big Tiny knew there was still an Ace out. He figured to split the pot would be the worse outcome. Snake thought long and hard. He had a full house; but the Ace caused him major concern. He had too much invested. He really didn't put anyone on an Ace or the last King. Both thought I had trip deuces, a losing hand. His chips went into the pot with confidence.

The dealer turned over the river card, a queen. It was at that moment I realized I had won. If an Ace or King would have shown, I might have been up against four of a kind higher than my hand. Big Tiny, still thinking his boat was the best hand, pushed all in ($150,000). Snake had to call with all his chips. I called as well.

Everyone stood up looking over the table. Tiny through his Ace's onto the table with a wide grin. Horace slammed his Kings down on the felt cussing loudly. I cherished the moment as long as I could before slowly turning over one deuce. I played with my final card as I glanced back and forth at my two adversaries. I smiled and laid down my second deuce face up revealing my four of a kind.

Luck is a nice thing. Experience is another. I find that when destiny and luck come together, they rule.

RESURRECTION

JILL WILLIAMS LAY in an alley at 2 AM on a rainy Seattle Saturday night. Heroin flowing through her veins as the Grim Reaper hovered over her convulsive body. He reached out to collect his prize; but was interrupted by Simon Gibbons entering the alley. The Reaper retreated back into the shadows.

Seeing the young girl, Simon approached and knelt down by her side. He tried to ask her if he could help; but she was incoherent and unresponsive. He called 911 and reported their position to the emergency operator. He did what he could to comfort the girl until the ambulance arrived. Once there, the EMT's evaluated her condition.

Simon heard one of the EMT's say, "when will this hooker ever learn?"

"Her type will never learn until she's a slab on the morgue's table," the other EMT said. They ran IV's in both of her arms and transported her to the Seattle General Hospital.

During all of the confusion the police had arrived. They talked to Simon and took down his personal information and how he came to find someone at 2 AM. Simon explained that he worked two blocks away and got off work at 1:30 am and that he lived three blocks away, so he walked to and from work. The policeman told Simon that the girl was a known drug addict and prostitute. She had been arrested many times and had almost died from drug overdoses on several occasions.

Finally everyone left except Simon and he found himself standing in the rain reviewing the night's proceedings. He looked down and saw a small clutch purse on the ground. He figured that it must belong to the young girl. He decided to hang on to it until the next day. He resumed walking to his townhouse.

The next day Simon woke up at 10 AM. He viewed the purse and it reminded him that he needed to return it. He showered, got dressed and had a bite to eat. It was his day off so he felt no urgency to hurry. He went to the city bus stop a block from his townhouse and waited for the bus. He only waited a short time when the number 8 bus pulled to a stop in front of him. He paid for his ticket and sat down. He was glad that he had overheard the EMT's tell the policeman what hospital they were taking the girl to.

While he sat on the bus he took it upon himself to look in the purse. He found the name Jill Williams on several pieces of papers. He felt better now that he could ask for the girl by name. The rain had stopped as Simon got off the bus in front of the Hospital. He walked into the main entrance and went to the admitting desk and asked for Jill's room. He was told she was in room 327. He thanked the nurse and made his way to her bedside.

Jill looked up and asked, "are you the one that found me last night?"

"Yes I am, I brought you your purse. It was left behind last night." He gave it to her and she thanked him for his kindness.

As they continued talking a social worker entered the room and addressed Jill, "I've got you placed at Huntington House again Jill. This is the last time. If you fail, then you're on your own, is that perfectly clear?"

Jill snapped, "I don't want to go back to Huntington House." Simon knew that was one of the best rehabilitation centers in all of Seattle. He listened as Jill continued to refuse to go and throw a fit.

The social worker sternly said, "if you don't go, then the police are going to lock you up for ninety days in the county jail."

Simon interrupted their conversation and said," may I offer to help? Jill you can come and stay at my townhouse. I will help you get through this mess if you like."

"I don't know you, besides, why would you do something for a total stranger? I'm 23 and you're like 50. I'm not going to sleep with you if that's what you think will happen. What are you, a pervert or what?"

"First off I'm 55 so thank you for the 50 comment. I just want to help; I believe it was fate that I found you last night. Maybe this all happened so that I could offer to help you. It is your decision, your choice."

The social worker told Simon that if Jill accepted he would have to be fingerprinted and sign papers as a temporary custodian. He would also be responsible for her safety and actions. Simon said that he had some vacation time coming so he could be there and help her recover. Jill was thinking it over in her mind when a policeman entered the room.

"OK! I'll stay at your place," Jill blurted out; "now get me out of this place."

The social worker drove Simon and Jill to Simon's townhouse. She examined it room by room. It had two bedrooms and two bathrooms. It all checked out according to state regulations. Jill had her own bedroom and bathroom.

Once the social worker left Jill turned to Simon and yelled, "What's going on here? You touch me and I'll see you in prison for the rest of your life!"

"Do you want to get off drugs and stop being a prostitute? If you do then I will do everything I can to help you achieve that. You have to want to get clean, do you want it? I mean really want it?" Simon yelled back.

Jill had a small quiver in her voice as she said, "yes I want to get clean."

She was speechless while thinking that someone wanted to help her and didn't want sex or anything in return. It brought a tear to her eye and a feeling that she had never had until that moment. The feeling that she had worth as a person and that she deserved to be a happy soul.

It was a hard thirty-days for Jill that first month staying with Simon. She screamed with pain, vomited and flat out prayed to just die. Simon was there by her side every second of the day and night. He had ice bags and cold towels to wipe her face and cool her body. It took many days for the withdrawal symptoms to begin relinquishing its hold on her body and mind. She was able to keep light fluids and food down. Jill slowly began to regain her strength back along with her self-esteem.

Simon had quit his job by the time 3 months had passed. Jill had blossomed into a beautiful, drug free confident woman. She enrolled in a local community college to study being a nurse. She was falling in love with a fine young man that was also studying to be a nurse. Life was truly becoming a modern day fairytale for Jill.

Simon decided that it was time for him to have his last talk with Jill. She was packing and preparing to move into her own apartment. They sat down at the dining room table and Simon took Jill's hand. He smiled and began talking to her in a loving voice. "Jill, I remember like it was yesterday when I first saw you lying in that alley. It was no accident that I came along that day or that your purse was left behind. Things were taking place that you weren't aware of. Death was there reaching out for you that night. God however, had decided to give you one more chance to redeem yourself.

When I came to your hospital room you were faced with a choice. Remember, Huntington House, jail or an offer from a total stranger; you chose me. You had the opportunity to leave my home anytime you wanted. You chose to stay. You could have stolen from me; but you chose not to. You could have reverted back to drugs and not suffer those terrible days of withdrawal. Once again you chose to fight and beat the heroin demon inside you. You chose to go to nursing school and get a degree. You have chosen a life that is far from the one you lived a few short months ago. I am proud of you because you made all the choices and you were the one that stood and fought for your life. I want you to stop packing and accept this as a gift. It is the deed to this townhouse. I want you to have it so you can always remember me. You see my work is done here and I must return to my real home."

Simon stood up and he was immediately encircled with an aura of light. A large pair of wings appeared from behind his body as he slowly rose from the floor. As he was fading away through the ceiling and upward into the sky she heard his last remark. "It has been an honor, I am thankful that God sent me to be your heavenly angel."

Jill was stunned and it all made sense to her now. How a total stranger trusted her and believed in her. She flashed back on all the things Simon had done over the last few months. The thing that stood out the most was her hearing Simon telling her, you chose, you chose your life. She realized at that moment that it had always been inside her to change. It just took a stranger to make her see it for herself.

Jill married her nursing school classmate. They both work at Seattle General Hospital. Jill did however take a few weeks off to give birth to her baby boy. She of course named him . . . . Simon.

WISHING

JOSHUA JONES WAS eleven years old and only had one true friend, which was Sammy Johnson his schoolmate in his sixth grade class. Joshua had a tough life up to this point in his childhood. He had always been different and so he was teased relentlessly his whole life. Sammy was his next door neighbor so they had been together from the first grade. A typical day for Joshua was to start out from home with a smile on his face. He would meet Sammy and they would walk to the bus stop. They would laugh and horse around until the school bus would round the corner. The door would open and Bill Woods the driver would say "Good morning boys and how are you Joshua?"

"I'm fine Mr. Woods" Joshua would say as he climbed the three steps into the bus. After that was when the day would start to deteriorate. There was always a group of kids, some his classmates and some older ones from junior high on board. It was usually the older boys and even girls that made fun of him. They called him stupid or funny looking. Joshua kept on smiling and pretending as if it didn't bother him, however, it hurt him inside; but he wasn't going to let them know that.

Once in his classroom he had to endure his classmates who would throw wadded up paper at him. They all laughed and pointed at him; but Sammy would always stand up for him and demand that the mean kids stop. Teachers did very little to stop the abuse other than to say," Now class that's not nice." It was sad in a way that Sammy had to endure his life with him. He was always there to hear and see the humiliation plus be the one to put a stop to it all. Sammy would get angry; but Joshua would just smile and put his arm around him and tell him to not worry about it.

The time came when Joshua and Sammy became seniors at Waterford High School. Their life had not changed over the years. The bullies had kept on teasing and tormenting Joshua. There was one boy in particular that had made his life miserable and a living hell. That boy was Troy Butler. Troy was captain of the football team, basketball team and the baseball team. Not only had he ridden Joshua for years he was also dating Sarah Ann, the head cheerleader.

Joshua had liked Sarah since the first grade; but she too had abused him. That had really hurt his feelings in a totally different way from the way Troy and others had hurt his feelings. Joshua wanted so badly to take Sarah Ann to the senior prom; but he knew that was never going to happen. The best he could do was to volunteer to decorate the prom hall and then help clean up afterwards. He didn't mind any of that because he could at least see Sarah Ann glowing in her gown. Seeing Sarah happy always made Joshua smile and bright eyed.

Prom night came and it was a warm summer Saturday night. Joshua had helped decorate the hall with Sammy and other classmates. Sarah and Troy arrived at the hall. Joshua's heart dropped as they exited Troy's sports car. She was dressed in a strapless sky blue formal and Troy in a white tuxedo. Joshua thought that they looked like the little statues on top of a wedding cake. He was still thrilled as they walked by him without speaking a word.

The crowd cheered and applauded as they entered the room. Even Joshua and Sammy clapped; after all they were the most popular people in their school.

Joshua watched as Sarah and Troy danced the night away. He was ecstatic when it was announced that they were crowned king and queen of the prom. Oh how he wanted to be in Troy's shoes for just that one night. If only Sarah could fall in love with him. Truth be told, he would have been in heaven if she would even have spoken his name just once. Joshua felt abandoned by God because he had prayed a million times since the first grade that she would at least be a friend. It was heartbreaking that after all these years she still didn't know he was alive.

The prom came to an end and the people began to leave. Sammy and Joshua cleaned up the hall and locked up the building when they were done. Sammy offered a ride to Joshua but he said he would like to walk home and think about that night. Sammy understood so he slapped him on the back and told him he would see him in the morning. The car's taillights disappeared into the night as Sammy drove away.

Joshua lived four miles away on River Road. He loved walking along the river at night and seeing the moon's reflection on the water. This was to be a night that Joshua would contemplate. He wondered what to do with his life now that he had graduated from school. He had given it little thought until now. He had walked halfway home when he heard a car's high performance engine getting closer. River Road is a two lane road and has no streetlights or signals. There are only six houses on a three mile section of the road and his house and Sammy's were two of them.

The car suddenly appeared around a sharp corner at a high rate of speed. It was coming directly towards him. He jumped out of the way in the nick of time as the fancy sports car flew by him. The car had only traveled approximately a hundred yards when it tore through a wooden barrier and plummeted down a 350 foot embankment to the water below. Joshua heard a girl scream and he knew in his heart that it was Sarah Ann.

He ran to the river's edge where the car had just gone off the road. He arrived in time to see the cars red taillights slowly descend under water. He slid on his backside down the steep bank and without hesitation dove into the water. If it had not been for the red taillights still being lit he would never have seen the car through the murky black water. He pushed himself downward until he finally had the car's door handle in his grasp.

He could hear Sarah screaming inside the car. He had to make decisions and fast. He was running out of time, air to breath and so was Sarah. He pulled with all his might at the door handle. Then with one massive pull, the door opened and the water rushed in. He grabbed Sarah and began swimming to the surface. Thank God they were only in twelve feet of water. Had they been any deeper, they wouldn't have made it to safety. As their heads broke the surface they gasped for air. They were free from their dangerous depths, but were caught in the river's current.

They were being swept down stream at a fast pace. Sara reached out and grabbed a limb from an old tree that had fallen partly into the river. Once secure she turned to see where Joshua was. It was at that exact moment that Joshua was swept into a jagged limb on the same tree. It stabbed him through the neck and he was momentarily pinned there as his blood drained from his body.

Joshua looked up at Sarah as she called out his name and took his hand. He smiled and tears slowly left his eyes. He had finally gotten to hear her say his name and to hold his hand. She had noticed him and in his own little world, life was complete. Sarah could no longer hold on to his hand and as she released it, Joshua's body sank and the current carried him away. Sarah managed to pull herself to the shore using the tree's limbs.

They found Joshua's body the next day, two miles downstream entangled in a log jam. Troy's body was brought up by divers and a tow truck hauled up his fancy sports car. Sarah recovered from her minor physical injuries; but still has nightmares about that night. The accident had a solemn and mesmerizing effect on the community. The school commissioned a brass placard that is on the wall of the main hall inside the entrance to the school. The placard reads as follows:

THOUGH THERE ARE MANY BRAVE SOULS IN THIS WORLD,

LET JOSHUA JONES BE THE EXAMPLE THAT THEY COME
IN ALL SIZES AND STATURE.
WE ARE PROUD TO CALL HIM AN ALUMNUS
HERE AT WATERFORD SCHOOL
FOR THE DEVELOPMENTALLY DISABLED.

THE IMPOSSIBLE DREAM

SKY BROWN WAS your average little six year old girl. She played with her friends and her dog Hugo. All the children would take turns riding on the big Saint Bernard. He had an excellent and loving personality. Sky and Hugo were more than friends; they had a bond like no other.

There's really not much to tell about sky's life that we all didn't experience ourselves as children. That is until she turned ten years old, that's when her life took a terrible turn for the worse.

It was late one night when she awoke to find her bedroom filled with smoke. She ran to the door and opened it only to discover a wall of flames and intense heat. She began screaming for her mom and dad. She was soon overcome with smoke and fell to the floor unconscious.

Both her parents were trapped in their bedroom and had to jump from its second story window. Sky's father, Dick Brown, shattered his leg when he hit the ground. His wife suffered back and pelvis injuries after she jumped. They managed to crawl away from the burning house to a point of safety.

Dick cried out for Sky to no avail as Susan Brown sat crying with the realization that her child Sky might be dead. Then at that moment a massive ball of fire appeared from out of the flames and smoke. It was Hugo all aflame dragging the limp body of Sky from the house to safety.

Her clothes and hair were on fire. Dick hobbled over to her as fast as he could and began beating out the flames with his shirt. He held her in his arms until the fire trucks and paramedics arrived. "My daughter, please help her. Please," he begged.

The paramedics immediately examined her. "She's alive. She has second and third degree burns over most of her body including her face," said the paramedic. They got her in to the ambulance and sped away to the hospital.

Other paramedics that had arrived were taking care of Mr. and Mrs. Browns injuries. Once they were stable they too were put in to waiting ambulances. As Mr. Brown was being loaded he glanced over to see the dead burned body of Hugo lying on the ground. He said quietly, "you did good boy. Thank you, I know Sky would be so proud of you."

Everyone's injuries healed from that night; but it was Sky that was left with disfiguring scars. The flames were particularly damaging and relentless to her face; she was unrecognizable as Sky. She could still see, hear and speak, that was the only blessing besides still being alive. There were years of skin graphs and operations in the future for little Sky.

Sky had accepted living with her parents; she had no job or social life. This was surely her destiny. She still had dreams; but only allowed herself that luxury on rare occasions. She had never replaced Hugo with another dog. She felt no other dog could ever live up to him. He was buried in the back yard of the new house that was built on the same lot after the fire. Sky spent many afternoons talking to Hugo, which brought back memories of being loved and accepted.

The years passed slowly and Sky continued being in and out of the hospital. It was on her 21st birthday that she entered the hospital for her 17th surgical procedure. This was to be the last one that dealt with injuries from the fire. As she lay on the table in the operating room waiting for another skin graft she closed her eyes and drifted into a peaceful sleep.

PART 2

Blake Jacobs got out of bed and walked over to the dresser. He reached out and pushed the alarm clocks button down. The annoying sound came to a halt as he stood there in his shorts. How could 5AM come so early every single day, he wondered?

He grabbed all the clothes he needed and made his way to the bathroom for a hot shower. As the water hit his body he stiffened to attention with eyes wide open. His heart was pounding now; he was awake for sure at this point. He finished with his shower, got dressed and fixed breakfast.

The sun was just breaking over the horizon as he started his Ford F-250, 4X4. He had an hours drive to the shipyard where he worked. Blake was a certified welder and worked as a private contractor for the U S Navy. He was building a new battleship along with a few hundred other welders. The money was good; but the job is dirty, hard and dangerous.

He arrived just in time to punch his time card before the whistle blew to start work. His foreman sent him down to the third level, section 110. Blake and two other men were welding in a small room called the hole. As they were working they were startled by a loud explosion. Blake lifted his helmet shield and turned to see what had happened. It was at that exact second that a fireball and bright light rushed through the doorway and filled the room, then disappeared as fast as it had came. It was similar to a back draft and it caught Blake square in the face.

The heat singed off his eyebrows and most of his hair. The men behind him only suffered smoke inhalation. Blake's body had taken the main force of the fiery blast. Blake's two coworkers took him topside, by the time they got there the dock was covered with medical personnel. As the paramedic examined him, Blake stated that he couldn't see. He was told that it might be temporary and that the doctors at the hospital would tell him more.

Blake was taken to the hospital basically for minor facial burns and observation. His loss of sight was considered something that would return in a day. It was common in these kinds of situations to have temporary blindness.

They arrived at the hospital and Blake was taken to the emergency room. Doctor Bailey examined him. "Yea, all this burns are minor. They will heal without leaving scars. Get a CT of his head to make sure that there's no problems in that area."

Blake called out to the doctor as he starting to leave, "doctor! What about my eyes, will I be able to see again and when doc," he asked.

"Your eyes, no one said anything about them. What's wrong with them?"

"I can't see, I'm blind as a bat"

Doctor Bailey examined his eyes closely. "Nurse, after you get this man checked in call Dr. Johnson and tell him I need a consultation. Don't worry son, Dr. Johnson is the best opthamologist in the state. He'll get to the bottom of your lack of vision."

About an hour after Blake was in his room Dr. Johnson entered the room and introduced himself. He examined him and then ordered several test. Blake was wheeled away and put through several test before being returned to his room. All he could do was wait for the results.

It was mid day when the eye specialist entered Blake's room. "Afternoon Blake, there's no way to sugar coat this. I've looked at the results of your tests and sadly I have to tell you that your lack of vision is permanent. I'm sorry Blake; there was too much damage to the cornea from the light intensity along with the heat. If there's anything I can do as far as training or set up counseling let me know."

No one could tell you how Blake felt at that moment; but Blake himself. He laid there in silence and his body fell limp. "Leave me alone, just go away," Blake said. The doctor left the room and pulled the door shut behind him. He instructed the nurse to keep a sharp eye on him.

The last thing they wanted was for Blake to harm himself or worse yet fall victim to suicide.

Blake had no intentions of committing suicide or hurting himself. He kept asking himself what a 24 year old man was going to do now. He wanted to know how to adjust and cope to his situation; which is a great attitude to have. One thing Blake had was a strong will to survive.

A couple of days passed and he asked if he could go outside and get some sun. A nurse got a wheelchair and pushed him out on the hospital's sun deck. He sat there absorbing the suns warm rays when out of nowhere a soft voice said "It's a beautiful day isn't it, the river, city and Mount Hood off in the distance?"

Blake was startled at first, he thought he was alone. "Oh! I didn't know anyone was here. I like the warm sun on my face; but unfortunately I can't say anything about the beautiful sight. I'm blind; but if you say it is, it must be."

"I'm sorry, I didn't know. Would you like me to tell you what I see?"

"That would be nice if you don't mind spending time with me," he said. "By the way my name is Blake."

"Hello Blake, My name is Sky and it is a pleasure to meet you and to spend time with you."

She began describing the blue sky with puffy clouds off in the distance. She told how Mt. Hood still had a snow capped peak and that the sternwheeler was paddling up the river filled with tourist. They spent the entire day laughing, talking and enjoying one another's company.

This was the first time in Sky's life that she was having a conversation with a boy. She was mesmerized by his voice because it had no pity or apprehension in it. That afternoon was one that was without sorrow or inhibitions. It was a day where she felt 100% accepted and was treated as a real woman. It was all she could do to hold back her tears of joy.

She got her courage up to say, "forgive me; but are you married or have a girlfriend?"

"No, I've never had the time before. Look at me now, plenty of time on my hands; but who wants a blind person?"

"You're handsome; I can't believe someone hasn't swept you right up."

"You're too kind Sky. What about you? With that lovely voice and sweet personality, how can you still be available? You must have a boyfriend."

"I was in a fire as a child and was severally burned. I've had multiply surgeries. I think the one I just had on my back is the last, thank God. I tend to stay indoors. I got tired of being pointed at and called names. I have no social life, so to answer your question, no I haven't a boyfriend."

"Well that's their loss. I know after talking to you this afternoon that you have a loving heart and soul. I believe that fate has brought us together on this day for a reason. If you wouldn't mind leading me around by the hand; I would like to invite you out for dinner next week. I hope that RENARDO'S on the RIVER will suffice?"

Sky's heart dropped. She thought about a second before saying "you don't have to do that; I'm use to staying at hommmmm."

"STOP THAT!" Blake snapped at her. "I don't know what you look like on the outside; but I damn well know I like the girl that's inside her. I want to get to know both girls. Don't you ever give up on yourself. People without dreams or hope have nothing and you are so much more than nothing. Don't ever forget that you are as good as any other person."

Sky began crying, not from sadness; but from joy. She thought that no one would ever ask her out on a date. She managed to reel in her emotions and hold back her tears long enough to say "yes and you will never know what this moment means to me."

"No Sky, you don't know what this means to me. I've been thinking all afternoon about how much I wanted to ask you out. I kept saying to myself why you would want to go out with a blind guy. What a wonderful day for the both of us. I accept you as you are and you accept me as I am. Like I said, call it fate or Devine intervention, we were destine to meet."

He reached out and she took his hand. He lifted it slowly while she guided it towards the side of her face. He gently wiped away the tears that ran down her cheek. He then kissed her where the tears once were. He smiled and laid his hand on her arm and squeezed softly.

If there was ever a case to be made for love at first sight, this is it. Sky and Blake continued to date and grow closer to one another. Then on Sky's 22nd birthday Blake asked her to marry him. They were married in a small ceremony at Cathedral Park next to the river.

Blake and Sky are still living the fairy tale life and their love grows more each day. Their love proves that there is someone out there for everyone. It's just that some have to look harder than others; but their rewards will also be filled with happiness.

It wasn't long till Sky found out she was expecting a child. She gave birth to an 8 pound 6 ounce baby boy on the 8th of November. Sky already had a name picked out from the past. She looked down to the baby she held in her arms and said, "I've given you a special name. It represents love, trust, dedication and loyalty. Your name is Hugo and it will always remind me to love you and your father as much as he loved me."

A SWAN'S LOVE

RACHEL ADAMS WOULD leave her parents lakefront home and walk the lake's shoreline for hours. She loved one section of the lake particular. It was a place that some would call an inlet or cove. The wind didn't blow there, so the water was smooth as glass and just as shinny. Rachel would sit on an old log and watch as deer and other forest animals come to drink. She has spent every summer of her life at Lake of the Woods in southern Oregon and has never grown tired of it.

During the summer between her tenth and eleven grades she was once again at the lake house. She walked down to the cove and sat on the same log as she has done year after year. As she gazed out over the still water she noticed something far off slowly approaching. She stood and then walked knee deep into the water. She was amazed when she discovered that it was a beautiful white swan that continued towards her.

The creature stopped three feet in front of her. Rachel held out her hand and the swan floated to her side. She stroked its head and soon the swan laid its head against Rachel's side. She looked at the creature and decided to name it Lovely. For several days Lovely returned and played with Rachel. She fed bread to her newly found friend and they splashed about in the water.

A few weeks past and as Rachel and Lovely were playing the joyous interacting came to an abrupt halt. Lovely stopped and stretched her neck as high as she could and looked out over the cove's water. There on the horizon was another. It came closer until it finally stopped three feet in front of Rachel. There in all his splendor was a rare black swan. He slowly tilted his head and Lovely drifted to his side. She circled him twice before they intertwined their necks while making cooing sounds. They turned and swam towards the open waters. Lovely glanced back once and looked at Rachel. Lovely lowered her head slowly and then looked away. It was as if it were her way of saying good-bye.

Rachel hasn't seen Lovely or the black swan for the last two summers. However, on the third summer as she sat on her log at the cove she again saw something approaching from far away. Rachel's eyes opened with excitement with her expectations that this would be Lovely and the black swan. She wadded waist deep out into the water and waited for their return.

To her surprise it was neither. It was the rarest of the rare, a charcoal grey swan. Rachel held out her hand and the creature swam close. She stroked its head while it leaned against her side and made soothing sounds.

"I know your mother and father," she said. "I will name you Unity."

That was five years ago; but Unity has returned every summer to be with Rachel. They play in the lake's warm water like two kids without a care in the world. Rachel still hopes deep in her heart that Lovely or the black swan will reappear someday. Until then she not only has part of them in Unity; she also has them imprinted in her memories.

This piece has many interpretations. I have found that there are two major ones; but many others as well. I chose to leave it up to the reader to take from it what they feel. I will say that the two biggest ones are interracial marriage and opposites attract. It might just be a cute little story; I hope you enjoy it no matter your interpretation.

LAND OF SKETTELS DOWN UNDER

LITTLE 6 YEAR old Bobby walked with his eyes wide open as he gazed at the multicolored things before him. There were purple trees, yellow mountains, checkered colored bushes and a pink sky with bright green streaks in it to name a few. Candy canes hung from the trees and chocolate drops were sprinkled on every bush.

A red river ran throughout, leaving black beaches with white sparkles scattered in as its shoreline. As Bobby looked around in amazement a teal colored squirrel approached him and said "hello, my name is Henry. Welcome to the LAND of SKETTELS down under."

Bobby stared at the creature before he replied "squirrels can't talk."

"They do here as well as every living thing."

"It's true. Honestly," said the big lime colored oak tree behind him.

Henry escorted Bobby around the LAND of SKETTELS and introduced him to the trees, bushes and all of the different talking animals. Bobby was impressed with Manny the butterfly and Croaker the bull frog. Their actions and voices thrilled Bobby to no end. Henry was his favorite of all. Henry showed him everything there was to see and do in the LAND of SKETTELS.

Bobby loved eating the chocolate drops and cotton candy from the orange clouds that floated slightly above his head. Even when he had eaten his fill he still wanted more. It was Sammy the otter that told him where to get the best ice cream in the land. It was by the big rock on the lake's shore where Whiskers the badger gave away his cold treats. "Umm!" said Bobby as he licked the sweet treat and asked for another. OH! What a beautiful place the LAND of SKETTELS was; so much fun and laughter. There's no sadness or stress here. It was just joy and happiness for all that resided there.

Croaker the bull frog sang as he sat on his yellow lily pad. The red river's current slowly pulled the pad out into the middle of the river. "I'll see you again real soon," yelled Croaker as he drifted down stream.

Bobby's eyes shortly became fixed on a special bush that had teal colored popcorn balls hanging on it. He picked one and took a bite of the Caramel coated treat. Once again he was lost in the sweet tasting offerings of the LAND of SKETTELS down under.

Bobby's enthusiasm was interrupted as he felt the ground move. He looked off in the distance and saw a white volcano spewing tangerine smoke with plum colored lava running down its sides. The ground started to shake more intensely. Bobby closed his eyes and started calling out "mommy, mommy."

He opened his eyes after a few seconds. Standing there over him while he was in bed was his mother. She had both of her hands on his shoulders gently shaking him. "Time for you to get up young man and get ready for school; I hated to wake you when I saw that smile on your face. What were you thinking of?"

She left the room and Bobby sat up in his bed. He looked out his window and he saw a squirrel with a butterfly sitting on its head looking in on him from the oak tree outside. He grinned ear to ear as he heard a croaking sound in the distance. He knew right then and there that he would be returning soon to THE LAND of SKETTELS DOWN UNDER.

ESCAPISM, WHAT A CONCEPT

THERE COMES A period of indecisiveness in ones supportive system that analyzes the worth, ability and strong under towing questions of youthful endeavors. Even though generations of past lives prove that we adjust and then survive this constructive yet agonizing frame of mind. Some will deal with it as a biological function. Others will select the avenue of escapism as their prescribed remedy. Some use comedy to disguise pain as well as emotional scars. Many drink or use drugs to hide their inhibitions. I am drawn to the ones that use fantasy to alleviate reality. That's because fantasy is a painless injection into an arena where we control the elements. We can then rule over the ingredients that enable us to mold a new reality apropos to ourselves.

The need to call upon this inner stimulant occurs periodically at different times of an individual's existence. One accepted hypothesis aligns itself with middle age in the male of the species, because at this time it appears that self evaluations along with their inadequacies surface to form an introverted shield. It's composed of highly impregnable substances creating a formidable psychological adversary to comprehend. To warrant its presence, it arms itself with receding hair line, grey hair, aches, pains and the spare tire that's support the beer belly. The mind with its repertoire of facts and ability to summon up memories seems relentless in flashing back to midnight strolls. It recalls youthful encounters of years long passed.

Remember the energy channeled into impressing a high school sweetheart or your first love? Then when it ended you felt that special pain of being heartbroken. We seem obsessed in wanting to re-analyze our past events and personal history. No one can turn the hands of time back. However, that doesn't stop any of us from trying everyday. Be it through make-up, clothes, cars we drive or diet with exercise. There are only so many beats of the heart in all of us. We can combine the past, present and future together to form a coalition. Merely by closing ones eyes they can enter into a world of fantasy. It's as simple as following footprints in the sand to obtain admission to the wonderful world of escapism. The wanting desire to control ones destiny with the power to form their very own conceptual imagery is truly phenomenal in today's society. To vividly visualize a circumstance that one is capable of reenacting in reality is indeed food for egocentrism. To push the outer realm of vision and perception is adrenalin in enormous fibrillating proportions.

No man is so mentally solid or stable that he doesn't dream of the perfect mate at one time or another. Many will use escapism to fulfill that illusion. They can then create a lover hallucinated to every detail that they have depicted in their minds. Through interfusion comes believability. Allowing the vision to breathe in unity with you the participant, the interlude is complete. Reality and fantasy become your very own romantically orientated world.

Now capture your new loves light and her warmth. Keep the fires within both your hearts burning and glowing so bright that they will endure until the death of eternity. Let her become the Earth beneath your feet and caretaker of your soul. Indulge in the forbidden zones that once eluded you. Let her arouse every sensation that lives inside you. She is the ultimate entity disembodied from reality. She is attached to fantasy and the surrealistic realm. She is much more than the goddess of night. She is mystically possessed with the power to induce spells upon those who dare enter your subliminal world. She loves only you. Your subconscious cerebral ability easily assesses its masters newly acquired lover as all colors, light and wind. She is a creature born for giving life and with the ability to instill destiny to her lover.

Many may never want to return from their experiences at the outer realms of realism. When an individual is bestowed spontaneously the ability to tantalize with the possibility of destruction or creativity, it can have a powerful effect on their judgmental evaluations. Predictable as the ocean with its fury relentlessly beating its shores, man wants to explore and exploit the unknown. However, existing too long in an imaginary plane can cause irreparable damage to the trespasser. Everything has a price to be paid. The longer the indulgence, the higher the sacrifice given. I think that to satisfy self gratification along with one's ego surely warrants a dividend to be paid. Where that line is to be drawn is something each individual must find in their own time.

Escapism offers numerous interesting speculations. Opponents have trouble ascertaining the creditability of fantasy because it is self visual and freely induced by that person. Speculatively it is a world of enjoyment, pleasure and intellect. Unfortunately the only vindication of this theory to be offered is the vast number of science fiction writers along with the millions of their fans.

The sci-fi populace has found itself many times being abused. People seem to have a tendency to back away and casually retreat from science fiction lovers. These people are really being injurious because they lack supportive substance to substantiate their actions. If they would take the time to get to know people that love fantasy they would find that they are analytical and display supremacy in imagination. Sci-fi lovers only want to share their experiences with anyone that shows an interest. The writers want everyone to be included in a wonderful free passage into a mentally charged world filled with idealism and diversification.

The hypnotic trance that accompanies one's excursion into escapism has a fragmented kaleidoscopic effect on acceptable reality. This is one reason why it is hard to explain the pictorial cinematic imagery envisioned by any one individual. Everyone sees events through their minds eye and like a prism; the hue is different with the slightest turn of the subject being viewed. There is no understanding the sequence in the world of illusion. That's because there are no rules, no boundaries, no limits and most important of all, no inhibitions. The timeline is yours, enabling you to bring reality back at your desecration. You are the one that has that impeccable approval of decision making. You are the king of the land that lives in your mind.

Where else can one relieve frustrations and at the same time obtain a paragon? Life can truly take on a polymorphous state when even a novice has the ability to create without restrictions. It's true that the best things in life are free. Be it dreams, escapism, scenic wonders to view or love for that special person. Enjoy the world of mystical illusion that lives inside you. However, be advised to keep a small taunt line that is connected to reality. Without that you may never return to reality and no one can live within themselves without becoming comatose. So float upon the clouds and the winds that reside in your mind. All you have to do is believe in yourself and you will enjoy the Utopia that is yours.

THE PERUVIAN VIRACOCHA CROWN

SLADE ROCKINGTON WIPED the sweat from his brow as he pushed forward deep into a Peruvian cave. The light from his flashlight grew dimmer the more he descended into its depths. Thank goodness he had the sense to bring extra batteries; after all he was a world renowned archeologist and knew many of its downfalls.

He had spent years researching the Peruvian Viracocha Crown that had been worn by the High Priestess of the Inca civilization. Legend has it that it holds the key to discovering the Tomb of Atahualpa; the last sovereign emperor of the Inca's. It goes on to state that he was buried with millions of dollars worth of gold to give to their god Viracocha. His tomb was even kept a secret from his brother Huascar who Atahualpa had overthrown to seize power of the Incan empire.

Slade followed the small notches along the caves walls. They would go unnoticed by you and I; but not to a trained archeologist in Incan hieroglyphics. The clues had already taken him down six different tunnels when he came out into a large cavern. He saw that there were three tunnels to choose from in order to continue. He examined the walls closely and deciphered the writings before making the decision to go down the tunnel on the left side of the room.

He had only traveled a hundred yards when he came face to face with a dead end. This didn't discourage him at all; in fact it only heightened his expectations. He knew from past adventures that almost every time the treasure was behind such a dead end. He felt around and found a small hole on the left side of the wall. He then found another similar hole on the right hand side. He laid his flashlight down on the ground lighting the area. He reached out with his left hand and inserted his index finger into one of the holes. He then did likewise with his right hand. Once both fingers were in place he pushed hard against the wall. It made a grinding sound and then retracted downwardly until it was level with the floor.

There behind the once seemingly dead end was a medium sized chamber. In the middle of it was a pedestal with the Peruvian Viracocha Crown displayed on it. Slade approached it suspiciously and after carefully examining it, he picked it up and held it with a sense of great pride and accomplishment. It was solid gold and had diamonds embedded along the base. As he began to calm down he noticed that there were three large gems missing. The inserts were there for the three of them; but the gems physically weren't there.

According to legend there was suppose to be a Ruby, Sapphire and an Emerald in the crown. The three gems were what were needed to create the beam that pointed to the exact location of the Tomb of Atahualpa. That is, once it was placed on the Incan Pantograph of Souls at a specific time. Slade roughly knew the location and time; but lacked the exact coordinates at this point in time.

He followed his chalk markings back up to the surface and exited the cave to find a bright sun in the sky and his fiancée Emily patiently waiting for his return. He showed her the crown and her eyes lit up and a smile covered her face. "You found it Slade, you found it," she said.

"Yes; but I'm still missing these three gems. See, here, here and there. I've got a pretty good idea how to find them. Lets go back to Lima and the hotel. I remember in one of my books something that made a reference to the jewels on the crown being hidden in case Huascar ever found the crown." With that said he and Emily got in their Jeep and drove down out of the mountains and in to Lima.

It was refreshing to be back in the city and take a hot shower. Treasure hunting can be a dirty and time consuming ordeal. Moments back in civilization are icing on the cake when you're on an exploration. Slade spent most the night reading from his many books and factoids that he had about the crown that he was seeking. He got all the clues organized in the proper order and laid out his travel plans.

The next morning Slade and Emily checked out of the hotel and headed for Cuzco (three hundred miles, southeast) which is an Andean valley in search of the first missing gem, a bright red ruby. The city of Cuzco had been the capital city during the Inca empire days. Three fourths of the city has been destroyed over the years due to many earthquakes; but Slade hoped that the main city well was still in existence.

It took the entire day to arrive in Cuzco. They checked into a hotel, had dinner and then went to bed early. The next morning they took a shower, had a large breakfast and then headed out to find the ancient well. It didn't take long until they found themselves looking right at it. It was a tourist attraction and is openly marked for all to see.

Slade took his maps out and compass. He followed the directions that he had deciphered from his books in the exact order and their placements. According to his translations he was to look Northeast at 32 degrees from

True North of the city well and then he would see what were two camel humps. As he eyed the line of sight using those coordinates he saw high up on the mountain peaks two large hump like configurations. Emily saw the same thing at the same time he had. She squeezed his arm and whispered in his ear "we just might find this ruby honey."

They both smiled and loaded up their equipment. They stopped at a store and got supplies along with a map of all the back roads of the area. It was a good thing the jeep is a four wheel drive because the roads they were driving were nothing more than pothole after deep pothole. As nightfall fell on them they reached the valley between the two humps and set up camp. They would need a good nights sleep for their adventure the next day.

Emily awoke first and started breakfast over an open camp fire. Slade rolled over and smelled the aroma of bacon and hash browns sizzling in the skillet. He unzipped his sleeping bag and came over and sat down by the fire. Emily handed him a plate with hardy portions of both bacon and hash browns. He gobbled it down and got dressed. He was in a hurry to find the ruby.

Slade took his sexton and attached it to the tripod. He triangulated the two peaks with the latitude and longitude that were from the city well in Cuzco, 13 30'57.16"S and 71 57'56.15"W. Once he had the new longitudes and latitudes he fed in the number of degrees from the data he had acquired from the triangulation. That gave him an exact number to the opening of what should be the hiding place of the ruby. He took the hand held GPS from the jeep and entered the new coordinates. Emily stayed back at the jeep and Slade set out on foot.

It was only a mile to the location that the GPS had displayed. Slade was there in less than an hour after climbing rocks and diverting around some large boulders. He was standing in front a solid rock escarpment with no apparent opening. He took his rock climbing hammer and began striking the wall in different places. He suddenly heard a thud sound instead of the sharp ping he had been hearing. He rubbed the dirt away from the rocks and he saw what appeared to be a seam.

He continued to rub until he had exposed a square block of granite. This was not the rock that should be there. He rubbed more of the dirt away until he had exposed six blocks of granite; each being three feet square. He took his hunting knife and scratched between the blocks unearthing the material in the seams. Once he had one block loose he wiggled it back and forth. It was only about a half an inch; but he was able to move it slowly towards him. Once it was protruding out one inch he could pull on it with his fingers.

Finally he moved the block from its once secure place. It fell on the ground by his feet with a thud. It was only six inches in depth. Thank goodness for that, otherwise he could have never pulled it out without some kind of mechanical help. It was easy to pull the other five blocks away from the wall and expose the entrance to a cave. With a deep breath and flashlight in hand he entered the darkness of the tunnel.

It turned out to be only two hundred feet in length. At the end was a wall covered in Inca hieroglyphics. He took pictures with his digital camera so he could study the writings later. There was a large sun painted on the wall with a hole in the middle of it. Slade shinned his flashlights light into it and grinned as he reached in and pulled out the red ruby that he was searching for. He secured the gem in a leather pouch and quickly returned to Emily.

After celebrating and having lunch both of them returned to the mouth of the cave and restacked the blocks, sealing it again and hopefully hiding it from others. Slade studied the writings and with the information that he already had; he knew where to look for the second gem, the sapphire. It was late that night when they returned to the hotel in Cuzco. They checked in and went straight to bed; it had been a long but rewarding day.

The next morning Slade went to work on studying his charts and graphs. He had what he thought to be the key in solving the exact location of the gems and the Pantograph of Souls. He had interpreted the drawings and symbols from the caves pictures he had taken. He made a major breakthrough when he realized that the location of the crown and the three gems as well as the Pantograph of Souls were laid out in this one hieroglyphic writing. If he would have found the ruby first it would have saved him months if not years that he spent just on the crown.

The sapphire was the next closest gem from Cuzco. The symbols showed that it was high up on an escarpment overlooking the Pacific Ocean. With little sleep he and Emily loaded up the jeep and set out for Desembocadura Del Rio Loa, Chile.

Slade had figured out that all the locations to the Incan treasures were based on the stars. They had used the planet Venus as their focal root. It was no coincidence that the locations of the dismantled pieces were based on their own properties. For example, each letter of each gem represented one degree that was added to the base latitude and longitude from the city well from the capital city Cuzco.

The ruby gem was the only exception to his findings. That baffled him; but he thought that it might reveal itself later on.

Slade had taken the base number from Cuzco and added eight degrees to it and got the location of the sapphire (eight letters). His new destination was 21 25'34.10"S and 70 03'20.17"W. Those coordinates were for Desembocadura Del Rio Loa, Chile. It was a long drive and took three days to arrive. They had a little trouble at the Chilean border; but both their passports were in order so they were only detained for a couple of hours. Americans are thought of as trouble. They might be FBI, CIA or worse DEA.

Slade stood on the beach with his GPS in hand; but he was still 150 yards from where he needed to be according to his signal devise. He rented a boat and followed the signal until he was right on top of the coordinates. He stared up a solid 200 foot rock cliff approximately 200 yards in front of him. He thought a moment before he had an answer that explained his pending situation. Chile has had many devastation earthquakes over the last several hundreds of years. It was plausible that part of the escarpment had fallen into the Pacific years ago.

Slade and Emily were both certified divers; its one of the things that all fortune hunters have in their repertoire of talents. He returned to the docks where he had rented the boat and then rented scuba gear for himself and Emile. The both of them returned to the spot above the coordinates. Emile tossed the anchor overboard and then the two of them jumped in the water.

It was just like Slade had thought. There at approximately 75 feet below the surface was what had clearly been the face of the rock cliff that he had seen earlier. Even though it was covered with moss and muscles they began searching for any kind of an opening or something suspicious looking. Emily signaled for Slade to come and see what she had found. It was an opening the size of a basketball. Slade reached in carefully after shining his light into it to make sure there wasn't an eel or other dangerous creature inside. He pulled at the edges and multiply rocks fell revealing a secret room.

They both entered to find the sapphire still sitting on a pedestal as unbelievable as that sounds. Slade gave Emile a nod and she picked it up with a grin and admired its beauty. Slade reached out and took the gem and put it in his leather pouch. They went back to the boat, pulled up anchor and returned to the small Chilean port. Their hearts were pounding as they realized that they had indeed broken the code to find the crown, gems, The Pantograph of Souls and the Tomb of Atahualpa.

The emerald was the only gem left to acquire and it was relatively close by. Slade knew that it was near Salar Grande, Chile; next to Sal Punta Lobos. There are several Salar Grande's in Chile ; but this one fit the mathematical formula that he was using and had been working up to this point. This was a high desert area with many high mountain peaks surrounding it. Slade was praying that his GPS coordinates were not top of one of the almost inaccessible peaks.

When Slade and Emile reached the small outpost of Salar Grande the GPS diverted them off the main road and onto a dirt one. After three hours of following the winding and pot holed road they heard the GPS voice say "you have arrived at your destination." Slade stopped the jeep as they both sat in bewilderment.

How could this be the correct place? They were in the middle of a valley. According to the coordinates they were right on top of the emerald. The terrain was dirt, flat and rocky. Slade had to believe in his math along with his instincts. He took a shovel from the back of the jeep and began to dig where the GPS indicated. He had only dug for a few minutes when he hit something solid. He started to shovel at even a faster pace. Soon he had uncovered a rock slab eight foot square. It was approximately eleven inches thick.

Both he and Emily knew they could not move it manually. Slade dug underneath one edge of the slab about twelve inches inward. He pulled the cable for the jeeps winch and wrapped it around the rock slab. As he reeled in the cable the huge stone began to move. It pivoted as it swung around exposing an opening beneath. "Stop" Shouted Emily. They approached the once hidden opening and looked in to see what they could. However they could only see blackness.

Slade unhooked the cable and hit rewind on the control box that operated the winch. He drove the jeep up to four feet from the edge of the hole. He made a loop in the cable and inserted his right foot. With a flashlight in hand Emily slowly lowered him down into the dark pit using the winches control box. She had almost let out the entire fifty feet that was on the winches spool when Slade yelled up to stop.

He stood on solid rock and was astonished to see more Incan hieroglyphics painted on the walls. He took more pictures and then followed the direction that he had translated from the drawings. It was almost two hundred yards when the tunnel he was slowly walking through opened up into a large chamber.

There on what appeared to be an alter was the emerald. However it was located on an island that was surrounded by ten feet of water. Slade swam out to the small parcel of land and removed the emerald from its resting place. He retreated back across the water and then to his lifeline to the surface. He once again placed his foot in the cable's loop and yelled at Emile to pull him up. He began to slowly ascend to the surface. He kissed the emerald as he broke the darkness and was bathed in the suns warm rays. He handed the stone to Emily and she to kissed it and then put it into Slade's leather pouch along with the other gems.

Their excitement was more than anyone could ever explain. As they grew closer to the Tomb of Atahualpa the more visions of grandeur they had. Now was the time to finally find the Pantograph of Souls and discover the last clue to the legend of buried gold.

Slade drove to the opposite side of the hole and pulled the rock slab back into place with help from the winch. He and Emile took the time to spread the dirt back over the rock slab in order to hide any evidence that anyone had been there. They felt confident that it would remain unopened for many years to come.

It was a long trip back to Cuzco, Peru from Chile. It was plenty of time for Slade and Emile to talk about getting married, having children and settling down once and for all. The crown with the three gems now inserted in it was worth easily two million dollars they thought. However if the Tomb of Atahualpa indeed held roomful's of gold, that find would be worth ten's of millions of dollars.

Once back at the hotel in Cuzco they both needed a day of total relaxation. They got massages, enjoyed the steam room and soaked in the hot tub. They ordered a wonderful meal and danced the night away. It was a great day and evening; one that had been long overdue for two in love and sharing a dream. All things must come to an end, so the next morning arrived bright and early.

With the aid of his maps, books and pictures he had taken recently; Slade knew positively the location of the Pantograph of Souls. Every hieroglyphic writing that he had seen always had the symbol of a snow capped mountain top with a sun sitting atop its peak. What better place for the Pantograph of Souls to be; the highest peak in the Incan Empire; which would make it closest to the sun and heavens.

It was also the place where the high priestess would go to bow down to their god Viracocha. Slade and Emile couldn't wait till the next morning to travel to Mount Huascaran National Park, Peru. How ironic that such an extraordinary archaeological find was hiding in plain sight all these centuries. Mount Huascaran is 22,204 feet. Slade hadn't given much thought to how they would conquer such a difficult task as climbing to this altitude. He would wait until he saw first hand what they had to deal with in order to reach the summit and the Pantograph of Souls.

Once at the National Park and they were looking up from the base of the mountain they had a sinking feeling in the pit of their stomachs. They were relieved after talking to several villagers that guides were available and that it was the perfect time (July) to climb the mountain. It was a hard climb; but nothing close to Everest in Tibet or K-2 in China. Still it would be dangerous and not to be taken lightly.

Slade hired a guide, Pedro, who would go ahead and set up a base camp. Pedro would also stock the camp with food, clothing, oxygen tanks, camping gear, radio gear and accessories. He would return in a week after everything was set up and then Slade and Emily would start on their tedious journey with him. In the meantime Slade and Emily had to attend a six day climbing course that is required of all climbers before they are allowed to attempt the climb. It was fortunate for both of them that they had climbing experience already under their belts. Knowing how to rappel and use crampons is something that treasure hunters must master to complete many of their adventures.

When Pedro returned Slade and Emile had their certifications and were ready to go. Much to their surprise they were helicoptered to base camp. Half their work was done in just a few minutes and that was OK with them. The weather was fantastic and the sun was warm on their faces as they ascended the mountain by the north face. They were tethered as all good climbers are and were making excellent time. Even Pedro was astonished by their speed and determination. He of course didn't know what their motivation was.

It took a few days to reach the summit. They had not run into any major problems or any setbacks to speak of. They were breathing oxygen from their tanks as they stood at the summit in total awe of the 360 degree panoramic beauty. Slade almost forgot why he now stood atop Peru's highest peak. Luck was surly on Slade's side. According to all of his computations at exactly 12 noon on the 23rd of July he was to place the Crown of Viracocha in the center of the Pantograph of Souls facing true north.

July 22nd was the day they summated Mount Huascaran, leaving Slade one day to figure out where the Pantograph of Souls was laid out and the center of it. There were no hieroglyphics or symbols etched on walls this time. He studied the small area that he stood on and the only thing that struck him as strange was four pillars that stood about 24 inches high. He asked Pedro what they were for and who put them there. Pedro told him that as far back as his family's history that they have always been there and that no one knew why or how they came to be.

Could this be why the ruby in the beginning was three degrees and not four? Now was the time to utilize the four letters in ruby to represent the four pillars. Each pillar could represent a gem and the crown. Bring all four together; they united with the four pillars that were the architectural points of the Pantograph of Souls. It was an easy task to draw a line diagonally from opposite pillars and find dead center.

It was 11:30 AM July 23rd and everything was ready. Slade had placed the Crown of Viracocha on the center mark where the lines had crossed. It was facing true north and was tilted at 32 degrees upwardly. The sky was clear and the sun was approaching its 12 noon position. He had no idea what was going to happen; but he had every tool and instrument he had laid out and ready to use if necessary.

The three waited with impatience for noon to arrive; but then the sun's rays struck the crown at precisely 12 and a beam of reddish light extended from the crown off into the valley below. Slade had only a few minutes to take his sexton and triangulate exactly where the beam was indicating where he hoped was the Tomb of Atahualpa.

Pedro was confused at what he was witnessing and finally asked Slade what was going on. Emily told him that they were explorers and following a family diary to find information about their ancestors. Pedro seemed to accept that explanation and that was all that what said about the subject.

Descending the mountain was as tough as ascending it had been; but they arrived at base camp in time to meet a party of ten on their way up to the summit. Pedro stayed at base camp to disassembly it and to bring any supplies back to the village. He would meet up with them in a few days to return any refunds and settle up any accounts. Pedro looked happy with a smile on his face as Slade and Emily waved good-bye to him as they departed in the helicopter.

As they waited for Pedro to return they stayed in the local inn and studied the triangulation figures that Slade had calculated from the beam and suns angles. It was a fairly easy thing for him to do on his laptop. He used the center of the Pantograph of Souls latitude and longitude to start, 9 06'25.89"S and 77 31'03.13"W. Ignore the 32 degree tilt of the crown and only use the established angles that were exposed during the beams visibility.

It took only an hour to pinpoint where they had to go to finally end this search for once and all.

It was a short distance from where Slade was sitting. Mount Chopicalqui, located in the White Range of the Andes in the Ancash Region of Yungay Province. Though its elevation is 20,846 feet their destination was only at the 6,452 foot level of the south face. Strange that when you translate the word Chopicalqui it roughly means (fits in the center). Slade put the mountains coordinates in his GPS 9 05'07.76"S and 77 34'25.80"W.

Slade and Emily hung out and played like tourist. It was nice to take a rest for a few days. The climb up the mountain was stressful and took a physical toll on the both of them. They wanted to get started on the next clue; but they realized that they needed to rest their bodies. Pedro returned and accounts were paid or refunded along with thanks and handshakes.

Slade inquired about a guide for Mt. Chopicalqui and Pedro said that he had a cousin that was a guide at the mountain. He said he would call him and tell him they were coming and wanted to climb the south face; but only up to around 7000 foot level. They parted friends and with the jeep loaded with new supplies they headed for Mt. Chopicalqui.

It was the middle of the first week in August when Slade and Emily drove into the small village at the base of Mt. Chopicalqui. They met with Juan at the local inn after Emile had called and told him that they had arrived. He informed them that there wasn't much work to their climb since you could drive almost two thirds of the way in a four wheel drive truck. That sounded great to Slade and Emile, they had been on a long journey and they were mentally and physically beaten down. Maybe the finish line will be an easy one after the hard work that it took to arrive at this point.

The next day the three drove up the mountain in the jeep. The last two miles were bumpy and slow going. Thank God they had the Cherokee. When they could no longer continue on the road they started to hike up the mountain. The seven thousand foot level still had snow on the ground; but only two feet. It caught Slade by surprise when his GPS stated "you have reached your destination."

It was 11:45 AM so Slade got his sexton and laptop and then waited for 12 noon. When 12 arrived he used the angels that he had acquired from Mt. Huascaran so that he could duplicate that moment. He took in the fact that it was eleven days later and he had to adjust for the earth's rotation and the movement of the suns position.

In order to duplicate July 23 Slade had to move coincidently 32 feet west and 32 feet higher up the face. He then began to pick at the ice and snow. He was standing on what could be a wide path and looking at a shear white wall of snow covered rock. As he picked away and got down to the rock he noticed like before in this quest what seemed to be seams. He again scratched the seams with his knife and soon he was pulling stone blocks from the wall exposing a cave entrance.

It wasn't like a cave as much as a tunnel. The walls, roof and floor were polished granite and smooth as glass. The light from his flashlight reflected off the walls witch lit the tunnel like sunlight. He and Emily walked down the long path as Juan followed several feet behind. The tunnel led straight back deep into the heart of the mountain. After half a mile they came to an abrupt end. The wall that was in front of them had colorful hieroglyphics with a bright sun two feet across in the center of it.

Slade took a deep breath and pushed at the center of the sun and the wall dropped straight down revealing a chamber. This was no ordinary chamber; but the Tomb of Atahualpa. Emile guessed that it was one hundred yards square and one hundred feet high. Gold cups, platters, vase's, bars and thousands of precious gems filled the room. At the far end of the chamber was a solid gold platform with a gold sarcophagus atop.

Slade and Emile went ballistic with their emotions. They were jumping around like little kids on Christmas morning that just got everything they asked for from Santa. It was short lived when they were interrupted by a loud voice yelling "Mr. Rockington! The governments of Peru and Chile thank you for discovering their lost fortunes."

Slade turned around to see Pedro and several armed military personnel with guns pointed at him. Pedro continued "You must have questions so I will explain and that may answer many of them. I am the chief of police in Yungay Province and do guide duties on the side. Once I saw the Crown of Viracocha I knew that you were searching for the Tomb of Atahualpa. This gold and wealth belong to the Peruvian and Chilean people; it is our history and ancestral roots.

Both of our countries honor the international treasure hunter laws and will abide by them. If you don't know what the law is I will explain them to you. Everything here will be appraised by experts and once they arrive at what is a fair price in today's marketplace you will receive 10 percent. Mr. Rockington, You may have the honor of this discovery, you have indeed earned that honor. I see a wonderful career for you on the archeology speaking tour as well as a book.

As you can see sir, we have no desire to dishonor you in anyway. We are grateful for all you have done to enrich our poor countries. My cousin Juan is also a police officer. I followed you here after I contacted the government and they sent these army men to assist me. Juan kept you under surveillance and he was instructed to make sure no harm came to you or your party. You are free to go, you have not broken any laws and all you passports and papers are in proper order. I have your information on how to contact you back in the United States. When the value is finalized I will notify you and see to it that your just reward is given you."

It was a somber walk from the burial chamber and down the mountain to the jeep. Slade and Emile didn't even stop driving until they reached Cuzco. Exhausted and emotionally deflated they checked into the hotel and then collapsed on their bed. The next morning they got up and went to the airport, turned in the Cherokee and caught the morning flight back to San Francisco.

By the time they arrived at San Francisco International at Daily City the discovery of the Tomb of Atahualpa was front page news. Slade's picture was on the front page with a full page of text to explain his adventure. The press was there as he and Emile walked up the ramp and into the concourse.

Flashes went off by the hundreds and questions were flying at him so fast he didn't have time to answer a single one. He said "no comment" as he and Emile hailed a cab and disappeared into the heavy traffic.

It had been a long time since Slade had been home. It was like heaven to sleep in his king-size bed. He and Emile stayed in and hid out from the press; after two weeks they quietly slipped away to Las Vegas and got married. A year passed without incident and everyone forgot about his find. He had his fifteen minutes of fame and then the press moved on.

Then on a quiet Sunday afternoon there was a knock on Slade's door. He opened it and saw Pedro standing there dressed in a suit and supporting a grin ear to ear. "Come on in my friend" said Slade.

"Nice to see you again Mr. Rockington" Pedro said.

"What brings you to America?"

"As I said a year ago my friend; when there was a value accessed to the Tomb of Atahualpa you would receive 10 percent as a finder's fee. It is with great pleasure that I give you this check. Please come back to Peru someday and see the museum that we built in Lima to display many of the relics from your find. Once again the people of Peru and Chile thank you. I must go; I have a meeting with the Peruvian Ambassador in an hour for dinner. Thank you again my friend." He shook Slade's hand and left.

Emile arrived just in time to see the black Peruvian Embassy car pull away from the driveway. They both looked at the envelope for what seemed a lifetime. "Open it honey" said Emily. With a trembling hand he carefully opened it and pulled the check out to reveal, Pay to the order of Slade Rockington 125 million dollars.

Slade and Emile left San Francisco shortly after that day and no one knows where they went or where they are to this day. Some say they bought an island and they want to spend the rest of their life's there in private. Others say That Slade always wanted to find the legendary or the mystical elephant graveyard in Africa. You draw your own conclusion, are they living in paradise on an island or they on another great adventure in the jungles of Africa?

MAKING MEMORIES

SETH BELIEVED IN love at first sight the second he saw her, her being Amber Warren. She sat at the high school cafeteria table with three other cheerleaders. He was a virtual nobody and had just transferred to Washington High. He gazed at her in wonderment and an inner voice told him they would someday fall in love. He was still in a daydream when the bell rang interrupting his thoughts. The students scattered to their class's leaving Seth standing alone in the cafeteria.

A teacher approached him and asked if they could help. Seth said that he was a transfer and was lost. The teacher guided him to his ninth grade scheduled math class. Fate was surely shining on him that day because he was assigned to the desk next to Amber. He introduced himself to her and told her she looked nice in her cheerleader's uniform. She smiled and welcomed him to Washington High. Being a freshman is hard enough; but trying to win over the head cheerleader to be your girl friend was not an easy task for anyone.

Days turned to weeks and little by little Seth got closer and closer to Amber. He finally got up enough nerve to ask her out on a date and she accepted. He was shocked in a way, yet convinced that being a gentleman and making her a friend first had paid benefits. Seth's older brother Jake had to drive Seth over to Amber's house since he was still too young for a license. Jake dropped them off at a nice restaurant and said he would return in two hours.

Seth might have been young; but he knew that for a first date you don't go to the movies. You want to talk to your date, not be in a situation where you must keep silent for the most part. Their dinner was excellent and they had grown closer after the two hour interlude together. As the weeks went on their feelings grew stronger and stronger for each other. By the time summer past and they started their junior year they were a couple in love.

Seth and Amber continued to be a couple throughout high school. They were selected their proms king and queen. They enrolled in a local community college and got an apartment together after graduating from high school. Both of their parents loved them as a couple and accepted them being together.

Two years at Hillsview Community College flew by for the both of them. Each was achieving B averages in difficult classes. The work was hard and at times stressful. Seth decided to do something unique for Amber because their third year anniversary of being a couple was rapidly approaching. He thought about it for awhile and came up with what he considered the perfect gift.

He went around to several stores in town and talked to the cashiers. When he had everything in place he anxiously waited for Amber to come home after her last class. She walked through the door announcing that she was home and then gave Seth a kiss. He looked into her eyes and told her she had to go to J C Penny's and ask for Carrie the cashier.

"Why" she inquired?

Seth said "I don't know, they called and said that they need to see you about your Penny's credit card."

Tired as she was she left and went to Penny's and asked for Carrie. She was directed to the correct checkout and she approached the cashier.

"Are you Carrie?"

"Yes I am, are you Amber?"

"Yes, what did you have to see me about" she asked?

The cashier reached under the checkout counter and gave her a beautifully wrapped box with a big red bow tied around it. The box was accompanied by a card as well. She unwrapped the box and inside was a beautiful black sequent evening gown. The card read happy anniversary my darling, now go to Sac's Fifth Avenue and ask for Bridget.

Amber hurried off to her next destination filled with excitement. She arrived and as instructed asked for salesperson Bridget. She was introduced to Bridget who gave her a pair of Prada shoes and another card. This card required her to go to Harry Winston's and seek Ramon. Once again she followed the directions and entered the highly status and elite store.

Ramon met her at the door and said "welcome Miss Amber, I have been expecting you. You are just as you were described to me." He handed her a velvet box. She opened it to see a gold tennis bracelet and earrings set in platinum.

Ramon continued "I am to instruct you to return home were your final gift awaits you."

She raced home with tears of joy and her heart pounding like a drum. She opened the door of the apartment to find it lit in candle light and rose petals scattered about the floor. The table was set with fine china and a beautiful rose centerpiece. She laid her gifts from all of her store adventures down on the couch. At that moment from the kitchen stepped out Pierre Barron, one of the best chefs in town. He was followed by an accomplished violin minstrel playing THE ROSE.

Amber stood there with her face in her hands crying as Seth came over to her and said "happy anniversary."

"I love you. This is the best day of my life honey, nothing could be better than this" she said.

It was at that moment that Seth dropped to one knee and displayed a 3 caret diamond ring while asking "Amber my love, will you marry me?"

"Yes, yes, yes" she replied between her sighs of joy.

He kissed her and whispered "I love you and together we will never stop MAKING MEMORIES."

COMPLICATIONS

IT WAS A hot humid day in June when James Jones walked into the New to You Pawn shop in Key West. He had his eye on a model F-75 metal detector for months. He knew that a thousand dollars was a lot of money for a used detector; but it was a good price for this one. It was top of the line and sold new for 1,500.00 dollars. He had Big Tommy (the owner) take it out of the display window so he could inspect it more closely. It was still in mint condition. James thought a moment before he laid down nine one-hundred dollar bills on the countertop. He told Big Tommy he could take it or no deal.

Big Tommy didn't like customers giving him ultimatums like that. If this would have been a fifty or sixty dollar watch transaction he would have laughed James right out the door. This however was a few hundred dollars, so he held his tongue. He had only paid four-hundred dollars to a poor desperate guy for it, so this was a five-hundred dollar profit. Plus he was getting his initial investment back as well. Still he might have rejected the deal if it were an item that was drawing a lot of interest. However, James was the only person that had shown any interest in it in eight or nine months. "Sold" barked Big Tommy as he scooped up the cash off the counter top in one swiping moment.

James left with his prize in hand feeling that he had beaten Big Tommy at his own game. Naturally nothing could be further from the truth; thinking that scenario made him feel like a shrewd businessman. James lived in Florida on a five acre parcel of land that had a thousand feet of ocean beach frontage. He had always been told stories that his ancestors moored their boats and ships at the waters edge. The land has been in his family for over 250 years. His family tree read like a book of who's who. There were sea captains, pirates and export-import gentlemen among the many branches of his family tree.

The next day James went out to his private beach and began searching the sand for hidden treasures. After an hour he had only found a cheap ring, a quarter and several bottle caps for his effort. As the tide began to go out he ventured outwardly with its retreat. He finally got a weak signal coming from deep under the sand. The detectors screen showed that it was gold and in the shape of a coin. He began to dig with his hands. He had dug down twenty inches when he found what indeed was a gold coin. He examined it closely before he put it in his pocket with a smile. He grabbed the detector and resumed searching, only this time feverishly. He had visions of a chest full of gold coins dancing in his mind. His search soon became one of disappointment as there were no more hits or images on his detectors display screen.

James couldn't find any information on his newly found coin so he decided to approach Dr. Horace Bateman. He was the curator of the Maritime Museum in Key West. Dr. Bateman's face lit up as he held the coin and examined it under a magnifying glass. He told James that in 1618 Queen Elizabeth commissioned a 20 dollar gold piece to be struck in honor of Christopher Columbus and his maiden voyage to find a new land in 1492. Christopher Jones (the Mayflowers Captain) was to bring a chest full of these coins to the new world to start an economy with when he set sail in 1620. This money was to help start a settlement and help establish a British colony. The chest containing the gold coins were believed to have been lost when the ship Queens Reign that was accompanying the Mayflower sank. It is a little known fact that there was another ship that sailed with the Mayflower.

Dr. Bateman told James that there were three other coins of this nature at the Smithsonian Institute. He needed to take the coin there and inquire about it in more detail. They were the experts on the history and facts about the coin. James thanked The Doctor and immediately drove to Miami. He booked a flight that afternoon and was in Washington D C that evening.

He got some of the bureaucratic run around trying to get to see the experts he needed to about his coin. It wasn't until he mentioned a rare gold coin from 1620 commissioned by Queen Elizabeth and that they had three like coins there and he had a fourth one that he finally got some attention. He was soon approached by Rachel Bines. She shook his hand and asked, "you have a coin that was commissioned by Queen Elizabeth in 1618"?

"Yes I do," as he handed it to her.

"Come with me please" as they went to her office. She began examining the coin in great detail. She even viewed it under a microscope. She weighed it and tested for the gold's purity. "How did you come in possession of this coin sir," she asked James.

"I'd rather not say right now, I was told that you had the history of this particular coin."

"Please tell me what part of the world it was last, that you know of that is," she asked. James thought that it would be ok to say, so he told her.

"I will tell you all that is known about this coin. The Columbus Coin as it is called." She walked over to a glass display cabinet that was down the hall from her office and showed James the Institutes three coins. As she pointed to one of the coins she said "this coin was found at the Eiffel Tower in Paris France in 1888. It is not certain exactly how it came to be there. This second coin was found in the pocket of a dead soldier at the Battle of Little Big Horn in 1876. The soldiers name, General George A Custer. The third and last coin was found by the doctor who attended to the body of assassinated President Abraham Lincoln in 1865. Thank goodness that the doctor, like the other two individuals turned the coins over to their governments at the time. It is sad that today's people probably would not do that. Now you show up with a fourth coin from Key West and in my expert opinion it is authentic in every way. It is priceless and you need to protect it at whatever the cost."

James was somewhat stunned to hear that one of his relatives was involved in the history of the Columbus Coins. He was a direct descendant of Captain Christopher Jones (Captain of the Mayflower) of Mayflower fame. When he relayed that piece of information to Miss Rachel her eyes opened wide and her back stiffened to an upright position.

She immediately suggested an alliance between them in order to try and discover the complete story behind the Columbus Coins. James knew that he alone would never be able to follow all the facts and legends to find the real truth among the old wise tales without expert help. He agreed to work with her, so they became partners in what was to be the journey of their lifetime.

Rachel got a sabbatical leave from the Smithsonian and returned to Key West with James the next morning. They went to the Maritime Museum to use its books and Horace's knowledge of the area to start their investigation. The three of them had figured out they had to find out what was so special in the time frame from 1620 to 1865. That was the time frame from when the coins left and the next time anyone saw a coin. If the entire chest of coins sank with the Queens Reign then there could only be one reason for the four coins.

Someone or a few people had stolen them. If that was true why did they only appear 245 years later and not sooner? Maybe one individual stole all four or more and some event happened in 1865 that brought them to light once again. It was obvious that they were hidden for over two-hundred years and then they were found. Who, where and how did they get discovered was the questions to be answered.

After days of brainstorming every idea that they had were collectively laid out in a theoretical plan. Since the first coin was found on Abraham Lincoln they would backtrack his movements. There were entire books of his life and his movements. They thought that somewhere in all that information it might show where he could have obtained the Columbus Coin. The search began from the day he was born and worked itself forward to his death.

It was during the first year of the Civil War in 1861 that the south appeared to have a surge in monies to finance the war. It would have gone unnoticed if not for the name of Wilbur Jones of Atlanta, Ga. After further investigation it was learned that he was a rich import-export businessman that did not believe in slavery and he was from Florida. James thought the name was familiar and after looking over his family tree journal he was proven correct. Wilbur Jones was a rich descendant and had met with President Lincoln on two separate occasions. Wilbur Jones had died in 1890 while traveling from Atlanta to Key West when his horse threw him, breaking his neck.

The three then switched their search to the facts about Wilbur Jones only to find that he had started out in Key West and that he lived on the same property that was still in the Jones family. The exact piece that James lived on presently. As they studied the ancestry of the Jones's family tree they found the exact place where Wilbur Jones had docks and a warehouse on the waterfront. It was located in an inlet where James had not checked with his metal detector.

He got his detector and started to survey the beach looking for a hit; but to no avail. Feeling let down and beaten, Rachel and James went to his house to rest. They talked about how to continue with their adventure. They slept well (in separate beds and rooms) that night. James remembered a box of old family letters that were in a chest in the attic. He got it down and as he was browsing through it he found three letters and a will from Wilbur Jones to his son William. The interesting thing about all four documents was the mentioning of a well that was to always be kept a secret. Its location was 100 yards north from the most southerly property marker that separated their land from the states.

James was off to the county clerk's office to get the surveyors exact land point of registration figures. Once he had them he hired a local surveyor to come and show him the boundaries. It took the surveyor most the day to do the work and install the four brass markers that outlined James's property.

Once the man had left, James and Rachel, with a tape measure and compass marked off the 100 yards to the north from the correct marker. There was nothing there at first glance but sand and a few weeds. James got a shovel and began to dig. He had only dug down about two feet when he broke through wood planks and nearly fell in the hole himself.

Excitement was running through the veins of both of them as James ran to get his jeep with a wench. He drove it to the newly opened hole. He showed Rachel how to operate the wench then grabbed a flashlight. She lowered him slowly down the opening as he hung on to the cable. At thirty feet down James touched bottom and yelled for Rachel to stop lowering the cable. He looked behind him and found the find of the century. There staring him in the eye was a huge chest. He opened it slowly and his eyes widened and his heart began to race as he pointed his lit flashlight at the contents. He was staring at a chest full of gold coins.

It was all the wench could do to lift the heavy chest up to the surface. Rachel and James together could not lift it into the jeep so they towed it back to the house. They hand carried gold coins into the house until every one was in the house and stacked up on the floor. There were 1,254 coins in all.

Stuck to the inside of the lid of the chest was a ledger written in the same handwriting as the letters and will from Wilbur Jones. It read as follows, "met with President Lincoln on March 15th 1864 and gave him 50,000 dollars that was from melting down gold coins that I had found in a well on my property in 1859. I also gave him one gold coin as a souvenir for good luck. Mr. Lincoln was a great man and it was an honor to have helped finance the war.

I went to Washington and met with General George A Custer on May 12th 1884. He was masquerading as a democrat; but he had been a secret follower of President Lincoln. He was picked as the next Democratic presidential candidate when the Indian wars were over. I promised him 50,000 dollars for his campaign because he assured me that once in office he would support Republican agendas and not liberal ones. I gave him a gold coin as a symbol of my intentions and to seal my verbal promise to him. He should have never pushed so hard to be a hero and not waited for his support troops to arrive. It cost him his life as well as the presidency.

I traveled to France in the summer of 1887 to obtain a trade agreement with the French government. That however did not come to pass. The government was too busy with their plans for the worlds fair in 1889. While there I met with Alexander Gustave Eiffel, he had designed the Statue of Liberty. I admired his work and views. He was in a competition to build a monument (the Eiffel Tower) for the worlds fair. He showed me his designs and I was impressed by them. I promised him funding and upon my return I sent him a gold coin. I told him due to prior business obligations I could not return to France. However I would give his envoy 100,000 dollars in gold as long as he would say the word freedom so I would know he was indeed his envoy. I await for his arrival still."

That was the only three entries in the journal, but they answered long pondered questions by some of the greatest curators. These entries final erased many mysteries and conjectures in the historical world of experts. The only question that was left was how did the chest of Columbus Coins arrive and be in a well in Key West. That mystery was solved and I could tell you the long version of it. However I think I will just tell you the simple version of the story.

It took another five years to figure it all out. Once all the facts came out about the four coins the academic world began to compile their information. They put travel records and time lines of people's travels together and began to see history before their very eyes. The Queens Reign never sank as thought. Well not as it was recorded in obscure history text. During a storm it deliberately steered off course and set a new course to what we today call Florida. The Mayflower thought it was lost at sea and sank. However it was doing well as it continued to the Keys. At the helm of the Queens Reign was Andrew Jones, cousin of Christopher Jones, Captain of the Mayflower.

Many died on the long voyage, but those that survived hid the gold in what we have been calling a well. It was really just a hole in the ground that filled up with water during high tide. Over the years the waterline retreated further and further back from the opening. So it was covered with planks and dirt to hide it. Finally the last survivors from the Queens Reign died off from old age or disease. It wasn't until Wilbur Jones found the opening after a hurricane in 1859 that the lost Columbus Coins were found. He melted coins down for the gold to start his import-export shipping business. Gold was a common means of currency and drew no attention whereas the gold coins would have.

OH! By the way the Queens Reign after arriving at the Keys and the gold buried was taken out a mile from the shore and sank on purpose. It was discovered last year bringing all the loose ends and conjectures to a close and solving one of the great maritime gold mysteries.

Rachel, James and Horace now have a new occupation. They have a sponsor and unlimited funding to find Amelia Earhart. Now their new adventure begins. If all goes well I will report to you their findings. We may be able to solve another mystery that is hidden in history.

MOVING ON NO MATTER WHAT

SO LATE ONE night you ask yourself why you're always sad
maybe because I was the best thing you ever had.
But I didn't make what you thought was enough money
so you couldn't ever think of me as your honey.

Now that you finally found yourself sad and alone
Sitting by the mirror, cold and with your heart of stone
I hope you are not thinking I will come crawling back?
All the qualities and love I seek you truly lack

Now that you have realized that when push comes to shove
you would rather have my once unquestionable love.
Now the time for us as a couple has come and gone
all my feelings for you have been totally withdrawn

I take my time while proceeding to find my treasure
while reaching out for someone to bring me new pleasure.

13 Count Sonnet

LET'S HAVE A TALK

I'VE NOTICED SOMETHING about people as they age. I've been watching human behavior since my high school days and their actions never cease to amaze me. Now keep in mind my observations are from a male's point of view, so some women may develop a frown as I continue.

I don't claim to know the inner most thoughts of a woman's mind; but I do know this much. They want a man that will give them security and protect them. If they can get that and at the same time the man is handsome and rich, JACKPOT. Most women however will tell you that it's a sense of humor, flat stomach, nice head of hair, cute smile, etc. Really! If only that was the total truth.

All though the majority of women will tell you the fore mentioned, there is a small percentage that are indeed gold diggers. You know the ones that say they fall in love with the bald, overweight, 30 years older than them, which seem to end up with the guy that just won the 80 million dollar power ball.

I think women are more sensitive and emotional than men. That's not a bad thing at all. I also think they are more caring and loving as well. I admit that they can endure more pain than a man too. Women have the great ability to have children and the nurturing capabilities to raise babies. I can't imagine a man having a baby; thank God we males were spared that magical gift.

I must confess that I have often wondered if women use the fact that they can have children as leverage to obtain control or gain favors while in relationships. I ask that question because as little girls they learn that boys will pay their way to movies, dinners; buy them presents, flowers, etc. This goes on for their entire life; it must give women some sort of entitlement mentality I would think. It may even bring on a feeling of being spoiled and thusly a little superior to men.

Now I bring that up because women usually want to change a man. They love the bad boys and they think that they are woman enough to change them. If they do manage to change them, they then become bored and their challenge is over. So why would anyone set out to accomplish a goal that if successful will end in catastrophe?

OK ladies; let's talk about men and some of their inner workings. Men as a whole are drawn to a woman by looks first and foremost. Like woman he will say it's your eyes, hair, your great smile, etc. Most men will truly mean those things; but they are only ribbons and bows on the prize. Sorry to be so blunt ladies; but when a man sees you in a bar or party you are only a prize at that point in time.

It is similar to when a woman sees a man that she wants, she will seduce him with all her little tricks. Men will say and do anything as well to win a woman over and get his prize. It is an interesting sight to watch and listen to as the game is played. Men will approach and smile and tell the woman she has a pretty smile, ask about her perfume. He will continue to complement her and show her all the attentiveness that she feels she deserves. Amazing how this approach has been so effective for hundreds of years.

Once again I am sorry to have to say to you ladies; that if a woman is lonely, sad and has low self-esteem she is vulnerable to the complementary approach. Sad that there are people that will take advantage of others when they are down. We all have desires of someone loving us; but many times when we trust another person we get hurt. If we ever learn to separate the lies from the truth we will have a better society for sure.

It use to be that more men cheated on their wife's or girlfriends than women. Today however, I think it's getting pretty close to becoming even/steven in the cheating department. So what is causing this to occur in such high percentages? Could it be that the thrill is gone or the need to have another conquest? I think it's the same for men and women. They have a need to prove to themselves that they are still sexy and can attract the attention that they got when younger. To once again receive that attention will positively boost their egos and self-esteem. So with that said, I ask you this. To again feel sexy, wanted, needed and appreciated, is that fuel enough to motivate one to new adventures outside their present relationship?

Let me get back to men for a second. Men feel pressure to provide as well as become successful. He has to be ready to perform when asked by his lover. He must prove that he is worthy of his mate. Even if he is single, he must prove it to himself that he can keep a job and earn money. Ego is a sword with many edges, not just two. Manhood is a man's greatest weakness. If a woman attacks that, it is a devastating blow that he will carry forever. It is also hurtful for a man to attack his mate's womanhood. Maybe because I am a man I think it is worse for the man; but I could be wrong and they are equal in mental hurtfulness.

Enough about young love and early in life relationships for now. I love looking at couples that have been in love for 40 or 50 years. They are the ones that got it right and have truly been blessed. They never let the little flaws become an issue and just accepted them as things that made each other that more special. They refused to see the receding hairline and the pounds that slowly were added on. They are the couples that got past physical looks and took the time to discover the heart, soul and love within each other.

These days it appears to be all about money, looks and possessions. If men and women would take the time to get to know someone they might find real love. Sure lust is great; but without true love it is fleeting. If both men and women would stop trying to manipulate each other, life would be so much more fulfilling. Mind games and controlling attitudes do nothing but destroy a relationship. Respect, trust and love are the foundation for everlasting love.

How many times have you heard about an elderly couple; when one dies that the other will die a few months later? Yes, a broken heart and the desire to be with the love of your life can overcome the will to carry on.

If I could talk to young newlyweds I would say this to them. Don't try to dominate the other; respect each other and their needs. Listen to one another with an open mind and heart. Last and most important, take the time to discover the person that dwells in your mates heart. That is the person to cherish forever and the one that will take you down the road to everlasting love.

CHILDHOOD MEMORIES

I FEEL FORTUNATE to have been raised in the rural part of the Pacific Northwest. I think it's sad that the kids today will never know what being a kid and having fun is really all about. While being on a farm during my youth and the chores that go with that lifestyle; my fond memories are priceless. Today the kids sit around and play video games and they seem lost when it comes to finding something that is constructive to do with their life's.

I could tell you many a story from my childhood; but one I enjoy the most is about fishing. My father taught my brother (Ted) and I how to fish and hunt as young boys. It was not uncommon for Ted and I to go fishing by ourselves. When I was 12 and Ted was 8, this one particular Saturday morning we decided to go fishing. We went in the back yard and dug up a coffee can of night crawlers, caught a couple dozen grass hoppers and away we went.

It was approximately two miles to Bear Creek where our favorite fishing hole was located. As we made our way along the same dear paths that we had walked a hundred times we talked about how today was going to be a great fishing day for us. We noticed a buck standing off 75 yards away eyeing us as we traveled on our merry way. A couple of pheasants and a wild turkey also caught our attention as we reached the banks of our fishing hole.

All these things were as common as day to Ted and I, yet we still took the time to admire the animals, trees and all that lived in the woods. Our fishing hole was about 100 yards down from a dam that was made of railroad ties and was only 6 feet high. We had never had any luck fishing the back waters so we stayed below the dam.

Some people had been working on the dam for sometime now; but we didn't know what they were doing. After an hour of fishing and without getting a bite we decided to move upstream and see what was happening at the dam. To our amazement we saw all these cement boxes going up from the creek to the top of the dam. There were 6 boxes and each a little higher than the other starting from the bottom up.

Our eyes grew to the size of baseballs when we saw all these fish jumping from one box to the other. We went running over to the boxes and stood there dumbfounded at the sight. I knew the difference between rainbow trout and these fish. These were silver salmon. We took our fish net and as they jumped one box to another we would snag them in midair with our net. We filled one gunny sack and started on a second one.

We were screaming and hollering so much that we didn't notice the man that came up behind us. "How's fishing today boys," he asked.

"Its great mister, look at all the fish my brother and I have caught. You can catch some too if you want, look, it's easy," I said as I scooped up another fine specimen.

"Well boys I'm afraid we have a small problem. I'm Officer Watson and it's illegal to catch fish from a fish ladder. You better come with me and bring all your fish." We got in the back of his patrol car and he put the gunny sacks of fish in his trunk. "What's you address and I will take you home."

I told the officer our address and he drove us home. When dad saw the police car in front of the house he came out immediately. He talked with the officer and dad told Ted and I to go in the house. We watched from the window as they continued to talk. They seemed to be getting along fine. They both were smiling and the officer burst out laughing at one point.

Well needless to say the officer kept our fish and dad scolded us for fishing not only at the fish ladder; but for fishing within 100 feet below a dam and for not having a salmon license. He shook his head and said he would take us fishing in the morning and show us the boundaries. We never got a spanking or grounded for any of it that day. I will always remember the look on that policeman's face when I told him look how easy it was to catch them fish. OH! The innocence of children can be fun; but what great memories.

STAR KNIGHT

AS STAR KNIGHT blew out the candles on the cake at her 4 year old birthday party; she made a wish. She wished for an imaginary friend, not just any friend; but for a Fairy God Mother. She was disappointed when she opened her eyes and saw that her wish had not materialized instantly before her.

It wasn't until little Star had went to bed that as she began to fall asleep; a beautiful Fairy appeared at the foot of her bed. Star's eyes lit up and her excitement filled the air. "OH! You came, I knew that you would," exclaimed Star.

"Why of course I did child. I am your Fairy God Mother and I will always be by your side."

"What is your name"?

"It's whatever you child want it to be. What would you like to call me"?

"I will call you Twilight," Star said joyfully.

"OH that's a wonderful name. Whenever you want me just think of me and touch your nose with your finger and I will appear. Now you go to sleep and remember that I am always near."

Star drifted into a deep sleep as a smile crossed her face. It was like magic that she could think of Twilight, touch her nose and her Fairy God Mother would appear. As soon as she woke up the next morning she summoned Twilight as instructed and there she was. Star talked to Twilight for an hour before going downstairs to the kitchen. Star introduced her Fairy God Mother to her parents and they both smiled and said hello.

Having an imaginary friend is not something to be concerned about unless it continues into adulthood. Stars parents played along with their child and they too would talk to Twilight and interact with her as if she truly existed.

It was a wonderful childhood for Star; but as she got older her parents began to worry about Twilight still being a major part of their daughter's life. When Star entered junior high she was still having conversations with twilight. She never made a scene while at school or in public. Star would call Twilight when she was home and usually at bedtime. She would talk to her for hours on end.

By the time Star entered high school her parents had long stopped pretending that Twilight was real. They had done everything they could think of to alter Stars behavior. Star was happy and told them that she was fine and in control of the situation. "Twilight will watch over me and keep me safe. She always has and I believe in her," Star said.

Star graduated from high school and went off to college. It was then for the first time she began to show interest in boys. That was something that she had never done before then. Being confused she spent many nights talking to Twilight about here new found feelings. She asked about relationships and what love felt like etc.

Star's first date wasn't until her second year at college. He was a nice young man studying to be an attorney. His name was Jake Smith and he was a true southern gentleman. He never tried any inappropriate moves or suggested anything that was not proper.

Twilight told Star that Jake was indeed a fine boy. He was one in a million and she should follow her heart. From all that Twilight had seen and heard she thought that Jake was perfect for Star.

The two continued to date all through college and by the time they graduated they had fallen totally in love with one another. That night of graduation they talked about their future. They laughed as they recalled their first kiss. It had been Jake's first kiss as well and looking back at it caused them both to giggle and smile.

Jake took a deep breath and looked into Stars eyes and asked her to marry him. She was caught off guard by the question. She hesitated and asked if she could give him an answer the next day. He was disappointed; it was not the reaction he had expected; but he agreed to wait for her answer.

That night, once home, Star called out for Twilight. She explained how Jake had asked her to marry him and that she loved him; but was scared of the unknown. The words she heard from Twilight were something that Star never would have dreamed of. "My child, I have been with you for many years now. I have watched you grow up. I have protected you and comforted you as well. We have talked and shared things and had our secrets. It is time my child for you to let another guide you. It is also time for me to move on as well. There are others that I can be with as I was with you. I say to you, let Jake now be the one to love, protect and care for you. Let him be the one you share and talk to. Marry him my child and let him be all that I have been to you and more. Go and tell him yes, for tonight I say goodbye, my job is finished." With that Twilight slowly vanished into midair.

Star didn't want Twilight to go. She reached out to her as she was disappearing. She cried as her long time friend left her side. She knew in her heart that everything that Twilight had said was right. She had to let go and trust her words and the love of Jake.

The next day with tears in her eyes Star told Jake that she would marry him. Her tears were tears of joy for the most part; but some were for the loss of her Fairy God Mother. It was going to be a whole new experience for Star from this day on.

They were married six months after Jake's proposal. It was a beautiful day in the park as they said I do. The blue sky and the sun's warm rays along with the birds singing made it that much more of a memorable day.

Jake continued his education and passed the bar exam and Star opened up a small clothing store that focused on high end dress's. Their life was picture perfect and they felt blessed; but not until Star found out that she was expecting did their emotions reach a new level.

They were in seventh heaven when the ultrasound showed that Star was going to have a little girl. They thought of names as they turned the extra bedroom into a nursery. They finally decided on the name Sarah Ann, Sarah was Star's mother's name and Ann was Jake's mother's name.

When the day came that Star went into labor she had a difficult time. She was in labor for 26 hours and had some complications. She was alright once she heard the cries of her baby after she had given her last push. All the pain disappeared for a moment as the doctor held up Sarah Ann for her to see. She smiled and slipped into a deep sleep from exhaustion.

When she woke up several hours later both Jake's and her families were there. The nurse brought in her little girl and Star held her for the first time. "OH my God, she is so beautiful. Look what we did Jake, look what we created together," Star said while crying with joy.

Jake's career was soaring and Star's dress shop was thriving. Sarah Ann was growing up faster than anyone imagined. There life was what we all dream that it would be for ourselves.

Sarah Ann had an elaborate five year old birthday party. There was a petting zoo, clowns, pony rides and everything that that a child could want. The smiles and laughter as Sarah Ann opened up her presents. It was a wonderful day not only for Star and Jake; but for Sarah Ann as well. However; at the end of the day Sarah was sleepy and she went to bed early that night.

Jake and Star were in the kitchen having breakfast as Sarah entered the room. Star looked up and was immediately stunned. There standing next to Sarah and holding her hand was Twilight. It was Sarah that spoke, "mommy I have a friend and her name is Twilight. She said I could be her friend, can I mommy?"

Jake couldn't see or hear anyone but he told his little girl of course she could. He glanced at Star and gave a wink. Star on the other hand could see Twilight and she smiled openly and said, "Yes my child, you can keep your new found friend for as long as you need her." Twilight bowed her head and told Star that she would protect Sarah and love her as she had done for her.

Star felt calm and a new feeling of serenity had now come over her. She knew she would never have to worry about Sarah's future now that she had her own Fairy God Mother. One that Star knew in her heart was the best one in the entire world. She knew that Twilight was what little girls dreams are made of.

WHEN THE TIME WAS RIGHT

BEATRICE CONNORS HUMMED Silent Night as she stirred her fudge simmering on the kitchen stove. She was in high spirits as Christmas was only a week away. She was thinking of her children and grandchildren coming to spend the holiday with her husband Hank and her. She glanced outside the kitchen window and smiled as the snow began to fall. Visions of the grandchildren making snow Angels and building snowmen captured her thoughts.

It was a ringing telephone that broke her concentration. She slid the fudge off the hot burner and placed it on a cold one for the moment. She then lifted the receiver and said, "Hello."

"This is Sheriff Bill Shaw, are you Beatrice Connors?"

"Yes, what's this about officer?"

"Are you the wife of Hank Connors and you reside at 2645 Harmony Lane?"

"Yes, what has happened is Hank OK?"

"I'm sorry to have to tell you your husband was in a traffic accident. He lost control of his car when he hit a patch of black ice and flipped over into a ditch. He has been transported to Mercy Hospital. There is an officer in route to your home and he will take you to the hospital."

She dropped the phone and fear took control of her emotions. As her head was swirling and her heart pounding she managed to somehow get her coat on and turn off the stove. The police car arrived with its lights flashing; but with no siren. She met the officer as he approached the front door. He helped her to the car and they sped away to the hospital.

Upon arrival she went to the emergency rooms admitting desk. She told the nurse who she was and that her husband had just been brought there. The nurse informed her that her husband was in surgery and that the doctor would come and update the family when he had news for them. Beatrice called her son Barry and daughter Cindy. They both lived about three hours away from Cedarville; but because of the snow it would now take longer for them to drive. She sat alone and waited for them to arrive and for the doctor to appear with news of Hank.

The time dragged by, each minuet seemed to be hours. Beatrice felt some relief when her children walked through the opening sliding hospital doors and ran to her side. "How is dad? How hurt is he? What has the doctors said?" Barry asked.

"No one has said a word to me son. I have no idea how bad your father is or what they are doing in the operating room."

Barry stormed up to the nurse's desk and started demanding some answers when a doctor pushed open a side door and approached the family. He walked up to Beatrice and asked "are you Mrs. Connors?"

"Yes."

"I'm sorry, we did all we could. His injuries were just too many and too severe; my condolences to you and your family." With that said the doctor turned and walked away down a long narrow hallway, leaving them all frozen in an emotional state of disbelief.

A nurse asked them if they wanted some time to be with their deceased family member. They answered yes and were then taken to a private room where Hank was being held before being taken to the morgue. After an hour of crying and comforting one another they left, still in a state of shock.

It was a silent yet tearful ride back to the Connor's home. Beatrice threw the pot of fudge away and started to wash the pot when Cindy took it away from her and told her sit down. Nothing more was said that night. Cindy and Barry slept in their bedrooms that they had grown up in as children.

Beatrice stood at her bedroom doorway looking at the bed that she and hank had slept in for a lifetime of marriage. She couldn't bring herself to enter. She closed the door slowly and then pulled out the sofa sleeper bed. She cried herself to sleep and thought of how she could go on without the love of her life. Hank was her knight, companion and protector. He was gone and she was faced with moving ahead without him. She questioned if she was strong enough to do just that.

The days that followed were filled with friends trying to comfort Beatrice and the family. Barry made all the funeral arrangements as well as financial and life policy matters. The house was paid for so that would not be a burden and the retirement account was sufficient to take care of all of Beatrice's needs for life. However, if you ask anyone they would have rather been broke, homeless and Hank still by their sides.

Christmas still took place at Barry's and Cindy's home back in the city of Elmwood. Beatrice stayed in Cedarville which was her request and spent the day no one really knows how. I guess that is for her to know so no one has ever pushed her for an explanation.

Time passed and Beatrice made friends by attending church events and joining a senior citizens center. These got her out of the house and occupied her mind and filled time. She still occasionally would open the bedroom door and stand on the outside looking in. She just couldn't bring herself to step across the threshold.

After several months had passed Beatrice found that she was crying less and was growing more confident in functioning alone. Sure her kids came and visited ever so often; but it was her that had to cope with the day to day existence.

It was seven months after Hank had passed away when one night Beatrice woke up in the middle of the night. She got up from her sofa bed and walked over to the bedroom door. She opened it and stood there looking at the bed. She envisioned hank sitting up in bed waving her into the room. She took one step inside and a warm breeze touched her face.

She walked over to the bed and got in. She turned and faced her mental picture of Hank. She knew at that moment that she would always be with her beloved Hank. She reached out, touched his cheek and gave him a gentle kiss. She fell asleep with the memories of her and Hank from the first time they met to their whole life together.

It was Barry who found her two days later lying in bed hugging a picture of Hank; with a smile on her face and a look of total peacefulness. The coroner said that she had quietly passed away in her sleep. I can only surmise that the good Lord above and her broken heart agreed that this was
WHEN THE TIME WAS RIGHT.

INTRODUCTION

I WOULD LIKE to introduce to you thirty-five year old Jacob Wayne Boatwright. First off however I want to tell you a little about him. He's six-foot three inches tall, weighs 350 pounds and has gray hair; balding slightly at the forehead back. His deep blue eyes are set far apart and the indentations on the bridge of his nose tell you that it supported glasses.

He wears dentures that are discolored and slightly pitted from eating high acid foods. That discoloration combined with his yellow stained fingers should indicate to you that he is a heavy smoker. His fingers are crooked and deformed which physically shows all the signs of him having rheumatoid arthritis. Even with this crippling disease he has calloused hands telling you that he is a hard working man.

His skin is dry and his forearms are covered with small pit marked scars. He is a welder down at the local shipyard which explains the dehydration and slag scars. He has a 14 inch vertical scar that runs down his left leg above the knee. He had the knee replacement probably due to a combination of his weight, arthritis and the small quarters inside the hull of ships at his work site.

Mr. Boatwright's appearance looks disheveled and your first impression of him understandably would be that he was a homeless individual. You would be close because he has lived a hard life. It's obvious that he has an unhealthy diet and the smell of alcohol tells you that he is a drinker.

Now that I have told you about Jacob, let me introduce you to him face to face. I should tell you that I myself only met Mr. Boatwright two hours ago; but he has told me so much in that short period of time. Come this way ladies and gentlemen.

Welcome to Autopsy room three. The man on table four is Jacob Wayne Boatwright. He suffered a massive heart attack yesterday. He chose to neglect all the signs and doctors warning for his entire life. During my examination I found that he had an enlarge heart, scarred lungs from the welding smoke. Even if he hadn't had a heart attack he had early stages of lung cancer from years of heavy smoking. His arteries were nearly clogged so he could have had a stroke at anytime.

What I am telling you is that you may be able to fool people; but you can't fool your body or your local Medical Examiner. You can't cheat death. Listen to your doctor and to your body; it talks to you everyday loud and clear. Don't you be Jacob Wayne Boatwright and be lying on my table long before your time.

I hope his story has encouraged you to get healthy and get check-ups on regular bases. Everything caught early nowadays can be fixed and taken care of successfully; so in the words of SPOCK "live long and prosper."
Thank you, John Travis M.E.

THE GUITAR

SCOTT SHIVERS WAS a boy that grew up on the road. His dad was Ridley Shivers, the front man for the hard hitting rock band SOULS UNLEASHED. Scott and his mother (June) traveled year round with the band all over the world.

What little time the front man had at home he spent making a hand crafted guitar. He was building it from scratch in his basement. The wood came from a Maple tree that he cut down himself located on the hillside behind their home. He bucked a piece three feet long from the butt of the tree. It was twenty-four inches in diameter. He also cut a piece that was only four inches in diameter and three feet long. He took the two pieces to a local cabinet shop. They milled the two pieces down for him. For the body he had an 18 X 26 X 2 inch piece of planed wood that captured the trees most beautiful grain. The other piece was planed to a 3 X 2 X 24 inch piece for the neck. The cabinet shop managed to also save him a planed piece that was 6 X 2 X 8 inches for the keys and nut assembly head.

Ridley designed the personalized body shape and cut away the excess wood. He sanded the edges and beveled them to precision. As soon as he would get lost in the project it would be time to once again go back out on the road.

That is the lifestyle that Scott grew up living. His father really had no time to spend with him. They never played ball or went fishing etc. His father did introduce him to all the great rock stars and celebrities of the music world over the years.

Time passed and little by little Scott saw how work continually controlled his father's life. Still when he was home his dad would spend hours working in the basement on THE GUITAR. Scott thought how ironic that everything in his father's life was playing or making a guitar and he was a second fiddle in his dad's life. When truth is known, Scott would have been overjoyed to have been elevated to second guitar level in his father's life.

The situation continued right up to Scott's 16th birthday party. The only thing that had changed over the years was Scott had started to learn to play the guitar and his parents health had started to catch up with their age. That wasn't the focus of today's events. Cake and ice cream was. Scott's mother called out for Scott and all his friends that had gathered to come to the dining room table for the present opening.

Scott and his mother sat at the table for a few minutes waiting for Ridley to appear. When he didn't show Scott went down the stairs to the basement to ask his father to come join the party. As he took the last step onto the basement floor he saw his father. His lifeless body was humped over THE GUITAR that was lying on the workbench. His fingers froze making an E chord. His lips stuck to the strings right above the two duel Humbucking pick-ups. A small blue ark of electrical current danced from the pick-ups to his lips.

Scott gasped as he pulled the plug out from the wall that supplied the power to the guitars amplifier. Scott yelled for his mother to call 9-1-1. He shook his father's body in hope he wasn't dead; but it was too late, Ridley was gone. There on the workbench was a card addressed to Scott. He opened it and found a note written inside that said the following.

Son I know that I have not been the best father in the world. In fact I've been a lousy one. I knew the day that you were born that I would never live up to fatherhood. I did know that your mother would be strong enough for the both of us. One thing I could do however was to put my heart and soul into making you this guitar. Every time you play it I pray that you feel the love and pride that I can't give you personally. That love is in THE GUITAR and I promise you son that we will always be together whenever you play it. Even though I let the road rule my life, you and your mother have always been and will be the love of my life. I think it is time that I start to slow down on all the touring and start to build on my family. That is if there is time to build that bridge with you son. I want to try, Happy Birthday. I Love you son.

Over five-hundred people from the music world attended Ripley Shivers funeral. Many said wonderful things and cried openly for one of the greats in the music world. The press was there with cameras and even a helicopter flying above. As the people slowly left Scott and his mother went back to their mansion in the hills that overlooked the city. That was all that was left now, material things, memories and THE GUITAR.

Scott had left THE GUITAR on the workbench and had not touched it. It was determined that a frayed wire in the electrical cord that Ripley used to plug in the amplifier caused the accident. The guitar itself was not at fault, it was only a conductor in the tragedy. Scott still could not bring himself to plug it in or to even move it.

His mother came to him two years later one night while he was sleeping. She shook him until he woke up. He sat up in bed looking befuddled at first, then realized who it was. She stared into his eyes and with a smile said she had something to say.

"Son your father worked for years and hundreds of hours building you that beautiful guitar downstairs. Go and hold it, embrace it and feel it's magic. Your father's heart beats within its body and his soul will sing freely every time you strum it. He can and will live on with you in the only way he knew how. Please son, let your father speak to you through the blood, sweat and tears he gave you in his gift, THE GUITAR."

Scott kissed his mother good-night and promised to sleep on her request. He couldn't fall back to sleep. He had a war battling within his heart and mind. It was 4 am when Scott got up and went downstairs. He stood over THE GUITAR and before long he imagined it was calling out to him.

He finally reached out and grasped the neck with his left hand. A tingle ran up his hand, then to his arm and shoulder. He plugged a cord into the body of THE GUITAR and took the other end of the cord over to the double stacked Marshall and plugged it into channel one. He hit the amps rocker switch and it lit up. He adjusted the setting to fit the sound he desired. He paused for just a moment pondering what 200 watts of power would sound like through THE GUITAR.

Scott was still a beginner and didn't know a lot of chords. He remembered the chord his fathers hand had been froze to that sad day. He made an E chord and struck the strings. Like magic he began to play like a professional. He didn't know what was happening or if he was dreaming. The sound vibrated the walls and soon his mother was standing at the bottom of the basement stairs. She stood mesmerized as Scott played lead riffs exactly like his father's. He couldn't stop playing, he was obsessed. He continued playing lightening fast leads and chords he only had dreamed of playing before that night. He finally stopped after hours of playing when he no longer could physically continue.

Scott Shivers went on to be the front man for the new band SOULS UNLEASHED. It is said that Scott is as good if not better than his father. His band has traveled the world and earned many platinum records and has countless number one hits.

Scott got married in his mid twenties and a few years later his wife gave birth to their son which they named Andrew. On his son's first birthday

Scott declared to his wife that he was not destine to make the same mistakes as his father had made with him.

He told her that during his spare time at home he would spend the first hour with his son and then half an hour in the basement making his son his version of THE GUITAR. With that said Scott grabbed his late father's chain saw and went out the back door. He looked up the hill and spotted a large Maple tree. Like his father, he had found the perfect Maple tree for THE GUITAR which he would pass down to his son when the time came.

THE TIME HAS COME

JEREMIAH BUSH WAS a scary man when I first met him. I was in the sixth grade at the time and he was a hermit type that lived two miles away from my house. We both lived high up in the back woods of the Pacific Northwest Cascade Mountain Range. He was a loner and a trapper by trade that lived off the land. I lived with my parents and my father was the foreman on a logging site. I would run into him once in awhile when I went down to the creek or walking the mile to my house from the school bus stop. I was the last stop that the school bus driver had to make. The one just before me was five miles down the mountainside. I'm sure that the school hated to have to put chains on the bus in the winter to reach my stop. Because of that extra work I made an extra effort to always be kind to the bus driver and my teachers.

It was during the summer between my 7th and 8th grade break that I ran into Jeremiah with his pack of dogs. I had heard them in the past; but never had seen them before then. They ran up to me and began to lick me and running around me playfully. "They like you boy" Jeremiah said. "You should come up to my place, with your pa's permission of course and meet all my other critters." With that said we parted when the road forked, me towards my house and him pushing on upwards to his place high on the Skyline Trail ridge.

I remember like it was yesterday when I asked my father if I could go up to Mr. Bush's house and see his animals. I told dad about the encounter that I had with him on the road the day before. I could see the look of concern on his face as he contemplated his answer. He knew that the old man was different; but he was not a dangerous man or really presented a threat to me. Dad had met him on several occasions and really spoke highly of him when he did talk about him. He looked right at me as he said, "OK Travis you can go and see the animals. You be polite and be back by dinner time at five."

I agreed immediately and started up the hill through the woods. It would have been a longer hike to his place to go down the road to the fork and then follow the high road. I could cut that distance in half by cutting over the top of the mountain and getting on the Skyline Trail itself. I was breathing pretty hard when I reached the trail head and approached

Jeremiah's cabin. The dogs began barking and Jeremiah came out the front door unto the porch with shotgun in hand. "Sorry boy, I didn't know it was you. One can't be too careful way up here you know. That old hound there that's licking you hand is Blue and leader of the pack. I knew the minute he took a shine to you back on the road that you were alright. Blue is never wrong when it comes to sizing up people."

The old recluse took be around back of his cabin and showed me all the animals that he had. Some were in cages, while others ran free. "Meet Jack and Jill" he said as he pointed to a doe and buck. "They're a pair of mule deer that just wandered up to the porch a few years back and never left. Go ahead and pet them if you like, they won't run away. Over here in the cages I have a skunk, porcupine, owl, adult cougar and last but not least Player the bobcat. I call him that because he will play with you all day. He's the friendliest animal I have ever seen, aint that right Player."

I stuck my finger in the cage and Player licked it. Boy he had a rough tongue. Jeremiah laughed and he unlocked the cage door and picked the bobcat up and handed him to me. Player just purred loudly and continued to lick the side of my face as I held him. It was a fascinating day that I will have fond memories of for the rest of my life. This rugged mountain type man was really a kind and soft spoken man at heart. He kept his cages clean and I could tell he loved them all, especially old Blue who stayed mostly at his side. I thanked him for the invitation that he had given me and for the tour of his place. I waved goodbye as I started down the Skyline trail towards home.

I continued to visit Jeremiah over the next few years and he taught me the secrets of tracking and trapping. I learned how to field dress a deer and how to properly handle firearms and reload ammunition. He showed me what was eatable and what wasn't in the forest, from mushrooms to berries. He revealed the hard to find ponds where beavers played and the elusive otters. Jeremiah was one of a kind and I looked up to him like a folk hero from a time long past.

I was a senior when one Saturday I went out side and saw smoke high in the sky coming from the direction of Jeremiah's cabin. I ran into the woods towards his cabin. When I arrived his cabin was totally engulfed in flames. I could hear old Blue and the other dogs howling in pain coming from inside the cabin. I tried to get close enough to kick in the door; but the intense heat held me at bay. Soon the cries ended and silence settled over the mountain. It was a sickening silence filled with pain and sorrow. As the smoke cleared, standing there was Jack and Jill as if nothing had happened.

I went over to the cages and opened them one by one. As the door opened they all went running to the forest. The porcupine, the skunk, the adult cougar exited his cage and stopped. He looked at me, then Jack and Jill. I thought for a moment that I had made a huge mistake; but he slowly walked past the three of us and disappeared into the woods. I opened the cage door that confined Player and to my surprise he didn't run away. Instead he walked out of his pen and sat down next to me while rubbing his head against my leg, purring all the time. I reached down and stroked his head and told him he was free and to go.

I left Jeremiah's cabin that day with Player by my side and Jack and Jill following. When I reached my house my father wanted to know what was going on and what this menagerie was that was following me. I told him over the years about the animals so after I told him about the fire and setting the animals free he knew the situation. He called the police on our shortwave radio and explained what had happened. The police came with all the proper personnel and investigators.

It was determined that Jeremiah had a heart attack, probably in his sleep, since his body was in bed. That was why the door was locked and the dogs trapped inside.

My father let me keep Player; but I had to build a pen for him. Jack and Jill continued to hang around so they to became our pets as well. A few months had past when late one night I heard strange noises coming from outside. I went out side to find another bobcat outside Players pen. I approached the pen slowly and the intruder backed off about 100 feet. I looked at Player and he had a look that I had never seen before. I opened the pen's door and he walked out. I bent down and put both my hands on the side of his head and talked to him. "OK boy, maybe the time has come." he licked my hand and then turned and went to the female bobcat. He sat down next to her and they nuzzled each other for a moment. They turned and walked away into the night. Player gave me one last glance and we stared at each others eyes till he vanished into the woods.

I still have Jack and Jill to help me remember the fond memories from the Cascade Mountain Range and Jeremiah. I graduate high school in a few weeks and will be off to college in another state. Like Player I have to realize that there is a new life with others to find and experience. Now that I have reached manhood I must embrace the simple fact, adolescence becomes manhood and I must face the fact that THE TIME HAS COME.

THE RUNAROUND

THE WIND WAS howling and the sky flashed with lightening as orderly Troy Collins walked the halls of the States mental hospital. The clock on the wall read 11:30 PM as the thunder claps made him flinch, catching him off guard. He swore that the halls of Evergreen Mental Hospital were haunted; especially ward C were the criminal insane were housed. The facility was well hidden in the Blue Ridge Mountains of Tennessee. It was built miles away from civilization so the general public couldn't hear the agonizing screams that were loud and often.

He checked each and ever room to make sure that all the inmates were accounted for. His rounds took an hour to completely check the 252 rooms that were his responsibility. All were there, sleeping like babies, after all they had all been heavily sedated. That was Evergreens standard procedure; drug everyone to the maximized limit that a human being could tolerate. The shadows on the walls reflected eerie and distorted shapes that played with Troy's nerves every time lightening flashed across the sky.

The lights would dim and the wind would play tricks with his mind as well. He was glad when the suns light replaced the night and brought forth daylight. He worked nights, and his shift never ended fast enough for him. He had considered finding other means of employment. However he had made friends with two of the inmates over his seven years of employment there, Carl Tombs in ward C and Anna Carlton in ward A.

Carl was a convicted multi-murderer and diagnosed as a homicidal schizophrenic and has been at Evergreen for 12 years. Anna Carlton was the name she had been using while on the street, so it stuck with her; even though there are no records with that name. She has been at Evergreen for 6 years.

Carl had killed and butchered 17 people (men, women and children); it had made no difference to him. He only loved the thrill of having power over others. Anna on the other hand was a completely different story. She had been a runaway at 13 living on the street. She had become a prostitute and crack head. Finally after 10 years of that life style she overdosed one night and nearly died. She survived, but suffered severe brain damage. No one could find out her real name or where she came from. It was easier to dump her at Evergreen than keep her at a clinic or standard hospital. I say easier; but the truth is the cost savings.

Troy drove the 33 miles to his home and let himself in. He turned on the Television and sat down with a bowl of cereal. The first story he heard on the morning show was that there was going to be a severe weather warning for the next three days, starting that evening. That's all he needed to hear living so far away from the hospital. What he didn't know was that the storm would be the event to create an adventure of a lifetime for him. He finished his breakfast and went to bed for a long deserved sleep.

He drove to work that night fighting heavy winds and rain showers. He got soaked running the hundred feet to the building from his car after parking. Nelson the day orderly was standing by the door, lunch pail in hand. Nelson ran past Troy as he was entering without saying a word. That was common actions for Nelson; he was a peculiar individual to say the least.

Troy punched in at the time clock among the screams and moaning of inmates. He walked around the activity room trying to sooth some of the loudest inmates. Inmates liked Troy because he would always treat them nicely, unlike all the others on the staff at Evergreen. After an hour things calmed down and many made their way to their rooms by themselves. At 9 PM the nurse's started down the halls with the nightly shots in hand. Room by room she went rendering the patients as close to being in a coma as possible. It was sad in away, yet understandable in another.

At 10 PM the staff left for home except for one charge nurse, Sally White and Troy. The doctors left before Troy ever got there. They left at 5 PM and started at 9 AM. Troy never saw them unless they had a major problem that caused them to stay late or come in early. That was fine with Troy. Most of the doctors were insensitive and were like robots instead of humans with any feelings. Nurse White was a middle aged woman who had requested the night shift for a reason only truly known to her. She has been at Evergreen for only 5 years and was a good person at heart and Troy got along with her fine.

Troy went to check on Carl in his room. He had not fallen asleep yet so he entered and asked him how he was doing tonight. "I'm doing OK I guess" Carl replied. "I keep having a dream that there is danger all around. I see my soul floating above me, I don't understand it and that scares me."

Troy told him that he had no real answers to give him about why or what his dream meant. He told him to ask one of the doctors the next day.

Troy went from ward C to see Anna in ward A at the far end of the hospital. Anna was sound asleep and Nurse White was sitting next to her bed brushing the young ladies long brown hair. That wasn't a rare sight at all. Sally spent many nights looking in on Anna. Anna was well liked by the entire staff from both day and night shifts. In fact if it were possible to spoil a person at Evergreen, Anna would be that person. She was always soft spoken and never trouble to the doctors, nurses or fellow inmates.

The storm continued through the night and into the morning. Several tree limbs had broken off and lay on the ground in front of the institute. The small creek that ran behind the hospital had crested and was out of its banks. The water was still a hundred yards away from reaching the building itself; but everyone would still keep a sharp eye on the waters level.

As the night shift ended Nelson burst through the doors cursing about the weather and the road conditions he had coming to work. He still said nothing to Troy as he punched in and Troy punched out at the time clock.

Troy went to his car and started his journey home. He got about three miles from Evergreen when the old wooden bridge that crossed that very same creek that flowed behind the hospital gave way. With a loud snap and cracking sound the bridge was swept away, leaving him stranded on this side of what had now become a river instead of a stream. He was forced to return to Evergreen.

Doctors and nurses began to file in as 9 and 10 AM came around. They all lived on the same side of the creek as the hospital. In fact, Troy was the only staff person that had to cross the bridge to return home. He got a hot meal at the commissary and found refuge in a staff room that was especially for any staff member that worked late or etc.

He was in a deep sleep when he was awakened with a shake. He looked up to see Carl kneeling by his cot. "I'm afraid. I keep having that terrible dream and its getting worse. Last night I was burning in my bed with fire engulfing my room. What does it mean" he asked.

There were tears in his eyes and it was easy to see that he was horrified. Troy sat up and tried to comfort his friend. Now I know that I told you that Carl had killed and butchered many people. However after being at Evergreen 12 years he had honestly became remorseful and was ashamed of what he had done. He had become a good person and if you didn't know his past you would give him the trust and respect of anyone in your community. After an hour talk with Carl he returned to the events room and Troy went back to sleep.

Troy grabbed a bite to eat and then punched in to work. He glanced outside and the storm was getting worse as the wind, rain and lightening continued to build in its viciousness. Eleven PM came and he started his rounds. First he stopped and said hello to Sally to see if there were any patients that needed any special care. She said no and that the day shift had said it was rather a slow day.

Halfway through his rounds Troy was startled by an explosion like sound that was deafening to his ears. The lights went off and screams could be heard over the wind and rain pounding on the roof. Windows were blown out and the wind blew in rain and debris. He looked up and saw fire in ward C. He ran to Carl's room only to find Carl's bed was on fire with him in it unconscious.

The lightening kept flashing and bomb like explosions could be heard throughout the hospital wards. Troy knew what had happened and was still happening. Mother Nature was attacking Evergreen with all her might. Lightening struck the main lobby and hundreds of small snake like bolts of lightening danced along the floor.

Troy beat out the flames that held Carl prisoner and pulled him to safety. He picked him up in the firemen's carry position and ran down the hall yelling for all the people screaming in the hall to follow him.

He got 60 or 70 patients out into the parking lot. There was no other place for them except out in the rain, wind and lightening. He ran back inside the burning building to bring others out to safety. All in all he made four trips in and out bringing people to safety. He knew that there were 252 patients plus Sally and himself for a total of 254. He counted only 252 including him. He looked for Sally, then Anna and they were not there. The institute was totally engulfed in flames at this point.

Troy ran to ward A and Anna's room. Sally was trying with all her might to pick Anna up; but she couldn't. Anna was still in the coma like state that was protocol. The smoke was thick and black as Troy carried Anna down the hall as Sally hung on to his arm. It was good he had worked there many years and had done rounds nightly. He didn't have to see through the heavy smoke, he had the route memorized by heart. Once outside and out of immediate danger he laid Anna down under a tree.

The inmates had wandered off and were everywhere on the grounds. Troy began rounding up the ones he could; but he would never be able to do it on his own. He went back to Sally and she was holding Anna's head in her lap rocking back and forth crying.

"Please tell me Sally that she's not dead" asked Troy.

"No! no! She's fine thank God" answered Sally.

The fire trucks sirens were a wonderful sound as they approached the hospital. Troy and Sally could see several ambulances and police cars as well following them. With everyone's help all 252 patients were collected and transported to another facility 300 miles away.

Carl had burns on his arms and legs but healed with little scaring. Anna was treated for smoke inhalation but also recovered. Many others had minor injuries; but all escaped without any major life threatened injuries. That was a miracle in itself and all thanked God for being merciful.

The hospital is being rebuilt and is expected to open in a year. Troy is drawing his unemployment and waiting for the day that the new hospital opens and he returns to work. Only Sally moved to where the patients were moved to. Everyone else is waiting for the reopening and then they will return to work.

One day Troy saw Sally as she was driving down the highway. He pulled up alongside her and motioned for her to pull over. She drove off to the side of the road and Troy approached her.

"Good luck Sally with your new job; but I've got to ask you though, why move away? You can get a job at the regular hospital until Evergreen reopens."

Sally explained "I'll tell you something that no one knows. Anna is my daughter. I spent years trying to find her and by chance I saw her on television when the police were trying to identify her. That was before she was admitted to Evergreen. She will never know that I'm her mother due to the drugs and her brain damage.

I will go wherever the doctors send her till the day I die. I am sorry that I never found out why she ran away from home and me. But now that I have found her, she needs me as much as I need her. She is my daughter and I will love her for the rest of my life."

THE LONELINESS ANTHEM

LONELINESS EATS AT every heart and soul
It doesn't care about a person's Goal.
With an appetite to hurt and destroy
It will take away happiness and joy.

Leaving behind the emptiness of pain
Making you ponder what is there to gain.
The smiles become absent from your sad face
And your tears cry out for someone's embrace.

The same four walls keep closing around you
As your life changes from what you once knew.
No matter how hard you push back, you lose
Cause the onslaught continues to abuse.

You sit alone in the darkness and cry,
knowing that loneliness will never die.
You pray for the tools to stand up and fight
delivering your soul from this dark night.

Is God the answer or is He with-in
Or is your courage what you should depend?
Who will claim the victory if you win
If you say I, then will that be your sin?

Would you ever take this challenge alone?
Do you feel this is your quest to atone?
Take the hand of God and his mighty sword
And smite the demon while praising the Lord.

The sun will shine again before your eyes
And no longer will your heart hear your cries.
You are free from loneliness' tight hold
God has blessed you with his anointed gold.

All those years you refused his helping hand
Because you thought it was only your stand.
Now you know that He is there by your side
So you have surrendered all of your pride.

Blessed be the ones that have turned to him
And praise the lord through their favorite hymn.

AA/BB 10 count

FINAL LAP

CHASE ROUNDS IS the most celebrated motorcycle rider of all time. He has more wins than anyone in history. He started riding at the age of seven and won his first race at eleven. As the years past he moved up through the ranks. He went from novice, apprentice and journeyman to the pro circuit by the time he was seventeen.

Chases best friend since fourth grade was Chuck Wetter (tools); he did all the bikes mechanical work. He would rebuild them and tune them to their highest performance level. Chase knew that a lot of his success belonged to Tools; he was a master at what he did.

Once Chase turned professional at the age of 15 he had a big time sponsor. They wanted their own support team; but Chase fought hard to keep tools as his main mechanic. The sponsor gave in easily once Chase threatened to leave.

After Chase won a couple of races he met Anna while she was on a pit tour. Feeling cocky he went right up to her and asked her out to dinner. She accepted and that was day one of a lifetime together.

They were married a few months after that first day and Anna found out she was expecting a few weeks later. It was the happiest day of both their life's when Anna gave birth to an 8lb 4oz boy, they named him Clay.

Chase bragged over and over how he and his son would ride together when he was old enough. Chase had a 1947 Harley Davidson that was his pride and joy. It was for riding when he needed time to himself to think or meditate. He had a race coming up in a few weeks so he went on a relaxing ride to the country. While on his ride he decided that he would give the Harley to his son on his 16th birthday.

Anna had been home for only three weeks when Chase entered the Race of Champions. He only had two weeks to get ready for the event. He kissed his wife and Clay good-bye and headed out to California where the race was being held.

Once he arrived he practiced long hours on the track. He felt out the tracks bumps and the banking on the corners high and low. He was satisfied come the day of the race that he had mastered the tracks little secrets and hidden dangers.

The horn sounder and the barrier dropped as the twenty bikes took off with a roar as the race got underway. This was a 250 lap endurance race in the 750cc class. Chase raced on a Bultaco motorcycle because it has great gearing for this particular tracks condition.

Chase was in second place at the 47th lap of the race. That was when he decided to try and take the lead. When he was side by side with the first place bike they both banked hard into a left-hand corner. The first place bikes rider leaned over too far and its tires lost their grip. His bike slid out of control sending its rear tire into Chase's front tire.

Chase didn't have time to make corrections so as his tire ran up on the other bike he was tossed 50 feet up in the air. Chase might have been able to survive; but when he hit the ground it was in front of the still racing motorcycles. He was bounced around like a pinball at the arcade as eight bikes ran over him and drug him a hundred feet down the track.

Chase died that day there on the track. It was determined later that he had 22 broken bones as well as fractured skull and a broken neck. It was a blessing that he died. He could never have lived the life that would have faced him. The entire motorcycle world mourned his loss.

Clay Rounds grew up on the stories of his father's races and seeing the many trophies throughout the house. Tools took Clay under his wing and taught the boy everything about racing and motorcycles. He coached him up through the ranks from the time he could walk. Like his father before him Clay won his first race at eleven. Clay was being talked about in the racing world and he was on the front cover of several motorcycle magazines by the age of fifteen.

On the day Clay turned sixteen Tools told Clay that he had something to show him. Tools drove Clay over to his house and then took him to the garage. He unlocked the door and slowly opened it. There standing all alone was Clay's father's 1947 Harley Davidson motorcycle.

Tools looked at Clay and said, "Your father had a dream that you and he would go for rides together. He wanted to give you this bike on your sixteenth birthday himself. After his death I did the next best thing. I have kept it in mint condition for you. Here are the keys to your father's bike. You see that eight inch long two inch round cylinder that is attached to the handlebars? That is filled with your father's ashes. I wanted his dream to come true. You take the bike and go for a long ride with your dad Clay, right now on your sixteenth birthday. It was his dream from the day you were born."

Clay hugged Tools and he tried to hold back the tears as he started the bike and put it in gear. He rode all day with the wind in his face and peace in his heart, from knowing that for this day, he was one with his father. As night began to fall, Clay went to the local track. He removed the cap from the cylinder. He slowly circled the track while sprinkling the ashes as he went along. After one complete trip around the track he had laid his father to rest in the place where he belonged. The place where his father could once again be part of every lap, including his FINAL LAP.

MR. HARDIN BUCKLEY

HARDIN BUCKLEY SAW himself as a modern day Indiana Jones. He continually got into situations way over his head; but seemed to always survive to live another day.

Once as a young boy of ten he found a cave on his Uncle Kevin's property in Tucson, Arizona. He was never without his Boy Scout knife and flashlight. He entered the dark cave with only the small pen light for illumination.

He hadn't ventured too far when he suddenly heard the rattlers of a diamondback rattlesnake. He froze in place and slowly panned the light side to side. Then right there in front of him was the reptile ready to strike.

Hardin had envisioned this exact scenario many times while daydreaming.

He moved his left hand, which held the flashlight, away from his body's side.

Once his arm was extended he began to make small fast circular motions with the light. The snake struck at the moving object. Hardin knew that he was just out of reach of the snakes striking range. As the snake reached its full extension Hardin grabbed the snake behind its head with his right hand.

He put the end of the flashlight in his mouth and then took his knife out.

He cautiously unfolded his knife with his left hand. Then he stabbed the snake repeatedly. Harding skinned the snake and had a belt made from it. He still has that belts memory to this day.

The older Hardin got the more he increased his level of danger. At the age of sixteen he went to Florida to visit his Aunt Lois. They went to Epcot Center and several others of the parks in central Florida. Hardin thought all that was fun stuff; but it wasn't something that got his adrenalin pumping.

He snuck out of the house one night and went down to a small canal. It was a mile from the house and was rumored to have a large alligator that patrolled the shoreline looking for food.

If there was an alligator to be found in those waters; Hardin was the one to find him. He shinned his light out over the water. He threw rocks and listened for any movement either in the water or the shore. He was ready to give up and return home when he saw two big eyes poke out of the water and stared at him.

They were approaching with great speed directly towards him. Once he realized that this was a big alligator he turned and ran for his Aunts house. He thought he was clear of it; but when he glanced behind him he saw the alligator still coming and was gaining on him. He couldn't believe how fast it could run. By the time he reached his Aunts porch he was yelling at the top of his lungs.

He burst through the door and standing there was his Aunts husband Joe with a rifle. The second that alligator crossed the threshold Joe shot it three times in the back of its head. That's the only place to kill an alligator quickly. As the eleven foot creature lay on the living room floor Hardin sat on its back while his Aunt took pictures. He has those pictures in his mind to this day.

When Hardin turned twenty-four he entered the X-Games as a snowboarder. He was real talented and set out to prove he was the best there was. He was the first person to do a triple in competition. He was the first to master the two and a half twisting double back flip as well. He won first prize at the X-Games and a six foot trophy that first year he entered. He was on the cover of Sports Illustrated as athlete of the year. He has that magazine and trophy to this day.

At thirty-three Hardin and three others climbed Mt. McKinley without oxygen. He canoed the Mississippi River from its origin to its finish in New Orleans. He raced a NHRA funny car and went 238 MPH in a quarter mile.

On Hardin's fortieth birthday an amazing event took place that would change his life forever. You see, Hardin was hit in the head at the age of nine with a baseball bat while playing Little League baseball. He has been in a coma for thirty-one years.

As Hardin turned forty, God decided to answer family prayers. He woke up, sat up and looked around his room. "Where am I" he said?

His parents, now in their late sixties were speechless. "You're in the hospital" his mother said as she held his hand.

The doctors and nurses came in to see him. They were crying and saying it's a miracle from God. The doctors examined him and did a few tests to evaluate his status. It turned out Hardin was forty in actuality; but he was still nine mentally. He was still the little boy he was the second before that bat struck him in the head.

Hardin could not believe what had happened. He tried to tell his parents about all the things he had accomplished. His mother took a compact from her purse and held it up so he could see himself. He started to cry as he began to realize that he had indeed been in a coma for thirty-one years.

Then out of nowhere it hit him like a bolt of lightning. "Mother, I want to go to Uncle Kevin's in Tucson" Hardin said.

"Why my son, what for" his mother replied.

"I have many picture and recollections in my mind. I just know there is a cave waiting for me there. I see a life of adventure for me to fulfill."

The last thing I heard about Hardin was that he found that cave and he killed a rattlesnake. He went to Florida and he killed an alligator since Aunt Lois's husband Joe had passed away. Rumor has it that he is now climbing Mt. McKinley with friends without oxygen.

Hardin is getting professional help and learning to become an adult mentally. He travels with good friends; but it is he that motivates everyone. He is living proof that you can do whatever you want. IF ONLY YOU PUT YOUR MIND TO IT AND MOST IMPORTANT, FOLLOW YOUR DREAMS.

NOT AS IT SEEMS

JILL JOHANSSON, J J to all her friends; lit up a room anytime she entered it. From first grade on she could mesmerize her classmates as well as most adults. Her popularity made the boys somewhat intimidated; because if she rejected you, you were automatically on the unpopular list and teased. Funny as it sounds there is a status level in elementary school.

She continued to be the envy of all the other girls and the one the boys stayed away from. It wasn't until Jill started junior high that a boy finally had enough courage to approach her. Rick Sinclair wasn't the captain of the football team or belonged to any clubs. What he was, was a boy that had self confidence and a total lack of fear. He knew what he wanted and would then go and try whatever it took to get it.

He had eyes for Jill the minute he saw her. He was polite; but firm when he introduced himself to her. "Hello I'm Rick and you seem to be the most popular girl in school. I must tell you that I think you're beautiful. Would you like to go to the movies with me Friday night"?

"I'm not allowed to date. I'm only 14 and my parents told me no dating until my 16th birthday," Jill replied.

"Would you go with me if you could go on a date"?

"Why should I go with you? I don't even know you. What makes you think I would ever go out with you anyway?"

"Because from what I hear from all the guys no one has ever asked you out. They all say that you will just say no anyways, so nobody tries. I however look at it in a different way. I bet you're a little sad that no one has asked you out. You may not be able to date; but you long for someone to ask you anyway. I think that you seek validation as a worthwhile person and being asked out would go a long way towards that goal. Well, have you ever been asked out on a date or am I the first? Tell me how close I am in analyzing the real you."

Jill had never been confronted like that before. She actually found it advantageous and it did make her feel validated in an unexplainable way. "No! No one has ever asked me out before, so what" she said as she turned and scampered away. Inside she was smiling ear to ear. She had finally been asked out by a boy. She was amazed at how close Rick's description of her inner self had been. He was almost 100% correct in all he said. She had to think, how a 14 year old boy could be that insightful.

Everyday after that first encounter Rick started walking with Jill in the hall. They ate lunch together and soon were the talk of the school. That was the way their relationship stayed until Jill turned 16. Then she and Rick expanded to going to movies, dinner and parties. By the time they started high school they were in love. Jill had stayed the most popular in school; but Rick was only Jill's boyfriend. He never took up sports or clubs. He was either with Jill or in his room studying.

Jill won the homecoming queen title and Rick had to endure her dancing with Lance Bond the homecoming king. Rick got over his dissatisfaction of seeing her with another as he was leaving the prom with Jill on his arm.

Jill and Rick got into the same local community college. That was when things started to change little by little between them. They had made a promise way back in junior high that they would not have a sexual relationship (it had been Rick's idea actually). Jill had agreed and they still had honored that pact between them. Since neither was pushing for anything different that was not the problem.

Much to the sadness of Jill it was Rick that was drifting away. He seemed distant and each day he was lost in thought that took him away from Jill and his relationship. Jill had fallen deeper and deeper in love with Rick over the years. She was terror struck when one night Rick came to her and said that he needed to tell her something. She already had tears in her eyes as Rick sat her down at the living room table.

"Jill I have something to say and it has weighed heavy on my heart for several months now. You know I love you Jill; but I am not in love with you. I thought I was; but I now know that I was hiding from my true feelings. I have had a growing love for another for sometime now. I must surrender to my true love. It breaks my heart to say these words to you; but I must fulfill my destiny with another. Please believe me Jill, you did nothing wrong. You have been wonderful, I just pray that someday you will understand and forgive me. I'm sorry. I've already packed my things. I have to go." He kissed Jill on her tear covered cheek and he slowly exited the room with out ever looking back.

Jill sat crying for hours. She felt betrayed, used and humiliated. She had spent eight years of her life with the one she had expected to spend all her life with. She felt she now wasted all those years.

With time Jill got on with her life. She finished college and went on to become a nurse. Shortly after starting work at Sam's Memorial Hospital she met a doctor. That was Dr. William Turner, the head of the heart surgical team. After a year of dating Jill fell in love with William; but she never truly got over her love for Rick. She loved William in a different way than the love she had for Rick. First loves are hard to forget and Jill was living proof. Rick got every part of 100% of her love. The good doctor got about 90% of her love. She held back some in case this relationship ended. This way she could limit the hurt and save a little love for herself.

Jill married the doctor and as the years passed she gave birth to three children, two boys and a girl. Since Jill's marriage she had longed for nothing. She lived in a beautiful mansion and money was never an issue. She had a wonderful husband and three adoring children.

As time passed the years took their toll. It was a devastating day in June when Jill found out she had cancer. She had all the tests and they all showed the same conclusion, the cancer had spread through out her body. Jill deteriorated fast and was soon on her death bed in the hospital.

With her husband holding her hand and their three children standing by her bedside they all said their last words. William called for a Priest to come and give Jill her Last Rites. As Jill lay motionless with her eyes closed the Priest began administering the Last Rites. When he finished praying he said "Amen."

Jill opened her eyes for the last time and looked up into the eyes of Father Rick Sinclair, then smiled and slipped away to eternity.

BLACK SAND

IN 1895 BLACK Sand was the fastest horse in the Arizona Territory. He was a black stallion that ran free across the plains until Jake Stone confronted him. Jake managed to trap Black Sand in a boxed canyon one hot July day in 1895. He dismounted his horse Patches and slowly approached the black beast.

It was man against wild horse, one on one. Once Jake got the rope around the big stallions' neck the war of wills was on. Jakes hands bled as the tug-of-war waged on. Black Sand had the will of ten horses' and their strength as well. Both adversaries weakened in the hot desert sun and their fierceness began to dwindle.

Finally Jake found himself standing alongside the black beast and petting its thick neck. "Good boy, we're gonna be the best of friends you and I" said Jake. He took a deep breath and cautiously mounted the magnificent animal. To his surprise the horse simply stood there refusing to move.

Jake dug in his spurless heels into the horse's flanks and he discovered in a hurry that he was air bound and then flat on his back. He had not let go of the rope that was still around the steeds' neck. He was being pulled across the ground approximately twenty feet behind as the stallion galloped away. Luckily the big horse stopped after only about a hundred yards or so. Jake stood up and slowly approached the black beast.

Black Sand stood still as Jake came closer. Once they were face to face Jake pulled on the rope as Black Sand lowered his head. As they looked into each other's eyes Jake said, "we're gonna try this again, only this time I'm gonna ride you until you know who's the boss. You better get ready big boy."

Jake once again mounted the stallion and in a flash the war of wills was underway. Black Sand would jump high into the air, drop his head and roll his neck. He would then raise his head fast and high as possible trying to head butt Jake as he leaned forward.

It was spirit against spirit and determination against determination as the confrontation went on. It took an hour before Black Sand walked slowly around the canyons floor; only this time he had Jake Stone on his back.

Jake went over to his saddle bags and got out two red apples. He gave one to his long time ride Patches. Then he faced the big black stallion and held out the other treat in his upright opened palm. The steed took it and began to chew. Jake patted the animals' neck while telling him that he was a good boy.

Jake had broken Black Sands' spirit; but he had also earned his respect. The black stallion would now be loyal to Jake forever and that was to become the secret to both their success.

Jake was three days ride away from Scottsdale. He rode Black Sand as Patches followed close behind. On the second day of his travels he was ambushed by an Indian scouting party. One thing for sure was that Indian ponies were some of the fastest horses on the open plains.

Jake gave the command and Black Sand took off in a full run.

Patches couldn't keep up with Jake and his newly found black steed, so the Indians quit chasing Jake once they had captured the slower horse. They were satisfied with a new horse for their tribe for right now. As Jake put more distance between himself and the Indians he realized the true speed on his big black stallion; he also new the value and importance of Black Sands natural abilities.

When Jake arrived in Scottsdale the next day he went into the saloon for a cold beer. After refreshing himself he took Black Sand to the stable for water, food and a bath with rubdown. This was going to be the first time that Black Sand would get a pair of shoes and the blacksmith wasn't too happy about that. That was because he would have to work slowly and take his time and that was time he could be making other money. Jake left Black Sand there and found his way to the hotel. He needed a hot meal, bath and a good nights sleep.

Next morning Jake was awakened by a tap, tap, tap of a hammer. He looked out his window and saw a man hanging up posters. After getting dressed he went downstairs and ate a big breakfast. Then he went outside and read the poster nailed to the porch support of the hotel. To his surprise it was for a horse race the following weekend. His eyes opened wide and a smile spread across his face when saw that first prize was $500.00 dollars. The race had a $20.00 dollar entry fee.

He went to the feed store to register as instructed by the poster. "What's your horses name mister," asked the clerk? Jake thought about it for a moment and then remembered how fast his black horse had run over the sand to escape the Indian ponies. "Black Sand," said Jake with smile. He paid the fee and received the number 5 banner to put on Black Sand.

He went to the stable to see how his new racehorse was fairing. Much to his amazement Black Sand was standing calmly and eating from a bucket of oats. The blacksmith had done an excellent job shoeing and rubbing down the big horse. Jake paid the blacksmith for his work and then put the saddle and bit on the horse. "Come on big boy, you'll love these new shoes once you get use to them. Trust me big fellow. By the way I named you Black Sand. I know you love to run so I entered you in a race. You can soon feel that wind in your face again and run as fast as you like big boy."

Jake led Black Sand out of the stables and mounted him. They rode off towards Jakes' cabin witch was a little more than half a days ride east of Scottsdale. It had been six months since Jake had left his home and went to work on the road. Jake caught wild horses for a living. He would brake them in and then sale them once they were tamed. He had done this for many years; but he had never broken a horse like Black Sand.

Jake was getting old and bronco busting was taken its toll on his body. Over the years Jake had broken several bones and had had many concussions. He was now thinking that he could win at horse racing. This could be his retirement from the dangers of breaking in wild horses.

As he neared his cabin he saw smoke rising from its chimney. He smelled the sweet scent of an apple pie hanging in the air. As he dismounted in front of the cabin his dog, Brownie, came running while barking and wagging his tail. The moment Jakes foot touched the ground he pivoted just in time to catch Brownie as he jumped into his arms. The dog licked his masters' face and squirmed with happiness. Jake smiled and lowered the dog to the ground.

Jake looked up and there on the front porch was Sarah, the love of his life. She too ran into his arms. They kissed repeatedly while Sarah kept saying how much she missed him and was glad he had returned home safely. Sarah was grateful that Jake had taken the time to get a bath in town before coming home. She loved seeing the well groomed man that she had married twenty years earlier.

Jakes cabin was a fine example of a quality home as was his barn. His homestead was built on 1000 acres of good farm land. He had some trees and a stream that ran year round through his property. He had a professional corral where he trained horses and broke them in. He used it for a place to show off horses to potential buyers. All in all Jake was very successful in his business.

Jake told Sarah about Black Sand. He went on and on about how fast the big horse could run. He talked about the horses' heart and his desire to run like no other. Jake went on to explain, "If I can race Black Sand and win we can breed him and charge a lot of money for that. I can't keep breaking in horses' honey. I've got to find a new way to make an income. I'm no farmer; but I know horses and how to ride in a race anywhere."

Sarah smiled and said, "I have always trusted you. I have never doubted you for a second. If this horse is all you say that he is, then race him. No man knows horses better than you. Let me meet this black wonder horse for myself."

Jake handed her an apple "bring this for him" he said.

They went outside and Jake introduced Sarah to Black Sand. She held the apple out in her outstretched palm up hand. Black Sand gently took it away. As he was chewing it Sarah came closer, hugged his neck and patted his head. Black Sand nuzzled his head up close to Sarah and nodded his head slowly. Sarah rubbed the bridge of his nose and from that moment on they were the best of friends.

It was the day of the race and Jake with Black Sand arrived in town. Jake scouted out the competition. He saw only one horse that he thought might somewhat be a challenge. In his heart he honestly felt that he had already won the race.

As he sat atop Black Sand he heard the starter call out for number five to approach the starting line. Jake eagerly walked his entry up to the starting line. Once all twelve entries were on the line the starter explained the rules of the race to the contestants.

The race course was 3 miles in length. Everyone would race out of town south to old man Turners barn. Circle the barn to the west and follow the trail to Johnson Creek. Ford the creek and run up the hill to the huge old oak called DeadMans Oak. Circle the tree and then backtrack the course to the finish line. Jake wondered if Black Sand had ever swum a river, forded a creek or stream. He would soon find the answer for himself.

"On your mark, get set, go," yelled the starter as he fired his pistol. Everyone bolted off the line in a flash in a cloud of dust. Jake held Black Sand back a little as the group became uncluttered. After one mile Jake was sitting in ninth place. He couldn't hold the big stallion back much longer.

"OK big fellow, it's all yours," Jake whispered.

Black Sand shot ahead like a bullet and Jake was thrown backwards in the saddle from the sudden thrust of speed. They moved up through the ranks of the competitors. Around Turners barn they went at a full run. Jake was now in third place. As they neared Johnson Creek Black Sand didn't lose stride. He entered the creeks' water at top speed and never slowed a step; up the hill and around DeadMans' oak. Black Sand had the lead coming out of the turn and he was pulling away from the other horses.

He ran down the hill and across the creek. The other horses began to slow; but Black Sand grew in strength and speed. As he circled Turners barn he was 200 yards ahead of his closest foe. When he crossed the finish line he had won by 350 yards.

The crowd cheered and Jake smiled as he waved his cowboy hat in the air and acknowledged the crowd. He got his prize money and headed for home to celebrate with his wife. As he traveled home he thought about the race and if he had made a mistake by winning by such a large margin. He knew word would spread fast to other towns that held horse races. Jake was faced with the possibility of having to travel far away to San Francisco, Sacramento or Denver in order to race his black wonder horse.

Sarah was ecstatic to learn that Jake had won and received the 500.00 dollars first prize money. "I knew you knew horse," she said. To celebrate she cooked a great meal of rabbit, potatoes and beans. It was a joyous night as Sarah thought up items to buy for their home.

Next morning Jake got up and went to the barn to check on Black Sand. As he neared the barn he noticed a lone rider off in the distance. He stopped, squinted and focused. He quickly realized that the horseman was an Indian scout. The brave sat stiffly upright and looked on as Jake continued to the barn. He led Black Sand out into the corral. The Indian then turned and road away.

Jake wasn't worried as much as bewildered. Indians rarely ventured this close to a major city; besides he had encountered the brave on friendly bases. He had also never seen an Indian on his property before. He had an uneasy feeling; but not one of immanent danger. He would however make sure that Sarah had extra ammunition for her rifle.

For the next few days Jake worked around the cabin repairing gates and fencing. Then one morning Jake was awakened by Brownie barking loudly and growling. He jumped up, grabbed his 30/30 and bolted out the front door.

He was startled to see six Indian braves on horseback and ten horses' tied together behind them. They did not point any weapons towards him or make any threatening moves. Jake lowered his rifle which he had raised as an automatic reflex from living in the open plains.

One of the Indians that was out front of the others began to speak. "I am Chief Eagle Claw's, son Night Hawk. I come in peace, my braves and I mean you no harm. We want to talk to you and maybe make a trade."

"I am Jake and what would any Indian want from me, a white man?"

"At the setting of the last full moon you trapped and took the black wild stallion that ran free across the plains."

"Yes I took him, he is now mine. I broke his spirit and I ride him. I am his master and he serves me."

"No! He is the spirit of my Grandfather, Chief Silver Wolf. He is the father of Chief Eagle Claw and when my fathers time is over I will become Chief. The big black stallion is my Grandfathers rebirth. It is his soul and spirit that lives in the black one."

"I can respect your beliefs; but I don't put much stock in their validity."

"I bring you 9 strong ponies and your horse we captured to trade for my Grandfathers soul and spirit."

"I'm sorry Night Hawk, I can't do that. I promise you that I will always respect this horse. I will give him everything that he needs and he will lack for nothing his entire life."

"He will lack freedom. He will cry from a broken heart if he is not allowed to run free. I will talk to my father and then return. I give you back your lost horse as a gift of friendship." Night Hawk and the braves as well as their nine ponies left. Patches stood motionless until Jake took the rope hanging for his neck and led him into the barn.

Jake went to town that afternoon and was told about a race in Sacramento the next week. First prize was 1000 dollars in gold. Jake went to the Western Union office and wired the 50 dollar entry fee. Once registered he thought about Sarah's safety while he would be away and wondered if he did the right thing in entering.

He remembered that the Indians had made no threats or shown any violence. He felt that even if they did return they would only talk to Sarah about a new trade for Black Sand. That put his mind at ease a little. He trusted Sarah not to agitate or challenge them in his absence. He felt confident that she would be safe since she was accustomed to being left alone at the cabin for weeks at a time.

Jake bought some supplies and went home. He told Sarah about the race and large prize money for winning. She was excited for the both of them. She just knew that Black Sand would win again. She also knew that the money would help out immensely towards the winter that was fast approaching.

Jake and Black Sand left the next day from the Scottsdale rail yard. Jake decided to stay in the rail car with his horse instead of riding in one of the passenger cars. He road there all the way to Sacramento and got little sleep.

This was going to be the race that told him if Black Sand could compete with professional race horses.

Once in Sacramento Jake went to the track to check in and be assigned a stall. Jake spied some beautiful horses. They were definitely bred for racing and nothing else. He had faith in his horse; but this race was on a circular track. Black Sand had never seen a track; he had only experienced free running and open courses.

Jake walked Black Sand around the track to familiarize him with its boundaries. It was three days before the race and all the horses were in training. Jake never let Black Sand open up to full speed; he held him back some. He didn't want to show the others just how fast his entry was.

By race day Black Sand was rambunctious to say the least. His desire to open up and run full speed was unbelievable. He was skittish of the iron gate he was being put in. Jake had not thought of that aspect of track racing so it was new to him as well. Black Sand however allowed himself to be loaded in the small area.

Black Sands anxiety reached a new level by being locked in that confining space. The bell rang out and the gate flew open. Black Sand shot out of the gate right into a full run and the lead. He hugged the rail and settled in to a methodic rhythmic pace. Jake had visions of grandeur. He knew Black Sand could run three miles at full speed. This was only a mile and a half track so Black Sand could run 100% full out with no problem from start to finish line.

At the half way mark a sleek horse by the name of Fireball came up from nowhere to run alongside Black Sand. Its rider was applying a strong hard whip and the horse was responding. As it began to pull away, Black Sand took a deep breath and took on the newly acquired challenge. Around the three/quarters pole and both horses were now neck and neck. Black Sand was a heavier horse as well as his rider Jake. The other horse was sleek, trim and had a lightweight rider that was still applying a hard whip.

Black Sand had never been in a position where any horse could run alongside him. From deep down inside himself Black Sand pushed and fought for more speed. He gained that speed and strength as Fireball begun to fade. Jake leaned over and rubbed Black Sands neck and said "run big boy, run." He got faster and faster. He was still gaining speed as he crossed the finish line ten lengths ahead of Fireball. Black Sand had set a new track record and had astounded the crowd that day.

No one could believe it; a wild untrained horse could have beaten some of the best race horses in the country. Jake walked Black Sand around the track waving to the crowd and accepting their accolades. He understood completely what had just transpired as he sat atop the first place winner. He received the 1000 dollars in gold prize money and rode off with the crowd still applauding.

As Jake and Black Sand traveled back to Scottsdale in a rail car he knew that word would spread quickly about his big, fast horse. It was nightfall as they arrived in Scottsdale. Jake stayed aboard the train car until daybreak and then he mounted Black Sand for the ride home.

Sarah heard Brownie barking as Jake approached the cabin. She went out on the porch to meet him. She could tell by the look on his face that he had won. She ran to his side and they kissed as he handed her the leather pouch with the gold.

The next morning Jake went outside the cabin to find Night Hawk and three braves waiting patiently. "I told you Night Hawk I did not want to sell or trade my big black horse," Jake said.

"My father Chief Eagle Claw would like for you to come to his village for a visit with him," Night Hawk said.

"Why would I do that? There's nothing he can say to make me change my mind."

"I could have taken my grandfathers soul and spirit as you slept during the night. We are a proud people and stealing is not our way. Do not disrespect the Chief of our Indian Nation. Come smoke the peace pipe and hear what he has to say."

Jake was actually impressed with what the Indian had said. Night Hawk could have easily stolen Black Sand during the night. He could return with a war party and burn his cabin to the ground. There were many options to consider. None of them good, so Jake spoke up "OK I will come and talk to your Chief. Let me say good-bye to my wife and ready my gear."

Night Hawks village was three days ride from Jakes cabin. Sarah was left alone once again. She was use to days or weeks at a time; but it was getting harder to accept quietly.

As Jake rode into the village hundreds of Indians reached out and touched Black Sand as he walked by. Night Hawk stopped at a large wigwam and dismounted. Jake followed suit then entered the wigwam behind Night Hawk. "Father, this is the white man called Jake. He has possession of Silver Wolf. He has come to talk to you and listen" Night Hawk explained.

"I am Chief Eagle Claw. My father is Silver Wolf. I became Chief after he died. My son Night Hawk will be Chief once I am no longer. When my fathers' time arrived he walked out to the open plain and laid down. I found his body the next day. Standing over him was the big wild black stallion. I saw the stallion lower his head to my fathers face. After a moment the black horse lifted his head and reared up on his hind legs. He then ran with the wind. I knew from that moment on that my fathers' soul and spirit lived on within the wild one.

For the last two years he has ruled the plains. He has defended his herd from others that challenged his dominance. We feed him treats and watch out over him so that no harm comes his way. He belongs to us; we are his Indian Nation ancestors. He is my father, his soul and spirit belongs free on our land.

I can understand your hesitance in not wanting to part with the black one. However he is more than a horse to us. He is one of us. We are sworn to protect him till he passes to the final spirit world. I know you rejected nine good ponies for his safe return to us. I have talked to the counsel and I can make you this offer.

In return for my grandfather the black stallion you can have any pick every year from all his folds. We will also break in 100 fine ponies and deliver them to your cabin. Finally, no matter what happens between Indians and White men; no harm will ever come to you or your family. What is your answer, white man called Jake"?

As Jake sat mulling over the Chiefs proposal Night Hawk lit up the peace pipe. He took a puff and handed it to Jake. He took a puff and gave it to Chief Eagle Claw. Scenarios were dancing in is mind as Jake thought about the pros and cons. First was how many more races could Black Sand be in before word spread and he would be banned from all race tracks. He could also get injured and never race again as well.

If he accepted Chief Eagle Claws offer Black Sand could run free for the rest of his life. Jake would get 100 horses to sell and he wouldn't have to risk getting hurt in the process. He would also get a colt of his choosing every year of Black Sands life. Security was another thing that was immensely important. Jake had the opportunity to protect his family and farm for life from any Indian wars or uprisings. His protection would be honored by all Chiefs from Eagle Claw, Night Hawk and all thereafter.

Jake looked into the eyes of the Chief and said "I respect the chief of the Indian Nation and I trust his words. Now that I see how much the big black stallion means to you I will accept your generous offer. I will return your grandfathers soul and spirit to you. There are only two small matters to agree on. Can you deliver one pony a week that is saddle broke, not bareback broke, for the next two years? Lastly, may I pick a fold from the black stallion now?"

"Indians have no saddles, if you provide a saddle or two we will learn to do as you request. When you have received your 100 horses they will be returned with the last horse. Yes you may pick a colt from the black ones offspring. There are three; Night Hawk will show them to you. When you select the one you want we will cut him from the herd. He is yours to break in, he is not part of the 100 and neither will be the other black ones folds you pick. If you agree, I agree," said Chief Eagle Claw.

"I agree," said Jake as he held out his hand and the two men shook. Jake went outside and removed his saddle. Night Hawk removed the bit and slapped Black Sand on the rump. The horse took off at a full gallop as the Indian village whooped and hollered. Jake laid the saddle on the ground and told Night Hawk it was his to use for the ponies that were to be broke in.

Night Hawk took Jake out to the open plain and pointed out Black Sands colts that ran in a herd of five hundred. To Jakes surprise Black Sand was out front leading the herd. Jake picked out one of the three that were available and watched as ten braves went in pursuit of him.

The Indians watched as Jake put the saddle on the wild horse and then started his breaking in procedure. He was bucked off a few time; but in the end he was riding around with a submissive animal. The braves were impressed and saw how to use the saddle for their obligation.

Jake rode home on his new horse that he named Buckeye, because he had to keep an eye on his twisting move when being broke in. Having left his saddle for Night Hawks braves the bareback ride home was a little painful.

Once again Sarah met her man as he approached the cabin by standing on the porch. Jake explained what had happened at the Indian village. He loved Black Sand; but now he could stay home and have an income from horses without any risk to himself. He explained that his families' safety was foremost in his decision.

Sarah thought the arrangement was a win-win situation for them. Her man was safe as well as herself. Jake wouldn't be getting hurt being bucked off horses. There would be a steady income from the horses that they could sell.

After a year had passed everything was wonderful with Jake and Sarah. The Indians were living up to there agreement and Jake had saved a lot of money. He loved being home with his wife; but he longed for something to do that made him feel he was contributing more on a manly bases.

The plains were growing and small towns were popping up all around. The stage coach line had a new route that went by Jakes cabin. So he built a store filled with the supplies that were needed for the times. He built a small place so that travelers could get a good meal. Sarah was a great cook and she enjoyed cooking for any and everyone. She even fed Night Hawk and the braves when they came to deliver ponies.

A year had passed and Jake traveled to the Indian Village to once again pick a colt from Black Sand. He lit up when he saw his once big horse running full speed across the plain.

There was only one fold this year and it was a solid white horse. To be exact, it was an albino. This colt was more than extremely rare; it was a sign from the Indian gods that only they could have delivered. Night Hawk had named him Spirit-God and he explained the legend of an albino horse that the gods said would come to free them from oppression.

Jake was a wealthy man by now and he respected the Indians. He felt that Night Hawk was like a brother to him. He knew what this horse meant to all the Indians and their heritage. Jake knew he would have a hard time selling the horse; but that played little in his decision.

Jake looked at Night Hawk and said "You are my friend as is your father Chief Eagle Claw. You are my brother; I want you to have the white horse. You can call it a gift from one friend to another."

Night Hawk smiled and loudly said something to the Indians that had accompanied them to the herd. They all cheered and hollered hearing the news. Jake gave Night Hawk a strong handshake then turned to ride back home. He watched the albino run by the side of Black Sand until they disappeared over a ridge in a cloud of dust.

Jake returned home where he and Sarah ran their successful business. Jake settled down and enjoyed his slower paced lifestyle. Sarah is expecting their first child and rumor has it that the railroad is coming right passed Jakes stores. So Jake is busy building a train station stop and water tower.

Jake sits on his porch on many a nights and looks out at the horizon. He thinks back about how his life has turned out. He never gets tired of smiling and saying aloud, "Thank you Black Sand, you were the one that led me to my destiny. Run free Black Sand, run free with the wind."

THE VISION WITHIN

KYLE UPTON STEPPED up to the plate with bat in hand. He was the heavy hitter on his little league team. Being twelve made this his last year to play in this league. It was the championship game and he wanted to win more than anything to go out a champion. After all he had dreamed of this day and this win.

He eyed the pitcher as he wound up and hurled a fast ball. "Strike one," yelled the umpire.

Kyle stepped back out of the batter's box and glared at the ump. He slowly regained his position in the box and readied himself for the next pitch. "Strike two," screamed the umpire once again. Kyle stood there a second and then took a deep breath. That pitch was actually a good strike ball that he'd laid off of. He looked up and saw the pitcher going through his wind-up routine. Kyle closed his eyes and imagined the ball floating up to the plate and him smacking it over the fence for a homerun and the championship.

Kyle's team won the game that day and they all held up high the little league trophy. The team had pizza and celebrated their win. Kyle had thought about his baseball life for a long time. He had it all figured out to the smallest detail. Winning the little league championship was only step one. He had now accomplished that feat in his life's plan.

Once enrolled in junior high he tried out for junior varsity baseball. He made the team easily as their shortstop. He practiced hard and longer than any other player and was rewarded by being selected as the team's captain. He was with no doubt the best all around player on the team. He proved that when his team was in the championship game. It was his homerun blast in the bottom of the ninth that won the school's first championship and his second one. All of Kyle's dreams just kept coming true.

At the age of sixteen Kyle was on the varsity team. He wasn't the all around best player anymore; but he was the batter with the most homers and highest batting average. No matter where Kyle went success followed him. He turned eighteen as a senior when his varsity team was playing for the state high school championship. No one expected that the big homerun slugger would do what he did to help win the state championship. It was the bottom of the ninth and two outs with a man stuck at third base; when Kyle laid down the perfect bunt and the man at third crossed the plate before any player put a glove on the ball, Kyle's third championship. Every detail that Kyle had dreamed of was still coming true.

Kyle always did whatever was asked of him to help the team win; he was the perfect team player. That fact did not go unnoticed by the college scouts. He was offered scholarships from some of the most prestige schools in the country. So far everything that Kyle had dreamed of as a young boy was playing out 100% to the letter. Kyle decided to accept a scholarship from the University of Oregon. It was where both his parents had attended college. He felt obligated in a way; but he wanted to make his mom and dad proud.

His dream continued to come true as if by fate. He held a 4.0 grade average and continued to improve as a super ball player. He was named college player of the year and was on the cover of Sports Illustrated.

It was at the college championship game that Kyle did what his coach asked him to do once again in order to help win the game. With the score tied at 2 runs apiece in the bottom of the ninth with one out and a man on third and second, Kyle got a surprise signal from the coach. Kyle had in his batting repertoire the ability to hit a ball that he called the flying eagle. He could hit a pop up really high and deep. The difference between his pop up and others was that he could make it come down on the warning track at center field. He smiled as the coach flashed him the sign again for the flying eagle.

Kyle stepped into the batter's box and stared down at the pitcher as he threw the ball. Kyle hit the pitch with just enough might and angle to accomplish his goal. The ball took off like a rocket with a guidance system. The center fielder backed up all the way to the warning track. The man on third led off while keeping one foot on the base. The second that the fielder caught the ball the runners took off for home plate. The short stop became the relay man; but before he even touched the ball the third base runner had already crossed the plate. The runner on second was already rounding third when the cutoff man touched the ball. That was the reason for the call; the ball would be too deep to ever throw out the second runner rounding third going home. The second runner came hard and slid cleats up right into the catcher as he caught the ball, "safe" yelled the umpire. Kyle's team came running out on the field while celebrating their championship win, another championship win for Kyle. His life was perfect; he was still living his dream.

Kyle got drafted number one in the first round of the major league draft by the L A Dodgers. He got a multimillion dollar contract as well as a five million dollar signing bonus. Everything was happening exactly the way he had seen it as a child. He was the talk on every sports radio station and was interviewed on ESPN's Sports Center.

Kyle was stupendous during training and fantastic while playing in all the exhibition games. He was ready for the big show to begin. He didn't have to wait long. Opening day came at Dodgers stadium and he was excited like he had never been before. He had butterflies as he made his way to the batter's box for the first time in an official MLB game.

Kyle was batting in the fourth position (clean-up). There was one out with runners on first and second. He stood there and took the first pitch, "strike one," yelled the umpire. Kyle glared back at the umpire for a second and then closed his eyes and visualized hitting a three run homer.

Kyle opened his eyes only to see his mother and father looking down at him. "Where am I?" He asked

"Thank God! Doctor! Doctor my sons awake," exclaimed Mrs. Upton.

A doctor and two nurses came running to the room. The doctor examined Kyle and then addressed his parents. "He's going to be fine," he said.

"What happened dad? I was waiting for a pitch. How did I get here?" Kyle asked.

"You got hit in the head by the ball son. You've been in a coma for six days," his mom explained.

"What! I was in the majors and playing for the L A Dodgers. I was standing at the plate getting ready to hit a homer," Kyle blurted out.

"You will my son, you will someday. You must have been dreaming or having some kind of amazing vision in your mind." said his father.

Kyle looked at his hands and then saw his reflection in the window by his bed. He realized that he was still a young boy and not reached manhood. He realized that it was all a dream. He took a deep breath and looked at his father and said, "I will dad; but when it really happens I won't close my eyes on that day. I will hit that homer, you just wait and see."

A HEARTBEAT AWAY

JILLIAN ADAMS THOUGHT nothing about how the sixth grade was going to affect her life. She was a little girl who ran around the playground at recess like any other child. That is until the day she fell and a little boy named Billy Turner offered his hand to help her up off the ground. The minute she touched his outstretched hand she felt a friendship. He smiled while looking down at her. She slowly rose with the aid of his helping hand to her feet, "are you OK," he asked her?

"Yes I'm fine. Thank you for helping me. What is your name? I haven't seen you before," she asked.

"My name is Billy and I just started school here today. I moved here from Denver, Colorado. My dad got a job at the Bonneville Dam. What's your name?" he inquired.

"My name is Jillian and my mom and dad both work for the Bonneville Dam Authority too," she replied.

That meeting turned out to be the first step in a lifetime journey filled with love and sadness. From that day forward they always managed to have all their classes together. They were inseparable through junior high and high school. After they graduated from Hood River High they decided to go to the University of Washington. Seattle wasn't that far away and they both loved the huskies. That decision wasn't much of a surprise to their parents.

The Bonneville Dam is on the Columbia River, basically half is in Oregon's and the other half is Washington's. Both families lived in Hood River, which is in Oregon; but the distance to U of Washington was only 250 miles up I-5. That was close enough to be out of state and yet close enough to come home on weekends. It was the best of two worlds for college students.

Their college days were like what most kids experience as far as parties and pulling all nighters studying for tests. The highlight of college for Jillian was the night that Billy asked her to marry him. That happened on the last day when their junior year came to an end. She said yes and they set the wedding date for June 17th the summer after they graduated college the following year.

It was during the fall of their senior year that tragedy struck Jillian's fairy tale life. Billy spun out in his car while driving in a rain storm and went hurling down an embankment. His car rolled and flipped before slamming in to a large oak tree. Billy died that night despite the efforts of the EMT's to stabilize him. The police on scene ran the cars plate numbers and found out all the information about Billy. They knew his name, address; he was an organ donor and was a college student. The medical personnel called ahead to the hospital with all of Billy's information.

The news devastated Jillian when she heard and she withdrew from people and all social events. She quit college and returned home to live with her parents. There wasn't much anyone could do for her except comfort her. This was something that Jillian had to mourn and cry her way through. It would be a hard heartache to overcome.

Days led to weeks, then into months. It took about a year and a half before Jillian ventured out into the real world again. She got a job working behind the counter at the local Les Schwab tire store. Once she had been there a year they gave her a wonderful one year anniversary party. Several men had asked her out while she was working there; but she always declined.

Jillian had her own plan to fulfill her life. She had hired an investigator and though it took months for him to close her case, it finally came to a satisfactory conclusion. There was another man Jillian wanted to find, ever since college. It took the investigator all this time to locate this individual. Jillian was excited and now she had a real purpose in life once more.

Jillian turned 24 a week after getting the news from the investigators report. She went to work and told Tommy Ray, the store manager that she wanted to transfer to the Gresham, Oregon store. Tommy Ray was sorry to hear that she wanted to leave. He called the Gresham store and they by chance needed a counter person. The girl they had was out on maternity leave. The job was hers; she gave Tommy a big hug and went home to pack.

Gresham is only an hour down the road (84) from Hood River; it runs parallel along the Columbia River Gorge and is an excellent road with great scenic views the entire 60 mile trip.

Finding an apartment was simple. Jillian had a place in less than two hours after arriving in town. She spent three days having furniture delivered and setting up house.

Monday came and Jillian reported to her new job. She was welcomed with open arms because already knowing the system she didn't need any training. She met everyone and they seemed nice and they in return thought highly of their new co-worker as well. When the store opened to the public Jillian was standing behind the counter. She was daydreaming about how finally it was time for her to get down to business.

She had to find a way for to meet Jake Alder; he was the man that the investigator had found at Jillian's request. He's thirty years old and works for the city of Gresham. She had received his name, address, phone number and his employment information from the investigator. She was deciding whether or not to basically stalk him to find out where he ate or what bar he might hangout at. She even considered going to his house pretending to be an Avon representative, just to meet him face to face.

Her deep thoughts were interrupted by a man coming up to the counter and saying "excuse me miss."

She looked up and said "oh! Sorry. May I help you?"

"Yes, I need four new tires for my pick-up truck. You must be new here? I haven't seen you before."

"I started today in fact," she said with a smile.

The man laid his credit card on the counter and told Jillian to charge it on his account. She picked up the card and read the name JAKE ALDER. Her mouth almost dropped to the floor. She took a deep breath and brought up his account on the computer. She immediately recognized the address. He was indeed the Jake Alder she had dreamed of finding. She felt that destiny was saying that she deserved divine intervention and she thanked God under her breath.

"I don't need your card yet. After you pick out your tires and have them mounted and balanced, with new stems installed they'll bring me the total bill. Then I will need your card. Let me get you a salesperson to help you get the right tires and get everything started. Jose to the front counter for customer service," she said. When Jose arrived he and Mr. Alder left the lobby and disappeared in to the tire aisle.

After awhile Jillian saw Jake return to the lobby and sit down in the waiting area. As he sat there reading a Road and Track magazine Jillian kept looking at him. He caught her several times looking at him and so he started looking back at her. Jillian was doing everything she could to make sure he knew she was flirting with him. This went on for approximately an hour before the technician brought up the keys and bill for Jake's truck. Jillian called Jake to come to the service counter. "That will be 1,158.54 cents," she said.

He handed her his credit card again with a smile. She ran it and everything cleared with no problems. She handed it back to him as she gave him one last hair flip and sheepish grin. Jake looked at her and asked "would you like to go to dinner with me tonight."

"Yes!" she blurted out with enthusiasm. She wrote down her address and phone number on his receipt.

"I'll pick you up at 8," he said as he made his way to the door and out to his truck.

Their date that night was picture perfect and their relationship flowered week after week. It took six months for Jake to ask Jillian to marry him. She accepted ecstatically and they set the wedding date for June 17th. They both had decided to wait till their wedding night to sleep together. That is a rarity in today's world; but it was something that they both wanted.

Time passed and their wedding day arrived. Jillian looked like a princess in a fairy tale, dressed in her white wedding gown with an 8 foot train. She had six bridesmaids all dressed in dusty rose gowns. Jake was dressed in a solid white tuxedo with a red rose in the lapel. His best man was dressed in a powder blue tuxedo with a white rose in his lapel.

The reception was just as beautiful as the service; her first dance, cutting the cake and throwing the bouquet. After the reception Jillian and Jake rode in a white handsome carriage that was accented with blue neon lights attached to its undercarriage.

As wonderful as the day was it wasn't yet what Jillian had dreamed. That night as she and Jake lay in bed she softly ran her fingers across his chest. She laid her head on his chest and when she heard a heartbeat she said, "I will always love you." You see she loved Jake; but she was IN LOVE with Billy. It was Billy's heart that was beating in Jakes chest because Jake had been the recipient of Billy's heart the night of that fatal crush. Jake had been the one that had Bill's heart for his transplant; now Jillian and Billy could be forever A HEARTBEAT AWAY.

THE FOUR HORSEMEN

I MET MY three best friends during our high school days . . .
The pranks we played and all of the games that we won,
were the foundations to our long time history.
Tommy, Tony, Earl and I were the four horsemen.

The day we graduated was the beginning . . .
to memories that solidified our friendship.
Through the years we compiled one after another . . .
even when we reached the middle age of our lives.

But then the good memories took a turn for the worse . . .
when at the age of forty Earl died from cancer.
It would be the first time being a pall bearer.
I soon repeated that action with my parents.

With three horsemen left, we continued to press on.
We still included Earl in our ball game parties.
We set out beer and some of his favorite chips,
and would toast his empty lazy boy chair and nod.

Twenty years passed and Tommy died in a car wreck.
The four horsemen had now been reduced to just two.
Then Tony and I stopped having ball game parties . . .
and reality took a front seat in our lives.

Tony lived only eight years after Tommy's death.
As I stood there at the funeral in the rain . . .
I faced the fact that I was now the last horsemen,
riding alone and facing my life's dead end road.

I ponder if I was lucky or have a curse,
or if God has given me this time as a gift,
To allow me to reflect back on my long life,
and ask for forgiveness and the time to repent.

I don't have any answers to all my questions.
Three horsemen are gone and I do ask, why not me?
When your friends are gone and you're finally alone,
It is easy to see the writing on the wall.

So until my time comes and takes me from this earth . . .

I will ride with the wind and float from cloud to cloud.
I will slide down rainbows and catch bolts of lighting.
I will reach up into the sky and touch the moon.
I will live for all the four horsemen . . . till . . . I . . . die.

SANCTUARY

THE FORTY FOOT waves along with seventy-five MPH winds tossed the thirty-six foot sailboat like a feather in an F5 tornado. It was all Joss Inlay could do to point the bow into the oncoming wall of water. This was the first time that he thought maybe sailing solo around the world was a bad idea. As he continued to fight the storm he began to tire and his arms ached and fatigue started taking over his body.

He'd had perfect weather for three months up until this point. The storm was getting worse. The waves were becoming larger and the winds were increasing. Joss knew his luck was over when he spied a sixty foot wave approaching. He lost concentration for only a second; but that hesitation and distraction caused the wheel to be jerked out of his hands.

The sailboat immediately turned sharply to the left opening up the boat for a direct broadside hit. There was no time to correct its course and the boat began to rise. After being lifted twenty feet she started to roll over. Joss hung on to the wheel for dear life; but as he looked up he saw the top of the waves crest break and falling down right on top of him. His life as he knew it was over. He was saying a prayer as tons of water crashed down on him.

Joss opened his eyes and was shocked to see a pair of woman's beautiful eyes looking down at him. "Where am I, am I dead, is this heaven," he asked?

"You are in the underwater city of Sanctuary. I rescued you as you were sinking to the bottom of the sea. You were unconscious and I feared for your life. I am Trinity and I am glad that you have awakened," she said.

"What do you mean by underwater city," Joss remarked?

"Sanctuary has been here for hundreds of years. It is inside a large underwater mountain. You can see that it's lit well; that is because of the reflective crystals and quartz that line the walls. There is a large five foot vent where fresh air blows in. There is another five foot vent that sucks the air out. That's why we always have fresh air.

The vents are believed to be old volcano lava tubes and they originate from some inactive volcano in the upper world that you come from.

Outside men are rare here. We are fortunate if one out of every hundred births is a male. Men that are born here only live for twenty years. Men like you from the outer world seem to die after a few short years as well.

There is no sickness here. The women die either by an accident or old age. We do not age in appearance. We just go to sleep one night and don't wake up. That is how all Sanctuarians die. Mortals like yourself do age in appearance; but like us die in their sleep.

There is no leaving the city for men. They cannot breathe outside these walls. It is wonderful that an outside man has arrived. We need new bloodlines here for the future," Trinity said.

It was at that very moment that Joss noticed that she was a mermaid. He thought he was dreaming or dead and all this was some kind of afterlife fiasco. He glanced around the city and saw there were many rock type islands with small cabins on them. Each rock island was approximately one acre in size.

All the islands had an arched foot bridge that connected each to the other. He saw other mermaids sitting on rocks that protruded out of the water scattered throughout the city. "What's with the cabins and other mermaids? Why aren't they in the cabins and on the island surface," Joss asked?

"The men live in the cabins. However most of the structures are empty. Mermaids can come on shore and walk with legs similar to yours; but for only a short time. If they stay more than an hour their legs become permanent. Once that happens we can never go back to being a mermaid. You will notice that all the mermaids still have their tales in the water.

Mermaids are the ones that catch the food and provide for the men. Mermaids can swim to the surface and the ones to salvage items from shipwrecks. The men have one function, that is to procreate and that can only happen when a mermaid is in her transformation period. That is what we call it when we have legs instead of a tail.

There are only five other men here in Sanctuary beside you. They were all born here and are reaching their age to die. You are the only outsider male here and the first one in fifty years. It is a blessing that you arrived at this time in our worlds history. You are greatly appreciated.

I found and saved you from the depths of the sea. According to Sanctuary law I am first to mate with you. Once it is confirmed that I am with child you are permitted to be with whomever you want and as many times as you want. I hope you find me worthy and that you desire me," Trinity sheepishly said?

"You are very beautiful; but you must give me time to adjust to all you have told me. I am a prisoner here and my world is now lost. You tell me that my life maybe shortened here and that I am nothing but breeding stock. I will need time to accept my new life and situation if I can," Joss remarked.

"I will give you seven tides to adjust and rest. Then you must make love to me. The women of Sanctuary are different than your outsider women. We are only able to conceive a child in a thirty-one day reproductive cycle. That fertile cycle takes place ever two years. I am in my third day of my reproductive cycle so time is relevant. I will let you sleep and will bring you food and fresh water later this day." Trinity swam away and Joss closed his eyes and fell into a deep sleep.

True to her word Trinity brought Joss a plateful of seafood delicacies. He was even pleasantly surprised by the taste of the seaweed salad that had muscle sauce covering it.

After his dinner Joss took a long walk around the city. He met the other men as he crossed the bridges one after the other. What was hard to fathom at first was how many thing were similar to his home back in San Francisco.

He recalled what Trinity had said about how the mermaids scavenged shipwrecks. That was where the dishes, silverware, mirrors, brushes, jewelry and the like came from.

While traveling through the city he met the Queen of Sanctuary who welcomed him with open arms. She had a strange name (Red Fire). The only explanation to Joss was that she alone in all of Sanctuary had long fiery red hair.

On the seventh night of the seven tides Trinity entered Joss's cabin where he laid sleeping. She shook him gently; but firmly. He woke and sat up. He looked at her as she stood there undressed at the side of his bed. Her long blond hair highlighted her face and dark green eyes. Her skin was silky smooth to the touch and her body called out to him. He could not resist and immediately fell under her spell.

There love making continued every other day for the rest of Trinity's fertile cycle. Joss was exhausted. What would seem to be nothing but pleasure and a dream come true; turned out to be work and took a toll on his fit body.

Everyone waited to see if Trinity was with child. Many women were in line to make love with Joss. He represented the new bloodline they needed so badly. The goal was for every woman in Sanctuary to mate with him. Joss knew of the goal and he didn't much care for it. However he was trapped and really had no choice at the moment.

He had been told by the Queen that if he refused to procreate she would invoke banishment. In his case he would be exiled from Sanctuary. He would be forced back into the ocean some two-hundred feet below the surface. He knew he could never hold his breath long enough to reach the surface. Even if by a miracle that he did, the bends would probably kill him. Finally he thought that if he beat both those odds he would still be stranded in an open shark infested ocean. He was indeed at Queen Red Fire's mercy.

It took three months before it was confirmed that Trinity was with child. Then as other women started their cycles Joss was on call every other night to make love. There were times when several women were having their cycles at the same time. Joss spent his time with only one woman for her complete cycle. So women that started cycling when Joss was committed would sleep with one of the other men.

Joss became fatigued so he begged the Queen for a month off from love making. She agreed to let him rest for thirty tides. There may have been an alternative motive because unknown to Joss, Queen Red Fire was to be his next lover.

Joss sat in his cabin and contemplated his life. He was fed up with his existence. Time had passed and it was coming up to his two year anniversary in Sanctuary. Trinity had delivered a healthy baby girl and Joss had fallen in love with her and their child. However in Sanctuary marriage did not exist; in fact the concept was unheard of. A woman was expected to mate to whoever was available when she started her cycle.

Two of the other men had died, leaving only three besides Joss. He knew that meant he would be pressed into more service and he wanted no part of it any longer. He began to pay attention to the air out and intake vents. Both were approximately five feet in diameter. The wind blowing in was between thirty and thirty-five MPH. The speed was the same at the out take vent. The two vents were a mile apart; one at the east side of the city and the other at the west side.

Joss had an idea; but who to trust. He turned to Trinity for support and to be his confidant. He asked her to bring him large kelp leaves and seaweed. She agreed to do so and brought him some everyday. He would dry it in his cabin and then stitch the large leaves together with the seaweed strands.

It took Joss six months to weave what looked like a small canoe. It was two feet across and five feet long. It was eighteen inches deep. The most impressive feature was the four foot square sail he had made. He was fortunate to have found a piece of driftwood that was perfect as a mast for the sail. He told Trinity what he wanted to do. She glared at him as if confused so he started explaining it to her in more detail.

"During the hurricane season the air speed in the air vents increases. I think I can escape to the surface through the exhaust vent in the makeshift canoe I have made with a sail affixed. I want to try, hell I've got to try for my own sanity. If I make it I will come back for you I promise. I know these exact coordinates and I will rescue you. I want you, me and our child to be together.

You told me that once you transformed from a tail to legs, after an hour they were permanent. The same is true with our child. I want you and her to come live with me in San Francisco if I make a successful escape. I'm asking you to leave this world and come to a new world with me. I know it's a lot to ask; but you must trust me Trinity, I will protect you always. Please, please say yes," begged Joss.

"You know I love you too; but it's hundreds of miles to the nearest land. Besides, there is no way of telling where the vent will open. What if the vent narrows and you are stuck there to die? Then I would never see you again. I would rather you stay here with me than risk injury to you. I am almost ready to start a new reproductive cycle and I want to be with you again for mating. So please do not do this crazy thing, stay here with me and our child Hope," she cried.

"I have to try. I cannot continue to have sex with all these women. You told me that outsider men die early here. I feel as if I am already dying. I must try; in fact I am doing it period. I need to know now, that when I come back you will come with me and walk the streets of my world."

"Yes! I will do whatever I must to be with you. You do realize that once I am no longer a mermaid I will start to age and grow old on the outside; like the women from your world do," Trinity sobbed?

"Yes I know; but we will grow old together. I love you and I will be back to reunite us and then become a true traditional family. The hurricane season starts in two weeks. I will watch the vents and when I think the air speed is sufficient for me to be successful I will leave."

Joss continued to make the final adjustments for his departure. He had some dried fish and three gallons of fresh water. He had an extra shirt and a pair of pants. He had no way of knowing where he would eventually emerge. He could only pray it was not in a high mountain range where snow was abundant.

It was sixteen days after Joss had had his conversation with Trinity that the wind speed increased to approximately sixty MPH.
Late during the cities sleep time Joss and Trinity dragged the canoe to the mouth of the escape vent. Joss kissed his love and told her he would return. He told her to keep an eye on the surface after the hurricane season. He stared into her eyes and wiped her tears away, told her he loved her and then turned away.
Joss placed the canoe as close as he could to the opening without being sucked in prematurely. He climbed in and strapped himself to the canoe tightly. Trinity pushed the canoe only a foot and as Joss raised the sail his transport vehicle immediately was sucked into the vent at sixty MPH and disappeared.
Trinity stood crying as she heard, I Loooooooov as the sound faded away and was drowned out by the wind. She returned to the water and her baby girl Hope. She could do nothing else but wait and pray for joss to return.
Joss had not given any thought to the fact that he would be in total darkness. It didn't take long for him to reach a high level of anxiety and paranoia. He had no idea if or when he would slam into a jagged rock protruding from the walls of the vent. As time became hours the thought of coming so far just to be trapped in a narrowing vent tube wore on his nerves.
Hours passed and his eyes were dry and he found it next to impossible to produce his own saliva. His skin was wind burned from the friction and his ears began to ring. He was already disorientated. Joss was literally within minutes of losing it mentally when the canoe shot out of the tube into the bright sunlight.
He and the canoe were air bound for several yards before they crashed to the ground. The canoe disintegrated on impact and Joss went tumbling down the side of the mountain he was ejected from. He came to an abrupt stop when he slammed into a large tree. He struggled to take a deep breath. The collision had knocked the breath out of him; but after a few minutes he returned to a regular breathing pattern. He did a self examination of himself and concluded he had no broken bones or other injuries.
Joss looked out and could see a modern city off in the distance. He was on the side of a mountain and he could tell he was in the south Pacific

by the vegetation and sultry climate. Where exactly he didn't know at the moment; so he set out walking to the city he saw.

It took him four hours to reach the bottom of the mountain and then he found a paved road. He had not gone far when a pick-up truck drove up to him and stopped. The driver offered Joss a ride and while on the drive to the city he found out that he was on the island of Viti Levu. The city he was going to was Nadi, which is on the west side of the island. Joss had heard of the FiJi Islands before; however he never dreamed he would arrive on the Island in the way he did.

Joss had no money or clothes except for the rags he had on him at the time. He called friends collect in San Francisco and they wired him several hundred dollars. He checked in to a hotel, ordered food and after a hot bath took a well deserved restful sleep.

Next morning Joss got on the hotels computer and started to figure out the who, what, where, when and how's to get back to Trinity and Hope.

He knew where he was when the storm sank his sailboat. He was in the Atlantic Ocean, 250 miles east of Miami, Florida. Some people call this area the Bermuda Triangle. Now that he was in Nadi, Fiji, he was approximately 8000 miles from where he had gone down.

If the wind speed had been a true 60 MPH it would have taken him 133 hours or five and a half days to travel to Nadi. There was no way to tell exactly how many days he traveled no knowing the precise wind speed. Joss did know it was an eternity to him and he was praising God that it was over safely.

Joss made arrangements to fly to Miami so he could start assembling a boat and supplies to go back to the coordinates he had memorized from that destructive day. Joss bought the most up to date maritime charts and bought the most sophisticated sonar and GPS systems money could buy. It was only early July and hurricane season is from June 1 to November 30. Joss had five months to wait before he dared to go back to 26*58'43.81"N and 64*55'41.84"W.

Joss had been president of Inlay Semiconductor Corporation before he sold his company just before the dot-com bubble burst. He sold his company for 273 million dollars so when he set out to sail the world solo he received a lot of press.

Joss had been missing for almost three years and the press was all over him for answers. He never said a word about Sanctuary or Trinity. He made up a story about a small uncharted Island and that he was finally picked up by a Russian fishing boat. None of the crew spoke English; but they took him to Fiji.

He knew he couldn't lie about being in Fiji because he had been seen there and had hotel and phone charges that would easily be traced. He spiced it up how he ate fruits, berries and speared fish to eat. He was lucky that during a storm lighten hit a tree and he was able to keep a fire going day and night. In fact that was what the Russian Troller saw that rescued him, his fire and smoke.

After a month the press found other stories and he was off the front page and virtually forgotten about. That was fine with him. He didn't want to be noticed when he left port the next time for obvious reasons. The time passed with agony and languishment; but the day came when Joss set out from Miami to the coordinates he had been dreaming of.

Without any fanfare at five AM Joss started his journey on the 32 foot cabin cruiser he had purchased. The two Royal Royce motors purred like the best and most expensive motors should. Once past the restricted speed buoys he opened the throttle and his boat took off like a bullet from a high powered rifle. With the wind in his face and the sun in his eyes he sped towards his hearts desire.

As he grew closer to his coordinates the bow of his boat bounced over the smooth sea. It took Joss over half a day to arrive at his destination. Upon arriving he shut down the motors and let the boat drift as he searched the water for any kind of a clue.

Nightfall came and joss got a good restful sleep. He knew the next day or days would be long and filled with stress. Joss had installed many more safety lights than were required by maritime laws. He had no concerns of a collision at night with passing ships. He was though worried about pirates attacking his boat while he slept in this highly infested drug running waters.

With that in mind he had also installed special motion detectors onboard his boat. They adjusted to the swells and rocking of the boat to prevent being activated. Their beams would penetrate water; but would reflect back only when they struck anything solid. If that happened several high wattage flood lights lit up and a deafening siren would blast. He also had an arsenal of powerful weapons and ammunition. He prayed that he would not have to use them or encounter any security problems.

Joss had stayed in the area for over a week and he was concerned about Trinity and Hope's well being. On the ninth day he sat atop his flying bridge scanning the glassy water when he saw movement a hundred yards off his starboard bow. He adjusted his binoculars and saw the face of Trinity with its infectious smile. He fired up the motors and approached her. As he shut down the motors and slowly drifted up to her; Hopes head popped up from beneath the water right next to her mothers. Joss lowered the rope ladder; but he couldn't wait for them to board. He jumped in to the water, swam to them and kissed Trinity. "I love you so much and I've missed you," he said.

Joss gave Trinity a minute as she looked at her tail. She stroked it and held it. Joss watched as her tail split in the middle and each fin like section transferred into a leg and foot. Hope then as well went through the ordeal. It was a common practice for mermaids; but it was the first time Joss actually watched it happened.

They climbed the ladder and boarded the boat. They talked about what they did while separated and rejoiced in their reunion. An hour was almost at end when Joss asked Trinity If giving up her world and her tail was what she honestly wanted to do.

"Yes, I want to be with you forever and to have the best for Hope," she said.

Hope looked at her mother and asked "will I ever have a tail again mommy"?

"No sweetheart, you will now have legs forever. We will live in a new world with your father." Trinity said.

That was the first time that Joss heard himself referred to as father, it touched his heart and that was immensely pleasing to him.

Trinity told Joss that she had refused to mate with another male during her last reproductive cycle. Queen Red Fire gave her a one time exclusion; but she had to mate next cycle or be banned from Sanctuary.

Joss was pleased that she was not pregnant with another mans child. One thing that could have been a problem is that all mermaids; both men and woman are born with a tail. The male fins transform to their permanent legs over a ninety day period. That would be hard to explain at any doctor's office or hospital in his world.

The next day Joss turned the boat towards Miami and headed back home. He had bought a beautiful home on Star Island with its own private dock for his boat. The property had all the seclusion and privacy that he desired for the safety of his family. He had sold his home in San Francisco and relocated his finances and other interest to Miami months earlier.

Time passed smoothly and the Inlay family prospered beyond all expectations. Hope became a Florida State swimming champion and is training for the next Olympics.

Trinity went to college as well and she has become a world renowned oceanographer. She gets published in magazines and is in high demand on the international speaking circuit.

Joss with the help of Trinity researched new sonar and sonic equipment. Mermaids can communicate with each other with mental telepathy up to five miles apart. He experimented and studied with Trinity and Hope. He discovered that it was a matter of frequencies.

Joss's new company is Reflective Enterprises. He sells his equipment to the military. It is top secret; but I can tell you that it works with obscure frequencies and their ranges within a beams parameters. This allows for a new revolutionary process of mapping and imaging the newly modulated waves that are bounced back and captured by a second unit and not the original sending source.

Trinity has never had any regrets of giving up her tail and becoming Joss's wife. They still take the boat out to Sanctuaries coordinates three or four times a year. Trinity still has her mermaid ability to communicate with the mermaids in Sanctuary. Several of them come to the surface and visit with them. Some even come aboard; but always return in time to keep their tails. They are happy for Trinity; but they choose to stay and live in Sanctuary.

Joss knows that deep in Trinity's heart she misses her home more than see lets him know. Joss is doing something to surprise her next summer. He's having a four man submarine built so they can actually go to Sanctuary and visit for a few days. That will then be the better of two worlds for Trinity and Hope.

OH! By the way, Joss is scheduled to sail around the world solo two years from now. His newly designed sailboat is being built. If there is one thing Joss has learned in his life, it is not to be afraid to dream; but more important is to try and not make them come true. Yes he has a family; but this he does for himself and is the reason he is who he his. A man that finishes what he starts out to do. We should all learn from Joss Inlay. Be true to your self and conquer your dreams.

This is a virtual short story. You (the reader) are one of the jurors. You are juror #7 and all conversation is for your consideration during the trial. It will be your base's to determine a mans fate.

GUILTY OR NOT?

TODD BUCKLEY SAT silently while he eyed you and the other jurors filling the jury box. There were only three, including you that made eye contact with him. It had been a miserable two days selecting the jury of five men and seven women. Todd was adamant that he was not guilty of killing a 23 year old woman during the holdup of a convenient store. He did look similar to the killer that was on the stores video tape; but he swore that it wasn't him.

Even though the FBI had enhanced the footage to obtain the best image they could, it still wasn't clear enough to make a positive identification. Todd had no alibi for that night of Friday November the 6th. He said that he was home fast asleep at 3AM; but there was no one to verify that fact. It was the day and swing shift personnel that said it was Todd in the video; because he fit the six foot one, tall, slender and white figure on the video. Todd definitely fit the description of the killer that was on the video; but so did his attorney, a couple of the jurors and even the bailiff. Making it even harder to make a positive identification was that the killer wore a black hooded sweatshirt and dark sunglasses.

Todd was a regular at the store and he lived less than two blocks away. He always used his debit card so all the employees knew him by name. After all he's the heir to the Buckley Electronics Corporation. I guess carrying cash wasn't necessary as long as one has plastic. Todd knew the stores employees by name from all three shifts as well. He couldn't understand how they could say it was him on the grainy tape.

The prosecution gave its opening statement and then the defense rebutted everything that they said when giving his opening. Once that was completed Judge Alcott asked the state to start with their case. The states Attorney Paul White called aloud, "Dr. Willows." The doctor approached the witness stand and was sworn in. He sat down and made himself comfortable. Mr. White continued, "Did you do an autopsy on Miss Cheryl Duncan, the deceased from the robbery?"

"Yes."

"Would you please tell the court how she died?"

"She died from a gunshot to her head."

"Were there any other contributing factors that led or brought about her death?"

"No! Just the gunshot, other than that she appeared to be exceptionally healthy and fit."

"Is this the bullet that you removed from the deceased?"

"Yes, it has my mark on it, right there on the side."

"Thank you doctor. The state would like to enter this bullet into evidence as people's exhibit #1 Your Honor. I have no further questions for Dr. Willows."

Judge Alcott turned to Todd's attorney Mr. Blackwood, "your cross Mr. Blackwood."

"Thank you Your Honor. Dr. Willows; I have only one question. How far away would you say the shooter was from the deceased when they fired the fatal shot?"

"I have no way of telling that for certain. That isn't my expertise. The CSI's are the ones to ask that type of question."

"Thank you doctor, that's all for this witness Your Honor; but I reserve the right to recall the witness at a later time," said Mr. Blackwood.

The Judge instructed the doctor to step down; as he exited, Mr. White called Ronald Sims to the stand. Once sworn in, Mr. White asked him, "Would you please tell the court what your job is."

"I am a ballistic expert with the FBI."

"Is this the 38 that you used to compare peoples exhibit #1 with?" He handed him the 38 from the crime scene.

"Yes sir it is."

"I'd like to enter this 38 as people's exhibit #2, Your Honor. What were your findings Mr. Sims?"

"The bullet in question definitely was fired from this handgun." He handed the gun back to the attorney and continued to explain. "The grooves and the twist were a perfect match as was . . . ."

"Thank you agent Sims interrupted Mr. White; no one is questioning your credentials. We only needed to hear that the bullet was fired from people's exhibit #2; your witness Mr. Blackwood."

"You're being a little modest Mr. Sims, are should I say Special Agent Sims. That's your full title isn't it?"

"Yes."

"Tell me agent Sims, didn't you ask Colt Henderson of the county crime lab to run a GSR (gunshot residue) test around the wound track of Miss Duncan?"

"Yes."

"I saved this question for you Mr. Sims because I felt that doctor Willows couldn't elaborate on the findings. What were the findings?"

"Mr. Henderson concluded that the weapon was fired from a distance of five to six feet away from the victim."

"Isn't it a fact that there was no GSR on my client either?"

"That true as well, replied Mr. Sims.

"Thank you Agent Sims, you may step down, I have no further questions of this witness."

"Redirect Your Honor, I'd like to ask Mr. Sims one final question," stated Mr. White.

"Go ahead counselor," said Judge Alcott.

"Mr. Sims is this casing that was found at the crime scene that night?"

"Yes, it was tested along with the gun and bullet. The firing pin's impression on the casing was definitely made with the 38 that was logged in to evidence. It has been proven that the gun, bullet and casing all are connected are one in the same."

"Thank you Mr. Sims, you may step down."

"Call your next witness," instructs Judge Alcott.

Mr. White calls out, "Special Agent Roy Lake."

Mister Lake approached the stand and took the oath, then sat down. "Special Agent Lake, would you tell the court who you are and what you do."

"I am an agent for the FBI and I investigate murder cases. I've been an agent for 28 years and have been investigating murder cases for the last 15 years."

Mr. White hands him the 38 and asks, "Is this the gun that was found at the crime scene lying next to the body of Cheryl Duncan?"

"Yes it is; I see the mark on it that I use to verify such evidence in these types of cases."

"What more can you tell us about this gun?"

"It's registered to one Todd Buckley. He bought it at Clayton Guns five years ago. He does have a conceal weapons permit to carry it with him. He goes to the shooting range every week and is a marksman according to the owner of Bucks Shot Barn shooting range."

"Boy! That sounds like he's good enough to shoot a girl right in the head at 5 or 6 feet away."

"I object Your Honor!" Screamed Mr. Blackwood. "That's an out right and disgusting attempt from the defense to plant a seed of guilt in the jury's mind."

"Sustained Mr. White. I will not have that type of inappropriate conduct or questioning in my courtroom. One more attempt like that and I will hold you in contempt, is that perfectly clear Mr. White?"

"Yes Your Honor, I apologize. Your witness Mr. Blackwood."

Judge Alcott then addressed the jury, "you will ignore the states last statement in its entirety."

Mr. Blackwood stood in silence for a moment before asking, "Mr. Lake, didn't my client report his gun missing four months ago?"

"Yes he did."

"You forgot to mention that fact in your attempt to crucify my client in your testimony."

"I object Your Honor. The defense is badgering the witness," screamed the states attorney.

"STOP IT! STOP IT! I will not tolerate this type of conduct in my courtroom. I will hand down fines to the both of you at the end of this trial. You both are here by officially guilty of contempt. Any more of this conduct your fines will keep doubling, so continue keeping that in mind gentleman," warned Judge Alcott.

Both attorney's said in unison, "Yes Your Honor."

"Good! Continue Mr. Blackwood; but watch your remarks."

"Mr. Lake, were there any fingerprints on the weapon?"

"No it was wiped clean."

"How can that be? In the store's video the shooter shoots Miss Duncan, then throws the gun down and runs. We can all see on the video that the gunman is wearing gloves so that explains why the outside of the weapon is clean of any prints? Agent Lake, please tell me why anyone who knows that the gun their using in a murder and is registered to them would just throw it on the floor at a crime scene? Further more he has a conceal weapons permit for said gun. Do you think my client is that stupid Special Agent Lake?"

"You can never tell what some people will do in a moment of fear or when they panic."

"True Agent Lake; but you tested the entire weapon didn't you? You took it a part and found nothing, not even a smudge from a print. You also tested the casing that was at the crime scene and it had nothing as well. So doesn't that suggest that someone cleaned this weapon to the point of sanitizing it and then deliberately left it there to frame my Client?"

"Speculation Mr. Blackwood, all my years in the agency and I have never heard such a defense."

"Your Honor, I would like to show the store's video from the night in question for the jurors, Agent Lake and the court."

Judge Alcott pondered the request for a second before replying, "Granted Mr. Blackwood. I warn the jury and the courtroom visitors that this is a gruesome and detailed account of the death of a young woman. Anyone in the courtroom may be excused during the viewing if this is unsettling to them. I ask the jury to try and watch the tape to the best of their ability."

This is the first time that you (juror #7) have seen this piece of evidence. You watched very intently and gathered all the information that you could. At the end of the viewing you had a better picture of what happened and gave you a clearer meaning to the attorney's questionings.

"I would like to enter this video as defense exhibit A Your Honor, said Mr. Blackwood."

"So entered."

"Isn't it true that the deceased broke up with her boyfriend D K a few months ago Agent Lake?"

"Yes and I questioned him on his whereabouts."

"What did he say about the night of November 6th at 3 AM?"

"He said he was sleeping at home, alone."

"That was good enough for you? I sure would be a little hesitant to believe an ex-boyfriend. Funny how you take his word; but you don't take my clients word that he wasn't there. No more questions of this witness I think we can all see the way the FBI investigates a murder."

"Mr. White call your next witness, said Judge Alcott.

"The state rest Your Honor."

"Mr. Blackwood is the defense ready to put on its defense?"

"The defense calls Duane Hicks."

Mr. Hicks approached and took the oath before sitting in the witness box. Mr. Blackwood began, "You work at the store where Miss Duncan died on November 6th?"

"Yes sir I do."

"You saw the killer on the tape; do you believe that is my client Todd Buckley?"

"Yes"

"Do you see this man in the courtroom here today?"

"Yes, that's him sitting right there at the defense table."

"How can you be sure, Mr. Buckley is my client and I can't say that that's him positively from that video, so how can you Mr. Hicks?"

"Well I think it's him."

"You think it's him! You're ready to send a man to prison for the rest of his life because you think it's him?"

"No."

"No! Well which is it Mr. Hicks? Is he or isn't he the one on the tape killing Cheryl Duncan?"

"Well I, um I, I don't know anymore."

"Seems you think and guess a lot Mr. Hicks, just imagine if you were a new agent at the FBI how effective you'd be. No more questions Your Honor."

"Any cross Mr. White," asked Judge Alcott.

"No Your Honor; but I reserve the opportunity to call him later if need be."

"I call Rachel Pond," announced Mr. Blackwood.

She like the others gets sworn in and takes the witness stand. "Good Morning Miss Pond," said Mr. Blackwood. "You're the stores daytime manager correct?"

"Yes."

"You knew Miss Duncan very well didn't you?"

"Yes."

"Did you know her boyfriend as well?"

"Yes."

"Isn't it true that he has the exact physical attributes as Todd Buckley?"

"Yes."

"Then tell me why couldn't the man in the video be him instead of my client?"

"Objection Your Honor, calls for an opinion," Mr. White interrupted.

"Sustained," snapped the Judge." I warned you Mr. Blackwood. You stay on topic and stop with these inappropriate lines of questioning."

"I apologize to the court Your Honor. Miss Pond I am going to ask you the same question I asked the previous witness. How can you make a positive identification from the stores video? What do you see that allows you to be 100% positive that's my client?"

"Well it kind of looks like him. I like Mr. Buckley; but that's who I think it is on the tape."

"You think! My God that's all I keep hearing from witnesses. No more questions for this witness. It's obvious why the state didn't call Mr. Hicks or Miss Pond. I move for a dismissal Your Honor. The states case is nothing more than circumstantial evidence based on witness's that think or guess that my client was the perpetrator. Your Honor, there is no DNA or physical evidence to put my client at the scene of the crime on the night in question."

"Motion denied Mr. Blackwood. The Grand Jury thought there was enough evidence for your client to be held over for trial. Call your next witness or summarize, unless Mr. White has any questions," the judge said as he wagged his finger at him.

"No Your Honor, the state has no questions at this time."

"Wait a moment Miss Pond. I was going to address this on cross; but since Mr. White has no questions I'll explore it now. Did miss Duncan talk to you about her love life and her boyfriend's?"

"Yes."

"Who was her last boyfriend?"

"D. K. His real name is Dirk King; but we called him D.K."

"Didn't they break up a while back?"

"Yes."

"Did she tell you why they broke up?"

"Yes."

"Please tell the court what Miss Duncan said about their break up."

"Objection Your Honor, hear say."

"Over ruled, I'll allow it. The witness will answer the question, "the Judge ordered.

"Because D. K. found out she was cheating on him."

"Did she tell you who she was seeing behind D. K's back?"

"Yes, it was Todd Buckley, your client."

"Then my client was her last boyfriend?"

"Yes"

"Did D. K know that it was my client that Miss Duncan was seeing behind his back?"

"Yes, during their argument she told him it was Todd."

"Thank you Miss Pond. I've nothing further to ask this witness. I'd like the court to know that this information was not made available to the defense during the discovery portion of the trial; your witness Mr. White."

"Thank you counselor. Miss Pond what happened after D K and Miss Duncan broke up?"

"Todd and Cheryl got real hot and heavy. Then when Todd asked Cheryl to marry him she said no. She told Todd that it was over and that she should have never left D K. That was a lie though. She just said that to make Todd mad. She had met a new guy; but I don't know who."

"So now this unknown boy is her last boyfriend," that's nice to know Miss Pond.

"How did Todd take the rejection?"

"He was furious."

"Objection, calls for a conclusion."

"Over ruled Mr. Blackwood, I'll allow it."

"What else did Mr. Buckley say or do?"

"He said she would be sorry. Then he pushed over a display of chips and stormed out of the store. That all happened a week before Cheryl was killed. D K came in the day after that fight between Cheryl and Todd. He begged Cheryl to take him back; but she told him she had a new man that was rich and twice the man he or Todd was. Then he stormed out of the store cussing and calling Cheryl names at the top of his voice."

"Thank you Miss Pond. You may step down. No more questions Your Honor."

"Mr. Blackwood any more witness's?"

"No your Honor, the defense rest."

"I think we will take an hour lunch break at this time. Every one be back at 2 sharp and counselors be prepared to give your summations," said Judge Alcott.

Everyone was back on time and the trial was back in session. Mr. White was first to give his closing statement. He does a fine job representing the state. He address's you and rest of the jurors; "Lady's and gentlemen of the jury. This is an open and shut case. The defendant Todd Buckley was having an affair with the deceased. It was his gun found at the scene. It was registered to him and he is a marksman at the nearest shooting range. He had a fight with Miss Duncan and was heard saying she would pay for breaking up with him. She even rejected his marriage proposal which had to make him very mad.

He has no real alibi other than he was home alone sleeping. He knew the stores location of their cameras by being a regular customer and he knew that Cheryl Duncan worked alone on the graveyard shift. Yes he reported his gun missing; but was it really or was he setting up a falsehood to protect his future actions? I surmise that Todd Buckley wiped off his gun, no sanitized his gun and deliberately threw it down at the scene. He thinks by reporting it stolen two weeks before the crime that would throw guilt away from him.

To answer Mr. Blackwood's question about do we think his client is stupid, well the answer is no! In fact he thinks he has out smarted us all; but no Mr. Buckley, the state knows you killed Miss Cheryl Duncan on the night of November the 6th at 3 AM. I ask you the jury to return a verdict of GUILTY as charged with first degree murder. Thank you members of the jury; your summation counselor."

Mr. Blackwood stands and shakes his head. He turns and looks straight into your eyes (juror #7), smiles then begins; "Wow what a story from the state. If that is all the state has we can all go home early today. Mr. Buckley had a lover's quarrel like millions of couples do everyday. You don't see massive murders because of it. I bet every one of you on the jury has had more than one in your lifetime. Hell, most of the time it leads to great make-up sex.

Mr. White has conveniently left out that there was no DNA or physical evidence to put my client there on the night in question. He loved Cheryl Duncan and he is still morning her death. Tell me why the state left out that D K got rejected twice? I'll tell you why, because he doesn't want you to consider anyone else but my client. Why couldn't D K stolen Mr. Buckley's gun and be the killer. Then again a total stranger could have stolen the gun and is the perpetrator.

Don't you the jury find it rather odd that the states attorney never even touched on these possible scenarios? Who knows? Miss Pond could secretively have loved D K or Mr. Buckley and she killed Miss Duncan to clear the way for her advances towards either one. For Pete's sakes, even Duane Hicks could have been jealous of Miss Duncan's multiply relationships and he thought if he couldn't have her no one could. What about this new mystery boyfriend, who and where is he? No one really explored this new boyfriend that she left both D K and Mr. Buckley for. If he does exist he should have been investigated by the state.

OK some of these scenarios seem far fetched; but all have been the reason for 100's of murder cases on file in our courtrooms and can not be totally overlooked as possibilities. REASONABLE DOUBT, members of the juror. No one can identify the man on the store surveillance cameras footage. Honestly it could be a man or a woman. You can not in good conscious find my client guilty. I leave Mr. Todd Buckley's future in your hands and I will rest assured that you will do the right thing and find him NOT GUILTY."

At this time Judge Alcott gives you and the jury their instructions. Once completed he inquires if the instructions were clear and all the jurors nod their heads in a positive manner. You all stand and are led to the jury room to start your deliberations.

The first thing that had to be addressed was picking a foreman. There were little conversations about it. You were chosen unanimously by every one to be the foreman; because they noticed how intently you listened and took notes during the trial.

You accepted that position and turned your focus on getting dialogue started. You asked for and received a blackboard. You wrote down the points that both attorney's had brought up during their summations. There was a knock on the door; it was the bailiff bringing all the physical evidence to the jurors for inspection.

Now I could go into detail about what transpired behind the jury room's door; but you're juror #7 and the foreman. It is up to you to control and lead the jury to a final decision. I too am juror #7 and I will reveal my vote much later on. This is your task now. I am sure you will discuss all the facts and come to a conclusion of some kind.

You have now spent a few hours leading the jurors to a final vote. Rumor has it that there has indeed been loud arguments and in fighting. However, many questions have been answered or resolved. The vote is taken by you starting with juror #1 and asking the question, "How do you vote?" The answer comes back loud and clear "GUILTY." You continue around the room and each respond "GUILTY." Your time has finally come; the vote stands at 11 guilty, are you in agreement? Do you see the same facts that allow them to find beyond a shadow of a doubt his guilt? Maybe you see something that they missed? Maybe you missed what it is that makes them so sure?

Everyone wants to go home and their tired and waiting for you to render your vote. Finally juror #3 barks at you "GUILTY OR NOT." You now hold Todd Buckley's life in your hands. You look up to the ceiling and say "I find Mr. Todd Buckley—?"

As the author of this short story I realize there are many facts that are not discussed at great length. There are some aspects to the crime that could have been investigated more deeply. However you only have the facts at hand. You available options are guilty, not guilty or a hung jury.

I as #7 juror would cast my vote as NOT GUILTY. I will not reveal why that is. The answer is in the story itself. Hopefully there will not be a re-trail or miss-trail.

DESTINY'S TWIST

TROY SIMMONS WAS a man whose life hadn't went very well. He couldn't keep a job due to being an alcoholic. His parents died when he was two and he was put in the foster care program. He bounced around the system for years until he turned eight-teen and then went out on his own.

He lived on the streets of Los Angeles, California and learned to survive by developing street smarts. He could have been anything he wanted if only he could leave the bottle alone. On his 28th birthday he went on a drinking binge that lasted for several days. His massive celebration left him so drunk that he walked out in to the middle of the 405 freeway; even though he can't recall doing it.

When he woke up, to his surprise he was in the hospital. He felt like death warmed over as the old saying goes. He noticed that his legs were elevated and they hurt immensely. The nurse came in the minute he regained consciousness. "Thank God, I see that you finally decided to wake up and join us," she said.

"Where am I? What happened to me?" he said.

"You're in the Los Angeles Memorial hospital. You staggered into traffic and were hit by a passing car. Both your knees were crushed and had to be replaced with new titanium ones."

"What the hell, I have knee replacements."

"Yes sir and except for a few minor cuts and bruises you will be good as new. You were a lucky man indeed."

Troy took a deep breath, rolled his eyes back slowly and slipped into a deep sleep. He spent a week in the hospital and then was discharged. He didn't have anywhere to go except for the mission. They took him in because of his condition. He had a walker; but could get around on his own. For a month he had food and a warm place to bathe as well as a bed while he healed completely.

He had time to reflect on his life and his so called memories during that time. He decided to find out more about his biological parents. For the first time in his life he wanted answers to who he really was. So the day he left the mission he went straight to the Los Angeles Times newspapers archive room. He knew his parents had died 26 years ago so he started scanning the obituaries for that year. After hours of searching he found what he had been looking for.

(Troy had been told what his parents names were when he was a teenager. It was not a secret because he was not taken away from them or left on a doorstep. They were killed in an automobile accident and he still had his given birth name.)

He was amazed to read that they left behind a two year old boy (Troy) and a one year old girl (Samantha). He had a sister, something that he never knew before that second. He wrote down the names of his Aunt and Uncle that were mentioned in the article. He searched the week before and the week after the article. He found a picture of his mother and father in the obituary section. The information there was more detailed than the news report of the accident. It answered many of the questions that now haunted him. He started this new journey by trying to find his Uncle Jim and Aunt Pamela. He prayed that they could tell him about his sisters' whereabouts.

It was an astounding coincidence that Samantha Simmons for years had been trying to seek out information on her biological parents as well. She knew that she had a brother named Troy and that they were separated at birth. She couldn't follow the countless moves he had in the foster home program. She couldn't understand why he didn't have a My-Space or Face book page. If only she knew the life he was living she would understand why he lacked any of the modern communication avenues.

Samanthas life was much different than Troy's. She was successful and highly educated. They were as different as day and night. With out knowing it, both were looking for their lost sibling.

Two years passed by from when Troy first began his search. He was frustrated. He couldn't find his Uncle or Aunt. He had no leads on his sister and that hurt him the most. He thought that she might have gotten married and that explained why she would have a different name. That was what he told himself in order to cope with his apparent failure to find her.

Troy was turning thirty and for the first time in two years he headed for the local bar. He didn't care too much for the pain and sense of failure; so he reverted back to the old Troy that drank his problems away. He drank until the bartender literally through him out onto the sidewalk.

Troy's bad luck continued that night. He pulled himself up off the sidewalk and staggered down the street. He hadn't gone three blocks when he stumbled out into the middle of the street. He was struck by a pick-up truck and died instantly. As his lifeless body lay there in the road many ran to his aid; but he was already gone.

It was a sad ending to any thirty year old person. It was also a shame that he never met his family or sister. He tried to turn his life around; but he just couldn't get there completely. His body was taken to the morgue in San Diego, since he was in that city and not Los Angeles.

There was no identification on Troy's body so the medical examiner sent his prints to the police. During the autopsy his two titanium knee replacements were discovered. All medical implants or replacement joints have a serial number assigned to them. The medical examiner ran the serial numbers right then and there on the hospitals computer.

At exactly the same time, the police report came back with Troy Simmons name, life history, where he was born and a list of foster homes. It had his parent's names and his sister's name as well as all his arrest facts.

The hospital computer beeped as the search for the knees serial numbers had found a match. It showed Troy Simmons as the man having these replacement knees two years earlier.

The question of who John Doe was had now been answered without any doubt. He had a name and history, Troy Simmons. All that was left to do was for the medical examiner to enter the cause of death, time, date and then sign the death certificate.

After all the appropriate boxes were checked and comments filled out the medical examiner signed the certificate, SAMANTHA SIMMONS.

Troy did finally meet his sister and she met her brother; but not in the way they had both envisioned. Not all ships pass in the night, they sometimes simply collide adding to the mysteries of our lives.

REMEMBERANCE

AS HE TURNED to leave he saw something lying in the brush approximately fifty yards away. He approached it carefully and to his amazement found an adult cougar with it's right paw caught in a trap. The big cat was exhausted and had lost a lot of blood. There was no fight left in the animal from the struggle it had endured.

Seth bent down and stroked the cat's belly. She just laid there too weak to be of any danger. Seth felt sorry for the animal and he decided to take a chance and help. He found a piece of wood that was the right size he needed for what he was intending to do. He put one foot on the lower jaw of the trap and then grabbed the upper jaw with his right hand. It took all his strength to open the jaws. As it opened he slipped the piece of wood in between the jaws with his left hand to hold the trap open. Seth slowly and carefully removed the damage paw from the steel vise that had held it captive.

The cougar never moved; but she started a faint purring. All Seth knew to do was pour some water over the wound from his canteen to wash out what dirt he could. He thought the cat would bleed to death if he did nothing more for it. He gathered up large oak leaves and wrapped them around the injured paw. He made mud and packed it around the leaves to hold them in place. His belief was the cat would lie there and the wound would coagulate on its own. Once the bleeding stopped maybe she had a chance to retain her strength. That was all Seth could do for her and darkness was falling quickly.

Seth took a large limb and triggered the trap shut. He patted the cat on the head as she opened her eyes just long enough to look up at him. He felt bad about leaving her there; but she was too big to carry and too dangerous even if he could have.

Seth got back to his truck hours after it had been engulfed in total darkness. He drove the 85 miles back to his house and explained to his wife what had happened that day. He told me about his adventure the next day at work. We worked at the local saw mill. We had started there right after high school 5 years ago. Where we live you worked in the woods or mills. Where as in Detroit you work in the car business or in Pittsburgh you work in the steel mills. Many jobs are regional.

The week finally came to an end. Seth and I had things to do Saturday that made hunting impossible. We agreed to go early Sunday morning. We wondered if the cougar would be gone are would it still be there dead and half eaten by predators.

Five AM came early indeed that Sunday since we had not gotten to bed until one AM. I was still putting on by boots when Seth blew his trucks air horn. I'm sure the neighbors loved it at that time in the morning. I ran out and got into the truck carrying one boot as I went.

We made good time arriving at Bull Run. We got our orange vest on and loaded our rifles. We hiked to where Seth had left the cougar. The trap was still there with the limb stuck in it; but the big cat was gone. Maybe she crawled away and died elsewhere or she beat the odds and survived. We had no way to know so we continued to hunt for a big buck. We continued to hunt the next three week-ends without filling our tags. The hunting season came to an end without either one of us getting off a shot. We swore that next year would be different.

Winter was mild, while the summer was a scorcher. We were glad to see fall and deer season come. When opening day arrived Seth and I were on the mountain as the sun peaked over the horizon for first dawn. As soon as we could see through our scopes we started down a well used deer trail looking for signs. It didn't take long for noon to arrive. We sat down and enjoyed our packed lunch of sandwiches and chips. as we sat there we were startled by a sound to the right of us.

It was a strange sound so we both grabbed our rifles and stood and faced the direction it came from. We quietly worked our way through the brush for about 100 yards when we found the source of the mysterious sound. A bear cub high atop a tree balling it's lungs out.

Danger! Danger! Will Robinson. We didn't have to say a word; we just turned and started to run. We had only taken a step or two when we heard limbs snapping and a roar that sent chills down our spine. Every hunter knows that where there is a bear cub, the mother is close and she will kill you for just being in the area. The mother wad about 200 yards up the mountain side and she was crashing her way downhill fast. Bears can run up to 30 miles an hour and she was closing in on Seth and I fast. For every ten feet we made she was doing 20. I can tell you our hearts were pounding as she continued to close the distance.

We final got out of the brush; but out into a level grassy meadow. We knew we couldn't out run her now. We had no choice but to turn and try to take her down the second she entered the meadow. In unison we turned;

but she had cleared the brush and had lunged at us before we could even get our rifles up. She was literally 10 feet away from us when out of the blue a large cougar blindsided her broadside. Both the bear and cougar fell two feet in front of us. We backed off forty or fifty feet and watched as the bear and cougar fought.

    Finally with a mighty roar the bear ran and retreated back into the brush headed for her cub. The cougar sat and looked at the both of us. Seth looked down and noticed that's its right paw was deformed. It was the cat that Seth had helped. Her paw had healed; but it was twisted. Seth walked up to her with no fear and scratched her head and the big cat purred loudly. He gave her a hug and touched his nose to hers. The cat licked the side of Seth's face as there reunion lasted for five minutes. She finally stood and gingerly walked backed into the woods and disappeared.

    We haven't seen the cougar since then; but we sometimes feel she is watching over us. You can call it a coincidence if you want to; but for the last five years on opening day of hunting. We both get our deer tags filled when bucks run right out in front of us as if someone is flushing them out for us to shoot. You be the judge, just luck or a cougar that has A FOND MEMORY.

LIFE AS I KNOW IT

I WAS TALKING to my roommate Bill from my bed in our hospital room when his parents and family entered our domain. I immediately stopped talking and allowed his mother and father to visit with their son. Bill introduced them to me after a short reunion. A beautiful creature that was approaching my bedside however mesmerized me at first glance. Bill smiled and shook his head as he said, "Larry that's my sister Cindy and beware she's a heartbreaker". She opened the conversation, believe it or not by just looking at me. She finally asked me what had happened to me that brought me to the hospital. I told her that I had injured my knee in a gymnastic routine at school.

She turned and walked to the end of my bed in a most alluring manner. I found myself gazing into her blue eyes intently. The more I studied them the more I was convinced that they were saying something much more than was being said audibly. Let me get to know you, I'm lonely and I need someone in my life, I imagined they were saying to me. However, our mental telepathy was broken by her mothers' words of "glad to meet you". I shook her hand and began to light a cigarette when the rest of Bill's family came over to see me.

Arlene was bills other sister. She was seventeen and very pretty and could hold her own in a beauty contest with anyone I concluded. Bill's two brothers were named James and Thomas and they were eight and eleven respectively. Bill's parents Jack and Linda Harrison were without a debut two of the nicest people that I have ever met. They were down to earth and did not try to be nothing more than what they really were.

After sometime they finished visiting with their son and got up to leave. Cindy had spent the entire time sitting on my bed and talking to me. Upon leaving Mr. Harrison invited me to come and visit them at their home when I got out of the hospital. That was an offer, that I would surly not pass on. I glared at Cindy as I watched her disappear out the door and my heart skipped a beat in disappointment from her absence.

Bill Harrison lived on a ranch and had been thrown from a horse and shattered his knee. That was why he was here at Saint Mary's Hospital. I on the other hand was on the school's gymnastic team. Four others and I were the school's trampoline squad. We put on half time shows at basketball games, demonstrating advanced trampoline routines.

I will never forget that I was doing a two and one halve twisting one and a half and got lost in the middle of the execution. As luck would have it the padding that is usually around the corners was missing at one end. I came down knee first on the steel frame and crushed my knee and was tossed out onto the floor a good twenty-five feet away.

Bill and I both had surgery on the same day as it turned out. Different doctors; but we both came out of recovery room at the same time and were wheeled to the same room. We were both high school seniors and nineteen years of age. We also now shared two matching pairs of four-inch scars on our knees. The only difference was I injured my left knee and Bill had hurt his right knee.

Bill was from Fort Jones, a small ranching community of eight hundred people and was about thirty-three miles from Hallandale, which is where I lived. Hallandale is a city of about twenty thousand people located in the mountains among the high timbers. Fort Jones was at the base of the mountains and was spread out into the valley.

Timber and cattle were all the industry that there was for a couple hundred miles in any direction. This collection of cowboys and lumberjacks was for sure a mess waiting to happen. I'm sure anyone could see and feel the tense atmosphere in the surrounding area.

Rednecks and mill rats had weekly run ins at the bars on regular bases. I don't recall any shootings or stabbing in all the years I lived there. I can remember one person who got beat up real bad and almost died; but recovered after a couple of months of intensive care.

Many of the locals think that there was more to that than just a difference of opinion. All in all it was a great place to live and grow up. Clean air and fresh water were of abundance. Despite the difference between the local folks all was really very peaceful. The tension between the rednecks and lumberjacks had absolutely nothing to do with me being here at Saint Mary's Hospital.

Good friends are hard to find, especially these days and I truly felt Bill and I were best friends. We spent nine days in those hospital beds and we had a lot of time to get acquainted with one another. I got to know his family better each time they came to visit him.

I learned real fast not to spend too much time talking with Arlene because I could visibly see that it upset Cindy. In my heart I knew that Cindy was the one for me and not Arlene so why rock the boat. After all

I didn't need to try and make Cindy jealous I knew she already liked me. She had to know I liked her because I acted like a normal high school kid in love. That is like a stupid idiot drooling all over themselves.

My biggest problem was that Jim and Tom wouldn't leave Cindy and me alone. They kept asking questions about Hallandale and the city life. They were normal kids with curiosity and inquisitive nature. The truth be known they probably saved me from saying or doing more idiotic things than I did. At the time they were a pain in the neck as far as I could tell. Yet Cindy and I still got some quality time to visit and get to know one another. I caught her mother smiling as she glanced over and saw we were holding hands as her daughter visited with me.

I wish you could have seen Bill and I working out in the physical therapy room. Between lifting leg weights, whirlpools and ultra sonic treatments, we had to walk and walk some more. Then there was always the itching and swelling.

My cast had to be split open because my leg swelled up so big that it wouldn't allow blood to circulate properly. The nun that cut my cast set the blade depth to deep and came through right on top of my kneecap. I've got to be honest, I let out a yell I am sure they heard down at the sawmill.

She didn't cut the skin because there aren't really any teeth on the blade. But the fact that the rotating blade broke through was enough to cause pain. The doctor had a close look at it and yelled at her, but all was fine. The doctor put small wedges in the cut on the cast in order to keep it split apart.

The very next day somehow I tore the stitches out and had to have new stitches put in. That felt as good as the saw incident. Bill got a bad infection and was sick for a few days. I remember him getting a lot of pills and having his dressing changed several times for a day or two.

Bill and myself were like experimental rats back then in 1966 and looking back at it I can tell you that they have come a long way in medicine since then. Now at the turn of the century one gets the same operation and goes home the next day. I have two four inch scars and today you get one three-quarter inch scar for the same procedure. Oh well at least we lived through it all and I'm here to talk about the good old days.

It was a sad day and a glorious day all in one when I checked out of Saint Mary's Hospital. The nuns wheeled Bill down in a wheelchair to the exit center and watched me get into the car to go home. I recall waving and yelling out the car window that I would call him as soon as I could. I knew he would be leaving the next day and that he looked forward to going home. I still remember seeing him sitting there until I was completely out of sight.

CHAPTER TWO

Recovery at home was slow yet steady. My armpits were sore and raw from having to use crutches. It had been about a month since leaving the hospital and I couldn't wait any longer to talk to Cindy. I had been begging my father to allow me to call Bill; but he kept saying no, that it costs too much. I know its long distance, but he's my friend and I want to hear how his knee is healing was my heart felt argument. My dad finally gave in one day and said I could call later that evening.

I nervously called the number direct that I had gotten from bill and was in a state of anticipation. I didn't know what exactly to say to Cindy. The phone began to ring and I became even tenser. It seemed to ring and ring until mercifully I heard a click followed by a low sweet innocent voice saying "hello". I asked if Cindy was there. There was an immediate answer that this is she. I told her who I was and she let out a scream of joy.

"I thought you had forgotten about me. How come you waited so long to call me? Well, what do you have to say?" she asked. I explained to her that I could never forget about her and that my father wouldn't let me call till now. Once she heard my story she understood and forgave me. I inquired about Bill and the rest of her family only to find that all was well. Bill was at whirlpool therapy and Cindy was home alone. Once I had started talking things started to flow easily. I completely lost all my anxiety and stressfulness that had built up over the weeks.

Cindy relayed that she was very glad that I did indeed call her. She wanted me to come over to her house and visit because she missed me and wanted to give me a big hug. I told her that I was still on crutches and would be for another three weeks. I promised that I would be over as soon as I could work it out.

After we had exchanged thoughts for about an hour I told her that I had to go. She was disappointed; but understood that I couldn't afford the long distance phone call. We said good bye and I hung up the receiver. It was only a few minutes till I felt like I hadn't talked to Cindy in years. I wondered at that time if that was a good feeling or not. She was so lovely and only thirty plus miles away from me. I sat down in a big overstuffed easy chair, closed my eyes and had thoughts of only Cindy. It wasn't long till I slipped into a deep sleep.

I awoke to my father's strong shaking of my shoulder. It was dinnertime and he wanted me to come to the table. I told him that I wasn't hungry and would like to go upstairs to my room and lie down if that was ok with him. He said that was fine, but don't expect to eat later on.

It was a funny sight to see me go to my room. I had to sit on the bottom stair and then slide up one stair at a time. I did this for each of the sixteen stairs. Once reaching my bedroom I turned on my television and sat down on my bed. My house was about as much fun as the hospital room. I managed to keep my thoughts and mind working in a suitable manner.

Many things run through a person's head when he or she is alone. It's a challenge to see if one can anticipate the coming events or look ahead and plan things the way you would like them yourself to occur. I carried on in this philosophical mood for several days. I was moping around the house not eating and remaining quiet. These were all give-a-ways to the way I really felt. However—my parents thought it was only a sign of withdrawals from the drugs I had been receiving in the hospital.

A few days had passed when I got a letter from Cindy and that was all it took to snap me out of my depression and return to my good old self. It was a three-page letter asking me how I was recovering and healing. She asked me in a round about way when I could come over to her house and visit her. The most surprising thing about her letter was the ending, which read I LOVE YOU.

I had never been told that before and found it highly unusually for a girl to say such a thing especially so early into a relationship and would write it in a letter. Though she shocked me with this statement, I must say however that I was overjoyed by it.

After many concessions I managed to get my fathers permission to call Cindy again. I remember the waiting as the rings continued one after the other for what seemed like a millennium. My heart skipped a beat as I heard her voice say hello. "It's me and I had to call you after receiving your great letter yesterday" I said.

That was followed by a shirk and girlish squeals and Cindy saying, "I knew you would call. I just knew it in my heart. I told everyone that you would honey."

We talked about how I was going to get to see her. I didn't have a car and there was only the Greyhound bus for any kind of a transit system at that time. I was nineteen and a senior in high school and I loved an eight-teen-year-old junior. Looking back I recall that everyone that ever met Cindy thought see was at least the same age as I was. When she put her hair up and did her make-up right she could pass as a twenty-year-old with no problem.

We as a couple did have some problems that we had to overcome. Her father would not let her go on a date with me unless Bill and his date or Arlene and her date went with us. The fact that she required a chaperone didn't bother me. It was just hard to coordinate all the people involved and to find a venue that was acceptable to all concerned. I didn't think of it as spying or not trusting me personally. Cindy's father loved his daughter and only wanted to feel she was in a safe situation. I would be lying if I did not confess that I would have jumped at the chance to be alone with Cindy.

I had no money, so I made up my mind that I was going to hitchhike to Cindy's house as soon as the weekend arrived. I wanted to see if she really loved me or if she was just pretending. I would have my answer in a few days or so I thought.

CHAPTER THREE

I was up at seven-thirty Saturday morning and found myself running around like a chicken with its head cut off. I was in a hurry to leave and was overcome with excitement over that I was going to see Cindy. One look out the window revealed that there was six inches of snow on the ground and that it was still coming down hard with flakes as big as oak leafs. However I did not allow that fact to detour me from my plans and I left the house full of high hopes and anticipation.

I walked the three blocks from my house to the highway and began to hitchhike to my destination. I was surprised by the number of cars that were out and about in this kind of weather. But snow was no stranger in these parts for it was a common winter companion. The slapping sound of chains against the packed snow was a familiar sound to me; but one I hated hearing on this day.

While I was slowly walking backwards with my thumb out I was at the same time trying to figure out what I was going to say to Cindy once I saw her in person. After a few minutes I knew that it would be useless for me to try and write a speech in my head. I would have to wing it once I was face to face with her.

It took me only a few minuets to catch a ride. The cars were after all traveling at a slow pace due to the weather. The man that stopped for me was a collage student from Southern Oregon Collage. He was a pleasant person, but on the shy side at first. As we drove along he began to open up more and developed into a chatterbox. The conversation found it self deeply rooted into Vietnam and the United States involvement in it. He had introduced himself to me as James Taylor and had made a joke by saying "no, not that James Taylor".

"Some people think that this was Nixon's war while others think that it was an Eisenhower war. Many people forget that it was John F Kennedy that sent the first fifty thousand troops to Vietnam.

"I don't even want to get started on Agent Orange and what the government is doing to our troops. I totally disagree with this war" James stated. I listened as he talked about other points of the war and the politics of it all. We talked about the draft and we both agreed on many subjects and disagreed on a couple of points of interest.

I can honestly say that I was disappointed when he had reached the Crater Lake exit off of I-5 in north Medford. He was continuing North on I-5 and I was headed East on Highway 62. James had brought me about fifteen miles leaving me another eighteen miles to go.

The snow was a good six inches of hard packed ice by now and it was still snowing. The traffic was becoming slower and less frequent. For the first time I began to wonder if I might have been a little eager and should have put this trip off till a break in the weather.

I stood there in a quiet white world and realized that I was all-alone. The stillness was intensified when James car disappeared and I saw nothing in any direction. I started walking east and listening for the sound of life from any direction. I saw only a couple of birds on a telephone line in an hour and a half.

I was almost dead from the cold when out of nowhere a car pulled up along side me and the door flung open. "Hop in young man before you freeze to death," a voice said. I didn't wait to be asked again. I jumped in as fast as my stiff body would allow. I didn't know that a car heater could feel so good till that moment. I looked over to the driver and was surprised to see Mr. Hall my woodshop teacher from Hallandale High School. "Larry" he shouted. "What are you doing so far from home on a day like this?"? I told him about Cindy and that was why I was out here. He wasn't impressed at my explanation because I had created the situation and the predicament I had now put my self in.

I told Mr. Hall that I needed to find a combination gas station and store along highway 62 a little ways past Eagle Point. He told me he knew it well and even though it was a few miles further than his true destination, he would take me all the way there because of the weather. It took approximately forty-five minutes to get to the store. Mr. Hall waited as I went in and asked the clerk if he knew where the Harrison house was. The clerk said that if I went outside, turned left and went half a mile down the side road I would find their house.

I told him I was walking there from the store. He told me it was the third house on the left side of the road. He also told me to look for a big flatbed truck in front of a two story white house with green trim. I thanked the clerk and went back to tell Mr. Hall that I had found the right place. I then thanked him and waved good-bye. I watched as he turned his car around and proceeded out of sight and I started walking down the country road towards Cindy's house as the cold bitter wind blew down the back of my neck.

As I neared Cindy's house I heard sounds of happiness. I stood silently and watched Bill, Cindy and jimmy having a snowball fight in the front yard. For some unexplained reason I thought about if I should continue or not. I had emptiness deep inside me for some reason. I made up my mind to continue so I gingerly advanced until I was standing in the yard just a few feet away from Cindy. I stood there a second or two before deciding to speak. I had just opened my mouth to say something when Cindy looked up. She screamed and ran inside her house as fast as she could. I must confess that wasn't the reaction that I was looking for.

Bill and Jimmy came over and began to talk to me and they invite me into the house. Mr. and Mrs. Harrison welcomed me with open arms. After a short re-acquaintance meeting, Cindy appeared once again. She was more beautiful than a thousand pictures. Her long brown hair was hanging down along the sides of her face and as she smiled her eyes cast a look of want and desire.

I could never describe to you the way I felt right then as I gazed upon her. She ran over to me and gave me a hug and a kiss on my cheek. "I couldn't let you see me all a mess before. I hope you will forgive me for running into the house" she said. I told her that I had worried there for a second or two. But, now that I understood why, it was fine with me.

Cindy and I had just sat down on the sofa when Arlene decided to get into the picture by coming over and trying to sit down between Cindy and I. Arlene knew I played the guitar and she wanted me to tune hers and play some songs. I agreed to play a couple of songs but it turned into about two hours worth. I could tell that Cindy was very upset and beginning to come to a boil with anger. I laid the guitar down by saying I was growing thirsty; but in fact I wanted to pay attention to Cindy.

We went to Cindy's room and she put on a record. I took her in my arms as the ballad began to fill the room with its slow beat and soft mood. I felt her heart pounding as I drew her close to my body. I am sure she felt mine also as I kissed her softly.

There came a time when she had her back pressed up against the wall and my body pressing hard against hers. We both might have been cold on the outside; but we were not on the inside. Our lips met as we were both consumed by one another. No matter how hard I tried I could not pull her close enough to me.

My head was spinning and things were progressing far to fast. I recall that I lost all self-respect in what I was doing and found my-self begging for more love. However—it was Cindy that kept things in perspective by stating that her parents might miss her and come looking for us both. We returned to the living room and I sat down on the sofa. Cindy went to get some drinks and a snack for everyone. Arlene immediately sat down next to me while Cindy was out of the room. Needless to say all hell broke loose when Cindy returned. Their parents put an end to all the bickering in a flash and with no ifs, ands or butts about it. When they had finished allocating their rules and disciplinary actions they left for work.

Arlene sat in a chair across the room and stared as Cindy and I danced the afternoon away to soft music. Time passed quickly and before I knew, it was five-o clock in the afternoon. I realized that I really had to be leaving soon.

We were interrupted by a loud knock at the door and Bill yelling that he would get it. I had forgotten Bill was even home as he came running out of his room running towards the door. He flung it open and revealed a man and woman standing in the cold shivering. They were introduced to me as Mr. Sam Irvine and his wife Julia. They were there to pick up James and Thomas for a church function being held in of all places Hallandale.

Bill told the Irvine's that he had completely forgotten about the church function. The children weren't dressed and because of the bad weather he thought it best that they stay home. Sam told Bill that he understood his concern; but that he and Julia were still going to endure the snow and continue to the revival.

I decided to speak up at this time and in actuality invite myself along for the ride back to my house. Sam said that I was more than welcome to ride along as far as I wanted to. I thanked him and began saying my good-byes. I got into the back seat of the Irvine's' car and rolled down the window. I leaned out and gave Cindy a goodnight kiss as she began to cry. I wiped the tears away and told her I would be back soon. I can still see her waving good-bye from her driveway as the car pulled away and we slowly disappeared from sight.

CHAPTER FOUR

The day had been as beautiful as one could have ever dreamed. I knew that I would never forget this Saturday at Cindy's house. What I didn't know was what everyone else thought. Mrs. Irvine asked me if I liked Cindy and if I was going to go steady with her. I did not know what to say exactly because I had seen her talking to Cindy and knew they were good friends. I answered her questions with yes's and no's when it was acceptable. I tried to stay vague and yet not be rude or disrespectful on others. Mr. Irvine turned to go into the downtown area of Fort Jones. He informed me that he was picking up his mother who was a little elderly woman who also wanted to attend the services. This does give me a moment to tell you about this little community.

I had been through the town many times' sense it was on the way to Crater Lake. Once one drove down the length of Main Street you had seen just about all of the sights. However—Fort Jones had something peaceful and pleasant about it. There were hundreds of oak trees throughout the city. Many of the trees were over seventy years old. There were also many enormous willows that let their branches fall to the ground. The entire town seemed to be hiding from the real world. I saw it as the perfect hideaway from the noises, confused and mixed up lifestyle of the big city.

There is a stream on the outskirts of town that winds itself along the cities edge which in my opinion adds to the town's beauty. One can walk the deer trail's that follows the stream along its path to the big river a few miles away. I find it relaxing to watch oak leaves floating down the streams current. You might even get to see a deer because there are many running free here.

You can always see fish jumping for flies at sunset and sunrise. I know that because I have fished Union Creek a million times. I will leave the fish stories for another time. If you continue your adventure along the creek you will about a half mile from town come across a spectacular sight.

A sight were man and Mother Nature have worked together to produce a breath taking view. It is a hundred and fifty foot covered bridge. It was built back in 1889 and even though it is closed to vehicle traffic it is open to foot travel. It is a tourist site and gets many visitors every summer. No one could ask for a lovelier site. It spans the creek right above a small waterfall and pond like reservoir. The town is indeed a beautiful place to visit.

The Irvine's children that were in the back seat with me began to grow irritable. Let me see if I can remember this. Melinda was six and Bobby was five. They had been waiting in the car when their parents had come inside to pick up James and Thomas. The car pulled up to the front of a little cottage and stopped. It had an old and peasant look about it. Not a shabby or deserted look, just different compared to all the houses around it. Melinda and Bobby began yelling as an elderly woman came out onto the front porch. The children kept screaming Grandma, Grandma as she opened the car door and got into the front seat. Once in and her seat belt attached and the kids quit calling out we were finally on our way to Hallandale.

My knee by this time was aching and hurting beyond description from being bent up in the back seat of a small compact car. However, please do not think that I am complaining. I am very grateful for a ride home. I am only telling you that at this time I was in severe pain.

By the time we got to Medford Sam stopped for gas and I took advantage of this and got out to stretch my legs. I had not realized it before but the snow was melting and the roads were almost clear. I felt better pain wise and at ease about the safety of the trip. Once the car was filled we were on our way again.

I gave Sam directions to my house as we entered the city limits of Hallandale. I reached in my pocket for my door keys as Mr. Irvine stopped the car in front of my house. I slowly exited the back seat of the car. I thanked Mr. and Ms. Irvine from the bottom of my heart and shook their hands. I hobbled into the house and got a bite to eat.

I then did my scoot up the stairs to my bedroom. Then after I finished a letter to Cindy I turned on the television and got into bed. I laid there thinking about Cindy till at last with the help of the now falling rain I fell asleep.

I awoke the next morning feeling as though I had not slept in my entire life. I was truly that worn out and beat. The rain had stopped and the snow had melted away. The sun was out bright and warm, which caused steam to rise off the street. The sky was a deep blue and not a cloud was anywhere to be seen. I saw two Robins sitting in the tree tops singing at the top of their little lungs. What a glorious day it was.

I got dressed and went downstairs and got a bowl of grape nuts. My parents, brother and sister were at Sunday services leaving the entire house to me. While still crunching my cereal I turned on the basketball game just in time to see Dr. J slam-dunk off of a breakaway. I sat down in dad's big recliner and dialed Cindy's number.

I thought she would be up by now since it was noon already. I was correct I found as it was Cindy who answered the only once ringing phone. We had a pleasant conversation; but it did un-nerve me somewhat. Now I am going to relay this meeting with you the reader and I want you to see if you agree with me or am I being paranoid.

I asked her if she had a good time Saturday and she said yes because she was with me. I told her that I hoped I didn't wake her up when I had called. She replied that she had just woken up and had gotten out of our bed. This response totally rocked me back on my heals. I had to ask her what she meant by that remark.

She just simply said that when we got married the bed would be ours. I hesitated a little bit and told her that was moving pretty fast. Her tone changed and asked didn't I love her. I bent over backward telling her that I certainly did. However, I personally had not even thought of getting married at this period of time.

Now hold on a second reader. I felt very uncomfortable with this subject, yet I tried to discuss it while at the same time be clear on my views about it. Anyway, Cindy continued to say how much she loved me and how many children she wanted. I was getting tense about now and decided to find a way to end this call.

She asked me when I would be coming over again and I said that I wasn't sure at the moment. I said it depended on the weather and my parents. When she implied that the next time I was over she would show me a really good time I had a giant lump in my throat. I don't know if I objected to what she was laying out as a relation or if it was the fact that she was being the aggressor and not me.

Perhaps I didn't like the fact that she was trying to control the relationship and not me making the decisions. I avoided an argument by telling her that I was looking forward to seeing her again. However, in reality I was not so sure anymore. I finally told her that my dad would blow-up if I didn't keep this call short by his standards. We said our good-byes and hung up.

I did not want to hurt Cindy; but on the other hand I didn't know what to do about this new development. I now knew that if I had sex with Cindy I would undoubtedly be in a trap that she would never let me out of. I had a decision to make. Should I go with the flow or should I explain my true feelings to Cindy and let the cards fall were they might?

Well readers, what is the way to handle this matter by your evaluation. Oh yea I hear the men saying go for it and score. I also hear the women saying tell her the truth. Isn't all-fair in love and war? Then there is right or wrong. I need some more time to ponder my plight so you continue to analyze the situation and I will do the same.

I spaced out the rest of the day and just enjoyed the nice weather. I cut and stacked some wood and played Frisbee with Cody my dog. By the time I went to bed that evening I was ready. I didn't lay there awake tonight. I fell asleep as soon as my head hit the pillow.

The next day I started off to school as usual. I was saying hello to all my friends as I walked through the halls. Mr. Hall gave me a big smirk as he passed by and slapped my behind. Don't worry it was a slap like a coach gives his players. That week passed slowly and uneventful for me. The only thing anyone ever asked was when I was going back over to Cindy's house. I told them next weekend if I was fortunate.

I walked into my living room on Friday afternoon just in time to hear the phone ring. I picked up the receiver and said "hello".

I heard Cindy crying as she said "I never want to see you again" and then the phone went dead as she hung up in my ear. I tried calling back, but a busy signal was all I got repeatedly. I had to find out what just happened. I was going to Fort Jones tomorrow for sure now. I was going to get to the bottom of this one way or another.

CHAPTER FIVE

I got dressed that Saturday faster than a bullet fired out of a rifle pointed down hill. I grabbed a fast breakfast of toast and a bowl of cereal. I had decided to take the Greyhound bus, so I was counting my money to see if I had enough for a round trip ticket. I was glad to find that I indeed did have seven-fifty for the fare. I lived only a few short blocks from the bus station. I said good-bye to everyone and departed for the station.

The sun was shinning and the sky was a bright blue that Saturday morning. I arrived at the counter and purchased my ticket shortly after leaving my house. I stepped onto the bus and sat down directly behind the driver next to the window. I remember my feelings of anxiety as the bus pulled away and rolled towards Fort Jones. The trip took an hour and a half due to all the stops along the way. When I stepped off the stairwell I still had approximately six miles to go to reach Cindy's.

I started walking with great anticipation, feeling confident that once I talked to Cindy face to face everything would work itself out to perfection. I had not gone more than a mile when an elderly man stopped and picked me up. He just nodded and I got to know him very little in the short time I road with him to the corner store next to Cindy's.

I started walking down the road to Cindy's. As I grew nearer to the house I could see Jimmy and Thomas playing in the yard. I turned into the driveway as they both began yelling that I was there and then disappeared into the house. I walked up to the door and raised my hand to knock when the door swung open. Arlene grabbed my hand and pulled me inside while laughing at the top of her lungs.

Cindy however just looked at me. Her eyes were red as if she had been crying all day. I approached her slowly in hopes of discovering what was wrong, before I could get to her side she ran down the hall and into her bedroom. I glanced around the living room to find that every eye was trained on me. I did feel better when Cindy's mother smiled and nodded her head towards Cindy's room. I walked to the bedroom and knocked as I entered the room.

She was lying across her bed crying as I sat down beside her. It hurt me to see her in such pain. I took her shoulders and pulled her up into a sitting position. I brushed the hair out of her eyes and as I looked deep into them I gently kissed her. She buried her face in my chest and began to cry more freely. I let her cry a few seconds before I lifted her head.

I softly began to inquire what was wrong. "I care about you so much Cindy. You mean the world to me. Please tell me what is wrong so that we can work through it. I can't think of anything that we can't work out together". There was a long pause before she said a word. I did not want to rush her so I gave her all the time she wanted.

She looked at me and began "there is a girl at school that say's she dated you last year. She said that she knows three other girls you've dated. They all say the same thing. The only reason your with me is to just get what you can and then your gone. I told them that that wasn't true; but she says that you're a real talker. In fact she said you're smooth as silk and that I would find out soon enough. I don't want to be a notch on your bedpost or your plaything. I love you but I won't be used. I deserve to be treated like a lady and with respect. So you tell me if you understand what I am saying to you? If you don't love me then go home now and never talk to me again".

I was stunned to hear such an unbelievable list of misrepresented facts as well as out and out stories. I took a deep breath and gazed into her eyes. "I can not say that I am in love with you. I do love you; but I am sure that it is not in the way you translate the word love. You mean more to me than anything else in the world. I would never do or say anything that would hurt you in a million years. When I am away from you it tears me apart. I miss you so that it hurts more than I can put into words. What you have to offer a man is a dream come true. A man would kill or go to earn your love. I am fortunate to have you love me. I can't believe that you could think that I would do anything that would jeopardize your love.

I have had other girlfriends before you, that's true, but only from my high school. So unless one has moved to your school district, I don't know who the girl is telling you all this crap about me. You will have to believe me when I tell you that I am not seeing you just for sexual reasons. You are beautiful, intelligent and a great judge of character. I am asking you to have faith in me and trust your own heart that fell in love with me. I do not think that that is too much to ask of you".

She looked at me and said, "I believe you, if you say it's not true then I will trust you. However, I must know if you know a girl by the name of Mary Ann Turner? She's the one who told me about you and said all those nasty things".

"Mary Turner! Oh yea, I remember her very well. She's a girl that back in the seventh grade wouldn't leave me alone. I had just started my first rock and roll band and she was like a groupie. The band played at after school game dances and homecoming. She would come to every dance we played. I felt she wanted me to be her boyfriend because she kept throwing herself at me continuously. I told her I was flattered, but I had a girlfriend already. She never accepted that and continued to follow the band to every dance for two years. I heard she moved away and I haven't heard a thing about her till now. I tell you she was a real loon. She was so far out there that it scared everyone in the band. I can't imagine the stuff she would say about me to you so she could get even with me. You have got to believe me when I say that she needs professional help. Next time you hear things about me, come and ask me about it before you stress out and cause yourself pain. I won't lie to you. I am not perfect. If something comes up that isn't so good, I will tell you about it or explain it to you. Now, is there anything else that I can do to assure you that you are the only one for me?"

Cindy shook her head no and I gently kissed her in such away that I have never kissed anyone since. I remember to this day that the feeling I had at that moment was one of total consumption. I was mad when Arlene burst through the door exclaiming at the top of her lungs that Rick was here. I was also at the same time grateful.

Arlene opened the front door and there stood a tall boy with the look of a jock-type. I recognized him almost immediately as he glanced right at me. I've been playing Church league basketball for four years and that's where I knew him from. Rick was the point guard for the Lutheran Tigers and I was the power forward for the Baptist Eagles.

The church league had finished its season two weeks before my knee surgery and I had won the scoring title. Rick had finished second and that had not set well with him. I averaged 33.8 points a game and he had averaged 33.2 a game.

Now, I would like to say to the lady readers out there. I can't explain the mood or tension at that moment. I know you hate hearing this, but it's a guy thing. Rick and I had had many wars on the court, nothing bad or dirty. I respected his ability as a basketball player and I believe he felt the same about me.

We did in the course of the year set some hard picks and hard fouls. A few that maybe considered flagrant by some, but not to Rick or I. We both loved the game and played it hard. Don't misunderstand me. We were not by any means friends or even friendly to one another. I guess you might say we appreciated the competitive animal that lived deep inside each of us. One could say in conclusion that the atmosphere was like two warriors or gladiators, before the confrontation in the arena begins.

"This is Cindy's boyfriend Larry" Arlene said as she walked over to my side. Rick reached out his hand and I shook it firmly with a small smirk on my face.

"We know each other well," I said. He nodded and confirmed that yes indeed we did. He went off with Arlene while Cindy and I did our own thing together.

When late afternoon arrived I decided I better get going towards home. Rick said he had to leave. He volunteered to give me a ride to the bus stop in Medford. We kissed our girlfriends good-by and Rick slowly backed his car out of the driveway.

Rick and I got along surprisingly well. We talked about certain plays that we had been involved in during the season. I got an entirely different opinion of Rick that day. I could tell he wanted to beat me next season, bad. No matter how many times I congratulated him on his season. I knew that in the back of his mind as well as mind was the fact that I won the scoring title, as well as my team winning the championship. When we reached the bus stop he stopped the car and I thanked him for the lift to Medford as I exited. Rick yelled at me as I walked away "next year, brother."

I shook my finger at him and said, "next year, you're on."

CHAPTER SIX

My day started off with a bang, literally. My father pounded on the wall of the hallway to my bedroom. "Pick up the phone" he screamed. I came running down the stairs and walked over and picked up the receiver.

"Hello, who is it?"

"It's me honey, guess what?" I couldn't believe that it was Cindy. Before I could answer she blurted out "I'm moving to Hallandale to live with my Aunt. I didn't say anything yesterday because I thought we were going to break-up. Then, I didn't want to get your hope's up if it didn't happen. I've been pressuring my parents for a month now. My Aunt is not in the best of health and she needs someone to help her out around the house. My dad was looking into hiring a live in nurse; but that turned out to be too much money. Dad said I could go and take care of Aunt Lois. I will be there later tonight. She lives two blocks from the state collage. Don't you live close to the collage? What do you say? Isn't that great?"

"That's unbelievable; I can't wait to see you over here. This is a dream come true for us. I live five blocks from the collage. I still can't believe it".

"It's true, but I have to go. I'll call you tomorrow night. Bye honey."

That afternoon my best friend Troy and his girlfriend Alice drove up in front of my house. I went out to the front yard and met them. Troy wanted to know if I wanted to go to the lake next Monday since there was no school due to a teacher's seminar. I told him that was fine and about Cindy moving to Hallandale. They both agreed that that was great. Troy and I also discussed the fact that the band hadn't practiced in a while and we needed to get back to work. That was in all honesty something that did need to be addressed. I told Troy to get the rest of the band together and we would talk at the lake Monday.

I should at this time introduce to you the band members and tell you a little about them. Troy Shaw was one of the finest lead guitars I had ever played in a band with. Rudy Sinclair was a great funk style, bass player. He could lay down a boogie beat that made it impossible for you not to dance.

Sticks, born Herman Tales, The bands drummer, was without a doubt just great. You can see why he went by Sticks, after all wouldn't you? He played a double bass drum set of Pearls. I never get tired of his solos. He is no less than amazing. Scott Reams the keyboard man. He can play classical, blues, country, rock or anything anyone can throw at him. Last but not least, myself. I play rhythm guitar and I am the lead singer. I also write all the band's original music.

Everyone in this band can sing good enough to be the lead singer. I got the privilege because I was the only tenor. However, we are the only band around that have four and five part harmonies. Our band's name is (Autumn Root) and we also have the best equipment of any band for hundreds of miles.

For everyone who are into amplifiers and the like. We had twenty-four Fender Dual Showman cabinets. Everyone except Sticks had four cabinets and two amp heads. Troy and Scott had Dual Showman heads. Rudy and I played through Baseman amp heads. The PA system had eight cabinets, four on each side of the stage. An eight hundred-watt Bose PA head connected in line with an eight-hundred-watt slave powering them. Everything was fed through a twenty-four channel mixing board. We used Shure d-56 microphones. We all had our own hundred-channel processor for every sound effort you could ask for. Each of the twenty-four cabinets had special d-140 fifteen-inch Altec Lansing speakers.

Finally, Troy played a Gretsch Country Gentleman guitar. Rudy played a Fender Jazz Master and I played a Gibson L-5 Byrdland. Scott had three keyboards mounted on a triple stack stand. One keyboard was a Yamaha. The others were a korg and Vox. We had a small light system, but that isn't worth taking up your time with. Now you know the band and you will be traveling with them shortly.

Sunday passed slowly for me as I waited to hear from Cindy. Finally she called late that evening and we both were esthetic. I told her about the party at the lake and she couldn't wait to meet my friends or see me.

I had a hard time sleeping that night anticipating the next day. Cindy had given me her phone number and address during our conversation Sunday. I was ready to go when Troy and Alice pulled up in front of my house at noon. I jumped in and we pulled away. I instructed Troy to drive to Mountain Street and go up the hill westbound. Cindy's house was about three blocks up on the left. She immediately came running out towards the car. I got out and ran to her. When we met I picked her up and swung her around and around. I put her down and kissed her and then led her over to the car and introduced her to Troy and Alice. We got in the back seat and Troy drove away headed for Lake Elderberry, eight miles East of Hallandale.

The most popular swimming hole at the lake was the place we called the Quarry. It was the place where construction workers had dynamited tons of rock for fill in building the freeway a few years back. The quarry had hundred foot solid rock walls. There were many platforms that all he kids dove from. I only witnessed half a dozen people that dove from the top ledge. The favorite heights were the twenty to forty foot ones.

I could see that everyone had already beaten us there when we drove up. Scott, Rudy and Sticks came up to the car and began pulling us out by our arms. Rudy and Sticks did not have girlfriends but Scott had brought his girlfriend Amanda.

I looked at the wide variety of personalities that stood there in front of me. Alice was the quiet type, almost to the point of being reclusive. I liked her very much because she kept a low profile and she allowed Troy to be Troy. She also kept his feet on the ground and kept him centered.

Amanda on the other hand was your average run of the mill bar fly type. By the time she was seventeen she had been with over thirty guys. She fit Scott perfectly. Both of them drank heavily and did drugs on regular bases. If Scott wasn't such a fantastic Keyboard player I really do not believe the band would tolerate his actions. However it was understood that if he showed up at practice or a gig loaded or stoned, he would be fired from the band. No one else in the band drank or did any type of drugs. We didn't harp on Scott or even talk about his personal habits. He knew when, who and where to do certain behaviors with and he knew where not to do them.

Everyone made their way down to a rocky platform that they were comfortable with, height wise. Before I had taken Cindy down to a ledge that was approximately ten feet above the water line I gave her a big kiss. We had stood at the top and looked down into the quarry. The water was crystal clear on this day and I had no problem showing her the hidden dangers of the quarry.

There are big rocks just beneath the surface at several locations around the rim. Every year at least one and sometimes two people come here and the water is muddy. They dive in and hit the rocks underwater. Last year two tourists broke their necks diving off the quarry walls.

Cindy felt safe because she had seen with her own eyes that the spot I had taken her to dive was free of any rocks. We took each other by the hand

and jumped while Cindy screamed the whole way down to the water. The whole gang spent the day playing water polo and roasting hot dogs.

I sure can appreciate now, being able to go swimming in ice water. If I tried to do that today I would have a heart attack or stroke. By the time the sun began to go down it was getting cold enough to put on heavy clothing. The guys went out and gathered up some firewood and started a large bonfire. We were all standing around getting warm when out of nowhere Paula Thomson walks up to the fire.

Paula was my girlfriend up to the time I met Cindy. We were having trouble before my knee surgery and we had really broken up a couple of days before I entered the hospital. She was dressed in a pair of cut-offs and a tube top. She looked right at me an asked "aren't you going to introduce me to your little friend Larry"?

I could see what Paula was up to. I had to somehow take control of this situation. When all else fails tell the truth. "Cindy this is Paula. She is the girl I was dating before I met you." I said. I put my arm around Cindy and glared back at Paula. She gave me a look that could kill, but then smiled.

She pulled her top down exposing her breast. She cupped them in her hand and jiggled them up and down. Your loss you son-of-a-bitch and stormed off up the path to the parking area. Rudy chased after Paula, for what I didn't understand. Paula wasn't as wild as Amanda, but I could see that she was now well on her way to giving her some competition.

Cindy had a complex look on her face and before she could say anything I started. "She was nothing like that before. Honestly, she has completely changed into a different creature. I didn't sleep with her or anything else, I swear. I can't believe what I just witnessed was the same person I once dated. It's getting late so let's get going guys. Starting Wednesday night we get back to band practice. I'm talking long hours and hard work. See you at practice at Scott's at five on Wednesday," I saw Cindy home and told her I would talk to her later. I felt great when I got home and went upstairs to lie down on my bed for a great night's sleep.

CHAPTER SEVEN

I got up the next morning and headed off to school never realizing that my life was about to change in away that was beyond believe. I had an uneventful day when at three-o-clock as I walked across the parking lot and a police car pulled up and stopped. Two officers got out and approached me slowly.

"Your Larry Hayden aren't you?" said one of the policemen. I shook my head in an affirmative motion. "I'm Officer Watkins and this is my partner officer Bentley. We need you to come with us down to the station and answer a few questions". My first instinct was to take off running as they reached out to grab me. I demanded to know what this was about. I got no response except having my arms forced behind my back and having handcuffs applied to my wrists.

I kept asking, OK yelling, what the hell was going on as we drove to the police station? Shut up you creep was all the response I got till we arrived at the station. After being drug through the front door and pushed down into a chair a well-dressed man came and stood in front of me. "I'm Captain Brockview young man and I think you and I need to have a long talk. Do you know a lady by the name of Paula Thomson? Before you answer you should know that she's not happy with you right now. You see Miss Thomson and her mother Mrs. Polly Thomson paid me a tearful visit this morning. Seems Paula is twelve weeks pregnant and according to her, you are the father.

Mrs. Thomson has filed rape charges against you. Her daughter said you forced yourself on her and threatened to kill her if she told anyone. After seeing your record and your brothers' record I don't have a problem in believing it at all. Do you know Miss Thomson? If you do, do you want to say anything at this time?"

I started off in a low voice slowly that I could not believe what officer Brockview had said to me. I wasn't allowed to call my parents or have that famous phone call you always hear about on television. There was no reading of rights or anything. I decided to stay calm and say nothing once it was clear that they would not believe me for a second.

I sat there twirling my thumbs and humming loudly. It didn't take long before the interrogators became upset and angry with me. I was actually happy when I heard the Captain say to call my parents and then everyone left the room. I stood up and paced back and forth in the dimly lit room waiting for my father to come. I knew that when he got there all hell was going to really break lose.

I wasn't wrong; my dad flung the door open and literally ran over to me and knocked me to the floor with a good right cross. The old man was good at being the tough guy and being greater than thou. "You've done it this time. You get your crap and get out of my house. I don't want a damn thing to do with you ever again. I hope they lock your sorry ass up twenty years you loser," he screamed.

The old man was a real piece of work. He had good points and some bad ones that were way over the top. I give credit were credit is due. Albert Hayden was an ex-alcoholic and hadn't had a drink in fifteen years. I give him a salute for that will power and commitment. He was a reformed bar room brawler and bully for the most part.

He was without a debut the perfect example of do as I say and not as I do. Dad preached a good line about how we the children should act, but he did the complete opposite. Yea, dad talked about being a man and being trustworthy, yet he had affairs on my mother. He never missed the opportunity to give us kids a beating. I said beating instead of spanking because that was what we got.

Yet on the other hand the old man taught us kids' responsibility and pride. He showed us hard work had its own virtue. My father taught me to hunt fish and work with wood. Dad was a master wood carver and craftsmen. Thanks to him I can run any power tool and shop saw there is on the market. He showed me how to stain woods and make beautiful furniture by the time I was fourteen.

Albert Hayden never once in his life omitted that he was wrong about anything. He was always right no matter what was said or done. It was hard to live with a man that was perfect in his own eyes, while you were nothing in his. He made it perfectly clear that my brother Ted was his favorite and that I would never amount to anything.

Dad jerked me off the floor and shoved me through the door. I stumbled towards officer Brockview and would have fallen to the floor again if he hadn't caught me. I was still drogue from dad's slug to my face. The room was spinning, but I managed to stay alert enough to see dad sign papers. I remember getting into the family truck, but I don't recall any substance of the screaming dad did on the way home.

Next day I was shocked to see the headline in our local paper. LOCAL YOUTH ARRESTED FOR RAPE. Thank God the paper didn't give out my name or Paula's. I felt sorry for my mother because she was so ashamed and embarrassed. I had never had something like this happen to me and was honestly frightened at the prospect of going to jail. I knew I hadn't done anything with Paula. I also knew that a blood test would prove that I wasn't the father.

By late afternoon I was feeling relaxed about the fact that there was no way anyone could prove that I was the father of Paula's child. I was startled by a loud firm knock at the front door. I opened the door to find a well-dressed man holding a packet of papers. "You Larry Hayden" He asked? I gave him an affirmative nod of my head.

He stated that his name was Mr. Talbert. He handed be several pieces of papers and told me that Paula had had a miscarriage during the night. The paternity suit was dismissed. However, I was still being charged with rape. I over heard him say good luck kid as he walked away down the sidewalk to his car.

My heart and jaw hit the floor at the same time. I didn't like my situation now at all. How can anyone prove they didn't have sex with someone unless that woman was a virgin and Paula was certainly not that? My outlook on the future was growing dimmer by the minute as I stood there contemplating the days to come.

My train of thought was broken by the sound of squealing tires. I looked out the front room window to see Troy and Alice parked at the curb and the sound of a blowing horn. I went outside and got into the back seat and we sat there silent for a minute or two.

I final broke the tension and told them that they had to believe me when I say that I did not rape Paula. I continued by saying that I had only felt her breast on one date. I could tell that they believed me as they looked and listened intently. I asked Troy to take me to Cindy's house so that I could tell her in person. I sat back and took a deep breath as we rolled away from the curbside.

Cindy came running out of her house with newspaper in hand crying and screaming "please don't tell me, this is you, Please don't tell me that". I met her somewhere in the middle of the front yard. I held her tightly as she continued to cry uncontrollably.

"I swear to you Cindy that I am not guilty of any of this. Paula is a bitch and she's pissed off at me," I explained.

As coincidence would have it Mr. Talbert drove up and stopped. He approached Troy and Alice and handed them subpoenas. He also walked over to Cindy and gave her one also. We glanced over the documents and noticed that the court date was March fifteenth at ten AM.

I realized that I had a short time to get a lawyer and prepare my case adequately. James Caldwell was a personal friend of the family and had represented my dad a year or so ago in an overtime discrepancy case. I don't think that I can call him the family attorney, but he was the only one I knew of.

I told Cindy everything would be all right as we departed. I had Troy drive me to James Caldwell's office. I got out of the back seat and told Troy I would see him at band practice later at five.

I entered the office of Mr. Caldwell and approached the front desk. There sat a beautiful lady who was intensely engulfed in typing a document. I read the nameplate on her desk, Mary Sullivan. She looked up and ceased her typing. "May I help you sir?"

"I need to speak to Mr. Caldwell".

She pushed the button on the intercom and announced me. She pointed down the hall and said, "Last door at the end of the hall". I stopped long enough to knock on the doors and hear the words come in. I took a deep breath and pushed open the double doors and entered.

Mr. Caldwell sat behind a huge oak desk in a black leather chair. He was a little man in stature and approximately eighty pounds overweight. He was a man in his fifties with gray hair, which was balding severely. I noticed yellow stained fingers from what appeared to be the results of smoking for years. He was dressed immaculately and actually had a pleasant disposition about him. I can't explain it but I liked him right off. I sat down and told him that I was the youth that the paper's headlines were talking about. I reminded him about my father's case and that did jog his memory. He asked me several questions and after an hour of discussion he agreed to represent me. He called my parents and got their approval to represent me and finalize his fee.

He informed me that he would be calling my friends in one at a time over the next few days to question them. I told him to do what ever he had to do. I stood and shook Mr. Caldwell's hand. He walked me to the front door and told me that everything was going to be OK. I left his office feeling better than when I had entered; but not completely as optimistic as he had displayed.

CHAPTER EIGHT

While walking home from my lawyer's office I kept trying to imagine why Paula would do something like this to me. We had never had a real torrid love affair or deep felt relationship. I wanted to talk to Paula badly, but Mr. Caldwell had instructed me clearly to stay far away from her and her house. I just knew that if I could be alone with her for an hour I could fix all this.

Once I got home I ate a late lunch and reflected on what the day had offered so far. I truly needed a diversion and was happy to get on my ten speed bike and start peddling to Troy's for band practice. The fact that I had ditched school for the day finally hit me.

I was huffing and a puffing when I dismounted my bike at Troy's. His garage door was open and I could see all of our amps stacked up. A calm came over me once I saw our musical equipment set up. I turned my amp and the PA system on and strummed my guitar. Everyone took their places and we began playing our favorite warm up song, (Feel a Whole Lot Better) by the Byrd's.

It took only a couple of verses for me to forget my problems. I was totally engulfed in the world of music; it always took control of me. We practiced till our ten o'clock curfew that had been placed on us by Troy's parent's years ago.

Thank God we had a place to play all these years. Mr. and Mrs. Shaw had always been supportive of their son's music. They loved our rehearsals and just having the band there. Mrs. Shaw fed us and encouraged us on a daily bases. She was our second mom and we were like her kid's. We as a band had a few rules, which were no smoking, no alcohol, no drugs and lastly no making out with our girlfriends. It was fine bringing girls to practice, just no necking. I can tell you over the years and with all the different band members that come and go in a band. There was never once a violation of the rules. That should tell you how much respect we had for the Shaw's.

Ironic that Scott was the only band member that did drugs, smoked and drank alcohol; but even he kept that part of his life away from home. He loved his parents and knew how special they were. He was petrified that they might find out about his secret lifestyle. He told me on many occasions how much he wanted to stop, but couldn't. I can tell you that he sincerely did not want to hurt his parents. Scott said that he was trying to stop, but I saw little headway. I think he meant what he said, but didn't know how to get started. I was glad to see a little improvement at a time rather than no improvement at all.

The next few weeks passed by slowly yet full of interesting events. Having meetings with Mr. Caldwell and my friends giving depositions and being interviewed by the police had its toll on me. It didn't take long for every person in Hallandale to figure out who was who in the newspaper stories.

I can tell you that seeing headlines in your local newspaper about yourself is not an enjoyable experience. That is when the text is branding you as a criminal. Schoolmates and the general public glared at my friend's and me with a consent ongoing day to day judging. Even my teachers treated me differently than before.

My house had been egged and Tee-Peed several times and my father's car had obscenities spray painted on it. The closer March fifteenth came the more the town was split into two diametrically opposed sides. Believe it or not I was begging for court to start. I wanted to get this started and get it over with.

I got my wish faster than I had anticipated, as the time seemed to accelerate to the speed of sound. I recall waking up on the morning of March fifteenth, getting dressed and dad driving us to the courthouse. This was it, the time to tell my side of what seemed to be a one sided story against me. I longed to say my piece in open court and to put a different spin on this case, the truth.

PART TWO

I could feel the cold stares as I walked down the aisle and took my seat behind the defendant's desk. I couldn't help but to glance around and see the faces of the town's people, studying my every move. I saw no smiles, only deep and intense looks upon everyone's faces. I soon tilted my head to my left and for the first time, since the quarry, I saw Paula.

She and her attorney were seated at their desk and exchanging conversation. Her eyes lifted and we made eye contact. She had a hollow stare and yet still conveyed a hostile intention. She had cut her hair and toned down her makeup. She wore a conservative dress that completely covered her from head to toe. My mind immediately sized up the situation and I did not like my own conclusion. I was worried about not being acquitted. After all, nowadays it's not if you're guilty or not. It comes down to who has the best lawyer that money can buy.

The courtroom became quiet as the bailiff announced all stand for her honor Judge Sandra Black. I thought judges were supposed to be unbiased, but not by the look she gave me from entering the courtroom all the way to her bench and sat down. "Be seated" she said and then began to make a statement. She talked about not tolerating outburst or disturbances. It was not until she addressed the jury that I had even acknowledged their presence. I didn't know anyone in the jury box. With Hallandale being such a small town I can only imagine the selecting process that took place.

I listened as Paula's attorney, Mr. Travis Darwin, give his opening remarks. They were impressive compared to Mr. Caldwell's. Mr. Darwin was a well-dressed man; tall, thin and would fit in that category of a ladies man. I told you about Mr. Caldwell earlier, remember? I didn't want to be here anymore or endure this event in the least.

Upon his conclusion, Mr. Darwin called Paula Thomson right out of the box. It was obvious that he was planning to capitalize on the media and citizenry emotions. Paula rose slowly and approached the witness box. She took the oath and sat down with a huge sigh.

Once seated, Mr. Darwin began his questioning, simple ones to start. Like what was her name and where she lived, etc. I half heatedly listened until she was asked about me and to explain what I had done to her. The following is in essence her story as best as I can relay it to you to the best of my recollection of it. I will be as unbiased as I can. Paula began her story.

I saw Larry walking through the halls at Hallandale High School for the first time about a year and a half ago. I admit that I was immediately attracted to him. I went to an after school dance a few days later and was surprised to see him on stage with the band. I did not know that he was in a band. I remember the first song I heard him sing. Three times a lady, I feel in love with him right then and there as he sang that love ballad.

I asked around school about him and found out that he wasn't dating anyone. I tried to time my walks in the hall so that I could run into him. I wanted to meet him so badly that I thought I would just die if I didn't. Then one day at a pep rally I was shocked to find myself sitting next to him. I told him that I had been at the dance and heard the band and that they were great. I was flattering him and it must have worked because he invited me to a band practice.

I almost died when he asked for my phone number and said he would pick me up next Friday after school for band practice. I began going to all the bands rehearsals and Larry and I grew closer and closer. We were what you might say an item. I was his girlfriend; you can ask anyone. We went to movies and out to dinner. We hung out at the park and the lake. Everything was fantastic until that night, the night that he raped me. We had been going together for almost a year when it happened.

We were alone at my house one evening and we started kissing. Well, one thing led to another and before I knew it Larry was trying to pull my clothes off. I yelled at him to stop and asked him what he thought he was doing. I had never seen him that way before. He wouldn't take no for an answer. I started crying and fighting him off but he was too strong. He tore my top off and my jeans to.

I tried your honor to make him quit, but I couldn't. He hurt me and I'm so ashamed because of what he has done to me. Then he dumped me for some girl from Fort Jones. When I told my mother that I was pregnant she was furious. She forced me to go down to the police station and she filed rape charges since I am only seventeen.

I was so traumatized that I had a miscarriage. I spent several hours in the hospital that night and now MY BABYS DEAD. I didn't want to be raped; but I didn't want my baby to die. Why Larry? Why? She screamed as she sobbed uncontrollably.

I must admit that Paula had the courtroom in tears and had successfully painted me out as Satan on Earth. I just wished that the jury and the courtroom could have seen the little smile Paula gave me as she left the witness stand.

I was feeling defeated and needed that voice of hopefulness that my attorney gave me when he said "Don't worry Larry we have a killer ace in the hole." Mr. Caldwell stood and said he had no questions at this time but reserved the right to question at a later time. The judge accepted that and because Paula's testimony had taken so long we adjourned for the day.

I left my table to the looks of hate and disgust. Somebody even spat on me and others called me dirty names. Only my attorney gave me support. He once again told me that he had a few tricks up his sleeve and that I would indeed be acquitted.

The next day the trial was much more subdued. Mr. Darwin called doctors to give testimony about Paula's mental state. They explained in detail about the miscarriage and how stress had contributed to it. He called all my friends to show that Paula and I had indeed dated and in fact did do all the social things she had said we did. That of course showed that she was honest and was telling the truth about everything.

By the end of the day Mr. Darwin had concluded his case. He actually said "your honor the prosecution rests."

My mother, who was sitting right behind me leaned over and touched my shoulder. "Now it's your turn to tell it like it really was son," she said.

I still had no clue to what my attorney had up his sleeve as he called me to the stand the opening of the next day's trial. He asked me the basic questions and then asked me to tell in my own words my relationship with

Paula. I told the same story as Paula had. I liked her from the start and that we were boy and girlfriend. We had dated for almost a year and then she changed into a totally different person for no apparent reason. No matter how hard I tried to inquire into her personality change she would not talk to me about it. Because of this change in her, was why I broke up with her.

I told the courtroom that I never had sex of any kind with Paula Thomson. I was the one who is a victim here, not her. I didn't understand why they would take her word over mine. I said nothing happened and asked the jury to believe me. I told the jury that they had my future in their hands and I couldn't believe that they would send me to jail when there is no prove other than he said, she said.

Not one juror had the slightest change in facial expression. I felt like I was talking to a brick wall. One person in the courtroom was applying makeup. Some were reading a book and a couple of men were sleeping.

Mr. Caldwell had already asked my friends about my character when he examined them on cross. There wasn't much left for me to say. I stepped down and returned to my designated area. The courtroom came alive when my attorney loudly announced that he calls Miss Paula Thomson to the stand. James looked at me and said "I told you that we would win this case didn't I. I know I don't look like much to you or anyone else. However Larry, sit back and watch your old, fat attorney destroy this lying bitch for once and for all.

Miss Thomson, I would like to give you at this time the opportunity to change your testimony. I would also like to have the judge, explain to you, this states penalty for perjury. I am telling you that if you continue to hold to your story, I will personally see that perjury charges are brought up against you. Your honor, please tell Miss Thomson this states consequences of perjury."

The courtroom was silent as Judge Black informed Paula of the potential jail terms for perjury. She continued to tell her that she had a moral obligation to tell the truth. When she had finished Mr. Caldwell thanked the Judge and then turned to Paula. "What is your decision Miss Thomson"? She looked at Mr. Darwin and then said that she had told the entire truth and that she would stand on her testimony. "I am sorry to hear that Paula. However, I did give you every opportunity to save yourself."

CHAPTER NINE

"Miss Thomson, with a warrant that I legally obtained from Judge Carter I was able to recover from the hospital, blood and skin samples from your miscarriage. One week ago I got the DNA results back from the state's forensics lab. Would you like to tell everyone what the results were? You know that Larry Hayden did not rape you and so do the doctors and I. I honestly do know who the father of your baby is and I will blurt it out myself if you yourself do not reveal the truth right this second".

"Stop it, stop it now. I made her say that it was Larry," screamed Mrs. Thomson. Paula buried her face and cried and the courtroom exploded into frenzy. Judge Black hammered her gavel calling for order.

The courtroom was still when the Judge said "Miss Thomson please stand. I want you to tell me who would have been the father of your baby if the child had lived. If you don't tell me I personally will see that you are prosecuted for perjury".

With her mother screaming in the background NO, NO, NO Paula looked at the bench and said "my father raped me and my mother blamed Larry in order to cover it up."

I felt sorry for her at that point. I really did feel a hurt for her. No matter what she had tried to do to me, I would have never wished something like this on her or anyone. The courtroom was a clamor of gasps and whispers. It was then that I heard the sweetest words up to that point in my life, case dismissed.

I took the hand of Mr. Caldwell and shook it as firmly as I could. "Why didn't you say something to me for Gods sake" I said to him.

He smiled and said "I needed you to be as frightened and worried as you could be. The jury had to see that look of sincerity and desperation."

I watched as Paula and her mother were led off to a side room. I saw the hurt in Paula's eyes as she left the room. I can not tell you why; but I forgave her right then and there on that day standing in the middle of the courtroom as she disappeared from my sight.

That was indeed a wonderful day in my life and yet a terrible one for others. I will never forget that time in my life and still think about it on occasion. I can tell you that there is but one feeling worse than being accused of a major crime that you did not commit. I discovered that feeling thirty years later and will tell you of that when this story gets to that point. Right now I am nineteen and about to get started on a great adventure.

Cindy broke up with me that evening and I have never seen her again to this day. The next two and a half months went by uneventfully in comparison to the earlier three months before. Graduation was great fun and so was the party afterwards. I had taken Lisa Palmer to the senior prom and she was my date at the graduation dance. The night was something that I will always remember. That night was the night that we the band members decided to move to San Francisco.

Troy, Rudy, Scott and I wanted to go to the city and give music an all out career move, Sticks wasn't at the dance that night. He had been dating Paula ever sense the trail ended. Amazingly enough it never once caused any hard feeling or tension among any of us in the band, including myself. I didn't know if he would want to move or not to San Francisco. However, if he didn't the band was moving with or without him. Lisa was a friend and not a girlfriend. The only real relationship was Scott and Amanda. Perhaps Herman and Paula, but I didn't know for sure at that point.

I had gotten a used car a month before the prom so I was driving that night. It felt good to be on my own instead of riding with Scott. I escorted Lisa home and thanked her for being a friend during a hard time in my life. Like Cindy, I never saw Lisa again, after that night.

The band had practice the next day and that was when we told Sticks of our intentions. He immediately wanted in on the move. He did say that Paula would be coming with him. He said that they would find their own apartment. That was also the same for Scott and Amanda. It turned out that Sticks and Paula were contemplating moving and wished that they could talk the band in relocating also.

We came up with the plan that I would go down first and find a house for Rudy, Troy and myself to live in. Then Scott and Sticks would come down and find separate apartments close to where the house was located. We, the band that is, had been practicing long and hard for three months. We had a tight sound and were ready for any bookings that would present themselves to us.

Two weeks had passed when I loaded up my car and hugged my mother good bye. I remember that Saturday, filling up the gas tank in my 1959 Ford Fairlane 500 and then five minutes later I was on interstate five southbound.

My trip of three hundred and seventy five miles was uneventful except for a guy I picked up around Hilt California. The only reason that I mention him is because he opened my eyes as to what to expect in San Francisco. His name was Buzz High or so he said. He talked all the time I was driving.

He told me about what was cool and what nerdy was. He outlined what I could expect and what I would experience. I enjoyed his input and as I would find out later, he was right on the money in his predictions. I dropped him off in Berkley and watched as he disappeared into a wooded area of a park. I continued on down the road to San Francisco.

I found a pizza parlor and ordered a pepperoni and then checked into a motel across the street. I turned on the television and settled back for a well-deserved relaxing night. I had bought a newspaper while in the lobby of the motel. I opened it and began circling houses for rent that were in the right price range. I had a city map, so I spent the night mapping out the next day's itinerary.

I awoke full of anticipation and enthusiasm that following morning. I headed out with map, paper and a desire to find a house that morning. I had viewed four homes when I saw a for rent sign in front of a house that caught my eye as I drove by.

It must have been fate because the realtor was there showing it to an older couple. I walked up and introduced myself as soon as the couple drove away. The realtor said his name was Ted Wilcox and that he was handling the property. He told me that the house was a three bedroom, two and a half bath. The view of the city and the bay was fantastic. However, I will confess that I nearly died when he quoted me the monthly rent. I had to make a decision fast. Even though it was four hundred dollars more than what was decided on, by all concerned, I took it upon my shoulders and rented it. I thought that one hundred and thirty three dollars more to everyone would be fine once they saw the house.

I signed the papers and paid the deposits as well as the first and last months rent. The rent was nine hundred and fifty dollars. The security deposit was five hundred dollars. I wrote out a check for two thousand and four hundred dollars. I had gotten two hundred and fifty dollars from Rudy and Troy before I had left home. I just hope that they had more money when I told them they still owed five hundred and fifty dollars each.

I spent the rest of the day in a phone booth calling to have water, trash, phone, electricity and cable turned on. I agreed to pay the utilities deposits so that there wouldn't be mass confusion. Once I had completed my calls I went and got lunch. I then called Troy and gave him the address and told him to call everyone and come on down. I drove back to the house at 10587 Skyline Manor. I stood in the living room and looked out at the lights along the bay and the skyline of the city.

I slept uninterrupted for eleven hours until the sun shinning in my face caused me to wake up. It was two thirty in the afternoon and one look in the mirror told me the sun had been out for a long time. One side of my face was sunburned to a crisp while the other side was as white as a new dress shirt.

I started unpacking my car and setting up house. I was just finishing up when the doorbell rang. I was surprised to see the cable man standing there with toolbox in hand. "Hello, I'm Greg from the Cable Company and I am here to install your cable".

"Great", I said and showed him were I was going to put the television. We chatted as he went about his job installing the service. When he found out that I was in a band and that I was looking for clubs to play he gave me a list of popular rock clubs. I wrote down their names and brief descriptions of where they were located. Greg was a cool guy and I told him that I might see him again at one of the clubs he had told me about in the future. When Greg left I noticed that it was ten till five so I locked up and drove down to Target to buy a new TV.

Once purchasing a new Magnavox 27-inch television I hurried home and connected the cables and turned it on. The picture was perfectly clear and the color was excellent. I had gotten the Platinum package, which included all the pay channels. I watched three movies before I fell asleep. Yes, life was sweet or so it would appear to a nineteen-year-old.

I awoke next day to the continual ringing of the doorbell. I walk over to the door in a half conscious manner and through it open. There stood Rudy and Troy with a look of astonishment across their faces. I allowed them to carry on about how fantastic the house was and what a view etc. Finally I had to step in and tell them the rent was four hundred dollars more that we had agreed on and that they still owed five hundred and fifty dollars more. I explained that that was first and last plus deposits.

I showed them the TV I had bought and told them that I had paid out three hundred dollars for the utilities and that that was my responsibility. They were upset in the beginning, but when I told them what houses looked like in our original price range they understood. We all shook hands and agreed to stay at the house. After all, for only one hundred and thirty three dollars more a piece we could live in luxury instead of a dump.

Later that evening Scott and Amanda arrived. Then around midnight Sticks and Paula showed up at the door. As I looked around the room I was saddened by the fact that Troy had broken up with Alice earlier. I had always liked Alice and thought she was the one for Troy. However—relationships come and go as we proceed in life.

It took about two weeks for Scoot and Herman to find their own places. While they had been looking, we had turned the two-car garage at Skyline Manor into the bands rehearsal studio. Once Troy and Amanda moved out and Sticks and Paula were gone. It was time to get down to business and get a job playing.

I can not tell you how it came to be that I was the spokes person for the band. That was something that had just evolved over time. I will tell you that once and only once did I really abuse that position. That was when I went into a club and played a demo tape for the owner, Jay Miller and he wanted us to play that Friday night for scale.

He wanted to see how the crowd would react and promised that if we were well received that he would make us the house band six nights a week for an undetermined amount of time, but that it would be a minimum of six weeks. He asked me the name of the band for the flyers.

We had forgotten to come up with a new name. We had decided to get a new name, because no one liked our old name. I had a name that I loved and so I said JUST SLIGHTLY RICHER. I thought that was appropriate since we had four and five part harmonies and were tight. We had the best equipment and a good light show.

When I told everyone about the gig no body said anything about my selection of a name. They just shook their heads in approval and said cool. We were all fired up about the opportunity to get it on that weekend.

CHAPTER TEN

I looked out at the crowd from behind the curtain on stage and the club was packed to the rafters with a rowdy crowd. I suppose that was appropriate in lieu of the clubs name, Hells Alley. I recall taking a deep breath as I heard Jay, the clubs owner announce over the public address system, please welcome to Hells Alley, JUST SLIGHTLY RICHER.

There was a tremendous roar and applause as the curtains opened and we started playing our opening tune, Cream's, Sunshine Of Your Love. That night in retrospect turned out to be a major crossroads in all of our lives and the bands future. The band played at Hells Alley for six months as the house band six nights a week. The biggest surprise was that after six months in San Francisco both Scott and Sticks were still with Amanda and Paula respectively.

I had personally met a beautiful lady that first week we played at the club. Sarah Black was her name and she owned my heart from the start of day one of our relationship. Rudy had met a girl named Kitty. While Troy had also met a girl named Brandy.

I remember the first time I went over to Sarah's apartment and spent the night for the first time. It was in my opinion heaven on earth and I don't mean it in the way I know your thinking. Sure we made love that night; but more important was the fact that we talked and felt comfortable with one another. I have never felt so at ease with anyone in my life as I did with Sarah. We could actually read one another's thoughts and anticipate the others word's before they spoke them. Sarah made that first breakfast at her place special. I will always see it in my mind and smile in appreciation.

It took only about a month of playing at the club until there were three couples living at 10587 Skyline Manor. We had a lot of ground rules, but everyone, with open arms welcomed them. The girls even chipped in on the rent, even though we said no, they insisted.

We had been playing four months when a talent scout from Big Bang Records approached us during a break one night. He introduced himself as Roy Wilson head of new talent for Big Bang Records. He said that he had been dropping in a day or two for the last month and would like us to cut a demo record in his company's studio.

We said in total unison yes, yes, yes, talk about a no brainer. For the next three weeks Just Slightly Richer spent between eight and sixteen hours a Sunday in the recording studio. We recorded a song that I had written and an old song by the outsiders called Time Wont Let Me.

I can not explain to you the feeling one gets when you are in a studio for the first time. Seeing all the equipment and the attention everyone shows you. It is truly an ego rush and an exciting experience. I can understand how super stars get caught up in all the whoopla.

When we were finished with the demo we were exhausted. Everyone, including Mr. Wilson had a smile ear to ear as we listened to the finished product. I probably should not tell you this; but those sound technicians can and do make you sound ten times better than you really are. These technicians must have been some of the best because our recordings sounded fantastic.

Mr. Wilson told us that he was going to take the demo to Los Angeles so that his boss could hear it. The final decision would be up to the president on the record company. Roy took the demo and said he would be back in a week or two. He gave us a thumb up sign and winked. That was a stressful time of waiting that week. However, it was well worth it when we were signed to a record contract eight days after Roy had left for LA.

Roy told us that we were Booked as the opening act for THUNDERSTROM. They were a major rock band at the time with the number one record in the country. They were going on a four-month tour of Europe. Kicking the tour off in London, England and ending at Dublin, Ireland.

Something that had happened to me during that week I have never told anyone before now. While on a fifteen-minute break when playing one night at the club, I was approached by a representative of Chart Records, a rival record company.

Mr. Tree Rodgers was the manager of a world famous band. He had been watching our band play for weeks and had made a decision. He took out a contract that I read by the light from a lit candle on the table. To make a long story short, the lead singer of his band was being more of a problem than he was worth. The rhythm guitar player had quit and I was to replace the guitar player. I was to learn the material and the words to all their songs. The contract stated that ninety days after my signature the lead singer would be fired and I would then be inserted as the bands new lead singer.

Without even knowing what Big Bang was going to do I declined his offer. He offered me twice the money that was stated in the contract as an enticement to sign. I told him that I would never hang my friends out to dry. We were a team and as long as we were a band I would remain loyal to them. He told me I was making a big career mistake, but he rose and shook my hand, then left. I still wonder once in a while how things might have been if I had indeed signed that night. Oh Well, back to the now celebration.

We had one month before we were to leave on the tour. We gave Jay a month notice and the good news why. He was ecstatic for us and we knew that he really meant it from the heart. We would see Jay Miller many times in the coming years. He was then and still is to this very day one of my dear friends.

It was the middle of January and the fog was rolling in heavy. It was the first Sunday that we had off in a month, we fired up the barbecue. I am sure that our neighbors must have thought that we were crazy. Can you imagine seeing groups of people standing out in the drizzle and flipping burgers and dogs?

We had been living in our house for months and we had been almost invisible to the neighborhood. We never played to loud of music nor had parties that got out of hand. We got enough of that at the club and we all enjoyed the peace and quite of down time at home.

You also must remember that we played nights and slept days so it worked out perfect. I still see us soaking wet that night not giving a damn what we looked like. It is great to be young and not have a care in the world; sorry I did not enjoy it a hell of a lot more when I passed through my time line in the world of youthfulness.

I thought that my life was set at this point in time. I had a great girlfriend and a promising career in the music field ahead of me. I had good friends and I was living in San Francisco. The next three weeks would bring without a debut some of the most dramatic decisions I would or ever have had to make.

First, I went to the mailbox Monday morning and there I discovered a letter from the U S military. I will never forget the opening in that letter. You have been chosen by the President of the United States of America to serve in the armed forces of the United States of America.

The letter went on to instruct me to be in Medford, Oregon in thirty days in order to board a bus to Portland for my Army Physical. I immediately called the Army induction center in San Francisco. I wanted to take my physical there instead of Portland.

I was denied a transfer to San Francisco and was ordered to comply with the instructions in my induction letter. The big problem was that I was to be in Portland on the exact day that we were to leave on the tour. I had to call Roy and tell him about this new development.

I could hear Roy's heart sink to the bottom of his feet when I told him the news. "OH GOD" what the hell are we going to do Larry. He finally said, "Look Larry, The tour starts on a Saturday night in London. Everyone is flying out on Monday Morning. You do everything to fail your physical and then you can fly over in a day or two. You can still be there in plenty of time before the gig. I will get a local band in London as a back up just in case you can't make it."

I told Roy that if I had to go into the service could he get someone else to take my place. I did not want to be the reason for causing the band to lose out on a chance of a lifetime. I was disappointed in his answer. He told me that I was JUST SLIGHTLY RICHER and that it was my vocals that BIG BANG was pushing. He said that the band had a great sound, but so did hundreds of other bands. What made our sound complete were my vocal style and my songwriting abilities.

What he did not know was that the band was where I got my style and my inspiration. I took a deep breath when Roy hung up the phone. I now had to tell the band. I had no slick way of breaking the news so I walked into the living room and held the letter up and said, "I just got drafted."

Every cuss word known to man could be heard for the next few minutes. Naturally they asked about replacing me if I did get accepted. I did not go into detail, I just told them that I had asked Roy that and he had said no. I explain to everyone that they would still be flying to London and I would try to make it in a day or two. Needless to say, on that day somber set in and was to remain for weeks to come.

Sarah and I went off by ourselves so that we could talk. The rain was pouring down as we walked along the beach hand in hand. We watched as eight-foot waves broke across the rocky shoreline. Even though her face was wet with rainwater I could see tears flowing down her cheeks.

We had that night a conversation so private that only the two of us deserve to know its contents. I will tell you that I called Jay at the club and asked for the band to have a day off that Monday. He agreed to that request with no interpretation. Sarah and I that very afternoon flew out of San Francisco airport in Daily City.

We arrived in Boise, Idaho approximately three hours later. There we went to the County Court House on Monday morning. The only judge in that day was a traffic court Judge. I talked to his secretary and while he was handing out fines she went to his side and pointed to us standing in his chamber.

I swear to you. He adjourned court for a twenty-minute recess and entered his chamber. At ten-thirty in the morning on January 15th Judge Sam Renton married Sarah and me. His secretary, Mary Tile, was the signed witness on the marriage certificate.

We flew back to San Francisco that afternoon and arrived at six-thirty. My car was in short term parking right were I had left it. We drove down to Fisherman's Warf and checked into a fancy hotel next to the Grotto Restaurant. That night was the extent of our honeymoon until we had been together for many years. Then we had a real honeymoon. The next day we went back to Skyline Manor and told everyone the good news. They were shocked, yet at the same time overjoyed.

The band finished up at Hells Alley and got prepared for the tour. The day Sarah and I left to drive back to Oregon was a sad day indeed. We had no idea what the future was to bring. I kept it upbeat as much as possible. I hugged everyone good bye, including Paula. When I pulled out of the driveway I looked back and the site of the entire band standing there is still burned into my brain today.

Once Sarah and I got to my mother's house I now had to tell her that her son was married. I had called her and told her that we were coming. My mother knew about me going for my physical. It was obvious that she was caught total off guard when I told her I was married.

My mom did surprise me when see turned to Sarah and said welcome to our family. If my son married you, you must be a lovely person because he has great ability to find good people. For him to fall in love and marry you, you must be very special. We stayed at Moms that night and the next morning Sarah drove mom and me up to the bus station. With tears and hugs I boarded the bus and was on my way to Portland.

The next day I found myself standing in a long line of guys in their under shorts. The day lasted eight hours. I had been paraded from station to station all day. I had pissed in a cup and been blood sucked three times for lab work. I had a stress test along with eye, ear and x-rays.

I remember it was seven-thirty at night when I and a roomful of about a hundred and fifty young men were forced to raise our right hand and take an oath to serve in the protection of the United States of America. I was sad that I had passed my physical. With my bad knee and a doctor's letter to excuse me from service I really thought that I would be rejected. I knew that I was dead meat when the orthopedic doctor looked at my letter and x-ray and tossed them aside saying "You must be a spoiled little rich kid.

I see that your knee surgery was performed my Dr. Mackie, the great sports doctor. He does all the pro ball players knees and even movie stars. I don't know who the hell you are; but I couldn't give a damn what Mackie says. I'm God here and I say you're in perfect physical shape for military service."

I thought that I was going to go back home and report to boot camp in a week or two. I was flabbergasted to see armed soldiers enter the room we were marched outside and into waiting buses. Within ten minutes I was on my way up Interstate five headed to Fort Lewis, Washington. A shocking realization had sunk in. I was in the army now and only God could help me now.

CHAPTER ELEVEN

I fell asleep as the bus made its way up the interstate. I still hadn't absorbed the impact of what was happening in my life. However, that was made clear to me when I was awaken by a screaming drill Sergeant standing over me as the bus sat idling at Fort Lewis that night.

I will always remember my first meeting with drill Sergeant Talbot. He was spraying spit all over me as he continued to bark orders at me. Why the military thinks that it can get a foot away from your face and yell at you is beyond me.

I have learned over the years that most drill Sergeant's are real jerk-off's. They are little men and border on the line of being cowards. They thrive on the fact that underlings have to stand there and be humiliated and degraded. If you say anything at all you are forced to run, stand or be sent to the brig.

I would love to see one of these so-called men go into a bar in civilian cloths and shoot off their mouth. The reason you don't see that is because they know that they would get their ass kicked from here to the end of the universe. Being a career military bum is the only way they can stick out their chest and strut around like king Cock of the barnyard. I think they are roosters because they sure don't have any balls of their own.

After Sergeant Talbot got everyone off the bus and lined up in a single file line outside in the pouring rain. He continued to tell us how he was our mommy now. He made it clear that while we were here in the Army that our wives or girlfriends would be cheating on us. He said that if any of them were close enough to the base he would go and screw them personally.

Naturally, he was dressed in rain gear, while all the recruits were in civilian cloths. I stood there for over an hour. We were allowed to go inside at about eleven PM. Once inside we saw that everyone's belongings had been search. The Army bums had taken all books, magazines, pocketknives and many personal items.

They made every person sign a letter, which we were not allowed to read. I found out later that it was a form letter that said that you had arrived safely and that you were being treated well. I am not naive, but I was shocked that people could treat others like that. I have never encountered a more degrading situation as the U S Army. I swear to you that by the time you read the events that took place in my short military life, you will, I hope, have the same conclusion.

You will have to trust me when I say that all my recollections are one hundred percent factual and honest. One example was that we were not allowed to make a phone call until the next day. Sarah was expecting me home the night of my departure. She had to return to San Francisco to go to work. She and my mother were appalled by what had happened once I was allowed to call them. I couldn't see any difference from the old Shanghai days of getting a crew on a pirate ship.

That phone call was monitored by a Sergeant and restricted to two minutes in length. I hated every second I spent in the Army and still do to this day. There were approximately seventy-five men in my barracks. I still reflect on the nights when I heard men crying in their bunks. The drill Sergeant would get everyone up and make us do push-ups and tell us to thank the private that was keeping him awake by blubbering. That of course turned just about everyone against that person. Many times they beat up that person, as the brass looked the other way.

I personally witnessed a drill Sergeant that was pushing an overweight soldier while on a march. I had bad knees and also found myself at the back of the column on long marches. On this particular day the Sergeant was yelling in this guy's ear and calling him every dirty filthy name you have ever heard. Eventually the young man fell to the ground in a state of unconsciousness. This man was white as a ghost and as he lay on the ground twitching and what I assume to be, having a convulsion of some type.

The drill Sergeant called ahead to the other drill Sergeants on his walkie-talkie. Four other Sergeants walked up and surrounded the young man. They began to laugh as the Sergeant that had drove the man so hard said "that's the third son-of-a-bitch that I've driven to a nervous breakdown this year. You bustards pay up. That's twenty dollars apiece".

When the Sergeant had a fistful of money he looked up to see me standing there. He approached me and grabbed my shirt and pulled me up into his face. "You didn't see shit ass hole. You better not say a damn word to anyone if you know what's good for you. Get back with the others maggot". With that said he pushed me back and gestured for me to get away from him.

The last thing that I recall about that incident was seeing the soldier being lifted into an Army ambulance and being driven away. I never found out what happened to that person, but I have thought of him many times through out my life.

I had made a couple of good friends that were in my platoon with me. First there was John Small from Salem, Oregon. He was a thin-framed individual that wore thick horn-rimmed glasses. He slept in the bunk two beds down. Second was Denny Walker from Seattle, Washington. He was tall and muscular and slept in the bunk bed right above me. I would kick him from underneath and flip him out of bed onto the floor as a practical joke from time to time.

John had one eye that was a fraction from being certified as legally blind. He swore that he couldn't see anything but shadows and blurs. Like all of us he wanted out of the service. He tried so hard to get Denny or myself to poke a straight pin in his eye. I totally refused to help him in that action.

However after many days of pleading, Denny succumbed to the repeated cries for help and agreed to participate in this discharge scheme. John personally took a match and while lit, he held a straight pin over the flame. I actually watched as Denny did indeed stick that hot pin into the center of John's' eye. John fell to the floor screaming in pain holding his eye. John himself pulled the pin from his eye. He composed himself and placed his glasses back to their proper place on his face. He thanked Denny and went to bed for the night.

The next morning John reported to sick call as well as a few others and I. I complained about my knee aching and swelling. John was to say that his eye was infected or hurting him severely. By noon we were both back on the shuttle bus to the barracks. John had a patch over his left eye and I was told that I was fine. John said that he was now blind in one eye. He was told that he would be assigned a secretary job that didn't require perfect vision in both eyes. The self mutilation act was all in vain. John was not to have his medical discharge. In the weeks to come I would continue to go on sick call, every day, without fail.

CHAPTER TWELVE

Many hours went into planning how we could get out of the service. Denny had a plan of his own to reach freedom. Since he had helped John it was my turn to assist him. The army issues each person a little shovel. It's approximately two feet long and the head folds up. I was swinging the shovel with the head folded as hard as I could and striking Denny on his hipbone.

I repeated this procedure two or three time a week. The purpose was to bruise the bone and not the skin. Denny held a fold up towel to his hip when I would strike him. After several weeks he did indeed develop a limp. He then started accompanying me to the sick call shuttle bus. He was put on light duty but not discharged and I was still getting the same old, same old routine.

I kept getting this one old doctor who was convinced that I was a big fake. It had gotten to the point were he wouldn't even examine me or touch me. The doctors kept Denny on light duty and John was told he had to complete basic training before he would be reassigned. I must admit that there were a few things I liked during basic training. I real did like crawling under bob wire while a machine gun was firing tracer bullets six-foot over your head.

While I was there at Fort Lewis someone got shot in the head and was killed during this exercise. We were told do not stand up or run because you could be shot.

I loved the day when I got to throw a live hand-grenade. What a rush it was pulling the pin and counting to three and throwing it. I even liked the day I had to crawl in the mud and they gassed everyone. I liked the obstacle course and the firing range. I was not physically able to perform many tasks and that was what got me upset many times. The reason I hate the army was because of the way you were treated not the work it self.

I had my many days of fire watch and K P duty. I got my ass chewed out like everybody else did. However, since I was always reporting to sick call I was especially targeted as a girlie boy.

The most frightening point of my short military career was when an outbreak of spinal meningitis killed four men in my company. Only one man was from my barracks, but he slept only a few bunks down from me. I watched as he was taken away by ambulance at three AM. I prayed that night for the Lord to protect me. Shortly after that the army began a rigid shot campaign. Not because of the spinal meningitis; but because it was nearing the end of basic. We were all getting shots to go to Vietnam.

We got shots with a gun and not by needles with syringe. We were instructed not to move or jerk and don't tighten up your arm, just relax. I like shot's with the gun, but some guys didn't listen. One person pulled back just as the nurse pulled the trigger. His arm got a bad cut and he was bleeding everywhere. Those guns have hundreds of pounds of pressure delivering the serum. You don't want to move believe me.

The last march I went on with my platoon was embarrassing as could be. The platoon had marched over twenty miles when the drill Sergeant asked if anyone had to use the rest room. Approximately twenty-five soldiers including myself raised our hands. The Sergeant had everyone, but those of us that raised our hands sit down. He then marched the twenty-five of us two blocks down the road and made us stop in front of an office building. He made us line up and face the building and then blew his whistle.

About forty or fifty women came to the windows and started to wave and giggle. The Sergeant screamed that you said you had to piss. Start pissing and anyone that doesn't will have me to deal with. So, with the clapping and laughing by the women, we all urinated right then and there. I still can't believe that this was policy in 1967 and that you had no options as a private.

A few days after that incident, I was back at sick call. This time when I walked into the old doctor's office he had a young doctor with him. The regular doctor told the young one to make a complete examination and then they would discuss his findings.

The first thing he discovered was that when bending my knee it cracked and popped. He moved my leg and noticed how sloppy the knee joint was. He commented on my surgery and then asked me a question that I have never forgotten. What were you doing before you were inducted into the army. I told him I was going on a world tour; but being drafted put a stop to all of that for me.

He nodded his head and said that he hoped that I liked that lifestyle because there was no future for me in the army. I was sitting there trying to figure out what he was really saying to me when he said, "you're going home." He gave me several papers and instructed me on where to take them to start my medical discharge. He told me that it would take about two weeks to clear. What a great day it was as I left that office and walked down the hall to administration.

John and Denny were both happy for me. I felt sorry for the both of them though. Five days later I stood along the fence and watched as my friends boarded a plane and lifted off towards their destiny in Vietnam. Over the years I have tried to find them or find out what happened to them. I never did find out one way or the other. I was discharged after a total of eighty-eight days and because of that I can not receive any government FHA loans or benefits. That is a small price to pay for my freedom.

I had called Sarah and the day I walked out through those gates at Fort Lewis she was standing there. We went to Seattle and had dinner at the Space Needle. The next day we drove back down to Hallandale and stayed a few days with my mother. We then returned to the bay area.

CHAPTER THIRTEEN

I had spent the time while driving down to San Francisco telling Sarah about my days in the army. She had told me little, in as much as what was going on, while I was away. That in retrospect was the correct thing to do at the time. I was surprised when Sarah said for me to go to my house on Skyline manor. I thought we were going to her mothers or an apartment she had rented; during the time I was gone. The closer I got to the house the more she began to inform me of some major changes.

Troy and Brandy still lived at the house along with herself and two of her close girlfriends, Jennifer and Lisa. The five of them had managed to keep the rent up and the utilities paid. I was proud of her ingenuity as well as her initiative to take charge in my absence.

I hugged Troy and Brandy and met the newcomers. I sat down and Troy began to explain what had expired in the last three months. Scott and Amanda had moved to Los Angles. Rudy had gone back to Oregon and Kitty was still around locally. Sticks and Paula were still living in San Francisco, in fact, the same house.

Troy told me that when I didn't show up in London, they were replaced with a local band. Troy said that he would always remember standing backstage and watching that band play instead of them. He said that the worst thing was that WE were a hundred times better than that band would ever be.

He continued on telling me that Scott, Sticks and Rudy blamed me personally for cheating them out of being rock stars. When the band was fired because I was no longer there, that was the last straw. I know it probably didn't help when Roy told them he wasn't going to replace me and that I was the key component.

I never personally thought that for a second that I was better than anyone else was. We were a band, in which each had their own talent in where they excelled. I knew I would miss that special sound that comes but once or twice in a band's life. I still believe to this day that if I had not got drafted, that our band would have gone on to become a major force in the rock world.

However, that is water under the bridge and I will never know what could have happened. I did call Roy Wilson's office only to find that he had been fired because of the JUST SLIGHTLY RICHER debacle. I didn't understand that, it wasn't Roy's fault I got drafted; but that's how the music business goes.

I had one option left to me and that was to get connected back into the fast track of music. Sure I could hold auditions and put a new band together. That is a long and time-consuming process. I remembered an ace card that I could play. The next day when I could get off by my self, I would call Tree Rodgers. I could only hope that I still had something that Chart Records found marketable.

The next day I called Tree and told him of my current situation. He was beside himself once he found out that I was no longer in the service and did not have a manager. He invited me to come over to his office on the 37th floor of the Maxwell Towers the very next day. He wanted to have a serious talk about my future in music. I felt great as I hung up the phone. I was thinking thought I might make it yet in this wild and crazy world of music.

PART THREE

I held on to Sarah's hand tightly as we walked through the automatic separating glass doors of the office complex that housed the corporate offices of Chart Records. We stood in silence as I pressed the elevator button to go up. It took what seemed to be an hour till the car arrived and the doors slid apart. I gazed into Sarah's eyes and took a deep breath and we stepped inside the elevator while she pushed the 37th floor button.

With a slight jerk the car began to rise and I started to fill with anxiety. I had not seen Tree in a long time and since I had rejected his offer before, he might not be forgiving. However business is business and if I still had a commercial sound that would make money, there was no debut that he would be interested once again.

I was afraid that the percentages and signing bonus would be remarkably different than that of the previous offer. I expected the diminished numbers in monies. I really just wanted a record contract of any kind and at any sum.

The car came to an abrupt stop and we stepped out into a well-lit and decorative hallway. We studied the brass directory that hung on the wall till we saw Chart Records, Mr. Tree Rodgers, suite 3773. With one glance we saw the big Oak numbers 3773 at the end of the hallway attached to two huge doors. We turned and made our way to the entrance of the office and then entered through the massive doors.

There, sitting behind a desk was an older woman, who looked up immediately as we entered the room. I was reading her nameplate, Joan Turner, as she asked, "May I help you"? I informed her that we were there to see Mr. Rodgers. She buzzed him on the intercom system and then showed us the way to Mr. Rodgers office.

Tree was halfway across his office floor as we walked into his office. He embraced me and hugged me till it hurt. I introduced him to Sarah and we all sat down. He in his plush leather chair behind the desk and Sarah and I in a couple of contemporary cloth chairs in front of him. Tree immediately went into an explanation. 'Larry, I've got this band that's ready to hit the road on tour as the opening act for BLAKE JADE. This is a one in a million shot man. I've been trying to find somebody exactly like you so I could fire that son-of-a-bitch lead singer that's their now.

I can't believe the luck. We are talking about you right? You're not going to tell me you have loyalties to Big Bang or only with your old band crap are you? This band is called MOURNING and they are going to be hot. They need a fantastic singer to go all the way to the top and that my friend is you. What do you say old buddy? I will give you 10,000.00 dollars up front if you sign an exclusive contract with Chart Records. I am willing to work with you on a lot of things Larry; but I have to know right now dude. Shits happening fast and I don't have time to waste on this deal. What's your verdict man? I want to work with you and I will treat you fair and square." I must admit that I got a little cocky at seeing how desperately he wanted me to sign. Ten thousand dollars was a huge and unheard of deal for me. I know that if something seems too good to be true, then it usually is too good to be true.

Sarah's eyes were as large as a pair of hubcaps as she stared at me relentlessly. I smiled at her and then turned towards Tree. "What percentage are we talking about? How many days on the road a year do we travel? What about the songs that I write and the royalties from them Tree? How do we travel, air, bus, car and who pays the hotel bills? Hell, you're not going to pay me money up front without completely owning my ass and everything I do for the rest of my life. I will tell you this Tree, right now, I will not be owned.

I want Troy in the band. I don't care if he is the only lead guitar or the band has two lead players. Double leads are great in case you have forgotten. Remember Doobie Brothers, Lynyrd Skynyrd and the Eagles. I will take your word that this band is as good as you say they are. I want to rename it however to my old bands name, JUST SLIGHTLY RICHER.

If you submit to me a good contract that has honest figures and the right answers to those questions, I am your man. You know and I know what is fair and what would be ripping me off. I guarantee you my lawyer will be looking out for me 100 percent. I'm telling you if there is just one loophole in your contract that screws me over, no deal."

Tree was turning a pale shade of blue; but I never saw him blink one time. "Consider it a done deal. You can pick up a copy of the contract tomorrow for you and your lawyer. I promise that you will love every word in it or you don't have to sign. I will have a check for ten thousand dollars here also. Take these five hundred dollars so you and your lady can go and celebrate, on me. You are going to be a very rich man in a few short years."

Tree stood up and came back around his desk and once again embraced me. I kept a business like demeanor and shook his hand while telling him I would return the next day. Once out into the hallway and we were descending in the elevator Sarah and I explode into a screaming frenzy that lasted till we arrived at the lobby.

CHAPTER FOURTEEN

I could hardly contain my emotions as I ran into the house with the news of the millennium. Troy and Brandy were startled upon my bursting into the room. I began to tell all concerned the news about Chart Records, the tour and contract offer. It was a wild night at Skyline Manor that night for everyone. That was the night I also learned that Jennifer and Lisa were more than just friends.

It was my first experience with lesbians. I was surprised at how little of an effect it had on me negatively. I really found it to be exciting. I had no ideal that it would become a major issue in the months to come. I did enjoy watching Jenny and Lisa making their special kind of love that night I confess.

I walked into Tree Rodgers office the next day and picked up the contract he had had his corporate attorneys draw up. I am not a lawyer, nor did I have one. I read it over several times slowly and tried to interrupt the language from an in-between the line mentality.

I saw that I could change the name of the band to the one I wanted. I saw that any song I wrote I got credit for as well as all writer royalties. Troy was allowed to play lead guitar and was an equal member. The percentages were fine and broke down as follows.

Chart records got 40%. I was to receive 20%. This was a 5-piece band so each of the 4 remaining members got 10%. Chart got its forty percent of the top. Then all cost was to be paid. Then the band got its percentage after all the bills were paid. This is a simple way to look at it after a concert lets say. Take the $100,000.00 gate and give Tree his $40,000.00. The cost to put the concert on lets estimate was 20,000.00. That includes radio, television, flyers, security the venue and roadies etc.

The balance left is 40,000.00 dollars. I would get my 20% witch would be 8,000.00 dollars and then 10% for the rest of the band. That would come to 4,000.00 dollars apiece. The contract also had a merchandising clause built into it. After the cost was deducted, the profit would be split 50/50. Fifty percent went to Chart Records and fifty percent went to the band members at ten percent apiece.

The paragraph that caught my attention was that all studio time would be absorbed by Chart Records and was not in anyway accredited to the band. That is a totally unheard of accounting practice in the music world. It had to be a major oversight or a major gift on Tree's part. I was afraid to ask, so I didn't mention it to him on that day.

I felt that with my 10,000.00 dollar signing bonus and the ten-year renewal clause in place it was a good and solid deal. I signed the contract and told Tree that I would send Troy in later in the day to sign. I could have just made the biggest mistake of my life or one of the best, time will tell.

Tree set up an eight PM start time in the studio to meet the other band members and have a jam to see how we would mesh. I called home and told Troy to come on down and sign. I left the office and went to the music store and bought me a new Gretsch Country Gentleman guitar.

Troy, Brandy, Sarah and I entered the studio that first night with butterflies flying high. We were introduced to three new band guys and their girlfriends. First was Stuart the lead player and his girlfriend Tammy. Then Ted the bass player and his girlfriend Teri. Lastly was Bubba Ray the drummer and his girlfriend Mary Lou.

Stuart and Ted were born and raised in San Francisco as well as their girlfriends. Bubba Ray and Mary Lou were from Little Rock, Arkansas. They together truly represented the southern stereotype of good old boys if you know what I mean. There was a lot of sizing up and tension going on for sure. I am not saying it was unbearable, but it was uneasy to say the least. Our styles went together on an acceptably level as we jammed, but. I could see that even Tree knew we needed sometime to get tight as far as personalities and musically.

In the days to come we had many arguments among the bands members. Troy and I were constantly at odds against the other three. They resented the fact that we were crammed down their throats and that they had to change their bands name. They also disliked the fact that I replaced their friend Juan, the previous lead singer.

Once all this was said and had been aired out to the satisfaction of all concerned, the atmosphere began to calm down. At the end of three weeks I remember having a band meeting and giving a little speech. The highlights being that I did not fire Juan, Chart Records did. The band had a chance of a lifetime and we needed to take advantage of it. I commended everyone on their talent and abilities. They were surprised to find out that Juan was going to be replaced by someone even if I had refused to join.

I recall circling the room and shaking their hands. I feel that on that night the animosity was lifted and replaced by a willingness to try and work together. I say that because the next days band practice was really hot and tight. From that night forward the sound and the band got better and better each time we played. We were ready the night of opening for BLAKE JADE at the one and only Los Angles Coliseum.

Standing backstage and listening to thousands of fans screaming is an overwhelming feeling. Especially when you know that they are there to see one of the hottest bands on the charts and not you. Never the less, when I heard the MC's voice over the loudspeaker say "give it up for, JUST SLIGHTLY RICHER", my heart skipped not one but two beats.

We ran out as the strobe lights went into their computerized program. We plugged into the wall of Marshal Amps and hit it with San Francisco Girls by The Fever Tree. Even though we had only six songs it was evident that from song one to song number six we had made an impression. The crowd was deafening as we struck the last chord of our last song, Sunshine Of Your Love by Cream.

We had performed six heavy up beat tunes. I really wanted to do a ballad but Tree said that this was not the place, he was right. We were in shock as we rushed to our dressing room backstage. What a rush, one that I will forever remember.

CHAPTER FIFTEEN

Next morning Tree called and set up an appointment for three PM that afternoon. He wanted to get the band into the studio and start work on an album. I was excited at the thought of cutting an album. I told Tree that I was looking forward to talking to him about such a project.

The day seemed to drag on without mercy. It was torture not hearing the facts about Trees ideas and his future plans for the band. I recall how I felt a since of relieve as I walked into Trees office that afternoon. He stood up and came over to me and shook my hand. "Sit down man" he said as he pointed towards a big overstuffed chair in front of his desk.

I sat down and we exchanged pleasantries and talked about how great the gig had gone the night before. I was more than ready when Tree finally began explaining his plans for the band and for me. "Larry, I talked to the big boys in Los Angles last night. They are willing to go all out, putting up the money for recording, distribution and advertising for a start. I want you to write a dozen songs for an album. After last night I am convinced that I can promote and sell you and Just Slightly Richer, big time. Now, do you see any problems with anything I have said so far? Will the band go for being out on the road or making this album? Chart Records have big plans for you and Just Slightly Richer. Talk to me Larry, does any of this sound good to you? What do you think about all of this?"

I just stared at Tree in disbelief. My dreams and the bands dreams were coming true. "Are you kidding me" I said. "This is exactly what we have all worked so hard for all these years. I have already written about one-hundred songs. I will pick out a couple of dozen to work on. I do not have to talk it over with the band. They want to know when and where do we start?"

Tree smiled and said "how about Friday at eight PM at the Market Street studio. You know the one, just up from the wharf. I think we will use studio A-3. I like it best because it is the largest and the most up to date technologically. You and the boys just bring your guitars, we have everything there you will need. Smile Larry, you and the boys are on your way to being rich and famous."

"We will be there Tree. I also will make a tape of the songs I picked so you can put your input in deciding the final twelve. Thank you, thank you" was the last thing I said as I left Trees office that day. I was still stunned even after my thirty-seven floor decent to the lobby.

I broke every speed limit there is getting back to 10587 Skyline Manor. I literally ran into the living room screaming at the top of my lungs. "We are making a record" I announced. Everyone there, Troy, Brandy, Sarah, Jennifer and Lisa joined in the excitement. I called up Stuart, Ted and Bubba Ray and told them the good news and to come on over for one hell of a celebration. I must tell you that Skyline Manor was rocking that night till early in the morning.

During the next few days Troy and I spent many hours going over songs that I had written. We both wanted to pick out songs that were driving and had some of Troy's best lead riffs in them. Maybe we should have consulted the other members of the band, but I didn't. I felt I was asked to write the songs for the album, so I thought it was my responsibility alone and not the bands.

Eight PM Friday finally came and I remember the atmosphere when we all entered studio A-3 for the first time. The electricity in the air could have lit every light in Las Vegas for a year. Tree introduced us to the two engineers that would be mixing our album. Two real cool guys Bounce and

Stretch. True, not their real names, but the ones they used as technicians. Bounce got his nickname by being great at bouncing tracks back and forth. Stretch on the other hand got his AKA by being able to reach both ends of the sixty-four track board at the same time.

While the band plugged in, the guys in the booth were getting sound checks and doing their levels. I started showing the boys the chords for the first song that I wanted to do. This was the first time the band had heard any of my original material, except for Troy of course. They were so happy to be making a record that they did not seem to be upset about my songs or my selections. They just wanted to cut an album and play music. I was thankful for that and the fact that I wrote all the music in the band never bothered anyone that I know of.

Several weeks passed and many long hours spent until we finished our album. However, we all loved the finished product. It was truly worth all the hard work, arguments and do overs. I tell you, when you play a song thirty or forty times in a row one can get real irritable fast.

Tree had the band booked in several small clubs around the bay area for about a month once our album was released. We enjoyed playing the clubs; but we did want to get out on the road and tour. We played a club where a heckler in the very back of the room was just terrible to us. He kept yelling insults like YOU SUCK and GET OF THE STAGE etc. Everyone else was applauding and having a good time. That heckler sticks out more than all the other people combined. It is not always easy to satisfy a roomful of people with different taste in music. Yet that damn heckler always sticks in my mind, even years later.

I have got to tell you this one story. Tree had booked the band in a lodge up in the mountains. This community, Burn Falls, was about one-hundred miles from nowhere. The population was approximately two hundred and fifty people. Now keep in mind that this is in 1968 and the hippies are prevalent and at war with the rednecks. Especially in a logging community as is this place.

We do our gig at the lodge, were people just looked at us wondering who the hell these guys are. When we finish playing we go to the kitchen to get a bite to eat. Well, the people in the kitchen would not feed us. Not because they did not have food or was cleaning up. They said we needed haircuts before they would feed us. I guess they didn't like boys with shoulder length hair in that town, what a laugh we got out of that.

We left the lodge in search of the only little motel in area. Now it's about two AM and I see a patrol car coming down the street. When the policemen stopped at the stop sign I approached his driver side window slowly to ask him where the motel was located. He jumps back three feet and draws his revolver and with a shaky voice yells "what the hell do you want"? I explained to him that I had just played the lodge and was now in search of the motel. He pointed down the street and to the left. I walked back to the bands van laughing under my breath. As I drove away I saw that he was white as a ghost and physically trembling. To this day I have never understood his reaction on that night. I hope the poor man didn't go home and have a heart attack.

It was late July in 1968 when our album hit the music stores, thanks to Trees publicity and the media bombardment. Three weeks later the first single release, ON THE RUN hit number two on the billboard charts. It was getting a ton of play time everywhere in the country. Best of all was the fact that our album, JUST SLIGHTLY RICHER / DREAM AMONG THE CLOUDS, was steadily climbing up the charts as well.

Tree called me and gave me even more good news. He had us booked on AMERICAN BANDSTAND in Philadelphia that Saturday. He said "come get your tickets. I got them right here in my hand. You leave tomorrow on the redeye."

The band was elated as we boarded the United Airlines Friday night flight to Philadelphia. We touched down on the runway at about seven o'clock that morning knowing that we had to be at the AMERICAN BANDSTAND studio by noon. No one had slept a wink because they were so wired about the show. The band had brought their girlfriends and I had brought Sarah along too.

There was a white stretch limousine waiting for us as we exited the airport. The driver welcomed us and helped with the luggage. The driver told us his name was J.T. and that he was at our service anytime of day. He drove us to the Philadelphia Hilton and gave me one of his cards and reminded me to just call. He did say that he would be back at eleven o'clock to take us to the studio.

Tree had taken care of everything. Each person had their own suite. Breakfast was delivered to our door just minutes after checking in. Sarah and I had a beautiful room that overlooked the river. Life was truly great and was getting better day by day. We decided to take a little cat nap if we could for about two hours.

I felt refreshed when Sarah woke me at ten o'clock. I took a quick shower and got dressed as Sarah was showering. I called the guys, but they were all already up and ready to go. I heard a loud voice from the hall proclaim "let's go boys". It was J.T. who had gotten of the elevator and just yelled for us. Everyone piled into the elevator and to my amazement we rode quietly to the mezzanine. Silence reigned supreme in the limonene until we pulled up in front of the big A B letters in front of the AMERICAN BANDSTAND studio. That is when it hit all of us like a ton of bricks; we are going to be on Television and on AMERICAN BANDSTAND.

We were nervous as the makeup people did their thing. When Dick Clark walked in to meet us, I was for the first time in my life in total awe. I did overcome my state of speechlessness and soon was conversing freely with him. He was truly a wonderful man. He made us feel at ease and had the ability to erase all of ones stress and tensions. When he left the room, we felt comfortable and ready to do a show on television.

When the curtain parted and we began to play, the musician part of us took control over our bodies. We nailed ON THE RUN that day and left the stage to thundering applause. We were celebrating in the dressing room, thinking how great the band was doing when Dick Clark walked into the room. "Congratulations boys, a super job. I've got a telegram for you from your manager". He handed me the envelope and I opened it up in front of everyone. It read, Larry—the band is booked on the Tonight Show with Johnny Carson Monday night, stop. Come back to San Francisco Sunday. Stop. You can fly to Los Angeles Monday morning, stop. See you Sunday afternoon, Tree, stop. We rested the rest of the day Saturday and flew back to San Francisco on Sunday morning. We all slept on the plane ride home. Mental fatigue had finally caught up with us all.

It was hectic after arriving back home. Tree was there at the airport to meet us personally. He had a limo waiting there for us to take us to our individual homes. Stuart and Tammy were first to be let out because they were closest to the airport. Next was Ted, Bubba Ray, Teri and Mary Lou all lived in the same townhouse complex just down a mile or two from them. Finally Troy, Brandy, Sarah and I stepped out of the limo and made our way to Skyline Manor. Tree was hollering at us to be sure to be ready at noon Monday for the limo ride back to the airport. He wished us good luck on the Tonight Show as the car sped away into the California sunset.

I dreaded seeing that limousine pull up in front of the house that Monday. The driver honked the horn, but I had already spotted him. Troy and I kissed the ladies in our lives good-bye; they had decided to stay home this time. I asked where the others were and was told that two other limos were picking them up at their residencies. What timing, all three limos arrived at about the same time in front of the United Airlines check in counter. We were taken through a side door and were allowed to board first, before anyone else. As Mel Brooks once said "It's good to be the king."

As we sat in the dressing room at the Tonight Show I made a phone call to Tree. I told him the band had decided to do the next release from the album instead of ON THE RUN. Tree thought that it was too early for that, but consented after my persistence. The fact was that even though I had written ON THE RUN I was getting tired of doing it over and over. The band had unanimously agreed to do MOUNTAIN SO HIGH. That night was the debut of our second single off our album DREAM AMONG THE CLOUDS.

The response was overwhelming for what was the first time the public audience had heard our new song. Ted had the best part to play in MOUNTAIN SO HIGH. He really got a workout using three fingers and stretching. His part was the drive and body of the song. Troy and Stuart both had a solo lead. They did their solo leads in the middle of the song. However, at the end of the song they performed a double lead together. Their double lead along with Ted's bass run was like three leads being played at once. It was a colossal finish to a high energy song that rocked already.

I had noticed that Ed MacMan and Johnny both were taping their hands on Johnny's desk. I even saw Doc Severson and the boys in the band nodding their heads with the beat. That night was a magical night where everything was working one-thousand percent and was cruising in overdrive. I hated to end the song. We were lost in the music and were part of it. I had never seen Bubba Ray sweat so much for just one song. We had exited this comatose state with Ed and Johnny standing as we struck the last chord and letting it ring through our sustain boxes.

What a feeling to find yourself sitting on that famous couch next to Johnny Carson. He helped us promote our album and discussed how the band had gotten together. We touched on the bands future and the inspiration needed to write a song. The interview only lasted for about six minutes, but I will never forget the moment.

We left the NBC studio and went straight to the airport and flew back to San Francisco. We arrived at Daily City around ten o'clock that evening. Tree had forgotten to schedule limos, so Troy and I took a cab home that night. We got home in time to see the Tonight Show on television. The show may come on at eleven-thirty at night; but in reality it tapes at five in the afternoon. We had gone on at six-fifteen and had left the studio by six-forty five. I still have the VHS tape of that show I recorded that night to this day. I regret never seeing the show or having a tape of the band on American Bandstand. I tried to obtain one from MR. Clark, but for some reason he could not find one either.

CHAPTER SIXTEEN

For the next six months the band was opening for BLAKE JADE. We were on a U.S. tour with them as an opening act and we did not like that at all. That is however called paying your dues in the music world. Playing two or three nights a week in different towns for weeks on end gets to be very difficult. You lose all sense of reality and time, it becomes surrealistic. Sure it's fun in the beginning, but it does tear you down hard and fast without you really noticing it, till it's too late.

I finally realized that Bubba Ray was drinking heavily and Ted was popping pills and smoking marijuana. I did not know how to handle or really respond to these new developments. I called Tree to get his advice on these matters. He was not surprised, nor concerned at this point in time. He just stated, welcome to the wonderful world of sex, drugs and rock and roll. I was shocked by his complacencies in this development. I decided to ignore the problem at the time. I did not want to rock the boat unless it mushroomed into a major obstacle.

By the end of the tour we were like zombies. I had missed Sarah immensely, for she and all the girls had stayed home while we were out on the tour. I was happy to be home once again and to get some much deserved rest. I slept for thirty-two hours straight, a new world's record for me. Troy and Brandy were still living at Skyline Manor as well as Jennifer and Lisa. The six of us made up our minds to go on a short vacation. I had suggested it first, after going to the mailbox and getting a royalty check for the last six months. That check included my share for song writings, album sales, tour salaries, television appearances and merchandise sold at concerts, T-shirts and the likes. Troy had gotten his check that day also. I never asked the amount of his check and he has never told me. I have never said anything to him about mine, although it was for 752,000 dollars and change.

We all decided to fly down to Cabo San Lucas and before I knew it we were on our way to the airport. The next thing I knew we were in the air headed for Mexico. Fortunately we had only an hour and one half to wait till our flight departed. While were waiting to lift off we eat there at an airport restaurant and lounge.

We eat in the lounge part of the restaurant on purpose, so we could hear the house band that was playing there. My ears perked up as I heard the opening bass run to my song Mountain So High. Troy and I looked at each other, smiled and then sat back to listen. I think we were both very surprised at how well they had performed our song. All in all I found it to be a humbling experience. The first time you hear your words and music done by a band in a club; you can not help but be completely ecstatic.

Troy or I never went up and introduced ourselves to that band. I do not think that they knew who we were at that time; because they never made any jester to acknowledge us. When I heard the announcement for our flight to board; we rose from our table and walked towards the front counter to pay our bill. The last thing I heard as we passed through the front door to catch the plane was ON THE RUN being played at a loud volume.

Our flight was smooth and without incident other than one passenger that was afraid of flying. He was trying to keep himself together, but was failing miserably. I felt kind of sorry for him; but it was somewhat annoying to us all. I was relieved as we touched down on the runway.

Cabo San Lucas was ninety-two degrees under a beautiful blue sky, with a slight breeze. We caught the shuttle and checked in to the Hiltons best room on the top floor that overlooked the Pacific Ocean. We spent the next few days' body surfing, tanning, deep sea fishing, Para sailing and playing volleyball on the beach.

Time passed way to fast as far as I was concerned when the phone in my room rang out. It was Tree telling me to wrap it up and to be back in San Francisco day after next. That indeed was not what I wanted to hear; but I knew that this vacation could not last forever. We wound ourselves down and embraced the fact that we had to leave. Our mood was however, still jovial as we stepped off the plane in San Francisco.

The next day Tree arrived at Skyline Manor unannounced. I recall answering the door bell and opening the door and there he stood. He stated he wanted to give us the news in person. He had a grin ear to ear and a sparkle in his eyes. He began to fill Troy and I in on future plans he had for the band. He told us we had only three months to cut a new album. That was because we left in ninety-four days on a world tour. The tour would start in Hong Kong and end in Hamburg, Germany. The tour would be five months long and consisted of eighty-seven cities in one hundred fifty four days; with many back to backs built into it. It sounded better than fantastic at the time. I would learn in weeks ahead it was a double edge sword.

The entire band spent the next week getting shots and physicals. We did all the paper work including taking pictures for our passports. We began putting together songs for the new album. This time the whole band had input on the material that was to be used for our second album. In fact Stuart and Ted both wrote songs for the album. I had some songs that I had written from before and I had one that I was writing for the title cut of this album especially.

I wanted to keep with the bands imagery that the first album had created. Our second album as well as the title cut that I had written was called DREAM WITHIN THE WIND. This was personally my first attempt at a power Ballad. It was also the first time that I had used augmented and diminished sevens as chords in my song writings. I could see and feel myself growing and evolving into a better song writer and musician.

It was hard work, but we finished the album on time. It left us only a few days before we had to leave on the world tour. Sarah was thrilled about going on a world tour; but the day before we were to leave she became very sick in the middle of the night. We went to the emergency room at a nearby hospital. It was in a way embarrassing that not only was Sarah not really sick; but instead very much pregnant.

We were surprised, yet both happy as anyone could be. Upon learning this wonderful news Sarah decided to stay at home and not go traveling abroad. I had mixed emotions about her decision to stay home. I knew that she would be in good hands with Jennifer and Lisa there in case a problem did arise. I wanted to be with her, but I knew I had to leave.

I still remember when everyone boarded the plane. Stuart and Tammy along with Ted, Teri, Troy, Brandy, Bubba Ray and Mary Lou all boarded before I did. They were laughing and celebrating as we taxied out to the runway. I was in a sadden state as I waved good-bye through the window of the plane to Sarah standing in the lobby of the terminals concourse waving back emphatically.

The flight was long and boring. That was because there was nothing to see but water for ninety percent of the flight. The movie was one that I had seen before and truthfully was not worth viewing again. I basically slept for most of the journey and when I was awake I kept to myself. I did not want to put a wrench into everyone's enthusiasm.

Tree had the band opening for some mega bands along the tours schedule. We were for the most part the headliner act throughout the tour.

There were a few dates where we opened for bigger named groups. A good example was the first night on the tour in Hong Kong; we opened for THE BYRD'S. I was in no way offended by that. I had been a fan of their work for a long time. I was spellbound when I talked to them backstage and watched them play live.

It was a grueling five month tour, hotel after hotel and traveling day after day. It really all became a blur after about two months. However I still cherish the memorably moments like when we opened for JIMI HENDRIXS and when the GRASS ROOTS opened for us.

I called Sarah every night and she kept assuring me she was fine, but that she missed me. We talked about baby names and the hope that we would buy our own house after the tour. It was a five month love affair by way of phone lines.

I rejoiced at our last tour date in Hamburg, Germany. We opened for THE ROLLING STONES. The audience was filled with so much electricity it put to shame all other concerts we had played before it, combined. We partied with the stones after the concert and I realized what a great moment it truly was for not just me, but for all of us.

While on tour our second album DREAM WITHIN THE WIND had been released and was climbing up the rock charts. It was a fact that JUST SLIGHTLY RICHER was becoming a major force in the music world. That was great on the surface, but it also created a lot of pressure on me to be better next time out of the gate. I contemplated that fact on the plane ride all the way back home to San Francisco.

I had already begun to worry about writing new songs for the next album we did in the studio. I was also more concerned about Ted and Bubba Ray slipping deeper into their world of drug use. They both could barely function as they staggered of the stage in Hamburg. I personally debut if either one of them remember even being there that night. I would have to deal with this issue with or without Tree, once back in San Francisco.

With Sarah having our child looking for a house to buy, life was getting to be overwhelming. Especially for a young man who was just a few weeks away from his twenty-first birthday. Every worry I was pondering was erased as I walked through the departure tunnel and exited into the lobby and saw Sarah. She now showed her motherhood and we both cried as we embraced each other. "I have missed you more than any words will ever be able to say" I said as I looked deep into her tearful, but joyful eyes.

Sarah greeted the guys and girls as they all commented on her obvious condition. The girls sounded like high school-ers talking about one of them dating the football captain; or who had asked one of them to the senior prom. I gently pulled at Sarah's sleeve and she politely ended her conversation with the girls. We made our way outside the terminal and I flagged down a taxicab. I was exhausted as Sarah and I finally lay down in our own bed together at Skyline Manor for the first time in five months. I was content to just lay there and hold her until I fell asleep.

Next morning as we lay in bed I explained to Sarah about Ted and Bubba Ray's drug problems. She had a totally different approach to the situation. She wanted to discreetly talk to Mary Sue and Teri about the problem. She felt that they could then apply the right pressure to their boyfriends and get them to clean up their acts. Sarah told me she knew that the girls were also concerned about their dangerous lifestyle.

I agreed to let her implement her plan. I told her I would give the guys sixty days to get their heads together. If they did not, I would have to go to Tree and demand that he get involved with this and not look the other way. If he would not get involved I was prepared to leave the band, even though I was under a contract. Time would tell if this ultimatum would be put to the test.

Tree called that afternoon and began to spout good news, one story after the other. The word was out that the tour was more successful than anyone dreamed possible. Our album DREAM WITHIN THE WIND had gone double platinum and DREAM AMONG THE CLOUDS had made it to platinum. Merchandising sales were through the roof. He concluded by telling me that I would be totally amazed by my next royalty check. That check was due in a few days and I was curious to see the amount myself. Before we ended the conversation I told him the band needed a year off from touring. He emphatically said no, that we had to promote the new album. I told him we could talk about it later; but that I would not be doing any long term touring. I said that a gig once every two weeks or so I could live with but nothing more intense than that. That was how the telephone conversation ended that day.

I rested around the house for the next few days. Troy and I shared stories about the tour with Jennifer and Lisa. Sarah had heard them already from my calls, but the girls loved hearing about the rock stars we had met and played with. Jennifer and Lisa wished that they could have gone with us. I promised them that the next big tour they could go along with the band. They were after all part of our family as far as I was concerned and they were good friends of the entire band.

My life and Sarah's changed on Friday of that week when I went to the mailbox and retrieved the royalty checks. I handed Troy his and let out a huge sigh. Troy and I never compared checks or asked about how much they were for. Sarah and I went into our bedroom and sat on the bed. This day was my birthday and this check was my present. My hands trembled as I opened the envelope. My heart stopped dead in its tracks as I saw; pay to the order of Larry Haden, two million, two hundred and fifty-seven thousand dollars. You will not believe me when I tell you that there was no screaming or hollering. We did not jump up and down or go crazy. I looked at Sarah and told her to get ready, because we were going shopping for the rest of the day.

I drove our Camaro IROC to the bank and deposited my check. From there I went and paid cash (I wrote a check) for a white Ferrari GT 350. Once the sales manager called the bank and verified that the check was indeed good he handed me the keys. I told the manager to have someone drive the IROC back to Skyline Manor for me. He was glad to be of assistance. Sarah and I decided to give the Camaro to Jennifer and Lisa as a token of our friendship. Sara and I left the showroom and drove to Susan Bells office, a famous realtor that dealt only with million dollar homes in the San Francisco bay area.

Sarah and I walked into Mrs. Bell's office around three in the afternoon. Her receptionist asked how she could be of assistance to us. I saw her name tag and said "Rita, we are here to look at homes. I want to only deal with Mrs. Bell personally and no other sales person."

"Who should I say is requesting her," she said.

"Tell her, Larry Hayden" I replied.

She clicked the button on the intercom system an announced," Mr. Larry Hayden to see you Mrs. Bell."

The doors to her private office opened and out walked a beautiful woman in her late forties. "The Larry Hayden of JUST SLIGHTLY RICHER" she said walking up to me with outstretched hand. I reached out and shook her hand while I tried to judge her body language and demeanor. We engaged in a friendly dialogue.

"You know my music?"

"My daughter has posters of you, well your band, plastered all over her bedroom walls. She loves your new album. She thinks it better than your first one."

"Thank you very much. Please tell your daughter hello for me if you don't mind."

"I will MR. Hayden. What can I do For You today Mr. Hayden? If you are in the market for a house, what price range are you looking at?"

"We are looking for a very secluded home with a lot of trees. I would like it to have at least four or five Acres and a view of the ocean. I want a lot of glass. In fact the more glass the better I like it. It goes without saying of course that I want a swimming pool, tennis and basketball courts and a game room. I don't need a twenty bedroom place with stables and a guest house or a staff. Anywhere in the eight to ten thousand square foot range is acceptable.

We would like at least six bedrooms and six bathrooms. I know that you are not going to have our dream house ready built. I understand that in all probability I will have to remodel or even add on to achieve our goals and that is acceptable with the both of us. I am more concerned with the zoning, planning and the space to do all that is needed to complete the project if need be to obtain the finished home of our dreams. As far as a price range, let's start out in the two to three million dollar range. I will have a better idea when I see what I can buy in that range. When can we get started at seeing some houses?"

I was more than surprised when Susan fired back that she had two places that came immediately to her recollection. "Would you like to see them right now" she said. Sarah and I were impressed with that and we all left in Susan's Cadillac Coup-De-Ville to view both of the properties she had in mind.

We might have made a big mistake that day, because once seeing the very first home that Susan showed us; we were both in love at first glance. I know most people would spend several days if not weeks looking at several properties before considering a final decision to buy. Sarah and I fell in love with this house as we passed through the iron gates and up the driveway.

The home was located in the hills above Mill Valley at the north end of the Golden Gate Bridge. The view took in all of the San Francisco Bay, including the bridge, Alcatraz and the cities skyline itself. The back yard opened up into a panorama view of the Pacific Ocean and the Northern coastline.

The house sat on eleven point three acres that was heavily wooded. This beautiful split level home was facing Southwest with glass galore. It had a pool, tennis court and an outside full size basketball court. There were five bedrooms and five and a half bathrooms. It also had a huge game room that was big enough for a snooker table and pinball machines.

The master bedroom was twenty four by thirty six with his and hers walk in closets. The sunken tub in the master bathroom, along with the eight by eight foot skylight overhead was beyond Sarah's and my wildest imaginations. The act that left us both speechless was when Susan flipped a switch by the nightstand and above the bed the ceiling parted to reveal a twelve by sixteen glass roof. The whole concept was built like a moon roof in a car.

The lower level of the house and the second level were accessible by a beautiful spiral staircase. The entire staircase was built out of English walnut wood and inlaid with Mother of Pearl along the handrails. I will point out other features later on when applicable, but for now I will move on.

Susan told us the asking price and Sarah and I conversed before making an offer. Mrs. Bell made a phone call and told us that the seller would accept our offer. I wrote a check for two point one five million and handed it to Susan Bell that afternoon as I grinned ear to ear. That was a fair price for nineteen sixty eight in the bay area.

My bank account would now be low of funds compared to its previous balance earlier in the day. Without being pretentious, I still had a few hundred thousand dollars to last till my next royalty check.

Susan Bell had a lot of clout in the bay area as far as a realtor was concerned. She managed to push our sale through closing and the title company etc in one week. The next Friday after we had viewed the house; I was handed the keys as I signed the last papers to complete the transaction of buying a home.

Everyone back at Skyline Manor was sad that Sarah and I were moving out, but they understood why completely. Sarah and I had spent that waiting week shopping for furniture. I called the stores involved and told them that they could now deliver the furniture the next day on Saturday. It was a very hectic weekend, but we managed to get completely moved into the house by Sunday night. Amazing what big tips and money will accomplish these days.

CHAPTER SEVENTEEN

I called Tree Monday morning to tell him about my new home and to give him my phone number and address. He was happy for the both of us. He had good news of his own to tell me also. Just Slightly Richer had been nominated that morning for best new group, best album (Dream among the Clouds), and best song (Mountain So High).

That was great news, but as Tree said, along with that came promotional appearances and photo opportunities. I made an appointment for the entire band to meet in Tree's office, Thursday at eleven o clock; to discuss how to do as little as possible in light of the nominations. No one in the band wanted to tour or anything yet, accept enjoy their private lives.

It took a lot of yelling and flat out screaming to finalize a deal that embraced only a dozen appearances; ten concerts, all on the West coast and two television shows, one on the East coast and one on the West coast. We had seven weeks till the music awards to complete our gigs witch did include a performance at the awards show itself.

Time flew by as we fulfilled our obligations for the next seven weeks. We finished our appearance on the Michel Douglas show in Philadelphia and got back into Los Angles the day before the music awards show. The girls were already there checked in to the Hilton waiting for us as the limousine let us out in front of the hotels lobby.

Quick as a flash I realized that I was standing backstage at the Grammy's. It was a mind blower meeting so many great superstar musicians and song writers. It is easy to get a big head when so many influential people come up and tell you that you're great and other accolades. I remember hearing the roar of applause as our name sounded out over the speaker system. We walked out and plugged in to the amplifiers and did Mountain So High flawlessly and then waited to find out who would when in our category.

That night was one of the most astounding, unbelievable moments in my life. We won all three of the categories that we were nominated in. Between all of us we were able to thank everyone that had made our success possible. I even remembered Jay at Hell's Alley and Roy at Big Bang records.

We were celebrating at the behind the scene parties when Sarah began to look like she was in pain. She continued to say she was alright, but I could see that there was a problem. Much to her disapproval we left in the limousine and headed straight to the nearest hospital.

PART FOUR

Sarah did not want to give birth in Los Angles; but at this point she did not have much of a choice. Upon arrival Sarah was rushed into the maternity ward and the doctor on call followed her into the examining room. I didn't like the fact that Sarah's own obstetrician was not present. The doctor now was a stranger to us, but we were grateful to indeed have a doctor present right now.

The nurse kept me busy signing papers and consent forms since Sarah was in no condition to respond herself. The doctor came out. In what seemed to be hours and introduced himself as Dr. Chan. "Your wife is in severe pain. We have her prepped for surgery right now, but I wanted to touch base with you first. The big problem is that the baby is in a breech position. I will have to perform a Cesarean section in order to deliver the baby. This procedure is common and I see nothing that indicates any other complications. You can see your wife in a moment as she is transferred from here to the elevator that will take her to the fourth floor. That is where we operate. She will be in operating room number two". I held her hand as we went down the hall way. I told her how much I loved her and needed her as the elevator doors closed leaving me to only watch as the arrow went from one to four before it stop moving.

I sat nervously in the waiting room for almost three hours before Dr. Chan reappeared. "Sorry to take so long. Your wife is fine and so is your new son. There was some damage to your wife's reproductive system. Your son weighed five pounds and ten ounces. I have put him in an incubator. I just want him to gain a little strength for a few days. He will be fine, but I would like to keep him and your wife here for a couple of weeks as a precautionary measure. Sarah is total exhausted and needs some rest. Now, I have talked to Sarah and she wanted me to tell you some bad news. Sarah in all probability will not be able to have any more children. She is really hurt by this and I hope that you will understand that this is not her fault in anyway. She needs your support and she needs to know that you still will love her as much as before. Your wife is in room 322 north so you go see her now and GOD bless you and your family."

I shook his hand and made my way to the elevator and pushed three, once entered. I rushed to Sarah's side; but not before she had fallen asleep.

I held her hand and watched her sleep for the next few hours. When she awoke I leaned over and gently kissed her softly and told her how much I loved her. She began to cry; but I pressed my finger up against her lips and told her that my life was complete with her and our son in it.

That night we spent several hours talking, crying and consoling till we both slipped into a deservedly deep sleep. The chair in the hospital room seemed like a good idea at the time. However once wakening to my neck pain it was obvious that it was a wrong decision to fall asleep in it. With a crack here and a pop there it began to feel much better.

It was approximately noon when Troy and Brandy showed up at the hospital along with Jennifer and Lisa for a visit. They could not see the baby because he was in the neonatal wing of the hospital. Only Sarah and I were permitted in when she breast fed our son.

Everyone had a baby name that they wanted to submit for consideration. We appreciated their interest and desire to help out: but Sarah and I had spent that morning making that decision on our own. We had already came to the conclusion was that our son's name would be Wade. I must say though that the names Cole, Travis and Joshua made us waver a little. We told them all to go back to San Francisco and we would be along in two weeks.

It was a wonderful day at the end of the two weeks when I took Sarah and Wade home from the hospital. What a site to see, Sarah holding Wade and myself driving down the freeway in a Ferrari. I know about car seats and how unsafe it is to hold an infant; but it was the first and last time it ever happened. I hadn't bought a car seat or anything those two weeks because I was a total mental basket case. I know that doesn't make it OK, but that is what happened. It was nice of Troy to have my car brought down to L A for me while I was there. What a trip driving from L A to San Francisco.

We arrived home safely in spite of the unsafe transporting conditions. Sarah had just gotten Wade down for a nap when the doorbell rang. I answered the sound to see and meet for the first time one of three people that was to interview for the position on Wade's nanny. I had completely forgotten that I had set up three interviews at one hour interval for the job.

Wade slept through the afternoon and through all three interviews. When the last person had left Sarah and I quickly decided on the second lady we had seen. Rose was her name and she was from El Salvador. She was a young lady of twenty-four and spoke perfect English. She came highly recommended by the agency and had a green card to work in the United States.

I had stipulated to the agency that any applicants for the nanny position had to be a U S citizen or a legal immigrant. I personally have a big problem with illegal aliens. It is not that I think they are bad people or anything like that. It's the word Illegal that gets me started on a rampage. Why should I reward people who are committing a crime by giving them money? I refuse to support crime in anyway or criminals. I do reward people like Rose who gets proper documentation and goes by the book to obtain a green card and get a social security number.

The next few months went by without a lot of fanfare. I did do several things that I thought would be financially beneficial to my family years down the road. I had received another royalty check similar to the previous one. I bought ten-thousand shares of a little company called Microsoft. I diversified by also buying ten-thousand shares of Wal-Mart and Home Depot. All three companies were small at the time I purchased them in comparison to IBM or General Electric. I thought that smaller companies would grow faster than giant ones.

I also bought five fast food restaurants. Taco Bell had only been in the San Francisco Bay area for about three years; but they seemed to be doing a great business. The fact that I ate there a lot myself helped me to make the decision to buy the franchise rights to five restaurants. I picked out five locations that I thought would be profitable and had them constructed.

I hired a financial consulting firm to watch over and to run my investments. The firm put me into several properties that they felt would return large profits in years to come. Time would tell if any of my speculations would be profitable or if I would lose it all.

During this hiatus from touring I started collaborating with well known musicians and songwriters. I co-wrote songs with Eric Clapton, Elvin Bishop and Joan Baez. I was seeing music in a completely new light these days and I liked what I saw in the future.

The year off came to an end and I was ready to get back into the flow of things again. It was early 1970 and the sixties had come and gone, leaving behind a new world of thoughts and lifestyles. The beginning of the woman's movement was in full swing as well as the wacko environmentalist movement.

CHAPTER EIGHTEEN

Tree didn't take long to tell us to get started on our third album. The band spent hours as well as weeks in the recording studio writing songs for the album. Keeping once again with the bands identity I titled the third album DREAM IN FANTASIES FUTURE. This album was very different from the two previous ones. It leaned heavily towards blues Instead of pop or commercial. For that reason we dubbed it DIFF, because in reality it was indeed different from our past work.

Troy and I were spending hours late at night writing two songs that we wanted to put on the album. Stuart and Ted had also written a few songs that were good and would surly be recorded. I still see Bounce and Stretch mixing songs in a lot of combinations in order to get that ultimate sound for us. It took four months to record the album and then six more weeks until it was released.

Sales were sluggish at first. Our fans had to adjust to the new sound. It was approximately seven weeks when the sales began to climb the charts. The title of the first song released had people wondering what was going on. I admit that SUN SETTING LILAC was way out there in left field as far as lyrics and musically. It did however have a sound that grew on you the more you listened to it. I still feel to this day that was what happened. The song was accepted after it had time to sink in. I was more surprised, when it was brought to my attention, that we now had a hard core blues following. They had accepted the album as blues and it met with there high standards of approval.

With the success of our third album came the world tour and promotional appearances. I did not want to leave Sarah and Wade, but neither did the rest of the band want to leave their loved ones. That's part of this entertainment world that has to be done.

It was a long, hard tour that took its toll on all five of us personally. The highlight of this tour was when we played with Led Zeppelin in Scotland. I can say in all honesty that was no where near the rush I got when I stepped of that plane and saw Sarah and Wade for the first time in six months. Trust me when I say there is no bigger thrill than to see your loved ones after a long absents.

We were tired and physically worn out to the point of exhaustion. We did not waste our time on the flight back from Europe. The band had come to an agreement that we would never do another world tour. We also agreed to flat out tell Tree that we were taking two years off with no ifs ands or butts about it. I was so thankful that we were in total agreement on these issues.

The problem that was a year and a half old was no better. Ted and Bubba Ray were still doing drugs on a large scale. They played the tour in an incoherent state of mind; but they did perform their duties as musicians one hundred percent to perfection. I can't understand how they did; but they did. If Tree balked on the time off or anything I would use their drug abuse to get the bands wishes consummated.

You can call it blackmail if you like; but alls fair in love and contract negotiations. We had spent three years with Chart Records and had seven to go before we reached the ten year clause. There was no way we could keep this schedule and maintain our health or sanity. We were as a whole beginning to lose interest in being rock stars or anything to do with being celebrities. I would call Tree tomorrow and set up a meeting with just him and me, one on one, to set forth the bands demands.

I could not believe it when I met with Tree and he listened intently as I informed him of what the band wanted. When I had finished talking he stood up, reached out his hand and said "no problem; you've been working your asses off. I can see that you are reaching the point of a major burnout. I was thinking the same thing for you guys as far as the band taking time off. The bands not worth a nickel to Chart Records if you burnout and your work starts to suffer. So go ahead and be with your families and kids for a couple of years. I can book one of you on a local television show once in a while in order to keep your name out there in the public can't I? Then we can orchestrate a colossal come back tour. Surprised you didn't. I'm not really a big jerk or relentless bastard. You've all earned it, so get the hell out of here and start enjoying your time off."

I rushed to the door before he could change his mind or yell something like just kidding. My heart did skip a beat when Tree called out "one more thing Larry. I expect two guys in the band to clean up the drugs and booze if they want to continue in this band."

That last statement got my attention, especially when I knew Ted and Bubba Ray were the two. I was glad Tree had spoken up and put a very serious problem out on the table officially. It was now up to them to get straight or be fired from the band. I would make sure they got Tree's message.

Sarah's talk with Teri and Mary Lou had no effect on Ted or Bubba Ray. Trees solution to the problem was the next step to be taken and I was happy that I did not have to bring it up again. I really didn't want to argue with them or try to get Tree to get involved in the situation again.

Many things happened in the two years that we were off after that meeting in Trees office. My parents died in a head on automobile crash on interstate five. My step father was driving north of Hallendale when the accident occurred. The best conclusion that investigators could agree on was that my dad fell asleep at the wheel. There was no other explanation as to why he would have come across the center line and run head on into an on coming vehicle at a high rate of speed.

Sarah and I as well as Troy and Brandy went back to Oregon for the funeral. While there I hired a financial consulting and management firm to sell my parents home. I also told the firm to handle any and all of the money issues. I instructed the firm to split the monies from the bank and the sell of the house between my brother and sister. I personally did take care of picking out the headstones for both mom and dad.

It was just a few short months after that that my brother died from a drug overdose. Brandy's mom was diagnosed with breast cancer as well as Stuart's sister. Both ladies are undergoing chemotherapy. I know that sounds like a lot of trouble and sadness. However, not everything was depressing in that two year period.

Bubba Ray and Ted had been in rehab and were now doing great. Teri gave birth to a baby girl and Mary Lou was starting a modeling career. Stuart's girlfriend Tammy had been appearing in rock videos. She now had a part in a new movie that got rave reviews at the Conn film festival.

Two years to the day after the band started its leave; Tree called and said he wanted the band in his office the next day at eleven AM. During the time off each of us had appeared at one time or another on local television shows as well as MTV and VH1. The bands name was still out there and remained popular with the public as well as fellow rock musicians. The best news was that Bubba Ray and Ted were clean and drug free. They really had kicked the habit. I give them praise for that to this day.

We had a little less than five years left on our contract before the ten year clause became effective. We were ready to return to work in the studio and record our fourth album. The truth was we really wanted to flat out quit, but we knew our responsibilities and contractual agreements.

Tree had aged a lot over the twenty-four months. We sat down in front of his desk and watched as he took a deep breath and cleared his throat. "Boys I have decided to retire. I am getting to old for all this high pace lifestyle. I have a dilemma staring me right between the eyes. I do not know what to do under these circumstances.

First of all I have been trying to sell Chart Records for about a year now. I don't want to run the label any longer. I don't want to sell your remaining five year contract to another label. The irony of all this is that I am in the position to sign two new bands that are great. Both of these bands want to sign here at Chart Records because JUST SLIGHTLY RICHER is on the label. I'm asking you boys to please go home and help me to come up with a solution. I want an answer that is fair to you and to me at the same time. You're my family and I want nothing more than a solution that we can all live with."

Everyone turned and left the room except Sarah and I. "let's talk Tree. You know the answer to the situation as well as I do."

He smiled and nodded his head up and down. "Yes I do Larry. What you don't know is that I am going to sell you Chart Records for the outrageous price of half a million Dollars. You know that as the owner of Chart Records you can tear up a contract if all parties agree. I know half a mill is a fraction of what its worth; but you have made me a millionaire ten times over and over again. Let's just say it is my way of giving back OK."

He knew that the band really did not want to work anymore. We were all multi-millionaires and we never had to work another day in our lives if that was what we choose to do. I personally did not want to tour, but did want to work in the music business. Tree's offer of owning Chart Records as well as running it appealed to every fiber of my being. Images of being my own boss began a barrage of expectations.

Sarah looked at me and I at her. I knew what she was thinking as if she was screaming it out at the top of her lungs. "Draw up the papers Tree. I will run your business to the best of my ability. I will try to be fair to all concerned. I might be buying the company; but it will always be yours as far as I am concerned. I want to see and hear these two bands you spoke of. If you were going to sign them, then I want to sign them. I trust your judgment explicitly."

It took about a month before I was the sole owner of Chart Records. To everyone's approval I tore up JUST SLIGHTLY RICHERS contract. No one in the band ever knew how much I had paid for the business. They were just glad that I had bought it, because they didn't want the responsibility of running it. They also knew that by me purchasing it they got out of a five year contract.

I signed the two bands that Tree had liked. He was right; both bands were tight and had excellent chemistry. I instructed Bounce and Stretch to mix these guys as if they were JUST SLIGHTLY RICHER. Over the next five years both groups had a couple of number one hits and two successful world tours. They were on top of the charts, so Tree and I had made a good decision.

In the summer of nineteen seventy six I sold Chart Records to Capital Records along with every bands contract that I owned. I sold Capital the buildings and all the equipment. I actual had in the sales contract that Bounce and Stretch could stay mixing as long as they wanted to work at Capital. The bands under my umbrella were excited about moving to the Capital label. After all Capital is a major worldwide respected label. When it was all said and done the lawyer handed me what was the biggest check I had ever seen up to that point in my life. Sarah and I gasped as we looked at a check for forty six million dollars even.

I celebrated by doing something that I expect no one will ever understand. I went down to Hells Alley and met Jay Miller. I gave him a check for one million dollars and told him to remodel the club. I told him that I would try and round up the old band to play his grand opening after the remodeling. Trust me when I tell you that he was reduced to a puddle of quivering jello. It had been so humorous that Sarah and I laughed all the way out of the club.

Sarah and I then drove up to Skyline Manor where Troy and Brandy still lived. Troy had bought Skyline Manor once I had torn up the JUST SLIGHTLY RICHERS contract. Believe it or not; Jennifer and Lisa, still in the house with Troy and Brandy. They were for the lack of any other description, housekeepers. I gave each one of them a peck on the cheek and a hearty hug.

I told them that seven years ago I had promised them that they could go on a world tour. Well in fact, that did not happen for them. They did not go on that last tour because I had forgotten all about what I had promised them. I reached into my sport coats pocket and then handed each of them a check for twenty-five thousand dollars. "You take that world tour I promised you years ago. I'm sorry that it took so long to come true for the both of you."

I informed Troy of what I had done as far as finalize the sale of Chart Record and Jays check to remodel. He was a little upset with me for not asking him to chip in on the check to Jay. He would like to have contributed half the money to show his gratitude as well. He was enthused about getting the band back together for a one night bash at Hells Alley.

Jay had told me that he would be ready to reopen by the Fourth of July. Troy and I began to contact the guys from the band. Bubba Ray had moved back to Little Rock Arkansas. He now owned a car dealership. He never worked there, he just owned it. Bubba Ray sounded good on the phone. He and Mary Lou were doing wonderfully. I had seen Mary Lou in past months in Vogue and Cosmopolitan magazines.

Ted and Teri lived in Miami Florida. Ted owned many high-rise buildings and apartment complexes that made up the greater Miami skyline. Ted had not only become a good business, but he was also a father. He and Teri had three children, two boys and one girl.

Stuart and Tammy lived in Los Angles. Tammy had been in several movies over the last few years. Sarah and I had seen her many times on HBO as well as Showtime. Stuart was her manager and agent. He, like Ted and Bubba Ray, wanted to participate in the big Fourth of July bash at Hells Alley. I could tell by their voices that we were going to rock San Francisco like it had never been rocked before.

Five months passed by slowly to me before the guys flew in and we started to jam. I was amazed at how good we sounded despite the many years apart. It just all came together as if we were never separated. We had a play list that was tight after only one week of rehearsal. True it was only eighteen songs that we had done on our own albums, but what the hell. You got to play what it was that got you there.

CHAPTER NINETEEN

Hells Alley was the new club that was beyond comparison in the rock scene. Jay had spent every penny making his place the talk of the bay area night life. He had spared no expense in lighting and sound system. He had imported crystal chandeliers and Italian marble countertops. He had what I think is the first ever stainless steel polished dance floor. You had to sprinkle this granular stuff from a container in order to dance without sliding and falling down. But who cared when you were at the hottest club in town?

It was a night to remember forever in time; five guys and their wife's walking down memory lane. I wished that it could have lasted a month long, but as four AM came upon us, the party ended. The San Francisco police crashed the party and fined Jay for being open past the two-thirty city closing law for clubs. It was sad as Sarah and I watched everyone depart on their flights back home. This was the last time that all five of JUST SLIGHTLY RICHER members would play together. I thank God that I had Bounce and Stretch bring in a portable recording studio and record a great live soundtrack that I will cherish forever and a day plus one more day.

The eighties and nineties passed by faster than I would have liked. My life as a whole was similar to anyone else's during all that time period. Wade broke his arm in nineteen-eighty playing midget football. He was the star power forward on his high school basketball team that won the state championship. Finally Wade was off to southern California attending collage at U C L A. I think he turned out fine for being a rich kid and all.

He's studying to become a microbiologist. He knew that he was worth millions of dollars and really never had to work a day in his life if he chose not to. He insisted on taking the hard classes that were required in order to become a microbiologist. I truly admired him for his hard work and disciplined dedication.

Sarah and I have traveled the world several times. The last time we went to Wales and Ireland for our vacation. The word beautiful is not even the tip of the iceberg in describing both of these wonderful countries. We had flown the Concord our last three trips and that was an experience all to itself. I only mention it because the Concord was discontinued May 31st 2003. I feel privileged that I was able to fly on her before that happened.

I heard through the grapevine that Scott had been shot to death in a barroom fight back in 1987. Jay Miller died of lung cancer in 1993 as well as Bounce. Tree had his seventy-ninth birthday and I gave him a gold cane and a Rolex watch. I lost track of Bubba Ray and Mary Lou once she disappeared from the cover of fashion magazines. I did hear that he sold the dealership in 1990. I often think about the guys. I even think if any of the guys in Autumn Root ever wish that they would have stuck it out till I had gotten out of boot camp?

Sarah and I through a big party at our house to usher in the New Year 2000. The Y2K controversy did not seem to hamper any of our guests that night. I admit that I did think that something might happen with computers or terrorist attack of some kind. Thank God none of that happened and the country was fine.

The stock market had been going crazy for the last few years and I really started to think how much higher it could go till it crashed. For the first time in thirty years I decided to see how much the three stocks I had purchased back in the sixties were now worth. I swear to you that I had forgotten about them for years, it's not like I needed the money or anything.

I discovered from my broker that all three stocks had split many times over the thirty years of my ownership. For example, my ten-thousand shares of Microsoft had split six times. That translates into 640,000 shares. I sold them early in 2000 for 93.00 dollars a share or in other words 39,040,000.00 dollars. My Wal-Mart and Home Depot were almost as good a return respectively.

Other than the Mill Valley home, the only investments I had left were several parcels of land that my financial adviser had bought back in the sixties. I never had taken the time to learn were they were actual; until a conglomerate made me an offer to purchase the entire seven lots.

It seemed very strange to me when I learned that all seven lots were separate from one another. One was in Monterey and one in Santa Cruz. Two were in San Jose and three were in West San Francisco. Each lot was One to three acre's apiece in size. The long and short of it is that I sold the entire grouping for twenty-eight million dollars.

I had sold all my stocks, properties and other investments by mid 2000 just before the market did indeed crash. I felt sorry for the millions of people that got wiped out by the dot com companies. They all went to the poor house and the rich S O B's went to the Bahamas. They should hunt them down the crooks and just out right beat them right there on the spot.

The good Lord has watched over me during my lifetime. Looking back on my life I do see some bad things, but I still feel blessed. With Gods help I overcame cutting my foot off as a child. I was one of the first kids to have a foot sown back on successfully. I had a stick thrown at me that stuck in my eye. Well, the doctor said that if it would have been about a sixteenth of an inch closer I would have been blind in that eye.

When I was twelve a lady jumped off the diving board at a local pool and landed square in the middle of my back. When I woke up twenty minuets later I was receiving CPR from an EMT. I was in three automobile accidents and walked away from them all.

Eleven high school buddies and I, in one car, on senior skip day decided to race some guys from our rival high school. Going north out of Hallendale there is a train trestle when you start going downhill on old ninety-nine. There is a small dirt road to the right of the trestle before you go under the trestle. The driver of the car made a sharp turn of 99 in order to get on this road so he could lose the car racing along side of us. We were doing 105 MPH at the time when we hit the cement pillar head on. I know this for a fact because I had just looked at the speedometer and was going to say slowdown.

The other two were just as violent in comparison. Rudy and I left Troy's one afternoon in Rudy's dads new Nova. It was the first time that I heard a voice in my head, and it said to fasten my seat belt. I had never wore a seat belt in my life, I mean NEVER HAD. I saw and heard it snap together when I looked up to see the car go air bound. When the front tires hit the dirt road both blew out and the rims dug into the dirt. We flipped end over end three times and then rolled like nine times before slamming into the bridge that crossed Bear Creek. I remember the car spinning on its top in the middle of the bridge and some guy running up yelling if I was all right. I had a small cut on my elbow from when my arm had swung around and broke out the side window. Rudy had only a cut on his finger he got from the horn ring that is on a 1965 nova.

The other car wreck was when I was very young. I was with riding with my uncle when a car ran a red light and T-boned us. He hit our car square in the middle of my door and forced our car up on to its side. My uncle's arm was pinned beneath the car against the payment. I can still see the policeman that had climbed up on the car and reached down inside and lifted me out through the window. I did not even have a scratch; to show for my ordeal.

The good Lord not only saved me from all of those incidents, he let my path cross with Roy Wilson's. God has really put me in the right place at the right time through out my life. Even the part of seeing that I got out of the military in a short time I feel was Devine intervention. Getting a second chance with Tree and the success of the bands music; God orchestrated all of it I believe.

Now that it is the year 2003 and I am fifty-five, life's been good to me, in the words of Joe Walsh. Everyone as far as I know (less the ones I mentioned) are still alive and kicking, even Tree himself, even though he's getting way up there in age. Maybe if I live long enough I will get enough stories to write a sequel to all this. God willing everyone will be around to read it. Take care and live life to its fullest and remember that NOTHING, NOTHING, is more important in life than FAMILY and good FRIENDS. Don't ever be fooled into believing that it's money, IT JUST AINT SO.

SECRET LOVE

CRYSTAL JOHANSSON stood in front of six girls on the West Hamblin High School gym floor. She was in the middle of teaching the cheerleading squad her new routine. She had been working on it at home for several days.

Working up new moves and picking the right music was part of her duties as head cheerleader. Being beautiful and having a perfect body didn't hurt in the schools voting for the envious position.

"5-6-7-8" she yelled as she started the new moves and the other girls copied her to the best of their abilities. It took a couple of hours of hard work; but they got it down perfectly.

Even though Crystal was seven-teen she had never had a steady boyfriend. She had liked a few boys; but none of them showed any interest in her. She tried not to dwell on that fact so she wouldn't become depressed. She spent her time focusing on cheerleading and its dance moves.

"Good practice everyone. We're ready for next weeks opening game against Jackson High," Crystal said. As the squad dispersed she put her pom-poms away in her gym bag. She turned around to leave and saw Principle Wagner with two boys that were identical twins. She was immediately attracted to the both of them.

"Oh! Hi Crystal, I'd like you to meet sophomore Terry and Jerry Tigard. They just moved here to Bakersfield from Seattle, Washington. I'm showing them around their new school. Terry is an all American quarterback and Jerry is an all state wide receiver.

Coach Billings is ecstatic to have them joining our football team. We may make the California state championship game this year," said Principle Wagner.

"Hello, welcome to West Hamblin High," Crystal said with a smile.

"Hello," said both boys in unison.

"Crystal, could you show Terry and Jerry around Monday to their class's and introduce them to everybody," asked Principle Wagner?

"I'd be honored to," Crystal said as she glanced at the new students.

Crystal's weekend was one full of excitement. She told all her friends about the two new cute boys and how she was the school ambassador to them come Monday.

As she got dressed for school on Monday she made a point of wearing her nicest outfit. She took her time doing her hair and applying her makeup. As she was driving away from her drive way she was checking her lipstick in the rearview mirror.

When she arrived at school she immediately saw the twins in front of the school talking to Coach Billings. While she approached them they shook hands and Coach Billings turned and walked away. The boys pivoted and stood there face to face with her.

She then put her hand out and they shook it. Terry handed her their class schedule. She glanced at it, nodded and said, "Your first class is math with Mr. Jones. He's a nice man and a great teacher. Come with me and I will take you to your class, its room 215 on the second level. The three entered the schools main entrance and made their way to the math room.

As they made their way to the second level Crystal asked, "How was it in Seattle?"

"Cold and rainy," answered Jerry. "We're looking forward to living here in Bakersfield."

"You'll love it here I promise. Well here we are at Mr. Jones's math class. I will return at the end of the class and show you to your next class which is Mr. Turner's biology class in room 195," Crystal remarked.

She watched as the boys entered the classroom with a look of apprehension. She had already developed visions of dating Terry the quarterback. After all that was a tradition at every high school. The head cheerleader dated the quarterback. She intended to keep that tradition alive.

She enjoyed the day escorting the guys around the campus. That excitement let down when she guided them to their last class of the day. It was gym class with Coach Billings. Her duties were complete and her time with them was over. She started then and there thinking how to reunite with Terry.

For the next several weeks Terry and Jerry were the talk of the school and Bakersfield. The both of them were fantastic on the football field. They were everything a coach could want in an athlete. Talk of a State Championship was on the entire communities lips.

The day before the homecoming game Terry stopped Crystal in the hallway. "Hey Crystal, would you like to go to the homecoming dance after the game Friday night," he asked?

She didn't hesitate a second in saying "Yes, I'd love to."

"Great, I'll meet you after the game outside the boys' locker room."

Crystal's smile was ear to ear as Terry exited the locker room. Hamblin High had won the game 38 to 17. "You were wonderful Terry, You're going to be all state for sure," Crystal said.

"Thanks; but I just want Hamblin High to win the state championship. Everything else will take care of it self," Terry fired back.

That night was the start of what developed into a loving relationship. It continued through that year and their junior and senior years, growing stronger with each day.

During those three years Hamblin High won the state championships in football and basketball thanks to Terry and Jerry. The only concern with the twins was that even after three years no one could tell them apart. They were moody, dressed alike and their mannerisms were identical as their appearances.

It wasn't until the start of Crystals and Terrys senior year that they made love for the first time. One thing she noticed in time was that when he was in a good mood the love making was unbelievable. When he was depressed or sad it was miserable and left him withdrawn. He always had an explanation and an apology for the inconsistencies.

Crystal began to worry if Terry was playing some terrible thing by switching with Jerry once in awhile. She had heard stories about twins switching for all kinds of things. She couldn't believe Terry would do such a thing, however it took her all night to get up enough courage to ask him flat out.

A couple of days passed and as they sat in Terry's car at Diamond Lake she asked "Terry has Jerry ever pretended to be you while we were having sex," she asked sharply?

"What! Are you on drugs or something? Of course not baby. I'd kill him if he ever touched you. Why would you ever suspect or say such a thing to me"?

"Because you're so different every time we make love. It's like I'm with ten different men and I don't know which one is going to show up on any given night."

"I told you, I act differently based on how I feel at that moment. For Pete's sake, think of it as experiencing several lovers; but it's really only me."

"OK! OK! Don't get mad. I had to ask. Now that I've asked and you've answered, it's fine. You know I love you, I'm sorry I questioned you," she said sheepishly.

With that said Terry took her in away she had never experienced before. It was as if he had to make a point to her. He did, she completely forgot about any reservations she had and melted into his touch and her womanly feelings of desire.

After graduation Crystal, Terry and Jerry enrolled at the University of Oregon in Eugene with a four year football/basketball scholarship and Crystal on a four year academic scholarship. Terry was immediately thrusted into the limelight as the beavers starting pac12 quarterback.

Jerry on the other hand was distraught because he was relinquished to the bench as a third string wide receiver. It was hard for a high school all American/state championship wide receiver to now be a benchwarmer. He was mad; but he was determined to work hard and get that starting position.

Terry was in all the local newspapers and considered to be a celebrity in Eugene. He had an arm like a cannon and could run the ball as good as his backs if the situation called for it. No one in college ball could scramble like Terry Tigard.

Finally after three years Jerry earned the starting wide receiver position. The day he was told that he and his friends went out for a night of celebration. However, after he left the bar that night he lost control of his car and hit a tree at a high rate of speed. They say he died instantly and didn't suffer any pain.

It was a solemn service that was held for him. He will surely be missed by everyone that knew him. Crystal and Terry flew to Seattle for the service. Mr. and Mrs. Tigard had flown Jerry's body back home to Seattle. He was buried in the family plot in Renton.

Terry was never the same after his brothers' death. His play suffered and his moodiness rose to a noticeable concern. Coach Billings had to sit him down and let the second string quarterback run the offense.

Terry was on course for the NFL draft and a career in professional football; but that all evaporated once Jerry died. He graduated from the U of O and went to trade school to become a welder. Once he earned his certification he went to work at Eugene Welding Corporation.

Crystal had studied meteorology and after she graduated she got a job at local channel 12 as their weatherperson. She and Terry got married a year later and soon had their first child, a baby girl which they named Monica.

As the years passed they had two more children; another girl (Jill) and a boy (Toby). Their marriage had its up and downs like all relationships; but they always managed to work through it. They never stopped loving each other nor did they ever regret their decisions in life.

Then on their thirtieth wedding anniversary Terry found out that he had lung cancer. The doctors informed him that he only had three to four months left to live. The disease had progressed too far to be slowed by any treatment.

Weeks passed and he became weaker as he began to slip away physically and mentally. Then one late night he called out Crystals name and she came to his side. "I have something to say to you. Sit down and I will explain," he said.

He coughed, hesitated and then continued. "You know that I love you with all my heart; but before I can't think correctly or speak properly I must tell you something. I have kept this secret far too long. It was Terry that died in the car crash back in college.

I'm Jerry, not Terry. We traded places hundreds of times right up to the day of the accident. We traded off being quarterback and wide receiver during high school. We trade off being quarterback in college; but not at wide receiver, the others were better than the both of us at that position.

I'm so sorry; but we took turns dating you as well. I know that was wrong and deceitful. I wouldn't blame you if you hate me for that. It started out as a joke; but we both started falling in love with you. I know that's no excuse, but we didn't know how to stop or how to tell you. You always thought you were with Terry so we let you think that. You seemed so happy and we didn't have the courage to tell you the truth.

You were with me the night Terry died. He was driving my car and we always traded wallets when we were with you. That's why the identification with Terry that night was in fact mine.

I told my parents the truth when we were in Seattle at the funeral. They said that they would say nothing because it was my place to tell you. They were disappointed in both of us for deceiving you. They have kept this secret for all these years. They love you and don't wont to hurt you. So they keep silence because it's all they know to do; but be assured they never let up telling me to tell you the truth.

Many of your memories are with me as well as some with Terry. I know I am asking a lot; but could you please forgive me and Terry for lying to you? I only wanted to make you happy and your dreams with Terry come true."

Crystal took his hand, looked in to his eyes and said, "I know, I've always known. The week before Terry died he told me what he and you had been doing. He told me that both of you loved me and that you both were trying to find away I could make a choice.

The question was, did I fall in love with Terry or Jerry based on our dates, conversations and as you said my memories. We discussed it at length and I told him I wanted some time to think about it. I told him to carry on the charade as I reflected on what dates made me fall deep in love. Terry outlined many of the dates we had and told me the ones that Jerry had been on with me. I told him I would make a decision in two weeks between him and you.

Terry died the night before I was going to tell him my answer. Maybe he was spared a broken heart, because after everything I did with him and you I had picked you my darling Jerry.

So even though you have gone by Terry Tigard for all these years I knew it was you Jerry. You have made my dreams come true over the years. I have no animosity towards you or Terry, I never have. I love you with all my heart and always will my darling."

Jerry smiled, closed his eyes and let out one last sigh as Crystal kissed his forehead. He passed away peacefully. Crystal never has told their three children what had taken place with Terry and Jerry. That is now her secret.

Crystal goes to the cemetery once a month and puts flowers on Jerry's grave. Below the name Terry Tigard and the dates, reads the following

Jerry and Terry are again as one; united to share the crystal clear love that lasted both their lifetimes.

FROM HAUNTED TO REALITY

I WOULD LIKE to tell you a story about two brothers, Wade and Edward Jones that lived in Medford, Oregon. When wade was fourteen and Edward was eight, they lived next to what everyone in the neighborhood called the old haunted house. No one had lived in it for over twenty-five years.

It was the place where at one time or another everybody was dared to go in and spend the night. What made this house different was that it was still fully furnished. It was left exactly as it was the day old man Peterman had died and it became the property of a far away relative. They never came to see it in person; they just kept paying the taxes year after year.

In the summer the weeds would grow to three feet tall and the oak trees would shade the entire house. As years passed the house became full of mold, mildew and moss had taken over the roof. There were many stories about how old man Peterman had died; everything from a heart attack to being murdered and cut up in to a hundred pieces.

Wade and Edward had lived next door to the empty house for only three years when they were dared to enter it by all the other kids. They had to prove they weren't chicken, so on a hot summer day they opened the back door and cautiously went in. The boys that had dared them to go inside stood across the street looking on in suspense.

What Wade and Edward saw inside was unbelievable, painted walls, graffiti on everything and furniture with ripped upholstery. All kinds of food thrown over the floors and eggs had been splattered on every wall. They noticed mirrors broken, doors torn off their hinges and shattered light bulb glass in all the rooms.

They spent an hour investigating the two story house when they discovered a door that led to the basement. There was just enough light to see coming from a small 6 by 12 inch dirty window. There was little to see except for an old dust covered tarp thrown in the corner. Wade pulled it back to find a box of what looked like a box of road flares. It was a full box of forty-eight sticks.

Their eyes widened and smiles spread across their faces; after all what boys don't love fire and flares? They carried the box back to their garage. They took a few sticks out and then put the box in their underground fort.

The next day they tried to light the flares; but to no avail. The sticks just smoldered and oozed. So boys being boys they did the next best thing. Since they lived next to the railroad tracks and rail yard they waited for the next train. When the noon train to Bakersfield pulled out they threw a stick into boxcars that had their side doors open. They took turns doing it, laughing all the time. When the caboose passed by they still had sticks left. They decided to wait till the next day and repeat their actions with the next noon train pullout.

They went in the house and made peanut butter and jelly sandwiches. They sat down to watch some television and take a well deserved rest. After an hour or so there was a loud knock on the front door. Their mother answered it and to her amazement stood two policemen asking if Wade and Edward Jones resided there.

She told them yes and inquired what this was all about. They informed her that they had a report from a neighbor that Wade and Edward had trespassed on the property next door. They added that they were also told that the boys were doing major damage to the house.

"Boy's, did you go into the Peterman house? You better not lie to me or your father will spank the both of you," she said.

It was Wade that spoke up, "yes mom, we went in there on a dare from the other guys. Everyone has been in there a hundred times. Gee, it's the haunted house, we didn't do anything except look around," he said.

The policemen asked the boys to show them how they got inside the house. They took the men to the back door and then the four of them entered. Wade showed the officers exactly where they had walked from room to room. All along the way the officers were taking notes and asking questions about the vandalism. Wade told them that that was already there when they came in.

"I swear to you. We didn't do any of this writing, eggs, broken mirror and glass. We only walked around and looked, really," Wade explained.

One of the officers (Officer Tom Black) asked, so after you walked around you went home? You're telling me absolutely nothing else happened and you didn't find or take anything, is that correct?" he asked.

Edward piped up and said, "we found a box of road flares. We couldn't light them so we threw some away. We still have some; but there no good for nothing."

"Can I see them young man?" asked Officer Black.

"Sure," Wade said. "Come on, I'll show you. There over at our house in our fort."

The boys led the officers back to their underground fort. The opening was too small for the men so Wade went inside and pushed the box up through the forts entranceway. Edward grabbed the rope handle on the box and pulled it up onto a level surface. Then the policemen yanked him back yelling "Stand clear kid, get back."

As Wade began to exit the hole in the ground the other officer (Bart Jenny) pulled him away from the box. Neither boy knew what was going on as both officers were on their radios and barking numbers that made no sense to them. Officer Jenny started yelling at the boys, "where did you throw the others away and how many were there?"

He didn't wait for an answer as he went back to talking on his radio. Wade and Edward decided not to say anything else. They were in trouble and the more they said, the deeper they seemed to get.

In a matter of minutes three police cars came to a screaming halt with lights on and sirens blaring. A big white van followed the police cars. It stopped behind the cars and a man in a white hooded space looking suit got out its back door. The police guided him to the box. He knelt down and examined it. He made everyone stand far back as he slowly carried the box back to his van. He put it in a big trunk and spread foam all over it before closing the lid.

With a police car in front and one behind the van; they slowly left and headed back to the police station.

Finally the police left and all the excitement ended for the day. The boys were grounded and sent to their room. It didn't take long for a detective to show up to ask more questions of them. "Hello boys, I'm Detective Anderson. You told the other policemen that you threw some of your flare sticks away. Can you remember where you threw them? If so, could you tell me?" he asked.

The boys looked at each other before Wade said, "we threw them in open boxcars as the train was pulling out."

"What time was that?"

"Around 1:30 I guess."

"Which way was the train going?"

"South, towards California."

"Excuse me boys while I call the station. Thank you for all the information, you have been a great help."

Detective Anderson got on his portable radio and called into headquarters. "John, get all the information on the southbound train pullout that left approximately at 1:30 PM from the North Rail Yard."

He turned and said, "I want you boys to wash your hands real good right now, just for safety. Scrub them really good you hear, while I talk to your parents." The boys went off to the bathroom to do as instructed.

Detective Anderson turned his attention to their father, Robert Jones. "As I was driving up to your house I got a preliminary report from the police lab. As we suspected, the box didn't contain road flares; but dynamite. It has crystallized and the report found that if the glycerin was only a half a percentage point less it would have blown up in your kids faces. Now each stick is similar; but some sticks could still be in a state of being explosive. Your children were more than lucky, it's a miracle they didn't get killed. We have to account for every stick immediately," he explained.

The box was a full one when the boys found it. It had a total of forty-eight sticks stacked in it. There were now thirty sticks left, leaving a total of eighteen missing that had to be found.

What happened in the next twenty-four hours is nothing less than a miracle as well. The police did a fantastic job in tracking down the missing sticks of dynamite. They found out that the Southern Pacific train #377 left the North Yard at 1:15 PM headed for Bakersfield. It had 101 cars in the pullout. They got the car number for each individual car.

They got the delivery destination for every one. They found that twenty-six cars were dropped off in San Francisco. The other seventy-five went to Bakersfield where then thirty was sent to Phoenix, Arizona, leaving forty-five there in California.

The police were able to stop the train in the Phoenix rail yard before proceeding eastwardly. The police then in each jurisdiction checked each car thoroughly and noted the cars number where a stick was found. In less than ten hours the authorities in each city had accounted for every stick.

They discovered five in San Francisco, nine in Bakersfield and four in Phoenix. The found sticks were brought back to Medford and united with the other thirty to once again fill the original box. After more intense Investigation the dynamite was destroyed. Law enforcement were able to find out exactly when the dynamite was manufactured, purchased and by whom.

Old man Peterman was a miner and he had bought the explosives back in 1942. There were no strict laws on purchasing dynamite back then as long as you were a licensed business. Mr. Peterman at the time was CEO of Peterman Mining Corporation making it all above board.

The main thing that happened after all this was that the county contacted the owners back east. They had the home torn down and the basement hole filled. Today there's an eighty-seven unit apartment complex where the old haunted house and Wade and Edwards's house once stood. The ordeal is nothing more than a memory today to those that wish to recall it at all.

However, for Wade and Edward; they drive by every so often and think back of how close they came to being blown up because of their own reckless actions. They cherish everyday knowing that the good Lord spared them on that dangerous day.

We all have stories where we almost died or had close calls. We need to reflect on those times and give thanks; not only at Thanksgiving, but everyday we experience in our life.

SLOW DOWN AND VISUALIZE

WHEN YOU DRIVE down a road and look out the window, how much do you really see? Do you think about what is passing you by as you travel along your way?

I was in my forties before I realized that I subconsciously did something that most people do not do. The good Lord gave me the ability to process in a fraction of a second to visualize anything's history. For example; when you pass by an old oak tree by the road, what do you honestly see?

Be honest now. I bet you just see an old tree standing there; unless it has something extraordinary about it. Other than some rarity you go on by without much notice.

I see that tree in its entirety. In only a few seconds I see that mighty oak as an acorn bouncing along the ground and coming to rest where it stands today as a new life. I see microscopic roots leave the acorn and start penetrating the earth's soil. Deeper and deeper they force themselves establishing the root system for the future.

I see it when it reaches six inches tall as an infant tree and the wind blowing hard against its little trunk and limbs. The roots anchored it safely in place and its limbs bent; but never broke. I see the sunlight as it shines down on its branches on a hot summer day.

I see how over the years it continued to reach out towards the sun and its roots searching deeper for security and water. Everything it does shows its determination to survive whatever harsh weather comes along.

I see many bird nests that have been made in its branches over the years. I see the scars from lovers carving their initials in its bark. I see the children that have climbed in its branches and the many picnics held under its umbrella of shade.

I see that as mighty as he is standing there, that time has begun its decent upon his very existence. I watch as the oldness of his might is exposed. Once dying is evident, the process is unforgiving and swift.

Then for the safety of all of us he falls victim to the chainsaw. His trunk and limbs are cut into fire wood; even in death he will serve useful to all that enjoyed his presents.

I count the rings on the stump that still stands and I count eighty. A smile comes to my face as I see an acorn roll across the ground and settle in a rut. I know that little acorn will follow in the steps of the one it came from.

    I swear to you that this is how I view all things. It happens so fast for me that it is easy to take it for granted. I have made a point to slow down and visualize what is all around me on a daily bases. We have heard the old saying stop and smell the roses. That is a wonderful idea; but if you really want to enjoy the moment, visualize whatever catches your eye from start to finish. It can be a barn or a bridge, whatever it is, thoroughly enjoy the moment.

DISPARAGING

I HEAR A lot these days about the rich and how they need to pay more in taxes. I personally am not one for wealth distribution. I will share with you my reasoning based on facts later on. It bothers me deeply that so many think the rich are cold blooded arrogant bastards that don't give a damn about you and I.

The perception is they live in mansions, have expensive yachts and fancy exotic cars. They thrive in a world of luxury while the rest of us struggle to just survive day to day.

Maybe the above is true, or is it only a matter of sour grapes covered in pure jealousy? With an open mind lets' take a real hard look at the rich and wealth.

First off the top 2% of the people with money (the rich) pay approximately 75% of the taxes collected by the government. The sad fact is that 51% of Americans pay NO TAXES, their on some form of government assistance. America has the highest corporate rate in the entire world at 30%. Is it any reason that big business is sending jobs overseas?

On top of paying that high tax the employer pays Social security, unemployment contributions, state and federal taxes. Then there are huge water, sewer, electric, trash, insurance and property taxes to pay at all business locations.

If you are fortunate to have you boss paying for your health care you are receiving a wonderful lifesaving gift. If you have a 401 program at work, again you have another gift from your boss as well because neither is mandatory for him to do. Both are extremely expensive and should tell you that your employer does care about you.

Have you ever thought about the personal life of the rich? I don't mean the things I mentioned at the beginning of this piece. At night you go home and for the most part you enjoy your family while forgetting about the workplace.

As far as the rich man; he too goes home to his family. He lives in a gated community where his home is protected by the best security system that money can buy. He has to worry about his wife or children being kidnapped or worse.

He thinks about how to keep the business up and running with all the new government mandates coming down the pipeline. He worries about hostile takeovers, lawsuits and loss of revenue. He tries to figure out how to show a profit at the next companies' quarter meeting that will keep the shareholders happy and not bail out of the stock market lowering the company stock.

I am not saying that it's hard to be rich and I understand completely that we all would pick being rich and we would then try to handle all these situations if allowed. Could we really deal with the decisions to keep hundreds at work and make a quarterly profit?

Lets get down to the bottom line, I mean the real bottom line, the one at the bottom of your paycheck. Do you think that's some poor slobs name scribbled along it? NO! It's a rich guys signature; because without them you would have nothing except what a socialistic government would give you.

Remember with no rich people for the government to tax to death you can only get what the government says it can afford. You have to get realistic and face the fact that you would get far less than you receive now in your weekly paycheck.

In conclusion, I don't envy Bill Gates, Warren Buffet or any other rich person. They worked hard and long for their money. They took the risks and long shot chances. Yes they got lucky or were in the right place at the right time. Be thankful that they are rich and are willing to share it in charitable donations and yes, YOUR PAYCHECK; because the poor don't sign any paychecks, only the rich do.

Edwards Brothers Malloy
Thorofare, NJ USA
July 23, 2012